Public Middle Schools:
New York City's Best

ALSO BY THE AUTHOR

The Parents Guide to New York City's Best
Public Elementary Schools

Public Middle Schools: New York City's Best

Clara Hemphill

The map for this edition was prepared by the Institute for Education and Social Policy, New York University, under the direction of Dorothy Siegel. It appears here with the Institute's kind permission. © 1997 NYU Institute for Education and Social Policy.

Published by
Soho Press Inc.
853 Broadway
New York, NY 10003

Library of Congress Cataloging-in-Publication Data
Hemphill, Clara, 1953–
    Public middle schools : New York City's best / Clara Hemphill.
        p.   cm.
    Includes index.
    ISBN 1-56947-170-3
    1. Middle schools—New York (State)—New York Directories
2. Middle school education—New York (State)—New York.
3. School choice—New York (State)—New York.   I. Title.
    L903.5.H48   1999
    273.747'1—dc21   99-36305
                                                                           CIP

10   9   8   7   6   5   4   3   2   1

To Judy Baum

for her many years of service
at the Public Education Association

Acknowledgements

This book was made possible with the generous financial support of the Public Education Association, a non-profit research and advocacy organization; and grants from J.P. Morgan & Co., Inc.; the Charles Hayden Foundation; the Stella and Charles Guttman Foundation; and the Taconic Foundation.

Particular thanks go to PEA's Judith Baum, whose unusually thorough knowledge of the public school system provided the foundation for my research; and Jessica Wolff, whose good humor and enthusiasm while visiting schools, and meticulous fact-checking of the manuscript, were critical. Linda Jefferson was good company on school visits and, as the mother of four children in public school, provided a useful reality check. Raymond Domanico, PEA's executive director, believed in the project from the beginning and gave me an unusual degree of freedom and independence in carrying it out.

The generosity of district officials, principals and teachers cannot be oversated. They opened their doors to me, allowed me to sit in on classes and to write about everything I saw—the good and the bad.

Tim Copper of Proteus Design was tireless in his efforts to translate the Board of Education data from computer disks into a readable form. Soho publisher Juris Jurjevics offered encouragement as well as editorial support. Colleen Michael lovingly cared for my children when I worked.

My children, Max and Allison, were the inspiration for this book.

My husband, Robert Snyder, has been my greatest supporter, cheering me on when my energy flagged, picking up the slack at home when I worked late, and reading and editing various drafts. Without him, this book would not have been possible.

Contents

Community
School
Districts

Public Middle Schools: New York City's Best

INTRODUCTION

Turning Point.

The middle school years are difficult for both children and parents. Young people struggle with peer pressure and puberty. Parents, watching their children develop more independent lives, fret about safety and unwholesome influences. Both worry about what's happening in school.

Finding a good middle school in New York City is more work than finding a good elementary school. There simply aren't as many good programs for 6th, 7th, and 8th graders as there are for young children. But don't despair.

Energetic reform efforts of the last decade have born fruit, and there are many more first-rate middle schools than are commonly recognized. Dozens of small, safe, and academically challenging programs have been created in recent years, based on new research into how young adolescents learn best. Many traditional junior high schools have been reorganized into mini-schools, where grown-ups and children get to know one another well and teachers pay attention to kids' social and emotional development as well as their academic skills.

The Board of Education has a policy of "school choice," which means children may apply to schools outside their own neighborhood. It's not always easy: overcrowding and problems with transportation limit your options, particularly outside Manhattan. The educational bureaucracy treats the most basic information as something akin to a state secret, and the admissions process can be as time-consuming and nerve-wracking as applying to college.

But persistence and careful planning pay off. There's no need to send your child to a large, chaotic junior high school, or to cough up private school tuition, or to move to the suburbs.

If you're looking for a good school anywhere in the five boroughs, this book will help you make an informed choice. If you're trying to improve your neighborhood school, this book will show you what works and describe successful efforts by parents to start new programs or fix existing ones.

This book is the result of a two-year research project by staffers and volunteers at the Public Education Association, a non-profit organization that gives parents information on good schools. We looked at test scores, safety records, and records of high school and college admissions. We spoke to hundreds of parents, teachers, district officials, and school-reform activists. We visited nearly one hundred programs in

3

the city's thirty-two semiautonomous districts. We didn't love everything we saw, but a few programs were so good we found ourselves envying the kids and wishing we were eleven years old again.

We found a few schools that serve all children well, from the highest-achieving to those in special education. More often, however, we found one program or mini-school that was good, in a school that was otherwise not yet ready for prime time. Lesson one: Finding a first-rate program within a larger school is one way to begin to secure a good education for your child.

As you visit schools yourself, you'll see the formidable obstacles that teachers and students face. Many buildings are in a poor state of repair. Class size sometimes tops thirty-five.

What saves the city's public middle schools—and what makes me committed to them for my own children's education—is the high quality of teaching combined with the opportunities provided by the city itself. Where but in a New York City public middle school could your child study biology with a professor at New York University's School of Medicine (page 54), drama with a Broadway actor (page 85) or ballet with a dancer from the Dance Theatre of Harlem (page 83)?

The city's public schools attract teachers who are committed to urban education as a profession, who believe that equal opportunity is the cornerstone of democracy. The best teachers have thought carefully about how to bring together children of different races and social classes, how to tailor instruction for children with different talents and different ways of seeing things. Those who are successful are real masters of their craft—as good as the best anywhere.

The best teachers have kept up with new research on adolescent development and have continued their own education with graduate courses at schools such as Bank Street College in Manhattan. In a city that changes as rapidly as New York does, teachers can't afford to be complacent. If they're good, they're always adjusting and readjusting their strategies and approaches.

The best middle school teachers have a special affinity and affection for kids this age. Rather than roll their eyes and moan about raging hormones, these teachers will tell you why they'd rather teach 7th graders than anyone else on earth.

"They're crossing that bridge between childhood and adulthood, and there's this great chasm and there's a rickety little bridge like in *Raiders of the Lost Ark*," said Ira Gurkin, former principal of MS 141 in the Riverdale section of the Bronx. "And I'm standing over on the other side of the bridge, like the Catcher in the Rye, saying 'Come on over.' It takes them three years to cross that bridge, and we're there to catch them. I love it."

Early adolescence *is* a time of tremendous physical and emotional change. Children from eleven to fourteen grow faster than any time except infancy. The onset of puberty brings with it exciting and confusing sensations and emotions. Friendships become more important than ever. Children begin to turn away from adults and rely more on their peers. These can be troublesome years, even for a child in a good school. In a bad school, these years can be disastrous—both socially and academically.

Most traditional junior high schools, with enrollments of 1,200 or more and class changes every forty-three minutes, have not served children well, in New York or anywhere else. Children in early adolescence need a school that offers them a sense of community, a feeling of belonging, and a few adults who know them well. Most traditional junior high schools can offer none of these.

The notion that children this age are merely miniature high school students—as the name "junior high school" implies—can lead to inappropriate teaching practices and unwholesome social situations. Many young adolescents are incapable of switching gears from English to math to social studies five times a day. Teachers who have entrusted to them 150 to 180 pupils each day are simply unable to take more than a passing interest in any one child. The results, too often, are low levels of academic achievement and high levels of bad behavior: truancy, playground fights, or precocious sexual activity.

Luckily, recent research in adolescent development has sparked a revolution in the way schools teach 6th, 7th and 8th graders. New York City is in the forefront of a national reform movement to transform traditional junior high schools into what are called "middle schools." This movement is based on the research of the Carnegie Council on Adolescent Development, which published a 1989 report called *Turning Points: Preparing American Youth for the 21st Century*. In New York, the Middle School Initiative spurred the creation of dozens of new, small schools in the 1990s and helped reorganize dozens of existing larger schools in ways that made them safer and more humane.

In schools organized according to the "middle school philosophy," kids may stay with one teacher for two hours or more—instead of changing classes every forty-three minutes. A teacher may have a total of fifty or sixty students—rather than nearly two hundred. A teacher may help children with study skills, such as taking notes and organizing homework, instead of concentrating exclusively on the subject matter to be taught. Teachers are encouraged to speak to children about personal or social problems and not to focus exclusively on academic performance. These schools organize the day in ways that give teachers blocks of time to talk to one another and to individual students. Teachers work in teams, organizing their lessons together. Children stay on one wing or one floor for most of the day, effectively creating a small school within a large building.

The most obvious and immediate advantage to the middle school model is safety. When the anonymity of a large school is replaced with the intimacy of a small school, when everyone knows everyone and children have close contact with a few attentive adults, children behave better. Schools that have adopted the Middle School Initiative have shown, almost universally, improved safety records and attendance rates. Race relations—often fractious in traditional junior high schools—seem to improve when small groups of kids learn to work out their differences with the help of a few adults who know them well.

The new research on early adolescence has offered new ideas about teaching methods as well as new ways of organizing the day. A good middle school looks more like an elementary school than a traditional junior high school, with colorful bulletin boards instead of bare walls, tables in groups instead of desks in rows, and kids working on group projects instead of listening to lectures. The curriculum isn't watered down—if anything, the subject matter is more advanced than what most of today's parents learned at this age—but material is presented in ways that are sensitive to the kids' level of maturity.

Rather than struggle through pencil-and-paper exercises on similar triangles in math class, for example, kids might be out on the playground estimating the height of a skyscraper from the length of the shadow it casts. Programs organized according to the "middle school philosophy" emphasize projects kids can touch and feel, as well as reading textbooks. Perhaps most importantly, they find ways to satisfy a child's yearning to be grown-up in ways that are more appropriate than wearing make-up or doing drugs—like organizing "community service projects" in which children volunteer in centers for the elderly, tutor younger children, or clean up their neighborhood. Such projects build a sense of belonging both within the school and in the community.

Good middle schools accommodate young adolescents the way they are, rather than battling to get children to conform to some idealized norm. If kids this age have trouble sitting still, good schools organize the day so they can move around a bit in class. If kids like to talk to their friends, good schools get them to work together in small groups rather than asking them to listen passively to their teacher. Good schools make sure kids have one adult who will be alert to signs of trouble with schoolwork, family, or friends. Some schools go so far as to organize outings and weekend camping trips for their pupils—supervised by teachers—to help develop what they call "positive peer groups."

Good middle school teachers manage to get on children's wavelengths. One science teacher told me she knows kids this age love disasters, so she spends lots of time talking about earthquakes and tidal waves. A history teacher, knowing kids at this age love descriptions of blood and gore, gave a memorable description of the guillotine in the French Revolution.

Good middle school teachers have the warmth of an elementary teacher and the specialized knowledge of a high school teacher. Find a school with such teachers and the roller coaster of adolescence can be manageable—and maybe even fun—for you and your child.

Getting Started.

When should you start your search? It doesn't hurt to start early, *really* early, like when your child is in kindergarten or first grade. Not to be obsessive or neurotic, but to get the lay of the land. Visit some schools in your district. If you like them, you can relax. But if there's nothing promising—and there are great swaths of the city in which the middle schools are pretty dreary—you may want to band together with other parents to pressure your district to do something to improve the situation. (More on that later.) Pressure from parents works, but it can take years to have an effect.

If you live in a good district, and you're happy with your child's elementary school, the best time to start your search is probably the fall of his or her 5th grade year. Most middle schools start in 6th grade. In Manhattan, most tours for prospective parents start in October and finish by Thanksgiving or Christmas—so if you delay you're out of luck. In Brooklyn and Queens, you may have a little more leeway, but not much. Entrance exams for the selective schools are generally the first week of January.

Some schools will tell you they don't offer tours, and that parents aren't allowed to visit classrooms. For these, try visiting during Open School Week in November. Board of Education regulations are vague on who may visit during Open School Week, and a lot of schools don't want to be bothered by prospective parents, but it's worth a try. Remember, it's your taxes that support these schools, and your child's future is at stake. These are public schools, not private clubs.

There are different kinds of schools serving kids in 6th, 7th, and 8th grades. The first thing you need to think about in choosing one is what organization of grades is best for your child. In some neighborhoods, middle school grades are included in the elementary schools, so children are in one building from kindergarten through 8th grade. Some districts start middle school in 5th grade, some in 6th grade, some in 7th grade. There are also "secondary schools" that include grades 6 through 12 or 7 through 12. There are advantages and disadvantages to each type of organization, and you might want to look at a number of different schools before you decide what's best for your child.

An old-fashioned organization that's recently become popular again is the school that takes children from kindergarten through to the eighth grade. Proponents of these **K–8 schools** say it's easier to adjust to early adolescence when you're with kids you've known your whole life. K–8 schools provide continuity and stability at a time when kids need it the most. Proponents also say young adolescents tend to behave better when they can act as big brothers and sisters to little kids in the school.

Many K–8 schools feel like small towns in the city. They may not have the fancy equipment of a large junior high school, such as science labs or woodworking shops, and the teachers tend to be licensed as "common branch" (elementary) rather than specialists (as high school teachers are). Yet many parents happily trade the fancy equipment and a high degree of teacher specialization for the safety and coziness of K–8 schools. These tend to be neighborhood schools, and it's often difficult for children from outside the school's zone to be admitted. But if you simply love a particular school, it's worth a try.

Most common in the city today are the **large middle schools** for grades 6, 7 and 8. These tend to be in buildings originally constructed for around a thousand students. The best have been divided into mini-schools, teams, or "houses," which provide the feeling of a smaller school. Each team or house might have two hundred to five hundred pupils. Rather than go from the first floor for English to the third floor for math and back to the second floor for science—as is typical in a traditional junior high school—children stay within their house or team for most of the day. Teachers and students get a chance to know one another well. In the most effective mini-schools, children and teachers have a sense of loyalty to one another and to the house. And at their best, each academy or mini-school has a cohesive staff that plans the curriculum together.

The big buildings tend to have good facilities—science labs, a large library, and a gym—and a wide array of special programs—band, orchestra, organized sports. Some children at this age feel claustrophobic in a K–8 school, or in a very small middle school, and are ready to test their wings in the larger world. For them, a larger school offers many opportunities. These tend to be neighborhood schools, although many have room for children from outside their zone.

There are a growing number of **small middle schools**, with two hundred or three hundred pupils. These are often located on the top floor of an elementary school or in a separate wing of a larger middle school building. They share a cafeteria and a gym with the main school, but have their own administration, their own admissions process, and their own distinct personality. They tend to be even more intimate and cozy than the K–8 schools. Every teacher knows every child's name. No one gets lost. The staff, by and large, has chosen to teach at this level and many have a particular affinity for this age group. There is one possible disadvantage of a very small school: the loss of one teacher can decimate a whole department. If the biology teacher takes a maternity leave, the school may have to do without biology for a few months. Also, they may not have a sports or music department. But many parents happily trade such extras for the intimacy and personal attention that a small school provides.

These tend to be unzoned schools rather than neighborhood schools. Children must fill out an application to be admitted. Some are open only to children living in a particular district; others accept children citywide.

Secondary schools, with grades 6 through 12 or 7 through 12, offer continuity as well as the opportunity to use high school facilities. The more years a child spends in one building, the easier it is to build a sense of community. A high school student can pay a visit to an old 7th grade teacher for moral support or advice. A 7th grader can easily see how the lessons she's learning now will be useful in later years. Parents say it's easier to build a PTA in a school where children spend five or six years, and a strong PTA can help the administration build an effective school. Like their parents, children often have difficulties making transitions. The fewer shifts from one building to another, the easier the adjustment.

A few secondary schools, like Hunter (which begins in 7th grade), are well established, highly selective, and very successful. Others are quite new and just getting off the ground. For both new and old, the benefits include facilities such as sophisticated libraries and advanced science labs and the ability for advanced pupils to take high school courses. A number of secondary schools are actually located on college campuses and even allow students to use college facilities.

One possible drawback: there is a tendency for secondary school teachers to treat all children as if they were in high school, rather than tailoring their classes to the maturity of middle school kids.

The exposure to older high school students can be both an advantage and a disadvantage. Middle school children can be inspired and motivated by seeing high school students hard at work. Or, if the high school is disorganized, the rowdiness of the big kids can be threatening. (In my experience, the size of the school determines safety more than the age of the kids. Small schools tend to be safer—however old or young the students may be.)

Many secondary schools fall under the jurisdiction of the Board of Education's division of alternative high schools. Your local district, which controls elementary and middle schools, may be unfamiliar with the secondary schools in your neighborhood, which are unzoned, and admit children by application.

There are also a handful of **K–12 schools** where children spend their entire preuniversity education in one building. Talk about continuity!

A few districts have retained their **traditional junior high schools**, with grades running from 6 through 8, 7 through 9, or, in a few cases, 7th and 8th grades. These schools have defenders who say, in essence, "If it works, don't fix it." Their parents and teachers believe the old ways are best, and they resist efforts to change what they see as a winning formula. Parents seem comforted that the schools resemble the junior high schools they attended as children. In stable, homogeneous neighborhoods, where parents and teachers share the same expectations for kids, the old methods sometimes work well.

These schools tend to focus on preparation for standardized tests, and to mark their success by how well their students do on Regents exams and how many students gain admission to specialized high schools. Included in this book are the traditional junior high schools that do well by these measures. Some schools call themselves "middle schools" but really have more in common with such traditional junior high schools.

Principals say the organization of the traditional school allows them to "track" children into as many as ten ability groupings—super-high honors, high honors, honors, et cetera. A child may be assigned to an accelerated track for one subject and a slower track for another. Teachers like the fact that they are only expected to teach—not to be social workers or hand-holders. Students who are self-disciplined, organized, and unusually mature may flourish in such a school. Traditional junior high schools are neighborhood schools and generally are open only to children living within their zones.

What are your options?
Once you've thought about the various types of schools, you'll want to see what's available in both your immediate neighborhood and farther afield. Many parents prefer to keep their children close to home. Can schoolmates easily get together after school? Are parents nearby and able to volunteer?

But the middle school years are also a time when many parents decide that the benefits of a distant school with a specialized music program or a first-rate gymnastics club are worth the traveling. Children are old enough to get to school on their own, and many welcome the chance to widen their circle of friends.

In most districts, children are assigned to a **neighborhood middle school** based on their address. **To find out the name of your zone's school, call your district office or the central Board of Education at 718-935-3584.** If your child has received special permission to attend an elementary school outside your home district, he or she will probably be allowed to attend middle school there. (One exception: District 25 in Queens.) If the neighborhood middle school for which your child is zoned is good, you don't need to worry. Your child will automatically be admitted. Unfortunately, many of the zoned middle schools are bleak.

Several districts—including District 3 on the West Side of Manhattan and District 15 in Brooklyn—have abolished zoned middle schools entirely. Parents complained that various alternative programs drained off the best students, and that the neighborhood schools had become dumping grounds for everyone else. In an attempt to solve that dilemma, those districts turned *all* schools into specialized schools of choice. In these districts, all children must choose a middle school from a range of special programs and schools organized around a theme. Children are guaranteed a spot—not necessarily at their first-choice school, but somewhere in the district. Some of the programs are still grim, but the hope, at least, has been that forcing all children to choose a program and keeping the brightest mixed with all the others would eventually improve education for all.

If you're unhappy with your neighborhood middle school, or you just want to investigate all your options, you should look at other

11

programs and schools both within and outside your district. These include: schools for the academically gifted; special programs for children with artistic, musical, or athletic talents; "magnet" or theme schools designed to attract children from outside the immediate neighborhood for the purpose of racial integration; and alternative schools for children who are unhappy or unsuccessful in their neighborhood schools. Ask your district office for a brochure about middle school options. Other sources of information include: New York Networks for School Renewal, which publishes a free directory of innovative public schools (212-369-1288), and New Visions for Public Schools, which to date has founded forty small schools (212-645-5110).

If your child has had high scores on standardized tests in elementary school (generally, the 85th percentile or better in reading), he or she will probably be offered a spot in a **special progress (SP)** or an accelerated program at your neighborhood school. You may also want to investigate the SP track at schools outside your neighborhood, as well as various schools for the gifted. Years ago, the "special progress" tracks were set up to speed able children through junior high school in two years rather than three. (The rationale was never clear to me, but one SP alumna explained: "Why would you spend five minutes more in junior high school than absolutely necessary?") Now, SP refers simply to the top track in a school in which children are grouped by ability. All children stay in middle school for three years. However, many SP students take high-school-level math and science courses, called Regents, in 8th grade. Some districts also have a track that's even more accelerated, called "gifted" or **special progress enrichment (SPE)**.

For years, public schools functioned as a fierce sorting mechanism, separating the top students from everyone else. The top students, in SP, were offered college-prep courses. Everyone else was offered an education that often amounted to second-rate vocational training. In some districts, that's still the case. If you live in one of these, your choice is simple: get your child into SP, or get out of the district.

Happily, some educators are now committed to educating all children, not just the top 15 percent. Some schools have eliminated tracking all together, and others have found ways to make the effects of tracking less pernicious for those in the lower tracks. If you're fortunate enough to live in a district where this is the case, you may want to consider a school that refuses to group children by ability—even if your child is a high-achiever. Some parents are glad to have their children avoid the competition that's often found in SP classes. Some feel that the social and emotional issues that young adolescents face are such that it's better not to pile on the academic work at this stage. SP classes often are gigantic—with 35 pupils or more. Some parents feel it's a worthwhile tradeoff to have a smaller class with children of various abilities. And some are attracted by a nonacademic program—such as a first-rate drama department—in a school that refuses to group children by ability. Remember, SP refers to the kids—not the teachers. There are some lousy teachers in SP classes just as there are some first-rate teachers in non-SP classes.

Children in SP classes need to maintain a certain average in order to stay in the track, and sometimes the pressure to keep up with classmates can be stressful. I spoke to one mother who was thrilled with her son's middle school—until his grades dropped and he was bumped into a non-SP class. He was so demoralized by the experience that he transferred to another school.

That said, there are some advantages to grouping children by ability in these years. A good teacher can reach children with various abilities in any class, but the wider the range the more difficult it becomes. As children become older, the gap between the top kids and those who are struggling becomes wider, and it's very difficult, even for an experienced teacher, to bridge it. Some children are ready for high-school-level work in 8th grade, and it seems to be a mistake not to let them take the courses that interest them. Some very high-achieving children who have been bored in their neighborhood elementary school are thrilled to finally have classmates who are as bright as they. Even when the teachers are standard-issue, having very smart classmates can offer the stimulation that bright kids crave.

In addition to SP classes within a neighborhood middle school, the city offers a number of **selective schools** devoted entirely to children who are high-achievers. Some of these have a special entrance exam. Others don't have an exam, but do have a minimum requirement in terms of scores on standardized tests. Selective schools accept children on the basis of a written application and an interview. Some schools accept children on the basis of artistic or musical talent, or a combination of academic achievement and artistic talent.

Theme schools offer a concentration in a particular subject area, such as performing arts, journalism, or science. Admissions may be by lottery, by exam, or audition. The best of these offer first-rate instruction in all subject areas, while offering a little extra in the area of the school's speciality. In general, I believe middle school is too early for children to specialize. If you're considering a theme school for your child, make sure all subject areas are strong. A school that has a particular emphasis on art, for example, should also offer solid instruction in science.

Magnet schools receive special federal grants to encourage racial integration. These schools use the extra money to provide special classes around a theme such as journalism or law. The hope is that the extra programs will attract children of different races from outside the neighborhood. Magnet schools give preference to children of racial groups that are underrepresented. Admission is based on a complicated formula that varies from school to school—and districts jealously guard the exact figures—but in general, mostly white schools give preference to nonwhites and mostly nonwhite schools give preference to whites. Race is self-declared. Children of mixed race seeking entry to a magnet school should figure out which racial group gets preference at the particular school to which they are applying—so they can be sure to check the box that will give them the best shot at admission.

Special education is available for children who can't cope in a general education program because they are physically handicapped, learning disabled, or suffering from an emotional or psychiatric disorder. Even if your child functions well in a general education class, it's worth taking a look at the special education department of any school you're considering, because how a school treats kids in special education is a good indication of how it handles any child who is struggling, or who doesn't fit the mold. Schools that value their special education pupils, that identify and encourage their strengths and include them whenever possible in activities with general education pupils, are likely to be schools that are gentle and accommodating places for all children. Schools that keep special education children in the basement and exclude them from activities may be punitive and disagreeable places for other children as well.

I've tried to identify the best special education programs in the city and describe them here. I've also identified general education programs that can accommodate children with special needs. Many of the city's very old school buildings don't have wheelchair access. Those with elevators are listed here. A few schools have made extraordinary efforts to accommodate children in wheelchairs. The Museum School in Manhattan, for example, arranged for a special van to take a handicapped pupil to museums three times a week; classmates helped the pupil up and down stairs.

Children with **learning disabilities, psychiatric disorders, or**

behavior problems may be assigned to a "self-contained" or segregated class with other special education pupils. If their disabilities permit it, they may be placed in a general education class and offered extra help. The advantage of the self-contained or segregated class is size. By law, special education classes are much smaller than general education classes. For children who need the extra attention, small class size is a must. Unfortunately, many of the special education classes are dumping grounds. Teachers' expectations are often low. Children assigned to them rarely return to the mainstream, and few graduate from high school. If your child is assigned to a self-contained class, it's particularly important to visit the school to see whether it's appropriate for him or her.

If your child's learning disabilities are mild, he or she may be assigned to a general education class with extra help in a **resource room**, a special class of eight to ten children who meet for an hour a day. You should also consider asking the school to provide a **consultant teacher** who visits the general education class on a regular basis and offers the classroom teacher tips on how best to help the children with special needs. If your child is strong in one subject but weak in another, look for a school that's flexible about how kids are assigned to classes. One child flourished at the School of the Future in Manhattan (page 63) because teachers allowed him to move quickly in math—his strength—while giving him extra help in reading, his weak skill.

Some of the most interesting special education programs are **inclusion** classes. In these, special education and general education pupils are placed in the same class with two teachers: a special education teacher and a general education teacher. The advantage for both general ed and special ed children is smaller class size and more individual attention. I visited a class in which an autistic child began to speak for the first time (page 209) and a child with a psychiatric disorder became calm (page 246). Their teachers attributed their progress to the fact that they were in classes with general education children—rather than being segregated with children who had the same problems as they.

For general education pupils, having two teachers in the class can be a boon. If a child is having trouble, the special ed teacher may be able to help—without the bother of a formal referral. That frees up the general ed teacher to help high-achieving children move ahead at their own pace. The inclusion model is still experimental, particularly in the middle school years, and some programs have yet to work out their kinks. But if your child needs more attention than he or she can get in a regular general education class, "inclusion" is worth investigating.

Second chance schools and programs (also called **transfer alternative** schools) specialize in helping children who are chronic truants, or who have been thrown out of other schools for misbehavior. Included here are several promising second chance programs.

Things to think about before you visit.

You'll need to visit schools before you decide on your first choice—and what you consider adequate if your child isn't admitted to his or her first choice. (You may also decide your existing options are hopeless and that you need to work with other parents to start your own school. More on that later.) But before you visit, you should arm yourself with as much information as you can. This book will help you get started. You may also want to get **school report cards**, the Board of Education's annual listings of each school's reading and math scores, safety records, and other useful data. Call the board at 718-935-3783 for free copies of the schools' report cards. I've also included key data from these in each entry in this book.

Location is your first consideration. If your child's school is close to home, he or she can make friends who live nearby. You may be able to volunteer in the school. Your child won't be tired out by a long commute. But if the local school isn't great, you'll probably consider schools in other neighborhoods. Middle school kids can handle commuting better than younger children can.

Each entry here lists a school's **enrollment**, its **capacity**, and **typical class size**. Enrollment is the number of kids registered at the school. Capacity is the number of kids the building was originally intended to serve. Typical class size is the size of an average academic class. Each entry also addresses **Admissions** and **When to apply**.

Zoned neighborhood schools accept all children who live in the school's designated zone. **Selective** schools accept children on the basis of a test for academic achievement or an audition for artistic or musical talent. **Unzoned** schools accept children from anywhere in the district or occasionally anywhere in the city. Some require tests, some accept children by lottery. Others interview children and ask them to write an essay explaining why they want to attend a particular school.

Overcrowding has been very serious in New York City public schools since the late 1980s, when large numbers of immigrants moved to the city and the children of the postwar baby boom entered school. Some of the most successful schools are also the most over-crowded. Parents will fight to get their children into them, even if it means placing them in a class of 35 or even 40 kids. The SP or advanced classes tend to be the most crowded. One way to get your child out of a giant class may be to investigate smaller schools that refuse to group children by ability. Some of these schools have kept class size to 20 or 25.

Each entry lists the percentage of children eligible for **free lunch**, a very rough indication of the poverty level of the pupils' families. A family of four with an income of $21,385 a year or less is eligible for free lunch. The proportion of middle school children in the city eligible for free lunch is 71.5 percent. Schools with a free lunch rate of more than 66.3 percent are eligible for extra federal antipoverty funds.

Each entry also lists the percentage of children in various **ethnic** and **racial groups**. Schools receiving federal magnet grants give preference to members of groups that are underrepresented. Your child may have a better chance of admissions to a school in which he or she would be in the minority—that is a white child at a mostly nonwhite school or a nonwhite child wishing to attend a mostly white school. Citywide, middle schools are 37 percent Hispanic, 35 percent African-American, 17 percent white and 11 percent Asian.

Safety is every parent's biggest concern. You will want to talk to other parents, students, and staff about safety when you visit a school. But here's how to look at the published statistics. Each entry lists the rate of **suspensions**—the percentage of children suspended by the principal each year for misbehavior. The citywide average for middle schools was 7.5 percent in 1998. Most of my favorite schools have suspension rates ranging to 2 or 3 percent. For a good many, information is Not Available (N/A).

But a high suspension rate doesn't necessarily mean the school is dangerous. A number of effective principals have a take-no-prisoners attitude toward discipline and suspend kids for even minor infractions. Sometimes a brand-new school needs a tough suspension policy to send a message that bad behavior won't be tolerated.

It's important to remove disruptive children from class, but sending them home for five days isn't the only way to discipline them. Some schools have "in-house suspensions"—keeping troublemakers in the school office to help with chores such as photocopying. Some have old-fashioned detention—keeping kids in during lunch if they misbehave. Some have "behavior modification" programs that give kids prizes such as pizza when their behavior improves. Each of these is more desirable, I believe, than is suspending children for minor disciplinary infractions, because it keeps kids in school. They can't learn if they're not in school.

The school report card also lists a school's **incident rate**. This reflects the number of times school safety officers reported problems to the police. The citywide average for middle schools was 3.1 percent in 1998. That is, for every one hundred pupils there were 3.1 incidents that year. Most of my favorite schools have incident rates of less than 1 percent. The suspension and incident rates are based on 1998 data. Again, for quite a few schools the statistic is Not Available (N/A) from the Board of Education.

The data draw no distinction between a fistfight in the cafeteria and a call for an ambulance for a teacher who has had a heart attack. You'll sometimes find a good school that has a high incident rate because ambulances were called several times during the year. The incident rate may also increase if, for example, the school hires extra safety officers. In that case, the increase reflects better reporting. In general, though, if a school has a high incident rate, you'll want to grill the administration to find out what they're doing about it. If you're not satisfied with the answer, send your child to another school.

The Board of Education reports the percentage of children at each school who score at or above national norms on standardized tests in reading and math. In this book, I've given schools one to five stars based on their **reading scores** and **math scores**. Schools with one star (★) have 0 to 19 percent of children at or above the national average. Those with two stars (★★) have 20 to 39 percent at or above average. Three stars (★★★) mean 40 to 59 percent scored above average. Four stars (★★★★) mean 60 to 79 percent scored above average. Five stars (★★★★★) mean 80 to 100 percent scored above average. Some new schools don't have test data available, which is noted N/A. Reading and math scores are based on 1999 data.

These stars *don't* indicate how much I like a school, or how competent I found the teaching staff. They reflect only how well kids do on standardized tests. Some high-scoring schools are boring places where rote learning and memorization are the rule. Some low-scoring schools accept kids who are struggling and—with lots of work and inspired teaching—help them succeed. Still, reading and math scores are at least one indication of how well a school is doing.

When you compare scores, be sure you're looking at schools with similar populations. It's not fair to compare a zoned school that accepts everyone in the neighborhood with a specialized school that requires children to pass an admissions test (and that asks kids to leave if their test scores drop below a certain level). A first-rate neighborhood school with three or four stars might challenge children of all academic abilities, while a "gifted" program with five stars might offer uninspired classes to children who are so motivated that they teach themselves.

Each entry also lists whether a school offers **Regents**, or high-school level, courses in math and science in the 8th grade. Public high school students in New York City will soon be required to take five Regents exams to graduate. Some parents and children are eager to get started on 9th grade courses in the 8th grade, hoping it will free them up for more electives in high school. Some very good middle schools, however, have resisted offering Regents exams in the 8th grade, maintaining that the exams emphasize rote learning over real understanding. A consortium of progressive high schools, moreover, has petitioned the state to approve alternatives to the Regents curriculum.

Another way to judge a school's achievement is by the quality of the **high schools** its graduates attend. The entry for each school in this book lists the top three high schools attended by its graduates, as reported by the Board of Education. School report cards also have this data. The most selective high schools are the so-called "specialized" ones: Stuyvesant High School in Manhattan, Bronx High School of Science, Brooklyn Technical High School, and the Fiorello H. LaGuardia School of Music and Art and the Performing Arts in Manhattan. Admission to the first three, called the "science schools," is by a citywide competitive exam. Admission to LaGuardia is by audition.

The rate of admissions to specialized schools isn't the only way to judge a middle school, of course. In the neighborhoods that have excellent zoned high schools, parents may choose to keep their children closer to home rather than have them commute to a specialized high school. Some parents, moreover, prefer the intimacy of small, alternative high schools to the large, specialized science schools.

If you're considering a secondary school, with grades 6 through 12 or 7 through 12, it may be more significant to see how many children stay for grades 9 through 12 than to see how many leave for selective high schools. The best secondary schools retain most of their 8th grade class for the high school years. And it doesn't hurt to ask where their graduates go to college.

Once you've looked at the statistics and drawn up a list of schools that interest you, its time to look at them firsthand.

What to look for on a tour.
Touring schools can be stressful and irritating, or a lot of fun, depending on the school, your schedule, and the luck of the draw. If you can possibly arrange it, try to take a couple of mornings off work to visit schools—preferably with your child in tow. Children see things you don't see and often ask good questions that won't occur to you.

Although some schools offer both daytime and evening tours, it's more interesting—and illuminating—to visit when classes are in session. Daytime tours tend to be a bit less crowded. If the schools you're interested in don't offer tours, you may have to improvise. Call the Parent Teacher Association and ask if you can attend a meeting. Say you want to be active in the PTA. (You might leave a message in the school's main office for someone in the PTA to telephone you. Middle school PTA presidents are so desperate for help, they'll probably call you promptly.) Visit the school during Open School Week in November. Offer to volunteer in the school library, or to tutor kids through the NYC School Volunteer Program (212-213-3370). Attend a concert or dramatic production at the school. If all else fails, hang around the school at dismissal and talk to the kids.

Some schools offer "open houses" where hundreds of parents are jammed into an auditorium to watch a slide show and to listen to a presentation by the principal. This isn't really a tour, but it's better than nothing. Other schools offer tours with forty or so parents. You'll have to stay with the pack and move rather briskly through classrooms. The more schools you visit, the more you'll learn and the easier it will be for you to judge what's right for your child.

The first thing you'll notice is the quality of the physical plant. A few schools are bright and cheery, many are gloomy. Try to look beyond the peeling paint to the **quality of teaching**. Look at the kids' faces. Are they interested and engaged? Bored? Staring off vacantly into space? Are *you* interested in what the teacher is saying?

Do the kids' books look interesting? It's okay to have some textbooks, but I much prefer schools with rich **classroom libraries**— novels and biographies, science discovery books, colorful atlases and original source materials such as diaries and historical documents. The more books the better—in the classroom as well as in the school library. Schools that rely too heavily on textbooks are dull.

Are the walls bare, or are there lots of **bulletin boards with kids' work**? Look for examples of children's writing. Is the quality of work good? Are the art projects imaginative? Are the **bathrooms unlocked**? Are children allowed off school grounds for lunch? If so, the administration is confident of children's safety.

What's the noise level in the school? Chaos, of course, is bad news, but so is total silence. Kids should be talking to other kids and to grown-ups. Desks pushed together in small groups, or in a circle, encourage discussion among kids. If you see desks in rows, it often means the teacher tends to stand at the front and lecture. That's not a bad method of instruction for part of the day, but you don't want it all day every day.

Even more important, grown-ups should be talking to one another. In a good middle school, teachers meet regularly to discuss everything from curriculum to individual students' progress and problems. If every teacher is locked in his or her classroom, and never has scheduled time to meet with others, that's a bad sign. Look for collegiality.

Generally, there's time for questions after the tour. This is a good time to ask the principal or director to describe the school's philosophy of education. Like elementary schools, middle schools are divided into two camps: traditional and progressive. Some fall neatly into one or the other. Many are a blend of the two.

Traditional schools see their goal as transmitting a body of knowledge to children. They believe that children must absorb information, learn certain dates in history, facts in geography, grammar, spelling rules, mathematical formulas, and scientific concepts. Traditional schools emphasize content—that is, the notion that certain material must be mastered. Traditional schools emphasize preparation for standardized tests.

Progressive schools, on the other hand, see their role as providing children with the tools they need to explore a new topic, to solve problems, and to conduct original research. Progressive schools emphasize "process," that is, the method by which children learn to find the answers to a question. Rather than focusing on dates in history, a progressive school might encourage children to debate a topic such as "Was the arrival of Columbus in America a good thing or a bad thing?" and require them to do research to support their case. Children might work out the Pythagorean theorem themselves, rather than having it presented to them by the teacher. Progressive schools try to transmit what they call "habits of mind"—the ability to think well and to work independently—rather than specific subject matter. They criticize curricula based on test preparation as factoid memorization, a form of Trivial Pursuit, not learning.

Progressive and *traditional* are tricky words, and different people use them to mean different things. If you ask a principal, "In what ways do you consider your school progressive, and in what ways is it traditional?" you might elicit an interesting answer. Some schools have embraced the "middle school philosophy"—a progressive idea—for the organization of a school, but have retained traditional teaching methods. Others have a traditional organization to the school day, but have introduced interdisciplinary teaching—a progressive idea. Many of the best schools mix elements of progressive and traditional teaching techniques.

The question-and-answer period after your tour is a good time to get a feel for **security** at the school. You'll get a more revealing answer if you ask open-ended questions such as "How do you handle discipline?" rather than "Is your school safe?" Ask whether parents may visit the school and classes during the year. A school that welcomes parents is not afraid of what you might see on an impromptu visit.

Even at the best schools, you may hear about an occasional fistfight or a child selling drugs. No school is immune to these problems—not even the most exclusive private school or the fanciest suburban school. However, it is possible to find a school where such problems are rare and where those that do occur are dealt with promptly and effectively. Look for a school that confronts safety issues head-on, rather than one that pretends nothing bad ever happens. Look for a principal who is respected and liked by the kids, who anticipates problems and intervenes beforehand.

A good number of schools have seen an increase in discipline problems as the result of a contract agreement that relieved teachers of lunchroom duty and hall patrols. Aides are supposed to supervise during these times, but they haven't been as effective as the teachers. At the best schools, teachers and administrators voluntarily supervise kids during lunch and class changes. Be sure to ask what the school's policy is.

Some of the worst incidents of violence occur in the early morning or late afternoon, particularly off school grounds, where kids may pick fights or rob others of their lunch money because there aren't a lot of adults around. The best schools take responsibility for children's safety both inside and outside school, before class and after. Good principals make sure adults are outside at arrivals and dismissals to ensure kids' safety.

Good principals have a close relationship with the local police precinct. School administrators and police officers may coordinate plans for a safe dismissal time. They may call one another if a fight in school threatens to spill into the neighborhood—and vice versa. It's not too much to ask a school to take steps to make sure kids get home safely.

School administrators have some discretion in what incidents they report. A school with a low incident rate may have an unpleasant atmosphere in which kids feel free to hurl insults, often racially charged, or to shove one another in the hall. Ask students about the atmosphere of a school as well as its safety record.

The kids I interviewed were more interested in the grown-ups' response to violence than to the violence itself. A school with a low suspension rate can still feel very threatening if the principal is holed up in the office and the teachers are locked in their classrooms. A school with a somewhat higher suspension rate, on the other hand, can feel quite safe if the teachers and the administrators are highly visible during class changes and after school—and the kids believe that the grown-ups care about what happens to them.

Small schools are generally safer than big schools. Schools that provide wholesome ways for kids to have fun together—supervised school dances or camping trips—are less likely to have problems than schools that leave kids to organize their own social lives. Schools in which the principal spends lots of time talking to kids informally, in the halls or in the cafeteria, are generally safer than those in which the principal spends the day pushing papers in the office.

Some parents are wowed by beautiful facilities and equipment they see on the tour, then disappointed to find their child isn't allowed to use them. Be sure to ask. May everyone play in the orchestra, or only those who pass an audition? Is that beautiful botany lab for everyone, or only for the "gifted" students?

If classes are tracked (grouped by ability), ask how the school keeps the kids in the bottom tracks from feeling like second-class citizens. If classes are not tracked, how are the kids at the top challenged? How does the school deal with kids who are strong in one subject, weak in another?

If your child is in **special education**, you'll be particularly interested in how they deal with handicapped kids. How many children are "decertified," that is, returned to regular classes? What proportion of their day is spent with general ed children? Do they study non-academic subjects, such as art and music, together? Some of the answers are available on school report cards.

Good teachers expect progress from all children, even the most disabled. I saw a class for mentally retarded children in the Bronx (page 193) where teachers helped develop social skills. Their "exam" was attending the school-wide dance in the spring. Test scores aren't the only way to mark a child's gains.

Perhaps the most difficult challenge for parents is **evaluating a new school**. Dozens of new programs have opened in the past decade, and parents are dizzy with the changes. How is it possible to judge a school with no track record, no test scores, not even a group of parents of whom one can ask advice? Is it better to send your child to a tried-and-true—but boring—junior high school or to a new and exciting—but untested—mini-school? There's no easy answer. My advice is to look at the quality of the teaching and to listen carefully to the director or principal's spiel. A principal with a vision he or she can articulate—and a plan to carry out that vision—has a chance to create a good school. One who can only tell you he or she believes that punctuality is important, or one who parrots incomprehensible educational jargon, probably won't cut it. It doesn't hurt to ask the principal or director where he or she worked before. The quality and philosophy of that school may be a guide to what the new school will be like.

When it comes to establishing a new school, the quality of teaching is probably more important than the level of achievement of the kids. A new school with good teachers will, as word gets out, attract bright kids. A school with bright kids and boring teachers will probably always remain a school with bright kids and boring teachers.

What kids should be studying.

Middle schools are so different from the junior high schools that the majority of today's parents attended that it's hard for many of us to judge what's good and what is not. In some cases, teaching methods have changed dramatically. In others, the material that teachers believe should be mastered is different. How can parents determine—particularly in a brief tour—whether a school is doing what it should be?

One of the biggest differences between today's middle schools and yesterday's junior high schools is the way in which subjects are integrated. No longer are history and English discrete subjects, taught by teachers who never speak to each other. Rather, the history teacher and the English teacher (and possibly the math and science teacher as well) will meet frequently and plan lessons together. Children might read *To Kill a Mockingbird* in English class while they discuss the civil rights movement in history class. The science and English teachers might jointly assign a term paper that they both grade, with the science teacher judging its content and the English teacher judging its style, organization, and grammar.

English classes (also called Language Arts) have probably changed the least in the past twenty or thirty years. You'll recognize a lot of old favorites on today's reading lists, such as *The Diary of Anne Frank* and Shakespeare's *Julius Caesar*. You may see a nod to multiculturalism with, say, a novel written by an author from Brazil or China.

The method of teaching writing, on the other hand, has changed somewhat, largely influenced by the work of Lucy Calkins at Columbia University's Teachers College. In her method, known as The Writing Process, children are encouraged to write multiple drafts and to edit one another's work. At its best, the Writing Process teaches children to write the way professional authors do—constantly revising their work, always with a real audience in mind. Not the least of the benefit is the way in which the Writing Process allows children to work independently of their teacher. This gives the teacher time to help one child, while the others in the class are working productively on their own. Most important, it gives teachers the courage to assign long papers. In schools that have incorporated the Writing Process well, children typically write longer and more complex papers than is common in junior high school—ten to twelve pages or more.

The subject matter in history (also called social studies) hasn't changed much. Kids mostly study ancient civilizations in 6th grade, and American history in 7th and 8th grades. But the teaching methods have changed a lot. Textbooks are out. Primary source materials are in, such as actual documents and contemporary accounts of events in the past: court records from colonial America, the diaries of Revolutionary War soldiers.

Kids may study the contents of an Egyptian tomb on a museum visit, or perform a Greek play in translation. Many history teachers make good use of the excellent documentary films that have been produced in recent years, such as *Eyes on the Prize*, the history of the civil rights movement. Here, too, multiculturalism has made inroads. Children study ancient civilizations of India and China as well as

Egypt, Greece, and Rome. Children study not only military and political history, but the history of ordinary people, too, particularly the lives of women and children.

There is a great debate over how math should be taught in middle school, comparable in some ways to the phonics/whole language debate about reading skills. Proponents of the "new math" say the methods by which most of today's parents studied mathematics were often dull, routine, and irrelevant. The old methods concentrated too much on basic arithmetic and memorizing formulas—pencil and paper work made obsolete by the introduction of the pocket calculator. Proponents argue the new math curriculum, which introduces elements of algebra, probability, statistics, and geometry to middle school children, engages students' curiosity and better prepares them for high school.

In schools that have adopted the new math, you'll see kids rolling dice to figure out problems in probability. You'll see kids constructing rectangles from small plastic tiles to find factors or to determine whether a number is prime. I find these new methods very appealing. But, like anything else in education, the quality of the teacher counts more than the method. Some parents have dubbed the new math "fuzzy math" and have complained that their children are unable to do long division if the batteries on their pocket calculator fail. If the teacher is poorly trained, the new methods are no better than the old. An excellent teacher will inspire a class, whether the textbooks are old or new.

The teaching of science is another area that has undergone tremendous change. In the past, critics say, many science classes concentrated on rote learning and memorization. Teachers focused on covering material in a textbook so kids could pass standardized tests intended to show their mastery of the facts. The teacher might do an experiment in the front of the class, but the kids rarely got a chance to touch any materials themselves. Many places still teach science this way. Those that concentrate on learning from textbooks may prepare children fairly well for Regents exams, but some teachers complain that those exams rely excessively on children's mastery of facts—memorization.

Many passionate teachers of science say the old methods of instruction were tedious and missed the point of scientific inquiry. These teachers say textbooks shouldn't be the primary tools of instruction. Rather, children should explore science with things they can see and touch. They should conduct experiments themselves, not just watch the teacher. They should take trips to the city's parks to learn how rocks are formed and how ecosystems work. They should learn to think the way scientists think—by posing questions, making their own observations and hypotheses, and by predicting outcomes, rather than passively accepting information from an authority.

Middle school is when instruction in foreign languages begins in earnest. Unfortunately, language teaching was weak in almost every school I visited. Rarely did I hear spoken the language the kids were supposed to be studying when I entered a class. Rather, I heard the teacher—in English—rambling on about some arcane point of grammar as kids fidgeted. Obviously, kids learn languages best when they hear and speak them. English in the foreign-language classroom should be used sparingly. Unfortunately, the large class size in most public schools makes it impossible for kids to get much practice speaking a foreign language.

Surprisingly, some of the best foreign-language instruction I witnessed was in Latin, a subject that's seeing a modest revival after years of being considered irrelevant. In these classes, teachers strive to teach children the Latin roots of English, enriching their knowledge of their own language. A tiny handful teach children to speak Latin. More common are the classes that use Latin as an introduction to linguistics and the history of English.

Judith Baum of the Public Education Association was impressed by a "dual language" middle school in which Spanish and English alternate as the language of instruction—and kids leave the school fluent in both (page 112).

How to get in.

Once you've visited the schools that interest you, you'll have to fill out applications for admission—unless you decide on your zoned neighborhood school. Some schools have entrance exams; some, auditions. Others accept children by lottery. When you apply, you'll have to rank schools in order of preference.

The admissions dance is a bit like courtship: tell someone you love him (or her) only, and he (or she) is more likely to respond in kind. Tell someone they'll do if nothing better turns up and you're likely to get the brush off. So think carefully before you list your preferences. **Many of the best schools will consider only pupils that list them as first choice**. Don't try to tell two schools in one district that they're your first choice. Schools within a district communicate with one another.

However, usually schools in different districts *don't* communicate with one another. That means there's nothing to stop you from telling Mark Twain in Brooklyn's District 21 that it is your first choice, while also telling Lab School in Manhattan's District 2 that you think they're tops. Just don't tell one district you're applying to another.

Some of the schools have admissions procedures that are clear-cut and apparently incorruptible. But in many, principals have some discretion over admissions. Even if admissions decisions are made by lottery, sometimes there's a little wiggle room—in the late summer, for example, when a child who has been admitted unexpectedly moves out of town. So it's worth letting the principal know who you are. A little hero worship doesn't hurt, either. Let the principal know, in a letter, why you think his or her school is the best on the planet. Promise you'll work in the PTA. You can even go to a PTA meeting. Tell the principal why his or her school is particularly well suited for your child. Most principals aren't looking for geniuses, but they do want kids and parents who share their philosophy and who support the goals of the school. Don't be a pest, but it doesn't hurt to make friends with a school secretary or someone in the PTA who can take your calls when you're anxiously waiting for word on whether your child is in.

If all else fails: How to start your own school (or fix the one you've got).

What if you don't like any of the schools in your neighborhood and you don't want to send your child far from home? Parents with concerns about specific, fixable problems at their neighborhood schools sometimes find that pressuring the district office works. One Brooklyn father, distraught that his son's special education class had virtually no books, complained pleasantly but persistently to his district office and got results. PTAs sometimes raise money to restore popular programs, such as music and sports, eliminated because of budget cuts. If other parents share your concerns, band together and see what you can do.

Under new Board of Education regulations, every public school was required to establish a "School Leadership Team" by the fall of 1999. These teams of administrators, teachers, and parents are charged with setting school policy—a potentially powerful role for parents seeking to improve their neighborhood school. Ask your PTA about becoming a member.

Or consider starting your own school. It's not easy, but parents at Manhattan School for Children on the West Side of Manhattan did it (page 115), as did parents at Jonas Bronck Academy in the Bronx (page 187). District 15 in Brooklyn opened eight new schools in 1998 as a result of parent pressure (page 202) So if you're unhappy with your options, make a fuss. Talk to a member of your community school board. Ask your district office for the name of the board member who is the liaison to your school, and leave a message for him or her to call you. Or run for the school board yourself. Contact the Institute for Education and Social Policy at New York University (212-998-5874) for advice on how to do it.

The state legislature in 1998 passed a new law permitting the opening of "charter schools," small, independent public schools organized by community groups and free of certain bureaucratic rules and regulations. Even before the charter law, New York City was in the forefront of developing experimental schools. Many of these schools founder in their early years, but some others are flourishing. Parents who start lobbying for change early in their children's elementary school years may succeed by the time their children are ready for middle school. **Parents interested in starting their own school should contact New Visions for Public Schools at 212-645-6110 or New Perspectives, Bank Street College, 212-875-4649.**

"It takes longer than you expect or hope," said Lois Harr, a founding parent at Jonas Bronck Academy in the Bronx. "You can't start when your child is in fifth grade." When her child was in second grade, Ms. Harr and other parents approached New Visions and won a planning grant to start a new school in 1995. They worked with officials from District 10, a consultant hired by the district, and Manhattan College. The college leased them space for the new school, which eventually opened in 1997. In many districts, space is the critical problem. Ms. Harr advises collaborating with a community-based organization that might have access to buildings that can be converted for school use.

Lucy Wicks, a former school board member in District 3 on the West Side of Manhattan and a founding parent of Manhattan School for Children, advises parents to research existing options thoroughly before drawing up a plan.

"If you just come out of the blue, yelling and screaming, you won't get very far," said Ms. Wicks. "You have to go to the district and say: 'This is what I see as available. Convince me that I'm wrong.' "

She said parents gain credibility if they become active early in their children's school years. "If you want to start a middle school, you have to have a history of working with the PTA at your elementary school," she said. "You will have connected with other parents. By the time your child is in third grade, you should know what kind of middle school your child needs."

There are more middle school options than you might imagine. Large or small, traditional or experimental, well-established or brand-new, the city has dozens of programs worth considering for your child.

The middle school years can be exciting and challenging, frightening and exhilarating, hopeful and frustrating—sometimes all on the same day. These years are the first, difficult steps between childhood and adulthood. Help your child find a good middle school, and you're well on your way.

Reading Scores	Free Lunch
Math Scores	Ethnicity
Eighth Grade Regents	Enrollment
Grade Levels	Capacity
Admissions	Suspensions
When to Apply	Incidents
Class Size	High School Choices

MANHATTAN

MANHATTAN

When out-of-towners say New York City, they really mean Manhattan, that crowded, overpriced, exhilarating island of skyscrapers, tenements, and raw energy. The most aggressive Manhattanites are among the most competitive people on earth. These are the folks who think nothing of sending their three-year-olds off for I.Q. tests to be placed in special prekindergarten classes for the "gifted." So it should come as no surprise that some of Manhattan's middle schools are among the most selective and competitive anywhere. Manhattan is also a place where oddballs feel welcome, and, perhaps not surprisingly, there are some excellent schools for kids who don't fit the mold.

There are schools that specialize in drama, or dance, or computer studies, or science. There are secondary schools (with grades 6 through 12 or 7 through 12) that boast that they send every single graduate to college. Several dozen new schools were created in the 1990s, and others were reorganized in line with current findings on how young adolescents learn. Philosophies range from very traditional to very progressive. Neighborhoods range from the super-posh areas of Fifth Avenue and Park Avenue to the rapidly expanding immigrant communities of Washington Heights at the northern tip of the island.

Many schools accept children from any of the city's five boroughs, although preference is generally given to children from the immediate neighborhood. Unfortunately, quality varies tremendously from school to school. Manhattan may have some of the best schools anywhere, but it also has some of the worst.

District 1

The Lower East Side of Manhattan has long been home to an eclectic mix of poor and working-class Puerto Ricans, Orthodox Jews, Chinese-Americans, yuppies, squatters, bohemians, and artists. A multiracial group of parents helped create a network of small progressive elementary schools in the 80s and 90s that attracted middle class parents and began to reverse a long exodus of neighborhood kids who had gone to other districts. Middle school reform has been slower, and the neighborhood junior high schools are, for the most part, disappointing.

An alternative school worth watching is **East Side Community High School**, at 420 East 12th Street, New York, N.Y., 10009. The school is a member of the Coalition of Essential Schools, a national network of small, progressive schools, and New Visions For Public Schools, the Manhattan-based school reform group. East Side has five hundred pupils in grades 7 through 12. Its principal, Jill Herman, can be reached at 212-460-8467. The school welcomes parent involvement and seeks families who are willing to participate in what it calls "a partnership dedicated to academic excellence, nonviolence, racial, gender, and ethnic equality and responsibility to one's community." Reading scores are the highest in the district, with about half the middle school pupils reading at or above the national average.

District 2

District 2 includes some of the most expensive real estate on the planet: the Upper East Side, Sutton Place, Gramercy Park, Greenwich Village, and Wall Street. Even the West Side south of 59th Street— once known as Hell's Kitchen—has been gussied up and renamed "Clinton" or "Midtown West" by hopeful real estate agents who have been able, in recent years, to command astonishing rents for extremely modest apartments. There are some reasonable rentals in the neighborhoods such as Stuyvesant Town and a few sections of Chelsea, but turnover is very, very low and affordable apartments are few.

So it's the rare family who can afford to move to District 2 to take advantage of its first-rate middle schools. Luckily, the schools generally have some room for kids from outside the district. With planning and a bit of luck you may be able to get your child a seat if he or she is willing to take a bus or the subway to school.

Superintendent Anthony J. Alvarado, the quirky genius who ran District 2 from 1987 to 1998, transformed many bleak and threatening junior high schools into the promising experimental middle (6th through 8th grade) and secondary (6th through 12th grade) schools found in the district today. He attracted first-rate principals by offering them rare autonomy in hiring teachers and setting school budgets, while giving them an unusual level of protection from the bureaucratic dictates of the central Board of Education.

He adopted the Middle School Initiative with enthusiasm, reorganized large schools into smaller mini-schools, and encouraged principals and teachers to return to school themselves for retraining in new teaching methods. "He dispelled the gloom," one middle school director told me. Unfortunately, after quarrels with the city schools chancellor, Alvarado was lured to a job in San Diego, California. Still, by the time Alvarado left, there were enough good administrators, principals and teachers in the district—and enough politically sophisticated, demanding parents—to maintain the momentum he had created.

Parents who are interested in District 2 middle schools should begin their search in October of their child's fifth-grade year. If your child is in a District 2 elementary school, you'll receive a middle school directory in the mail. Otherwise, you can pick up a copy at the district office at 333 Seventh Avenue, 7th floor, New York, N.Y., 10001, or call 212-330-9400. The district conducts middle school fairs at several elementary schools in the fall, at which you can meet representatives of various programs. You should also arrange to tour—with your child—the schools that interest you. The schools have weekly tours during the fall. Applications are due before Christmas. When you send in your application, you must list four schools in order of preference. If you live in the district, your child is guaranteed a spot in one of those four. Acceptance letters are sent out in April.

The district has "zoned" schools as well as "option" or "unzoned" schools. Every child who lives in the district is entitled to attend a "zoned" school based on his or her home address. The schools also have some room for children from outside the zone. Several zoned schools are excellent. The two listed here, MS 167 and MS 104, group children by ability (known in educational jargon as "homogeneous grouping,") with separate classes for advanced or "special placement" students.

Some parents prefer an "option" or alternative program. Option schools are smaller than the zoned middle schools and accept children by written application, without regard to their address. Children living in District 2 have priority, but many of the option schools have room for children from outside the district. These have a variety of admissions requirements. Some ask children to write an essay. Some ask only that a child be "committed to the philosophy of the school." Some have classes that mix children of various abilities (called "heterogeneous grouping"). Some are "selective" schools that limit admission to children who have high scores on standardized tests.

Even if your child scores high on standardized tests, you may want to consider a school that mixes children of different abilities. In District 2, several of the option schools with mixed-abilities have managed to limit class size to 25. The classes for advanced students, however, are almost all oversubscribed—with class sizes of 35 or more.

Also included in this chapter are entries on Hunter College High School on East 94th Street, the Institute for Collaborative Education on East 15th Street, and the Professional Performing Arts School on West 48th Street. These three schools are in the geographic area covered by District 2 but are *not* administered by the district.

PS 89, IS 89
201 Warren Street
New York, N.Y. 10282

Ellen Foote, principal
212-571-5659

Reading Scores: ★★★★★
Math Scores: ★★★★★
Eighth Grade Regents: N/A
Grade Levels: 6–8
Admissions: Unzoned. By
  interview.
When to Apply: Weekly tours
  October-December.

Class Size: 30
Free Lunch: N/A
Ethnicity: N/A
Enrollment: 75
Capacity: 300
Suspensions: N/A
Incidents: N/A
High School Choices: N/A

This glorious school building—with commanding views of New York Harbor, the Statue of Liberty, and Liberty Park in the southernmost tip of Manhattan—opened in 1998 after a speedy eighteen months of construction.

Built by the Battery Park City Authority (rather than the notoriously inefficient School Construction Authority), this combined elementary and middle school, PS/IS 89, is unusual in that the architects consulted with administrators, teachers, and members of the community about what they thought an ideal school should look like.

The result is a building that has nooks in the halls for kids to work individually or in groups, spaces for community meetings, and large, sunny, quiet classrooms designed so kids can move around. Each classroom has a space for them to sit on a rug as a group and listen to the teacher, as well as tables for them to work in small groups or individually.

The corridors are unusually wide for a middle school, and at various points there are carpeted steps where kids may sit and talk to one another, put on a small theatrical production, or meet with a teacher.

The middle school principal, Ellen Foote, was a teacher at PS 234, a progressive elementary school in nearby Tribeca, and a math staff developer for District 2. She is committed to building a school where children of different abilities work in classes together.

"We have really made an effort to start small and keep it simple," Ms. Foote said. Instruction in instrumental music (strings, brass, and woodwinds) is offered as well as basketball and track and field. Other electives include the student newspaper, drama, and woodworking.

The intermediate school had only seventy-five pupils, all 6th graders, during our visit. The stress of opening a new facility weighed heavily on the principal, who seemed a bit harried. Not every teacher the first year was stellar, and Ms. Foote was working out the problems of a new building—getting the computers hooked up, getting books into the library.

But the promise for the future seems great, partly because the physical plant is so conducive to good teaching and partly because staff development—the district's program to continuously upgrade teachers' skills—is so good. Lucy Calkins, the renowned Teachers College expert on how to teach children to write, was in one classroom helping a teacher.

In a science class, kids were discussing how cholera is transmitted and the importance of clean water. In social studies, kids were talking about how ancient Greece was both a democracy and a highly stratified society. The level of instruction was very sophisticated. Obviously there were some very bright kids in the class. The children were attentive and well behaved.

Like PS 234, IS 89 is working toward an "integrated" or interdisciplinary curriculum. Sixth graders study the Hudson River in science class, for example. They learn about sewage treatment and the threat of pollution to local wildlife In social studies, 6th graders study the role of the Nile in ancient Egypt. In both classes, children learn about the importance of rivers to human civilization.

"It's progressive in the best sense of the world," said Judy Epstein, a parent. "The kids are extremely happy." She said she liked the fact that the students aren't competitive and that they don't have mountains of homework.

Ms. Epstein and Ms. Foote both said it was a "challenge" to have children of different abilities in classes together. Ms. Foote was experimenting with ways to pull out for part of the day small groups of kids who needed extra help.

West Street, a busy, noisy highway, divides Battery Park City from the rest of Manhattan. Children attending IS 89 from Tribeca or other neighborhoods outside Battery Park City must cross West Street on a footbridge that is shared with Stuyvesant High School.

PS/IS 89 is designed to hold 850 children in prekindergarten through 8th grade. When it is at full capacity, the middle school will have three hundred children in grades 6 through 8.

IS 89 is open to all children in District 2. The administration is committed to having a range of academic abilities, a mix of children from different ethnic groups and income levels, and a geographic distribution of children within District 2. There is no test for admissions. Children are interviewed in a group. Ms. Epstein said the interview is designed to assess how well children can work in a group, rather than their academic ability. Prospective parents may visit the school in the fall. The school is wheelchair accessible.

IS 897, Manhattan Academy of Technology
122 Henry Street
New York, N.Y. 10002

Melinda Leong, principal
212-962-2964

Reading Scores: ★★★★★   **Free Lunch:** 79%
Math Scores: ★★★★★   **Ethnicity:** 1.6%W 4.9%B
Eighth Grade Regents: yes   8.2%H 85.2%A
Grade Levels: 6–8   **Enrollment:** 61
Admissions: Selective. By test.   **Capacity:** 180
When to Apply: Weekly tours   **Suspensions:** N/A
  October-December.   **Incidents:** N/A
Class Size: 30   **High School Choices:** N/A

This tiny, new middle school on the top floor of elementary school PS 2, blends the values of traditional education admired by many Chinatown parents with the progressive teaching techniques favored by the staff. First opened in 1997, the school quickly rose to the top of the city's middle school ranking for reading scores. Even in its first year, it scored in the top 20 percent of schools citywide.

The Manhattan Academy of Technology was founded as a way for parents in Chinatown to keep their youngsters in a small school close to home. But the school's reputation has spread quickly and it draws children, mostly Chinese-American, from Staten Island, Brooklyn, and Queens, as well as Chinatown and the Lower East Side.

The students wear uniforms—white or blue polo shirts emblazoned with the logo of the Manhattan Academy of Technology—and skirts or trousers of their own choosing—mostly blue jeans or nylon warm-up pants with sneakers. The staff, on the other hand, is young and hip, not out of place in the East Village. One teacher is a recent MIT graduate; another a recent Harvard graduate.

It was the parents' idea for the kids to have uniforms, and the staff went along, reluctantly at first. But teachers came to appreciate the fact that a uniform policy helps free the kids from competition over wearing brand-names and anxiety about their changing bodies.

Parents wanted a school that emphasized old-fashioned standards of decorum and discipline, punctuality, homework, and high scores on standardized tests. The teachers wanted a chance to be creative. Both parents and teachers, it seems, got their wish.

"Homework is checked. We teach kids responsibility and account-ability," said the principal, Ms. Leong. Kids who are late or who don't turn in their homework on time must have a "detention" lunch in their classroom instead of the cafeteria.

"It's very strict. I like the structure," said PTA co-president Chris Lam. But it's not a regimented place with desks in rows. In fact, kids are likely to be sitting on the floor, working on projects independently or in small groups. One class took apart a bicycle and reassembled it, learning about mechanics in the process.

"Children here aren't always handed the facts. They have to figure things out for themselves," said Ms. Leong, who was a science teacher at PS 124, a well-regarded elementary school in Chinatown. "When I was a kid, to measure the slope of a line they gave me a formula and I just plugged it in," she said.

At Manhattan Academy of Technology, in contrast, kids study algebra by dropping a tennis ball from various heights, and graphing how high it bounces each time. Ms. Leong: "They say, 'Where would it fall if I dropped it from here?' and they begin to see a pattern. They develop the formula themselves."

There are computers in every classroom, and the school has its own website. Kids compare notes on projects via e-mail with other schools. When they tested the quality of water samples from the East River, for example, they compared their results with those of other schools in the district. Kids present projects via computer "hyperstudio," instead of ordinary term papers. In "hyperstudio," children can add film clips, music, and photos to their research papers. In an on-line chat with Madeleine L'Engle, the author of *A Wrinkle in Time*, children dis-cussed what it's like to be a writer.

"The kids were enthusiastic," said Jessica Wolff, of the Public Edu-cation Association. "They were into what they were doing and they really seemed to be paying attention to one another's ideas. The teachers talked to the kids with respect. There was a nice balance of noisiness and quiet."

Instead of changing classes every forty-three minutes as they would in a traditional junior high school, children have classes of ninety min-utes or more. English and social studies are combined and taught by one teacher. Kids only have to get to know a few teachers, and teachers have a total of fifty or sixty students instead of one hundred or more. Each teacher has an "advisory" of fourteen students in which they talk about any problems—social or academic—that kids may be having.

Parents praise the energy and dedication of the staff. "At three o'clock, they don't run out the door," said the PTA's Ms. Lam. "They play soccer with the kids after school, on their own time."

PTA co-chair Debbie Cox-Langley said the principal is always available to listen to parents' concerns. "The students have the teachers' phone numbers at home," she said. "You can call if you have a question about your homework."

Parents may tour the school in the fall, and should submit an application by December. Children are admitted according to the results of a test given by the school. The administration says standardized test scores play only a small part in the admissions process. The school's own test, which is administered at various times between January and March, includes an open-ended math question, a science question, and a computer question. It also attempts to assess how well a child works in a group with others.

Children from outside the district are accepted, but children from District 2 have priority.

MS 896, Greenwich Village Middle School
490 Hudson Street
New York, N.Y. 10014

Jacqueline Grossman, principal
212-691-7384

Reading Scores: ★★★★
Math Scores: ★★★★
Eighth Grade Regents: yes
Grade Levels: 6–8
Admissions: Unzoned. By interview.
When to Apply: Weekly tours October-December.
Class Size: 28

Free Lunch: N/A
Ethnicity: 29%W 32.3%B 35.5%H 3.2%A
Enrollment: 62
Capacity: 180
Suspensions: N/A
Incidents: N/A
High School Choices: N/A

Before Greenwich Village Middle School was founded in 1997, parents had long complained that there was no middle school in the West Village. Parents from PS 41, in particular, wanted the option of keeping their children close to home rather than sending them north of that great downtown Rubicon, 14th Street.

After several years of pressure from parents, the district agreed to open Greenwich Village Middle School and named Jacqueline Grossman, an experienced 6th grade teacher from PS 41, as its teacher-director. The school was assigned a few rooms on the top floor of PS 41 on West 11th Street in its first year. In 1998-99, it moved to permanent quarters on the top floor of PS 3 on Hudson Street.

Like PS 3, Greenwich Village Middle School has an informal, relaxed atmosphere, where everyone—kids and parents alike—can wander into the school office for a chat. Parents worked hard to beautify the new quarters in the hundred-year-old-building, painting the large classrooms in noninstitutional colors like lemon yellow with periwinkle. Classrooms are plastered with charts and lists; kids' completed work is displayed in the halls.

"I love the closeness, the fact that we know everything that is going on," said PTA co-president Thom Fogarty. "There's a real family feeling. You can come in anytime and sit in on your daughter's classes."

Augusta Kaiser, another mother, said the individual attention the children receive is invaluable. Teachers and even the school director will answer kids' queries about homework by e-mail in the evening.

"My older daughter came in as a mediocre student," said Ms. Kaiser. "She really wasn't living up to her potential. This school turned her around. She became accountable." Ms. Kaiser credited the school's small class size and the teachers' dedication for the improvement.

Ms. Grossman believes it's important for middle schools to establish traditions and routines that offer kids a sense of purpose and feeling of belonging. The whole school meets once a day for "community time." Kids are encouraged to read a newspaper every day, and to participate as a school in activities such as an AIDS walk or a "penny harvest" to collect coins for charity. Such activities, Grossman said, harness adolescents' natural desires to have their voices heard and to make changes in society.

"We want kids who are going to be problem solvers in their community," she said. "We say to kids: if you're not part of the solution, you're part of the problem."

Ms. Grossman, whose parents both survived Nazi concentration camps, believes academic studies should be infused with a sense of moral purpose as well as an acute sense of history. I sat in on a humanities class she taught in which kids discussed a passage from *The Diary of Anne Frank*, the story of a Jewish girl hiding from the Nazis.

Ms. Grossman said that her favorite passage in one of her favorite books was, "It's really a wonder that I haven't dropped all my ideas . . . in spite of everything I still believe people are good at heart." She asked children whether they agreed that people are really good at heart, and to support their view with evidence.

Most classes are ninety minutes long. Regents-level math (also called "Sequential I," or 9th grade math) and Earth Science are offered.

Parents are enthusiastic about both the classroom instruction and the frequent class trips. Children visit the offices of the Spanish-language newspaper *El Diario*, which publishes a few blocks from the school, for a lesson in journalism and Spanish. The science teacher organized a six-week program at the Bronx Zoo in which parents and kids visited behind the scenes at the zoo on Saturdays, meeting with the scientists who work there and seeing such sights as the animal's cafeteria.

"I wish every child could have the experience we're having," said Fogarty. But Ms. Kaiser mused that the school should perhaps remain the well-kept secret that it now is. "I don't know if I should publicize it, because it may ruin everything," she said.

The admissions process favors kids who say they are committed to working in what Grossman calls a "collaborative, activist-oriented environment." There is no test for admissions, and children of all academic abilities are admitted. A writing sample and an interview are required, however. A plus for late risers: the school's hours are 9 a.m. to 3:20 p.m.

IS 894, Ballet Tech, the New York City Public School for Dance
890 Broadway
New York, N.Y. 10003

Dania Vasquez, principal
212-777-7330

Reading Scores: ★★★
Math Scores: ★★★
Eighth Grade Regents: no
Grade Levels: 6–12
Admissions: Selective. Auditions four times a year.
When to Apply: Apply year-round, tours in March.
Class Size: 20 or less

Free Lunch: N/A
Ethnicity: 18.6%W 45.8%B 23.7%H 11.9%A
Enrollment: 59
Capacity: N/A
Suspensions: N/A
Incidents: N/A
High School Choices: N/A

An unusual collaboration between a professional dance company—Eliot Feld's Ballet Tech—and the Board of Education, the New York City Public School for Dance offers talented youngsters academic classes in the morning and trains them to be professional dancers in the afternoon.

"There's no other model like it in the country—a purely public school associated with a professional dance company," said school director Dania Vasquez, who boasts that the training children receive is as good as they would get at a private school such as Juilliard or the School of American Ballet.

The students perform with professionals from Ballet Tech at the Joyce Theater in Chelsea, at Lincoln Center, and at the Kennedy Center in Washington, D.C. All classes are free of charge. Even ballet shoes and leotards are provided. Interestingly, the school has more boys than girls. This is a place, it seems, where dance is considered a manly pursuit.

Founded in 1995, the school is an outgrowth of the Professional Performing Arts School on West 48th Street. Aspiring dancers at PPAS used to go to studios at the Wein Center for Theater and Dance, at 19th Street and Broadway, for rehearsals.

But the thirty-block commute cut into their academic studies. So the public school for dance was set up on the seventh floor of the Wein

Center, where Ballet Tech has its studios. A small academic staff was hired, and a few studios were carved into classrooms for students in grades 6 through 12.

It has the intimacy of a one-room schoolhouse. There are two humanities teachers (who combine English and history), one math teacher, and one science teacher. Ms. Vasquez teaches Spanish, and there is a part-time art teacher and a part-time French teacher. The school is so tiny that teachers need to mix kids of different ages to fill up a class. Sixth and 7th graders are in one class; 8th and 9th graders in another.

"The academic part of the school is modeled on the best that progressive education has to offer," Ms. Vasquez said. The curriculum is interdisciplinary. Children are more likely to work on projects than to read textbooks. They are more likely to have their work assessed by teachers looking at a portfolio of their written work than by a multiple-choice exam.

The day I visited, five kids in one high school humanities class were discussing character development in *Huckleberry Finn*, while a dozen kids in the other humanities class were comparing *Romeo and Juliet* to *Macbeth*. Kids in a middle school science class discussed the oxygen cycle and drew up plans to make terrariums. Kids in a middle school math class were working on algebra problems as a teacher walked from table to table to offer individual help.

With pleasant views of the mansard roofs of the Flatiron District, the school feels as if it might be in Paris. Shiny hardwood floors, high ceilings, and large windows make all the rooms—even the cafeteria—cheery and pleasant. Walk through the corridors, and you hear the sound of dancing feet, pianos playing jazzy tunes or classical numbers, and instructors putting their charges through their paces. Students in grades 6 through 12 have several hours of dance instruction each afternoon.

The studios are set aside for elementary school pupils in the morning. Ballet Tech, formerly known as the Feld Ballet, auditions thirty-five thousand 3rd and 4th graders each year from 450 public schools, and offers about a thousand the chance to study ballet once a week. No experience is necessary, and children are chosen according to their aptitude for dance, based on the flexibility of their feet and their musicality, rather than their level of skill.

Children are bused from their neighborhood schools to the studios at Ballet Tech. Those who show particular talent are invited to continue dance twice a week in the 5th grade, and a small number—about

20—are selected to continue at the preprofessional level in 6th through 12th grades.

Parents of children who want to audition in 3rd or 4th grade may ask if their school offers auditions, or they may call Ballet Tech directly. Auditions are held twice a year in the fall and spring.

Children seeking admission to the 6th grade who have not been part of Ballet Tech may also ask for an audition. Successful candidates generally have had several years of training in ballet.

One student told me he learned more in three hours of academic classes here than he did in a full-day program at his elementary school in the Bronx. Small class size, and teachers who made him focus on his work, made the difference, the boy said.

Prospective parents may visit the school in March. Call the school for details.

MS407, Institute for Collaborative Education
345 East 15th Street, 5th floor
New York, N.Y. 10003

John Pettinato, principal
212-475-7972

Reading Scores: ★★★★
Math Scores: ★★★
Eighth Grade Regents: yes
Grade Levels: 6–12
Admissions: Selective. Teacher recommendation, writing sample.
When to Apply: Year-round.
Class Size: 16

Free Lunch: 51%
Ethnicity: 20.0%W 46.8%B 25.5%H 7.7%A
Enrollment: 235
Capacity: 300
Suspensions: N/A
Incidents: 1.7%
High School Choices: N/A

A well-kept secret in its first years of operation, the Institute for Collaborative Education (ICE) is a small, progressive secondary school that has relied on word of mouth to attract high-achieving kids from across the city. Founded in 1993, the school established a small but devoted following among parents whose kids went to progressive elementary schools and even to the super selective Hunter Elementary School.

A member of the Center for Collaborative Education, ICE shares the belief of Deborah Meier (founder of Central Park East Secondary School), that schools should be democratically run institutions in which parents, teachers, and even students have a say in deciding what is taught.

ICE is a very informal place. Kids pile up on an old sofa in one humanities class rather than sit at desks. In a science class, a girl has a lollipop in her mouth and several kids have cans of soda on their tables. Students call teachers by their first names and sometimes use slang when speaking to adults. Blue jeans are the rule.

Nearly 100 percent of its high school graduates go on to college. About 80 percent of the middle school students continue at ICE for high school.

"Teachers and kids here are really striving for academic rigor, really pushing each other," said humanities teacher Greg Baldwin. "We want a balance between pushing the academic sphere and creating a safe

51

and comfortable place. Every kid here has probably two teachers they know well."

Although the school is firmly in the progressive camp, the staff attempt to strike a balance between progressive and traditional teaching techniques. Kids create their own newspapers, put on their own mock trials, and stage debates in their humanities classes. But the staff also teaches grammar and tests kids on vocabulary. The school offers Regents-level (9th grade) Earth Science in the 8th grade.

The Institute for Collaborative Education occupies the fifth floor and part of the fourth floor of the former Stuyvesant High School, which it shares with the High School of Health Professions and Human Services. Large cardboard gargoyles, which the kids made and painted themselves, sit on top of lockers in the hall. The school has a well-equipped gym with an elevated running track. However, middle school kids complain that they don't have enough access to that gym.

The principal, John Pettinato, has a degree in social work. He founded a school for kids released from juvenile detention, and he was assistant principal at City-as-School, a successful alternative high school. "Kids love to hang out with him, especially kids who are having a hard time," one teacher said.

The school has just 235 kids in grades 6 through 12, with an average class size of 16.

To ease the transition for incoming 6th graders, to bridge the gap between the older and young kids, and to build a sense of community in the school, teachers organize a schoolwide "opening project" in September. (Teachers stay an extra week after school is let out in June and come in one week early in August to organize it). The project centers around a single question. "What makes us human?" Or: "To what extent is the creator responsible for the creation?"

Students and teachers work together in groups for several days, organizing seminars, workshops, and various activities about the central question. New students have a chance to get to know old students, and teachers get a chance to know new students, because everyone has a chance to work with everyone else.

Many of the teachers come from Brown University's graduate school of education, a major influence in the alternative education movement. The school is a member of the Coalition of Essential Schools, a national network organized by Brown University's Theodore Sizer, who believes that small schools that concentrate on teaching a few subjects well are more effective than large schools that attempt to teach a wide array of subjects.

All kids take math, science, foreign language, and humanities each day. Technology, art, gym and music are offered once or twice a week. Sixth graders take a course called Introduction to Language in which they learn basic phrases in languages as diverse as Hebrew, Arabic, Japanese, and American Sign Language. In 7th grade, they choose either French or Spanish.

This school is administered by the Division of High Schools—not District 2. As a result, it doesn't appear in District 2's brochures on middle schools and has been overlooked by many District 2 parents. (One plus for kids in District 2: ICE is a separate application, so it doesn't count as one of their four District 2 choices. That means they may apply to four District 2 schools plus ICE.)

Children living in any of the five boroughs may apply. Applicants must score in the 80th percentile or above in reading and the 70th percentile or above in math, based on standardized tests. Applicants must also have a letter of recommendation from a teacher and a writing sample. The school offers monthly tours. There is no admissions deadline; applicants are accepted throughout the year for the following September.

IS 891, Salk School of Science
320 East 20th Street
New York, N.Y. 10003

Alexis Penzell, director
212-614-8785

Reading Scores: ★★★★★
Math Scores: ★★★★
Eighth Grade Regents: no
Grade Levels: 6–8
Admissions: Selective. By exam and interview.
When to Apply: Weekly tours October-December.
Class Size: 30-35

Free Lunch: 39%
Ethnicity: 35.8%W 21.8%B 15.5%H 26.9%A
Enrollment: 193
Capacity: N/A
Suspensions: N/A
Incidents: N/A
High School Choices: Bronx Science, Stuyvesant

At the Salk School of Science, kids have a chance to study with research scientists and professors of medicine from New York University Medical Center. They learn firsthand how the science they study in school relates to the questions they ask themselves about the world around them, and they learn how their curiosity about the physical world can lead to a career in science.

Located on the top floor of elementary school PS 40, Salk has fewer than 200 kids and only nine teachers. Classrooms are clean, airy, and newly renovated. There are cushy sofas in the corridors. And the school is unusually well equipped. Kids can culture bacteria, set up their own weather station, and build their own motors with elaborate sets in the classrooms.

The day I visited, a 7th grade science teacher explained how protons and neutrons work, with concrete examples: why a flashlight works, your hand hurts when you touch a hot pot, why you get a shock walking on a carpet. He challenged kids to think about what causes lightning and gently drew each of the children out as they discussed their hypotheses.

History and English are integrated, so children studying the American Revolution may read historical novels about, say, a boy who fights in the Battle of Lexington, along with real diaries of the teenage soldiers who witnessed the battles. Children are expected to do historical research from primary sources: soldiers' letters home, court records, and documents, such as the Declaration of Independence, which are all available in their classrooms.

In English, kids keep journals and study creative writing from teachers who've had special training in the Writing Process at Teachers College. In one class I visited, children wrote lyrical lines about the pain of war and the loss of innocence based on their readings about Revolutionary War battles: "It seemed my childhood had slipped away with the pull of a trigger," one poem began.

The Salk School of Science was founded in 1995 as an unusual collaboration between District 2 and the NYU Medical Center. The medical center had been offering special summer school programs for high school students and linking them with professional scientists, who acted as mentors. These "Programs in Preparation for the Professions" (PIPP) hoped to encourage kids—particularly girls and children of color—to consider careers in medicine. So Salk was founded with the hope that exposing middle school children to science in a systematic and serious way would engage them more intensely than traditional junior high school science programs. The school hopes eventually to expand to include grades 6 through 12.

Children attend weekly lectures at the medical center by volunteer research scientists and doctors on topics ranging from the effects of smoking on the cardiovascular system to the way in which drugs affect brain chemistry. Professors from the medical school regularly sit in on 6th grade classes to learn how to gear their volunteer teaching to the eleven- to thirteen-year-olds.

Eighth graders are required to give "mini-dissertations" to a panel of Medical Center professors at the end of the year. One child presented a plan for an invention that would trap and store electricity from lightning bolts. Another had a plan for saving the Chinese pandas from extinction by setting up wildlife corridors between their existing habitats.

Several parents have complained of high teacher turnover, and that communication between the administration and the parents is not always smooth. The struggle to open a new facility has left the director and the staff "overwhelmed," said one parent, who complained about a "lack of structure."

Director Alexis Penzell acknowledges there have been problems. Two teachers left because they really preferred teaching high school, she said, and one left because she was offered a job consulting on the use of computers in school for nearly triple her teaching salary. Ms. Penzell attributed the sometimes disorganized atmosphere to struggles over space as the school grew and took over more rooms in the elementary school in which it is housed.

Other parents praise the school's strengths. "They encourage kids to think," said PTA co-president Bob Simon. "Alexis [Penzell], the director, is really trying to build a corps of excellent teachers. She doesn't hesitate to replace a teacher who's not working out. With all the complaints that people have, it's still an excellent school."

Simon said the staff is responsive to kids' individual ways of learning. His daughter, who is mildly dyslexic, had a consultant teacher to help her with reading a few hours a week. More important, Simon said, the teachers seemed to relish her quirky, unconventional responses to questions. "She comes up with inventive solutions to problems," Simon said. "That's appreciated in the school and it might not be appreciated somewhere else. She is seen not as someone who is totally missing the mark, but as someone who sees things differently. It's a very warm, friendly kind of atmosphere that doesn't put pressure on her."

PTA co-chair Dorothy Klein said teachers gave her daughter individual attention when she was struggling in math. "The teachers said: 'Don't worry.' "

Salk doesn't have a large sports or music program, but Ms. Klein said her daughter enjoyed the early morning basketball program. "They're out there at seven in the morning," Ms. Klein said. "The coach believes it shouldn't be so competitive—everyone should get a chance to play. I think they have a basketball team that has never won a game, but they keep on coming because they are having a good time."

Traditional Regents' level high school courses are not offered in the 8th grade, partly because the teachers aren't satisfied that the material covered by the exam is what kids should be learning at this age. One science teacher said it placed too much emphasis on memorization, while Salk hopes to teach children to conduct their own research. However, the school recognizes many children will want to complete their 9th grade requirements while in 8th grade, and offers after-school programs to prepare them for the Earth Science Regents and the Sequential I mathematics Regents.

Perhaps the best indication of the school's success, Simon said, is the proportion of children who are accepted to the specialized science high schools. Twenty-six of sixty-two recent graduates were admitted to Stuyvesant, Bronx Science, or Brooklyn Tech.

Prospective parents and students are invited to visit the school in the fall. Children whose math scores are in the 80th percentile or above are considered for admission. The school doesn't look at reading scores.

All applicants are given an aptitude test—not designed to test their knowledge of science but their ability to approach a new problem. One year, the test asked children to think of ways to sink an eye dropper in a two-liter bottle of water. Applications are due in December.

Children attending District 2 schools have preference. In 1998, there were two hundred applicants for sixty-five seats in the 6th grade. The school attempts to enroll an equal number of boys and girls, and more boys than girls apply. The school can accommodate special education children with mild learning disabilities who need extra help in reading outside class, or a consultant teacher giving extra help in class.

MS 104, Simon Baruch Middle School
330 East 21 Street
New York, N.Y. 10010

Marge Struk, principal
212-674-4545

Reading Scores: ★★★★
Math Scores: ★★★★★
Eighth Grade Regents: yes
Grade Levels: 6–8
Admissions: Neighborhood school. Others may also apply.
When to Apply: Weekly tours October-December.
Class Size: 33-39
Free Lunch: 52%

Ethnicity: 29.3%W 16.2%B 22.3%H 32.2%A
Enrollment: 975
Capacity: 1183
Suspensions: 1.4%
Incidents: 0.9%
High School Choices: Bayard Rustin, Murry Bergtraum, Brooklyn Tech

Simon Baruch Middle School is spotless, cheerful, well-equipped, and offers first-class instruction for all children, from the most academically successful to the most disabled. It's worth a visit just to see how good a large neighborhood middle school can be.

It's organized in a way that allows the most advanced children—those in "special progress"—to move ahead without making average or slow students feel like second-class citizens. Everyone, from the gifted to those in special education, gets the same high-quality teachers and the same high-quality materials.

The school is divided into "houses" of four classes and four teachers who work as a team. Each house has one or two advanced "special placement" (SP) classes, one or two regular "academic" classes, and a class in "special education" or "English as a Second Language" (ESL). Children go from class to class within their house, so everyone has the same teachers.

Kids who are struggling get as much attention and respect from teachers as those who are high achievers, a rare thing in a city where too many schools give plums to the top students and ignore the rest. If the SP kids get classrooms with fish tanks and colorful bulletin boards, the special ed kids do, too. No one is consigned to the basement.

"The world can't survive on the backs of 'gifted' children," says principal Marge Struk. "We work very hard at providing gifted kids what they need. But it shouldn't be that you only teach the smart kids. You teach everyone."

The school is open to every child who lives in the zone on the East Side, from 59th Street to 14th Street. Others are accepted as space permits. It's a sign of the school's growing popularity that parents from outside the zone opt to send their children even if their test scores aren't high enough to get them into the SP track. More than half the children graduating from 8th grade go to the specialized high schools or to the small alternative schools known as educational option schools.

"It's a large, traditional school, and yet they have made changes to make it cozier, to have pockets where children can make friends," says Sharon Steinhoff, the PTA co-chair, whose twin son and daughter attend. "Marge Struk is a warm human being and she sets a great tone for the school. They call everyone 'Honey' in the office. The teachers have a good feeling for this age group—bless their hearts, I could never teach thirty-nine middle schoolers—and they seem to be on the kids' wave length."

Some principals are great administrators, some are great teachers. Ms. Struk is both. She recognizes and encourages good teaching. She mixes veteran and new teachers in each house. And she encourages everyone to acquire training in new teaching techniques.

She's circumvented the notorious School Construction Authority ("I won't let them in the building," she said) to build a computer lab quickly and for what she says was less than half the price it would have cost if she had gone through the normal bureaucratic channels.

She replaced every stick of furniture in the building with new tables and chairs, paid for with money she saved by delaying hiring an assistant principal for a year. (Under District 2 policy, principals are allowed what is called "school-based budgeting." That means they are alloted a pot of money they can spend more or less as they wish, deciding for themselves whether it's more important to hire an assistant principal or buy new furniture. Most districts don't have this flexibility.)

She even managed to get good lighting in the halls by persuading the school custodians to take down all the dirty light fixtures, wash them thoroughly, and replace them. (According to the Board of Education chain of command, custodians report to their own district supervisors, not to principals. Getting the custodians to do something outside their contractual obligations requires particular persuasive powers, something not every principal possesses.)

She's found parents to volunteer to keep the library open during lunch and after school, although middle school is the time when most parents disappear from their children's schools. She's persuaded the teachers to keep homeroom even though the teacher's contract doesn't require it. "Kids need the structure of homeroom," Ms. Struk says. "The tone is set in the first seven minutes of the day." Children keep their coats in closets in their homeroom.

Although all the parents I spoke to described the school as traditional, MS 104 is not your standard desks-in-rows, keep-your-nose-in-the-textbook kind of place. The day I visited, 7th grade math students were out in the playground, using mirrors and simple geometry to estimate the heights of buildings. A drama class open to all children, including those in special ed, was learning how to portray anger.

"How many times do I have to tell you!" the kids shouted.

"Are you annoyed?" the teacher asked.

"Yeah!" the kids responded.

"Then be annoyed!"

"How many times do I have to tell you!" the kids shouted again.

"Better!" the teacher said.

Sixth graders studying ancient civilizations were writing poems about gods in ancient Egypt, and comparing them to the God of the Bible.

A 7th grade history teacher gave a gruesome account of the invention of the guillotine and the French Revolution, geared to the ghoulish interests of adolescents. She skillfully tied it in to accounts of the American Revolution.

An 8th grade social studies teacher decorated her class to look like a campaign headquarters, with red-white-and-blue bunting on the walls. Kids were studying the political process firsthand: Everyone volunteered for a day in a local political campaign.

The children were also required to identify a problem in the city and come up with a solution to it. One of the most creative: kids complained that the subway passes given to students to ride to school for free weren't valid in the early evening, when they want to study at the public library. Through research, they found other cities offered more free mass transit to students than New York did. They marched on City Hall, wrote the city council, and eventually won the right to use their Metrocards until 8:30 p.m. instead of 7 p.m.

In a 6th grade science class, kids so small they had to stand on tiptoe to reach the lab tables were looking at pond scum and volcanic ash under a microscope to see the difference between living and nonliving things. A microscope, hooked up to a television, helped them watch a cell dividing.

Kids in a 7th grade physical science class put the finishing touches on their mobiles designed to classify matter: One mobile had a bag of dirt (a mixture), a Metrocard (a compound), a copper wire (an element) and a penny (a solution or alloy).

Eighth graders in a remedial science class made their own experiment: a wooden maze for a rat. They wanted to see if the rat "got smarter" over time and learned the maze. (It did.)

All 6th graders take Latin. Seventh and 8th graders may take Latin, Spanish, or French. A bilingual Chinese class is offered.

Special education classes include MIS I, for learning disabled children, and MIS III, for children with severe speech delays. In one special ed class, children were comparing the works of Ezra Jack Keats, a popular picture-book author. In another they were pruning plants.

The parents I spoke to were enthusiastic about the school, although all complained that classes were too big. "Class size burns teachers out," said Ms. Steinhoff, whose child was in an SP class of 39. "They're cooked by April."

Barbara Adams, a parent, said the "workload is incredibly heavy," and others said children often had three hours of homework a night. The parents were impressed with the teachers' accessibility and willingness to set up meetings with families whose children were having trouble.

Rita Danza, a 7th grade English teacher who chose MS 104 for her own child, said: "You see teachers who really like teaching, who really like kids. The advantage of a big school is everyone can find his niche, have the option of trying everything. It's easier for a kid to find what he's good at."

For example, as Ms. Adams said, everyone can play in the band or orchestra—no audition required—and children can choose whatever instrument they want. That makes some odd ensembles—an orchestra with one guitar, one violin, and lots and lots of flutes. But the kids enjoy it. "It's probably not the best sound, but nobody's left out," Ms. Adams said.

Similarly, anyone can be on the track team or play basketball. "If you want to play, you can play," said Ms. Adams, whose daughter came in next-to-last in a track meet but "keeps on because it's so much fun."

Weekly tours of the school are offered from October to December, and children must apply by December. All children living in the zone are accepted. Children accepted for the special progress class must

have reading and math test scores above the 80th percentile. For children from outside the zone, priority is given to students who demonstrate "social maturity, strong motivation and focus, and a serious
academic interest."

Ms. Struk clearly loves teaching children this age more than any
other. "Middle school is where you make the difference," she said. "If
the kid is going to be a quitter, you can see it and you have three years
to fix it. If someone takes that kid under his wing, you can save a soul."

IS 413, School of the Future
127 East 22 Street
New York, N.Y. 10010

Kathy Pelles, director
212-475-8086

Reading Scores: ★★★★★
Math Scores: ★★★★★
Eighth Grade Regents: no
Grade Levels: 6–12
Admissions: Unzoned. By interview.
When to Apply: Weekly tours October-December.
Class Size: 25
Free Lunch: 66%

Ethnicity: 20.8%W 25.1%B 38.9%H 15.3%A
Enrollment: 530
Capacity: 500
Suspensions: 4.9%
Incidents: N/A
High School Choices: Humanities, Environmental Studies, Health Professions

The School of the Future has an idealistic and energetic staff committed to sending every student who graduates to college. Amazingly, they succeed: the school has had a college acceptance rate ranging from 98 to 100 percent every year since it graduated its first class in 1996. One-third go to colleges that are considered "highly competitive." That figure is particularly impressive when you consider the School of the Future has no test for admission and that children of all abilities, including some in special education, are welcome.

Founded in 1990, the school is designed to be small—with just five hundred kids in grades 6 through 12. The small size, combined with the fact that kids stay for six years, means students and staff really get to know one another. If any student starts to slough off—or even if anyone gets a little depressed—some grown-up is sure to notice right away. Even the elevator operator is attentive and caring. It is a very welcoming atmosphere.

"The kids really feel they belong," principal Kathy Pelles says. There's a sense of community and a continuity in the curriculum from grades 6 through 12. And, because both students and teachers choose to be at the school, "There's nobody here who doesn't want to be," she says.

The school, which is wheelchair accessible, is in a newly remodeled former vocational high school for girls. The building is nothing fancy, but it's clean and pleasant. Girls' bathrooms are bigger than the boys', and lockers are inconveniently located in the basement, but there is a nice gym and an adequate cafeteria. The library is small, and students frequently use the public library nearby.

A member of the Coalition of Essential Schools, an organization that includes Central Park East, the School of the Future is progressive. Textbooks are out. Primary source materials are used. Desks are not in rows. Tables move and kids work in groups. No one is put into a track. Students of different achievement levels are all together in the same class. Standardized tests are out. "Portfolio assessment," where kids present their completed work to a panel of teachers and other students, is in.

The staff repeats the progressive mantra that it is more important to learn "habits of mind"—various ways of approaching a new problem—than to learn a particular set of facts. "It's not important to know the capital of Albania (which will likely change in our lifetime) but rather how to get that information," Ms. Pelles said. "It's not important to know the statistics about a country, but rather to understand and analyze how those statistics influence a country's policies."

But the school also has a traditional view of the material that children should master. The curriculum is standard: kids study ancient civilizations in 6th grade, American history in 7th and 8th. Algebra is still taught as algebra, and it's not unusual to see kids studying new vocabulary words.

The State Board of Education has recognized portfolio assessment as an alternative to standardized tests. Accordingly, graduates receive a Regents-endorsed diploma, although they are not required to take traditional Regents exams. (That may change as new state rules are imposed.)

There are lots of computers in each class. Instead of having a computer teacher with computers in a lab, every teacher is trained in technology. That means kids can do research in, say, the archives of the Smithsonian Museum without leaving their classroom. The school has a high-speed Internet connection, and students have their own e-mail addresses.

Still, what makes the school an exceptional place isn't the quality of its computers, but the talent and passion of its teachers and the vision of its director. Ms. Pelles has clearly thought about what makes 6th graders different from 7th graders, and what makes 8th graders different from high school kids, and has incorporated those thoughts into the teaching methods.

Sixth graders have two main subject teachers, one for math and science, one for humanities, history and English. This is less scary and confusing than having five teachers and changing classes each period, and it eases the transition from elementary school, where kids have one teacher.

The two teachers work in adjoining classrooms, and each knows, for example, what homework the other is assigning. That means kids don't get overwhelmed with five different major homework projects at the same time. Sixth graders have gym four times a week—an acknowledgment that they need more physical activity than older kids.

Seventh and 8th graders have three main subject teachers, for math, science, and humanities. They have gym three times a week. Seventh grade teachers move up to the 8th grade with their students, so kids have the same teachers for two years in a row—a way to ensure continuity in the curriculum and to make sure the grown-ups and children know each other well.

The day I visited, a 6th grade humanities teacher, David Paris, was leading the kids in a game of Simon Says—he calls it "Mr. Paris Says"—designed to teach vocabulary words while giving kids the chance to bounce off a little excess energy:

"Mr. Paris says, shake your hands!

"Mr. Paris says, say something completely irrelevant!!

"Mr. Paris says, take meticulous notes!

"If you think that's right, raise both elbows like a chicken!

"Commit a transgression!

"Do two serene jumping jacks!"

The kids jumped and laughed and learned words such as "irrelevant" and "meticulous" and "transgressions."

They were studying ancient Egypt, and the classroom was filled with interesting books. Not just history books, but historical novels, a guide to hieroglyphics, and books of archaelogy. Kids wrote their own newspaper called *The Egyptian News*, with headlines such as BOY KING MURDERED? They researched questions such as "How high was the Great Pyramid?" and "Why are pyramids no longer being built?" They visited the Egyptian wing at the Brooklyn Museum. They compared the class structure of ancient Egypt to that of contemporary America. "I try to relate society then to society now," Paris said.

Upstairs, in an 8th grade math class, a Wizard of Oz voice boomed from behind a big sheet draped across the room in what I eventually figured out was an unusual way to teach algebra. The kids, their teacher, and a student teacher had built what they called a "Function

Machine," a sheet trimmed with Christmas tree lights and poster paint and knobs in red, yellow and blue. A chart listed values for X: 2,3 and for Y: 4,6. A child asked: "Function machine, does the function equal 2X?" And the voice of the teacher, hidden behind the sheet, boomed, "Yes!" The class then worked on graphing the equation.

Down the hall, a class was discussing *Rifles for Waite*, an historical novel by Harold Keith about a sixteen-year-old Union soldier who infiltrated a Confederate camp as a spy during the American Civil War. The protagonist finds, somewhat to his surprise, that the Confederate soldiers have feelings much like his own, and he toys with the idea of defecting. The class, sitting in chairs in a circle, was discussing his dilemma. "If you really believed in the Union, could you ever go to the other side?" one girl asked. "I'm really against slavery, so I couldn't." The teacher was gently prodding the students to separate the emotions the protagonist felt from the political situation.

The School of the Future's system of portfolio assessment is based on the model of Central Park East Secondary School. To graduate from high school, children must demonstrate proficiency in math, science, and two areas of the humanities through a series of demonstrations. Each student is paired with a mentor-teacher who supervises the demonstrations, which are like dissertation defenses.

Parents describe the school as "cozy" and say the staff makes a big effort to help 6th graders acclimate. Parents of 6th graders are invited to breakfast the first day of school. On Fridays from 5:30 p.m. to 7 p.m. there are "Family Reads" when parents and kids read together and have a light supper of pizza at the school.

PTA president Susan Wolin, who transferred her son from a selective private school to attend the School of the Future, says she appreciates that the school has "kids of all colors." She says an unusual amount of time is devoted to to teaching children to write well, and she describes teachers as "tireless, energetic, and very creative."

Another parent, Nadine LaGuardia, raved about the college admissions counselor, who writes "extensive" letters of recommendation, takes kids personally to visit college campuses, and regularly calls colleges on behalf of the students. Recent graduates have been accepted to Cornell, Stanford, New York University, Wesleyan, Amherst, Fordham, and Penn State, all classified as "highly competitive" by *Peterson's Guide to Colleges*.

The school has space for a few special education children with learning disabilities, who are integrated into regular classes. Billy Holliday, a Brooklyn father whose son is in special education, said he chose the school because it allowed his boy to leap ahead in mathematics, where he was strong, while giving him extra help in reading, where his skills were weak. "It was clear the teachers were accepting him for what he was, and also had very high expectations for him," Holliday said. "It was clear no one was going to get lost, and everyone knew the kids." Class size is low.

Parents and students complain that the sports program is weak and the music program nonexistent. The downside of a small school is that it can't have the wide array of programs possible in a big school. But, in keeping with the philosophy of the Coalition of Essential Schools, most parents have adopted the notion of "less is more." That is, it's more important to do a few things well than to offer a taste of every imaginable discipline.

The school has many student teachers (who call themselves "preservice teachers") from Teachers College, New York University and The New School for Social Research, so there's usually more than one grown-up in a class.

Student applicants are interviewed by a committee of teachers, which reviews academic records, a writing sample, and teacher evaluations. The staff says it looks for students with a commitment to the school's philosphy, an interest in technology, and an ability to work independently. Children of all academic abilities are accepted. Children from outside the district are strongly advised to apply for 6th grade, because space is extremely limited in the upper grades.

IS 887, School for the Physical City
55 East 25th Street
New York, N.Y. 10011

Mark Weiss & Candy Systra, co-directors
212-683-7440

Reading Scores: ★★★★
Math Scores: ★★★★
Eighth Grade Regents: no
Grade Levels: 6–12
Admissions: Unzoned. By interview.
When to Apply: Weekly tours October-December.
Class Size: 25
Free Lunch: 33%

Ethnicity: 45.6%W 26.2%B 20%H 8.1%A
Enrollment: 300
Capacity: 400
Suspensions: N/A
Incidents: N/A
High School Choices: School for the Physical City, Humanities, Environmental Studies

The teachers at the School for the Physical City see themselves as activist-intellectuals committed to changing education and society. The school challenges almost every notion of traditional education, from the way the school day is organized and the material that children study, to the way in which students' work is evaluated. It aims to instill in its students new ways of thinking, doing research, and posing questions. Gone are the traditional trappings of a school day. There are no bells, no bathroom passes, no forty-five-minute periods, no tracking of children into honors classes and slow classes, no assistant principal in charge of discipline, no rushing through a textbook to prepare for a standardized exam.

Instead, children and teachers explore topics together, often without textbooks, often outside the school building. In science, children study meteorology, building their own thermometers and anemometers to gauge the wind in a nearby park. In history, they watch a documentary film about a slave ship and compare it to the dramatic film *Amistad* about a slave rebellion and the early abolitionists. In art, they study the Italian Renaissance and practice two-point perspective in a lesson that combines mathematical concepts, studio drawing, and art history.

Exams are rare; students are evaluated on the basis of the papers they write and their "portfolio," or a collection of their written work.

"The principal is very dynamic. The teachers are wonderful. The small class size is unbeatable," said PTA president Margaret Owen. "The kids all feel that it's their place." With its relaxed atmosphere and welcoming attitude toward parents, Ms. Owen said, the School of the Physical City is the "perfect extension of PS 3," a progressive Greenwich Village elementary school.

The School of the Physical City was founded in 1993 by two old friends: Mark Weiss, a former high school principal and Board of Education administrator, and Sam Schwartz, a former city traffic commissioner who writes the *New York Daily News* column "Gridlock Sam" about traffic conditions.

Schwartz had noticed that few New York City public school students went on to become engineers or urban planners and that the city had to import talent to keep its infrastructure in good repair. Weiss suggested starting a school where children would study the "physical city"—bridges and tunnels, subways and roads, sewer lines and powers stations—and, through that study, learn how to "take care of and take charge of their city."

The School of the Physical City opened with a grant from New Visions for Public Schools and the help of Cooper Union for the Advancement of Science and Art, a tuition-free university where Schwartz taught. Cooper Union and Schwartz help arrange internships for students to work with professional engineers, architects, carpenters, and policy-makers to learn how the city runs. Several students were interns at New York Public Interest Research Project, a nonprofit group that, among other things, works to improve subway service. Three other students had internships to study with photojournalists in southern Africa in the summer of 1999.

While the school isn't specifically designed to train children to become engineers or architects, the administration hopes to give a solid academic background to kids who might otherwise shy away from the difficult courses necessary to prepare for those careers.

For example, Weiss says, many children find standard textbook-style Earth Science courses deadly boring. But if kids have a chance to see how the city gets its drinking water by visiting the city's waterworks, the water cycle—the process by which rain flows down to lakes and then evaporates into the clouds—becomes comprehensible and interesting. A trip to the city's sewage treatment plant, or a walk across the Brooklyn Bridge, give kids a feel for engineering problems and their solutions.

The School for the Physical City has been named an Expeditionary

Learning Center. This national network of schools is based on the principles of Outward Bound, that learning is an "expedition into the unknown." Children typically take field trips once a week. In one high school course, called "Sludge, Seepage and Society," kids studied water quality and land-use planning and spent the night on a boat docked at South Street Seaport.

Ms. Owen said the progressive approach puts lessons in context. Instead of learning abstract rules of grammar, for example, kids learn the history of the language and find out where the rules come from.

The school's building design, a high-tech renovation of an old vocational school, is intended to be used as a tool to teach basic architectural concepts. Exposed air ducts are painted bright orange. Imposing columns are painted grass green, and walls are painted yellow. The paint-job is a constant reminder of basic engineering principles: that all buildings need a source of fresh air, for example, and that columns and walls are needed to hold up the roof.

The school is modeled after Central Park East Secondary School, the alternative school in East Harlem. Like Central Park East, the School for the Physical City is based on the notion that small is better. The school has twenty teachers and fewer than four hundred students. Everyone can fit comfortably in the cafeteria. Teachers have frequent staff meetings, and policy decisions are made by consensus, a sometimes time-consuming and frustrating process.

The day I visited, teachers were discussing how kids who are having trouble with reading should get extra help. The differences among the staff were palpable. The advantage of the lengthy discussion, however, is that once a decision has been made, everyone is united in implementing it.

Students have more freedom than is common in public middle schools. They can go to the toilet without a pass, and they can go outside for lunch. But students also have more than the usual number of grown-ups keeping an eye on them and leaning on them if they transgress. As you walk through the school, you see kids and grown-ups deep in conversation. Teachers—not aides—stay in the lunchroom and halls during class changes. And minor transgressions prompt major discussions. One class I visited was almost entirely devoted to a lecture about how kids shouldn't run through the halls.

Parents said the school is strongest in the early grades. But the academics are strong enough that several 8th graders were admitted to the super-selective Stuyvesant High School. One mother complained that some of the mixed-abilities classes allowed her son, who was bright but not hard-working, to coast, doing the bare minimum of work. Renee Ehlee, the college counselor and admissions director, said, "Schools that believe in heterogenous grouping are constantly struggling with how to challenge everyone." In math, in particular, she said, the school was experimenting with ways to group children to ensure that all were challenged.

Interested parents should contact the school in the fall and arrange a tour. The school does not screen for test scores, and the best way to get in is to tell the administration it's your first choice.

The administration is looking for a student body with a range of academic achievement, for an ethnic balance, and an equal number of boys and girls. The school is wheelchair accessible, and children in special education who are classified as learning disabled are integrated into regular classes. All classes mix children of different abilities. Children who fall behind in their studies are required to attend after-school programs and summer programs.

Most of the middle school children have continued at the school for high school. The School for the Physical City graduated its first senior class in 1999.

IS 412, NYC Lab School For Collaborative Studies
333 West 17th Street
New York, N.Y. 10011

Sheila Breslaw & Rob Menken, co-directors
212-691-6119

Reading Scores: ★★★★★
Math Scores: ★★★★★
Eighth Grade Regents: yes
Grade Levels: 6–12
Admissions: Selective. By exam and interview.
When to Apply: Weekly tours October-December.
Class Size: 32-36
Free Lunch: 13%

Ethnicity: 56.2%W 11.7%B 10.6%H 21.5%A
Enrollment: 641
Capacity: N/A
Suspensions: 1.1%
Incidents: N/A
High School Choices: Stuyvesant, Bronx Science, LaGuardia.

The Lab School for Collaborative Studies is a small, selective secondary school that consistently ranks in the very top in reading and math scores citywide. A demanding curriculum, mountains of homework, and an extra-serious student body makes Lab a rigorous academic program. Eighth graders routinely take high-school-level courses, and high school students regularly take advanced placement courses. Some seniors even take college courses at New York University, Borough of Manhattan Community College, and Parsons School of Design.

Founded in 1987 as the Lab School for Gifted Education, the current codirectors changed the name to the less pretentious Lab School for Collaborative Studies.

"We don't believe in the G word," says codirector Rob Menken, whose style sets a laid-back tone for the school—a graying beard, a small diamond earring, an open-collar flannel shirt, and blue jeans. "It's a collaboration, not a competition," adds codirector Sheila Breslaw.

The physical surroundings aren't beautiful. The Lab School shares space with several other schools in an ugly, fortresslike concrete structure originally built as a large neighborhood junior high school. Corridors are poorly lit, and the paint job is depressing.

72

But the Lab School classrooms, on the third floor of IS 70, are cheerful and well equipped, with colorful bulletin boards and mobiles. Class changes are pleasant, with kids talking quietly to one another, then settling down quickly to study. There are no bells, no PA announcements to interrupt the day, no passes required to go the bathroom.

Classes are interdisciplinary. Experiments and independent research are stressed over textbook learning. The day I visited, I saw kids in the hall outside their classroom giving critiques of one another's artwork—in Spanish. The kids had painted pictures in art class, which were posted on the walls of the corridor, and the Spanish teacher was asking questions about them.

Down the hall, a humanities and history teacher were working together on a project about the American South after the Civil War. The kids had read *To Kill a Mockingbird* and were working together in groups drawing posters depicting the period, drawing on quotes from the novel as well as lines from Langston Hughes.

In other projects, the kids read Lewis and Clark's journals, then wrote their own journals of fictional explorers. They wrote a make-believe journal of the Civil War from the perspective of a slave owner. They put together dioramas of Civil War battles with plastic toy soldiers painted blue and gray. "It's a lot more interesting than reading from a textbook," said history teacher Kerry McKibbin.

Sixth graders, in a project that combined history, art, and math, visited city landmarks including St. Patrick's Cathedral, the Cathedral of St. John the Divine, and Grand Central Station. They made sketches of the buildings, noting down such information as the number of cubic feet in the interior or the use of flying buttresses.

Math students, meanwhile, made architectural models of fanciful buildings and colorful cardboard polyhedra—geometric solids.

Eighth grade science teacher Suzanne Dwyer had one of the most imaginative approaches to the Regents Earth Science course I'd seen anywhere. She managed to cover the material needed for kids to pass the Regents exam—an exam some have criticized for being filled with facts to memorize—while still making lessons fun. Her classroom is replete with rocks, fish tanks, and plants. "I try to give them really visual stuff where they can get there hands dirty and really touch stuff," Ms. Dwyer says. When kids studied rocks, Ms. Dwyer took them to historic buildings in the neighborhood to talk about what stones are used in architecture. She and an art teacher took a class to the Metropolitan Museum of Art, where kids made sketches and learned about the stone used in Egyptian temples and sculpture. The children went "orienteering" in Central Park, using a map and compass to pick out geological features. They learned about glacial striations in the rocks and spotted the direction the glaciers receded. They took a trip to the beach and tested water for salinity. As for all those facts you need to know for the Regents exam, Ms. Dwyer gets kids to make their own board games to quiz each other on tidbits such as: What is the most common iron oxide mineral?

Lab school and the other programs in the IS 70 building have secured $2 million to build new science laboratories, Menken said.

In a 7th grade humanities class, a teacher was drawing kids out in an effort to identify what makes writing persuasive, part of an exercise that allows them to evaluate their own writing. Instead of having the teacher say, "This is an A project or this is a B project," a student explained to me, the children help set the criteria for grading themselves. "Most of the time you have two grades—a self-evaluation and what the teacher gives you," said Lena Imamura, an 8th grader who served as my tour guide.

The Lab School encourages children to take an active role in their education and their community. Students may petition the administration for electives of their own choosing. In one case, a student actually taught a course, on videotape editing.

Lab is part of a national network of Expeditionary Learning Schools that emphasize field trips in addition to classroom learning and that strive to build a sense of community between a school and its neighborhood. Children are required to take part in projects to solve problems in their community. In one, 7th graders sought to improve the physical conditions in their school and to build an alliance among students in the three programs in the building: Lab, Museum School, and the zoned neighborhood school, IS 70. They planned to paint graffiti-scarred bathrooms themselves and to plant a community garden for all the students to enjoy.

Parents I spoke to made such contradictory statements about Lab that I returned to the school for a second visit to reassess my own opinion. Some parents described the school as warm and "touchy feely," while one mother complained the school was "very competitive" and that teachers assigned "way too much homework." One mother, who withdrew her child from Lab after six weeks, complained kids were "spoiled brats" and "nasty" and "exclusive."

The comment that best sums up Lab was from one mother, Lisa Siegman, who said Lab is "staking out a middle ground" between schools with "crazy amounts of homework" and those that are cozy and nurturing without being rigorous. "It's academically serious, without being high pressure" said Ms. Siegman, who is an elementary school science teacher in the district.

Children do form cliques, and some are competitive. But most of the young people I saw seemed to be nice, friendly, normal kids. Teachers give lots of homework—two and one half hours a night is typical—and there have been complaints that the assignments aren't always focused or useful. A few staffers, while technically competent, lack the warm manner that makes middle school teaching effective. But the administration is responsive to parents. After a number of parents complained, through the Parents' Association, about particular teachers' assignments, Menken and Ms. Breslaw worked with the teachers to improve the situation.

Perhaps the strongest endorsement from a parent was that of former District 2 superintendent Anthony J. Alvarado, who chose Lab for his own daughter.

Part of the attraction of the school is the fact that it includes grades 6 through 12, so 8th graders don't need to spend half the year agonizing over where they'll go to high school. About half the class does leave Lab for Stuyvesant or Bronx Science. Lab has one of the highest rates of admissions to specialized high schools of any middle school in the city. But many students also choose to stay at Lab for high school, including a dozen who were accepted at Bronx Science. Lab graduated its first high school class in 1997 and has established its reputation by sending nearly every student to a four-year-college, including several to Columbia, Cornell, and Carnegie Mellon.

Parents and students say the advantage of Lab over a school like Stuyvesant is the small size. Not only do students say they feel they get more attention from their teachers, they also believe there's less competition for college. It's easier to get noticed by MIT if you're one of a few applicants from Lab, rather than one hundred from Stuyvesant. And the Lab guidance counselor is likely to know you well and to have the time and energy to advocate your cause.

Children are admitted to the 6th grade based on their reading and math scores, as well as a test and an interview given at the school. Children must score in the 70th percentile in reading and the 80th percentile in math to be considered. Children are also accepted in the 9th grade. The school is wheelchair accessible. Interested parents should arrange a tour in the fall the year before they want their child to attend.

IS 414, NYC Museum School
333 West 17th Street
New York, N.Y. 10011

Ron Chaluisan & Sonnet Takahisa, co-directors
212-675-6206

Reading Scores: ★★★★
Math Scores: ★★★★
Eighth Grade Regents: no
Grade Levels: 6–12
Admissions: Unzoned. By interview.
When to Apply: Weekly tours October-December.
Class Size: 33

Free Lunch: 21%
Ethnicity: 35.2%W 29.7% B 29.7%H 5.5%A
Enrollment: 300
Capacity: 420
Suspensions: 3.4%
Incidents: N/A
High School Choices: N/A

I'm standing on the No. 3 train en route to Brooklyn, clinging to a strap and chatting with history and English teacher Jonathan Spear, while twenty-eight kids from the Museum School are seated or standing in the car reading—really reading—quietly to themselves.

We're on our way to the Brooklyn Museum, one of the four New York City museums where kids at this unusual experimental school have regular classrooms. Think of it as postmodern education (or maybe an innovative way to deal with school overcrowding?) No walls, just teachers and kids and books. No single fixed place to study, but lots of places to work.

Kids spend two days a week at the school's home base on West 17th Street and three days a week in one of four museums: The Brooklyn Museum, the American Museum of Natural History, the Children's Museum of Manhattan, and the Jewish Museum. There's a lot of travel time involved, and to get anything accomplished kids have to learn to concentrate even while they're on the subway. But spend a day with them and you'll agree the education they're getting is worth the hassle of spending hours each week on the train.

The premise of the Museum School is this: The great museums of New York have the tools, the staff and the objects in the galleries, to give children a great liberal arts education, not just an appreciation of fine art but also a firm foundation in science, mathematics, history, and English. A collaboration between District 2 and the museums offers the kids exposure to a vast array of learning materials unavailable anywhere else.

Students learn to use the collections the way museum professionals do. They do research in the museum archives, learn how museums take care of their collections, and even become curators of their own exhibits. They learn that objects—a portrait from the Colonial period or pottery shard from Ancient Egypt—can be a source of information about history just as documents—the *Federalist Papers* or the story of Exodus—can be. They spend eight weeks at each museum, studying with both their classroom teacher and a staff member from the museum. Each museum has assigned one staffer to work with the students full-time.

The day I accompanied students to the Brooklyn Museum, they had none of the field trip silliness so common when excursions are a once-a-year thing. They filed smoothly and quickly through the grand entrance of the museum and down a flight of stairs to a windowless classroom in the basement, where another teacher, an educator on the museum staff, was waiting for them. They dumped their coats and lunch bags.

Half the class, fourteen kids, joined Spear in a gallery upstairs and the other half settled down in the classroom to work on American history projects. There were half a dozen tables in the room, each with a bin of history and art books on topics such as the Industrial Revolution and westward expansion. Children were working in small groups, coming up with research topics. "I want you to study something that intrigues you," the teacher, Katie Whitney, said.

The teacher walked from table to table, helping kids get started. She showed one group how to use an index in a book called *The People's History of the United States*. Two girls were interested in the role of women in the 1860s and Ms. Whitney helped them narrow their topic, and they decided to write about how factory life (where women worked outside the home for the first time) increased women's political power.

Upstairs, Spear was working with the rest of the class. Kids were sprawled on the floor of a gallery of nineteenth-century landscape painting. Equipped with colored pencils, clipboards, and paper, they were sketching silently, except for an occasional whispered question to the teacher. Their assignment: Pick a painting, imagine it as a series, and draw something that comes before and something that comes after. One child picked a painting of a river, then sketched what the river might look like upstream and downstream. Another showed a town before and after the arrival of trains. "These drawings are a different way of taking notes," said Spear. "The purpose is to make them look more carefully. Art is immediately accessible, but to really understand it you need to look at it for an extended period of time."

The Museum School was founded in 1994 by Ron Chaluisan, a former teacher at the Lab School for Gifted Education (now simply called the Lab School) and Sonnet Takahisa, a museum educator at the Brooklyn Museum. Their hope was to create a school that would accept children of all talents and abilities, all income levels and ethnic groups, and offer an education with the academic rigor of a traditional college preparatory school and the fun and excitement of a progressive elementary school.

They won a grant from New Visions for Public Schools and the support of District 2 to set up in IS 70, the junior high school building that houses a number of alternative programs, including the Lab School.

"Ron wanted to call it the 17th Street Collective or The Lab School for the Ungifted," said Ms. Takahisa, but they eventually agreed on the New York City Museum School. It does have the feel of a collective—teachers really talk to one another—and, although no one would call anyone here ungifted, folks do seem to have a highly developed sense of irony and they don't take themselves too seriously.

The school has children who have transferred from private schools as well as homeless children living in temporary housing, which, as Ms. Takahisa says, "makes for an interesting PTA."

Sixth graders study Earth Science at the American Museum of Natural History, concentrating on the rain forest. They study math at the Brooklyn Museum, calculating the mathematical formulas—in cubits—used to carve sculptures or build a mummy case.

At the Jewish Museum, they learn about Varian Fry, who helped Jews escape from occupied France in World War II. "We can also learn by his example of how to deal with moral issues," Ms. Takahisa said. The history lesson is then woven into a lesson in citizenship and social responsibility. Each child is required as a community service project to address a problem in the school—litter in the girls' bathroom or smoking by kids, for instance—and to come up with a strategy to deal with it.

In the home base on West 17th Street, classes are a shade more traditional. At least they have conventional classrooms with desks and blackboards. But they are still imaginative and quirky. One American history teacher assigned his students to draw an automobile that

79

would best represent Jefferson (A station wagon? A pickup truck?) and one that would best represent Hamilton (A monster truck? A stretch limo?) Another class wrote historical fiction about families moving West in the 1870s and 1880s. The level of writing was very impressive.

The school's teaching methods are evolving, and the staff is willing to rethink a program if it doesn't seem to be working. When teachers found that extensive use of museum trips was short-changing kids in math, for example, they put together a more organized math program with more classroom instruction.

By its nature, the school is not highly structured, and it works best for a student who is focused, engaged, and rather mature. One mother transferred her son out of the Museum School because he wasn't able to concentrate in such an unstructured environment. But the school has built a core of ardent fans. "I love the Museum School," said Laurel Adlouni, whose son attends. "If I were able, I would go there myself. It makes learning so much fun." She said one of the highlights of her life was a potluck PTA supper at the Brooklyn Museum during the Monet retrospective. To be among these wonderful paintings—in the evening, after hours in what amounted to a private showing—was a great privilege, she said.

But what she likes most are the open houses (two at the Brooklyn Museum and two at the Museum of Natural History) held as children finish their eight-week stints, called "modules." Parents are invited for cookies and soft drinks as the children explain different concepts shown in the exhibits. "You feel like you really have a handle on what's going on," Ms. Adlouni said. She noted that the atmosphere is very ordered and disciplined, despite the unconventional setting. "They are really, really strict," she said. "If you're going to take kids on the train, you've got to do that or you're going to lose them." She said Chaluisan, one of the codirectors, hugs and jokes with the children, but doesn't accept misbehavior. "It's not that they are afraid of him, but they really respect him." Here are some rules: No gum chewing. No being late for class. Two chalk-marks on the blackboard for misbehavior and you get detention. You also get gold stars for good spelling.

Children may be admitted in either 6th or 9th grade. All candidates are interviewed by faculty. They write an essay, solve a math problem, and observe an object and describe it. Children must also present a teacher recommendation from their elementary school. "We look at test scores just to make sure we have a heterogeneous balance," said Ms. Takahisa. "We have never rejected a kid based on test scores."

The school has resource room for children who need extra help with reading, but no self-contained special education classes. The school is wheelchair accessible. There was one child in a wheelchair in the program who used a specially equipped minibus to get from the home base to the museums.

In recent years, there has been room for children from outside the district, and the Museum School has been particularly popular among Brooklyn parents, who have hired a private bus to transport their children to the school. Weekly tours are offered from October to December.

IS 881, The Clinton School
for Writers and Artists
320 West 21st Street
New York, N.Y. 10011

Joseph Cassidy, director
212-255-8860

Reading Scores: ★★★★★
Math Scores: ★★★★★
Eighth Grade Regents: no
Grade Levels: 6–8
Admissions: Unzoned. By
interview.
When to Apply: Weekly tours
October-December.
Class Size: 27-32
Free Lunch: 32%

Ethnicity: 47.4%W 22.5%B
20.5%H 9.6%A
Enrollment: 249
Capacity: N/A
Suspensions: N/A
Incidents: N/A
High School Choices: Art &
Design, Environmental
Studies, Health Prof &
Human Services

Director Joseph Cassidy stood on the sidewalk outside the entrance to
the Clinton School for Writers and Artists, greeting each student by
name, urging them inside when they dawdled, and admonishing them
to take their hats off. It was just one of the ways he helps guide kids
through what he calls their "most interesting and most vital" years—
early adolescence.

The Clinton School, founded in 1976 and the oldest alternative
middle school in District 2, operates on the assumption that young
adolescents need more attention from grown-ups than elementary
school kids do, not less. A tiny school, with just 240 pupils, every
teacher knows every child and every child knows every teacher.

"It's small, it's very nurturing, and yet it's a pretty traditional education," says PTA president Nancy Blechman. "There's a routine and it's
kept to. They have tests and grades and an honor roll. They expect you
to know grammar and spelling."

Cassidy says that middle school students "start to look to their own
peers for validation and not to teachers. Adolescence is often a time of
turning off . . . to one's family, one's school, one's teachers. We don't
think that's inevitable. A good school doesn't take it personally and
doesn't back out of kids' lives."

If a child is having trouble in school, for example, Cassidy will arrange an early-morning meeting with a parent and every one of the child's teachers, Ms. Blechman said. "I'll be forever grateful to Joe Cassidy because he said, 'Let's be very, very careful because your daughter is rapidly approaching the age where girls go off a cliff,' " one Clinton mother said, referring to the common phenomenon of adolescent girls losing interest in academics. She also said the teachers went out of their way to find books that would challenge her daughter, dozens of books outside the regular curriculum.

Teachers have "advisories" with a small class—18 children—for forty-five minutes twice a week, where kids can talk about anything that's bothering them, "everything from how many times they wear their jeans before their Mom makes them wash them to asking how come people make fun of kids who get good grades," says Cassidy.

The class size for 6th and 8th graders is average for middle school—31 or 32 children. But 7th grade classes have only 27, the result of an agreement Cassidy made with the staff to give up one period of their course preparation time a week in exchange for smaller classes.

Cassidy, who became director in 1997, says 7th grade is a crucial year, the turning point between the elementary and secondary years. High schools look at 7th grade standardized test scores; and Cassidy hopes the smaller class size will pay off in terms of high school admissions for Clinton students.

The school has a grant from the Annenberg Foundation to integrate arts into the curriculum. Professionals from the Dance Theatre of Harlem, the Museum of Modern Art, and the School of Visual Arts teach regularly. The day I visited, a dancer from the Dance Theatre of Harlem was teaching a class with an English teacher. The children, in stocking feet and jeans, were divided into groups of four and asked to invent and practice a dance phrase of at least four steps. Then they were asked to write about the similarities between dance and writing. "Words are like steps of a dance," one girl said.

The school is racially integrated, with no ethnic group dominating. "My daughter was really proud of the fact that she went to one of the most racially integrated schools in the city," one mother said.

Several parents complained the science curriculum was weak, and a few suggested the school should give kids more homework and challenge them more academically. Still, the parents I talked to said their children were happy at Clinton.

The Clinton school occupies the fifth floor of an elementary school, PS 11. There's no elevator. The facilities are pretty basic. There's a tiny gym and the library looks home-made, with a couple of beanbag chairs and a few plants as its only furnishings. The coat closets in the class-rooms are too small, so kids carry their coats from class to class.

There's one big plus to the building, though: It's one of few middle schools with a swimming pool. Cassidy acts as lifeguard during the free after-school swim program. Other teachers also volunteer their time for after-school classes in art, computer, and singing.

The school offers tours for prospective parents and students every week during the fall. About 40 percent of the students come from out-side the district, including many from Brooklyn and a few from Queens. There is no test for admission, and Clinton is committed to accepting children of various abilities. The school looks for children with an interest or talent in writing and the arts. "I'm not picking fin-ished artists, or finished writers," Cassidy said. "We're looking for stu-dents who want to use art and writing throughout the schoolday."

The school has one special education class for children with speech and language delays. The special ed children have their academic sub-jects in their own class, but mix with the other children for art and physical education.

MS408, The Professional Performing Arts School
328 West 48th Street
New York, N.Y. 10036

Mindy Chermak, principal
212-247-8652

Reading Scores: ★★★★
Math Scores: ★★★★
Eighth Grade Regents: yes
Grade Levels: 6–12
Admissions: Selective. By audition.
When to Apply: January
Class Size: 22

Free Lunch: 48%
Ethnicity: 32.2%W 41.7%B 24.0%H 2.1%A
Enrollment: 338
Capacity: 350
Suspensions: 4.4%
Incidents: 1.2%
High School Choices: N/A

The Professional Performing Arts School was founded in 1990 to give aspiring actors, dancers, and musicians the technical skills they need to become professional performers and the academic skills they need in whatever career they choose.

About 25 percent of the students work professionally in film, television, or theater productions, both on and off Broadway. When they're on location, sometimes for three months or more, teachers send them their lessons through a computer modem, a fax machine, or by Federal Express.

When the kids are in attendance, they have academic classes in the morning. In the afternoon they study with professional actors, dancers, and musicians from the Actor's Institute, the Alvin Ailey American Dance Center, and the Lucy Moses School of Music. Some recent graduates include: Mike Demas, who starred in the TV sitcom *Teen Angel* and attends UCLA, and Sara Zelle, who played Liesel in *The Sound of Music* on Broadway and was accepted at Harvard.

Just off Broadway near the Theater District, the school shares a building with a popular and successful elementary school, Midtown West. The one hundred-year-old building is clean and the rooms are airy, although some are a little bare.

In every class I visited, the teachers clearly loved the students and the students loved them. The teachers display a willingness to work with each child, from the most academically successful to those who

85

are really struggling. The faculty enjoy planning lessons together, integrating, for example, history and English by using a historic novel in English class about a period they're studying in history. Students read a mixture of modern classics such as Richard Wright's *Black Boy* and contemporary fiction such as *Shabanu: Daughter of the Wind*, a novel by Suzanne Fisher Staples about an arranged marriage in Pakistan.

Teachers are attentive and protective of the students. They realize, better than the pupils, that today's child actor on Broadway may be tomorrow's unemployed has-been. On the performing side, that means the kids have to develop real skills they can fall back on when they reach an age where merely being young and promising won't get them a job. On the academic side, it means the kids have to master algebra and English grammar so they can go into other lines of work if their performing careers fizzle. "As a staff, we're not lost in Broadway," says science teacher Joseph Ubiles. "If anything, we're very cynical about Broadway." Drama teacher David Leidholdt adds: "You try to give them the skills so when they're not cute teenagers they'll have the professional skills to compete."

The school had a rocky start, with rapid turnover in staff and four principals in five years. Many of the teachers were unlicensed. One was even accused of assaulting a student. But Ms. Chermak has brought order and stability to the school. And students appreciate Ms. Chermak's warmth. "You're the first principal who really opens your arms to the students," one girl told Ms. Chermak as we toured the school. The current staff is all licensed, the teacher accused of assault is gone.

The school's safety record has improved. There was only one suspension of a middle school student in 1997-98; in 1998-99 there were none. Teachers are offering more high school level courses to middle schoolers and kids are passing more Regents-level exams.

"Our standards are higher, we're demanding more and they're snapping to," said Ms. Chermak.

There is only one class for each grade, and the classes are small. Children's reading ability within the class varies tremendously, "from zero to the one-hundredth percentile" one English teacher told me. "We have a couple of ninety-nine-plus kids who carry the whole class," the teacher, Betsy Pratt, said. "My only fear is that the very tippy top is getting a little too comfortable."

The school has a few special education pupils. These children, diagnosed with learning disabilities, are integrated into regular classes with the help of a consultant teacher, who visits several times a week and suggests approaches to the regular classroom teacher.

The performing arts traditionally attract more girls than boys. The school has 240 females and 90 males. There is no gym, no science lab. The science teacher shares a room with the drama coach. But the small class size and individal attention children receive help make up for the spare facilities.

The school is administered by the superintendent for alternative high schools, not by District 2. Children are admitted by audition. Middle school auditions are scheduled from January through the spring semester.

JHS 167, Robert F. Wagner Middle School
220 East 76th Street
New York, N.Y. 10021

Elizabeth McCullough, principal
212-535-8610

Reading Scores: ★★★★★
Math Scores: ★★★★★
Eighth Grade Regents: yes
Grade Levels: 6–8
Admissions: Neighborhood school. Others may also apply.
When to Apply: Weekly tours October-December.
Class Size: 30-36

Free Lunch: 17%
Ethnicity: 40.5%W 12.8%B 19.3%H 27.4%A
Enrollment: 1394
Capacity: 1601
Suspensions: 0.4%
Incidents: 0.3%
High School Choices: Bayard Ruskin, Bronx Science, LaGuardia

Robert F. Wagner Middle School is a high-achieving neighborhood school with a traditional, no-nonsense tone and wide range of programs and facilities. The floors shine, corridors are wide and well lit, classrooms are roomy. The modern building is spotless.

The school has two large gymnasiums, an exercise room with up-to-date rowing machines and treadmills, four indoor tennis courts, a music program than includes a full orchestra and band, and even a computer-equipped woodworking shop.

JHS 167 consistently ranks among the top middle schools in the city on standardized math and reading tests. It sends a high proportion of its students to specialized high schools: More than half the graduating class goes to Stuyvesant, Bronx Science, Brooklyn Tech, LaGuardia, or to small alternative programs.

There is a strong emphasis on math; the 7th graders have won the national Continental Mathematics League competition four years in a row. Nearly half the school's 8th graders take Regents-level (9th grade) math. Almost one-third take Regents-level Earth Science. The school has a magnet grant to improve math and science instruction.

Wagner employs an old-fashioned approach to order and discipline:

Bells mark class changes. No hats are allowed in class. Children are expected to wear uniforms for gym, and they never call teachers by their first names. Classes are grouped by ability, with children tracked into "special progress," "high honors," "honors," "merit," remediation, or special education classes.

"I believe at middle school you need structure," says John Wittekind, who was principal of JHS 167 for thirty-five years.

With the encouragement and direction of former District 2 Superintendent Anthony Alvarado, Wagner shifted from a by-the-book, desks-in-rows junior high school to a more innovative middle school serving grades 6 through 8. The teachers have been organized into teams of four, and classes are organized into "houses." Each team of teachers has common preparation time so they can plan classes together and talk about individual children's progress in different subjects. Each team has adjacent classrooms, so when kids move from class to class they need only go next door. Each teacher has a small group advisory in which children can talk about any academic and nonacademic problems they may be having.

When the school added a 6th grade, a group of teachers went out to good elementary schools in the district to learn techniques for teaching younger children, some of which proved useful in the upper grades as well. There is now more emphasis on projects children can touch, and less on chalk-and-talk lectures.

In one 6th grade science class I visited, for example, kids watched as a teacher floated cans of soda—one diet, one with sugar—in a fish tank of water. They made hypotheses about why the regular soda sank and the diet soda floated.

A 6th grade social studies teacher set up a make-believe archaeological dig in his classroom, burying shards of pottery, religious artifacts, and bones in mounds of kitty litter and gravel. Kids would dig and analyze their findings as part of their study of ancient civilizations of Mesopotamia, Egypt, Greece, Rome, India, and China. "We got away from textbooks as the driving force of instruction, to using them as a supplemental tool," Wittekind says of those days.

Simple things can make a difference, such as having the teacher use an easel with paper and a marker, rather than a blackboard. Teachers can then go back to review earlier notes, which haven't been erased. Every class in language arts, as English is called, has its own classroom library, so kids have ready access to a variety of books in addition to their textbooks.

Perhaps the most interesting innovation is the way in which old industrial arts labs have been transformed into "technology studios." In a woodworking shop, students use a computer to draft complex architectural plans, including detailed blueprints, which they then translate into 3-D balsa wood models. Children build suspension bridges and "magnet cars" that ride on a cushion of air from a vacuum cleaner. In another corner, kids create their own tiny film set of an Egyptian tomb for a class on "claymation"—animated film made by moving and photographing tiny clay figures.

The school boasts the largest music department of any public school in the city, with a chorus and orchestra. Children who pass a musical aptitude test given in the 5th grade are permitted to study a brass, woodwind, or percussion instrument five times a week in the 6th grade. Seventh graders, who are not in the instrumental program, study music history and theory and take part in the chorus. Seventh graders also study speech and drama.

Children play soccer, basketball, and do gymnastics in addition to taking part in free after-school sports clubs four days a week. Phys ed teachers direct activities on the playground during lunch. Children may leave the school grounds for lunch, with their parents' permission.

Parents I spoke to agreed the school is safe and well run. Its strength is the special progress program. High-achievers tend to do very well here. Parents of children in the general education track are less satisfied, and changing from one track to another can be a jolt. One mother complained that her son was bumped downward without warning when his average dropped to the 79th percentile.

The school has five self-contained special education classes for children with learning disabilities, speech problems, and hearing impairment. The special education classrooms are as cheerful and well equipped as the regular classrooms.

About half the incoming pupils come from the zone for the school, which includes the East Side from 97th Street to 59th Street. Children living in the zone are automatically admitted. Others come from the West Side or from downtown, particularly from Chinatown, or from outside Manhattan.

Children applying for the special progress program must have reading and math scores above the 80th percentile. About two-thirds of the school is classified as SP. Children applying for the academic program need only declare an interest in the school. Children applying for art, drama, or music programs must be applicants for SP or an academic program. Priority is given to students with an interest in math, science, or orchestral music.

IS 882, East Side Middle School
1458 York Avenue
New York, N.Y. 10021

Denise Levine, director
212-439-6278

Reading Scores: ★★★★★
Math Scores: ★★★★★
Eighth Grade Regents: no
Grade Levels: 6–8
Admissions: Selective. By
  interview.
When to Apply: Weekly tours
  October to December
Class Size: 32-35
Free Lunch: 21%

Ethnicity: 54.6%W 17.1%B
  15.1%H 13.2%A
Enrollment: 416
Capacity: 420
Suspensions: N/A
Incidents: N/A
High School Choices: Beacon
  School, Brooklyn Technical,
  Stuyvesant

When you visit East Side Middle School, try not to be put off by the physical conditions. You will—alas!—see 35 kids packed into rooms so small you have to turn sideways to get past the desks. You'll see hallways so narrow that kids have to duck into a classroom to let others pass during class changes. The floors are concrete. A few light bulbs are out. The light-blue paint job doesn't add much to the ambiance.

Try to concentrate instead on the quality of teaching and the level of discussion the kids are having. Look at the samples of their writing, the artwork on the bulletin boards in the halls, and the mountains of books in each classroom, books that are both serious and fun to read. Talk to teachers about the passion they have for their students and their work. Look at the kids—serious, articulate, engaged.

Crammed into the fourth and fifth floors of a pleasant hundred-year-old elementary school (PS 158), East Side Middle was founded in 1991 as an antidote to what one teacher called "the Henry Ford model of education." Parents who feel that traditional middle schools are too big, too anonymous, and too much like factories are attracted to the idea of an intimate, cohesive alternative.

While classes are big, the school overall is small, with about four hundred pupils. Teachers from different disciplines plan their lessons together, and it's not uncommon for kids to have one paper jointly assigned (and jointly graded) by their biology teacher, their social studies teacher, and their English teacher.

"There's a real esprit de corps because everyone knows everyone," said a mother, Katharine Flanders Mukherji. "The teachers don't underestimate these kids." The director is likely to answer the school's phone herself, and there's no bureaucracy or hierarchy for parents to contend with.

Unlike other middle schools where teachers are assigned by the central Board of Education according to seniority, a committee of parents, teachers, and the director hand-picks the staff. At East Side Middle, you get the sense that the teachers really like early adolescents, and really like one another.

East Side Middle School has an active Parents' Association, unusual in a middle school, and parents are frequently on hand during the day.

Kids typically read forty to fifty books a year, old favorites such as *Oliver Twist*, *To Kill a Mockingbird*, *1984*, and *The Catcher in the Rye*, as well as more contemporary fiction. The English, history, and science teachers integrate their lessons. Children studying the Civil War in American history will be reading *The Yearling* by Marjorie Rawlings, a story of a backwoods Florida family, with their English teacher. Their science teacher, meanwhile will discuss how geography affects where people settle, and the importance of rivers, water tables, and aquifers to farming. The teachers are knowledgeable not only about their own disciplines, but others as well. "Everyone is a Renaissance person here," says Susan Schwartz, whose Language Arts class combines art and English.

Children don't rely on textbooks or encyclopedias for their research. They are expected to use primary sources: articles in *The New York Times* on global warming for a science project, or the letters of fifteen-year-old soldiers from both sides of the Civil War for a history project. They learn to write, telephone, and interview experts and ordinary people to gather information. Some students conduct oral history projects.

Children write frequently, not just their weekly English papers, but also research papers in, say, the history of science. Typical topics for three-page papers: What were Bernoulli's contributions to science? What are modern applications of Leonardo DaVinci's inventions? How does physics help in the design of the Citicorp Building on Lexington Avenue?

One parent complained that the homework assignments were burdensome, but others said the workload, while heavy, was appropriate.

The school's graduates have a very high rate of acceptance to specialized high schools. Nearly 30 percent go to Stuyvesant, Bronx Science, or Brooklyn Tech, and eight to ten children a year go to art schools such as LaGuardia or Talent Unlimited.

Bathrooms are unlocked and no passes are required to use them. Children who have their parents' permission may go out for lunch or to John Jay Park next to the school.

Children who score in the 70th percentile on the city reading test and the 80th percentile on the city math test are eligible for admission. Children who pick East Side Middle School as their first choice are asked to visit the school for a morning, where they present a writing sample, solve a math problem, and take part in a group interview with other children and teachers.

"Don't worry if your child is shy," says Ms. Mukherji. "They make an effort not to allow kids who are the most self-confident to dominate the discussion." Priority is given to residents of District 2, but in past years there has been some room for children from outside the district. The school has a few special education children, who are fully integrated into regular classes. The building has an elevator and is officially listed as wheelchair accessible, although the hallways are very narrow.

Hunter College High School
71 East 94th Street
New York, N.Y. 10128

Susan Leung Eichler (acting principal);
Polly Breland, admissions director
212-860-1259

Reading Scores: N/A
Math Scores: N/A
Eighth Grade Regents: no
Grade Levels: 7–12
Admissions: Selective. By exam.
When to Apply: Apply in
November, entrance exam in
January.
Class Size: 25

Free Lunch: 1%
Ethnicity: 47%W 11%B 5%H
37%A
Enrollment: 1200
Capacity: 1200
Suspensions: N/A
Incidents: N/A
High School Choices: Hunter,
Stuyvesant, Bronx Science

Getting into Hunter is a little like getting into Harvard, except harder. Hunter accepts one in ten applicants, Harvard accepts one in six. Hunter has such a great reputation and it's so famous that nobody much cares what it's actually like to be a student there. Everybody who can, it seems, applies, even though the school doesn't allow tours. And most of the kids who are accepted go.

Hunter High School, which includes grades 7 through 12, is a highly successful, very academic school that prepares its students well for the country's most selective colleges. Half of its graduates typically go to Ivy League colleges. More than 12 percent of its staff has Ph.D.s; nearly all have master's degrees in their disciplines. It's known particularly for its strength in the humanities, but it also produced a Westinghouse Science Talent Search winner in 1997.

"I think it's so fabulous I can hardly believe it," said Karen Greenberg, whose son attends. "The teachers are so smart and so nice and so funny and they know your child so well. There's wonderful, thought-provoking, interesting work."

The surroundings are pretty grim, and the kids call the school the Brick Prison. The building is an ugly high-rise, with tiny slits for windows, designed, it seems, on the fortress-theory of architecture. Classrooms have no windows, ventilation is bad, and the heating system is dicey. The halls are strewn with occasional bits of litter and even

95

graffiti. The school has grungy, scuffed-up lockers, reading materials photocopied twenty-five years ago, and books held together with tape.

But you go to Hunter, after all, for the life of the mind. And most kids are so grateful to be there that it seems churlish to complain about some beat-up textbooks. What the school offers very bright kids is each others' company, some very good teachers, and a consistently high level of intellectual excitement in the classroom. Several parents I spoke to were envious of their children's experiences—the passion inspired for biology, the thrill of studying Asian art at the Metropolitan Museum of Art.

"She just loves it," said a mother, Sharon Kleinbaum. "For her to be around other kids whose minds are very supple, and to not feel she has to hide her smartness, is wonderful. The good teachers are phenomenal. Their level of knowledge is really high."

Like Hunter College Elementary School, Hunter College High School is touted as a "laboratory" school for the study of "gifted" education. It is tuition-free and supported by tax levies, but it's not part of the Board of Education. Instead, it is administered by Hunter College, part of the City University of New York. In fact, students may take college courses at Hunter while still in high school. The school hires its own teachers, sets its own admission criteria, writes its own curriculum and administers its own tests. Regents are not given.

Hunter was the first public high school for girls in New York City. Founded in 1869 as the Female Normal and High School, it was divided into a high school and college in 1903 and renamed Hunter College High School in 1914. It opened its doors to boys in 1974.

The high school shares a building with Hunter College Elementary School, but the two schools have very different personalities. The elementary school, on the ground floor, is a relatively laid-back, relaxed, progressive school where kids play with blocks and no one pushes them to read until they seem ready.

The high school upstairs, on the other hand, is a competitive, serious, traditional place where no one forgets that getting into a superselective college is the goal. One mother complained that a 7th grade teacher introduced a new vocabulary word by saying, "This is an SAT word," as if to remind them, even as they started secondary school, that they'd need to do well on the Scholastic Achievement Tests to get into a top college.

Children in the elementary school are automatically admitted to the high school. Others are admitted in the 7th grade, based on the results of a test administered to children in January of their 6th grade year.

Admissions to the elementary school is limited to Manhattan residents; children living anywhere in the five boroughs may apply to Hunter High School.

About fifty children enter Hunter High School from the elementary school. About 190 are chosen from other schools.

The middle school years are always a big adjustment for children. At Hunter, the transition can be particularly daunting. Depending on your child's temperament and elementary school background, the 7th and 8th grades at Hunter can be traumatic or enormously liberating.

"You have all these bright kids who were the smartest kids in their class and all of a sudden they are thrown in with two hundred kids who were the smartest in their class," said former principal Anthony Miserandino, who gave me my tour. "We don't separate the big kids and the little kids. We treat the 7th graders like miniature 11th graders."

One mother described the set-up as "cold" and her son's first years as "bittersweet." But another mother said her girl was extremely happy to be with very bright, motivated kids for the first time in her school years.

The 7th and 8th grades are organized like an old-fashioned junior high school, with 40-minute classes and different instructors for every subject. The school hasn't been influenced by the Middle School Initiative, which seeks to ease children into the middle school years by giving them two or three teachers at first—rather than five or six—and by setting aside time for teachers to plan their classes together and to share information about an individual child's progress.

Seventh and 8th graders are given far more responsibility and freedom than is typical in middle schools or junior high schools. In fact, children are sometimes treated more like college students. One math teacher, for example, doesn't collect homework. A mature child understands you need to do the homework anyway or you won't pass the end-of-semester exam. But a lot of twelve-year-olds simply don't have the self-discipline to cope with that much freedom. Children are allowed to leave campus anytime they don't have a class, a liberation for some and too much freedom for others.

The school has been so successful for so long that the staff and administration have been reluctant to change what many see as a winning formula. The curriculum is traditional, almost old-fashioned. There are no electives in 7th and 8th grades. All 7th and 8th graders take algebra, science, social studies, English, music and art.

Children may study Latin, German, French, or Spanish. (Italian

and Russian are offered to juniors and seniors.) Readings include
To Kill a Mockingbird, Julius Caesar, Great Expectations, and *Jane
Eyre*. Icons of Western civilization, such as Plato and Aristotle, are
introduced.

Serious study of contemporary fiction and non-Western literature
and history has also been incorporated. *Nilda*, by Nicholasa Mohr, a
story of a Puerto Rican girl growing up in New York, and *The Joy Luck
Club*, by Amy Tan, the story of four Chinese-American mothers and
their daughters, are required reading. The Bible, and early Irish myths
and sagas are read, along with stories of Islam, and tales of dragon
gods and spirits from Chinese mythology.

In a 7th grade social studies class, students were required to chose
two cultures—one they felt close to, one that seemed far removed
from their experience. They were then to find a creation myth from
each and compare them. Finally, they were assigned to write their own
myths, working in small groups.

In another social studies class, kids were showing off papier-mâché
models they'd made of monuments in the ancient world—Genghis
Khan's mausoleum, Aristotle's Lyceum with its open-air classes. One
child used his model to discuss ideas of government and equity. "Plato
had an Academy that only the smartest people could go to," he said,
"but Aristotle believed everyone should have a chance to learn."

Another led the class in an interesting discussion of whether Marco
Polo was lying about his trip to China. "Even if he was lying," the boy
said, "he still brought together those worlds. His book was the only
book in the West about China for hundreds of years and he did
encourage the exploration of America."

Because it's administered by CUNY—not the Board of Education—
Hunter isn't bound by the Board of Education requirement to teach
American history in the 7th and 8th grades. That means teachers can
use these years to introduce children to topics that form the foundation of social studies such as political philosophy, cultural anthro-
pology, and a smattering of economics—and give them tools to use for
research—such as how to use documents and primary sources. Children investigate these "global studies" for three years before they take
up American history in the 10th and 11th grades.

Kids study two years of algebra in 7th and 8th grades, as well as elementary probability and geometry. The most advanced 8th graders
also study less traditional topics such as logic, groups, and fields.

Kids study life science in 7th grade and physical science in 8th grade. The school recently updated its twenty-five-year-old labs. In a class I visited, kids were working in groups, chatting together happily and animatedly. One girl in blue jeans was digging for earthworms in a pile of dirt on the lab table as her group investigated ways to estimate the number of earthworms without counting every one. They divided the dirt into quadrants, counted the worms in one quadrant, then multiplied the result by four. The teacher, who has a Ph.D. in microbiolgy, had given other groups of kids related problems to solve: How can you estimate the number of birds in a park? Can you measure the intensity of an oil spill by estimating the number of brine shrimp killed in a certain area?

As I walked through the halls between classes, I saw groups of kids sitting on the floor, chatting. Two kids were eating cupcakes, and Miserandino explained to me that the older students are paired as "big siblings" with 7th graders; the older of these two had given the younger one cupcakes for his birthday.

Hunter has long had a reputation as a very competitive place, where a child's fear of failure can occasionally lead to desperation. A student committed suicide in 1989, which triggered much soul-searching into whether the school was too competitive to be healthy.

The school instituted a "peer counseling" program to train kids to help others with any problems and, most important, to recognize when a problem is big enough to call for notifying an adult. A guidance counselor is assigned to students for their whole six years, which parents say is a good way to make sure at least one adult is looking out for every child.

Still, the school is stressful and intense. One teacher described an "insane careerism" about where kids go to college and "hysteria about having a 1350 SAT score," a score that would be considered very good anywhere but at Hunter. I met a child who was visibly disappointed that he would be going to Swarthmore. (He'd been hoping for Yale.) One teacher said the "parents are just nutso" about their kids' college admissions.

Students who are grappling with any other problems in their lives—a death in the family, or a divorce—may find it hard to keep up. "It's not a touchy-feely place," one mother said. "The individuals are warm but the atmosphere is not." Another mother said the school "could be a little more accommodating to the eccentric kid."

Not every teacher is stellar. One mother said her daughter had one disappointing teacher every year. But she added, the good teachers were extraordinary, and even the classes with uninspired teachers were salvaged because the kids were so smart they were able to learn from one another.

The workload is heavy. "I think she's working harder at middle school than I did at college," Ms. Greenberg said of her daughter. "Unless you're incredibly motivated and organized, it could be a horror."

Former PTA president Eve Kravitz said children need to be "self-starters" with good study skills and the ability to work independently. "No one will say, 'This is how you do it,'" she said. She also said parents need to be involved, perhaps even more so than if their child was at a neighborhood school.

"For the kids it does fit, it's a wonderful thing," Ms. Kravitz said. "But it's not the kind of school where you can just send your kid off and everything will be fine."

She warns parents that they have to help their children organize their social life, particularly since children come from all five boroughs. Be prepared to open your home to other children, and be prepared to drive your kid to the far reaches of Brooklyn or Queens to friends, she said.

"The social aspect is hard," a Queens mother agreed. "My son doesn't have friends he can play basketball with right in my neighborhood."

Admission to the school is extremely competitive. Children who score in the 91st percentile in reading and the 93rd percentile in math on standardized tests given in 5th grade are eligible to take the entrance exam in January of their 6th grade year. (The cutoff scores vary from year to year.) Elementary school principals must give the names of all qualified candidates to Hunter by November. Parents of children in private or parochial school may register for the test if their school sends records of standardized tests. Call the school for a brochure explaining the application procedure.

Students must pay a forty dollar fee to take the exam. About two thousand kids take it each year, although that number fluctuates considerably. The test consists of multiple-choice questions in math and English, plus a writing assignment. The exact content is a "closely guarded secret," one mother said. That hasn't stopped various entrepreneurs from offering test preparation classes. Other parents pay private tutors. "I've heard of kids who started prepping for Hunter in the 3rd grade," a mother said. "If you can't afford the test prep or a private tutor, you're not going to get in." (Although many do.)

I spoke to a mother whose child had no more preparation for the test than a basic review from a study guide available from any bookstore and got in. (Look for *New York City Specialized Science High Schools Admissions Test* by Stephen Krane, published by the Arco division of MacMillan.)

The test relies heavily on the writing sample, which is graded pass-fail. The English section of the test—the multiple-choice section on grammar and vocabulary, plus the essay portion—counts for two-thirds. "Anyone who is weak in English skills won't get in even if he is a walking Einstein in terms of math," Miserandino said.

How awful is the test? It depends on who you ask. One mother called it a "cattle call," with hoards of eager souls crowding into the examining room, while another found it a "moving experience" to see children of all races, shapes and sizes competing for a spot in an extraordinary institution.

Parents of children who are accepted may attend an open house in the spring. Parents of current students may sit in on classes during "open school week" in the fall, but there are no tours for prospective parents.

The school makes accommodations for children in special education whose reading and math scores meet the cutoff. If, for example, a child is blind or hearing impaired, an appropriate aide may assist during the exam. The school is wheelchair accessible.

The 160 children who score the highest on the multiple-choice portion of the test (and who write acceptable essays) are offered admission. In addition, about thirty seats are set aside for children who are "economically disadvantaged"—children from low-income families. Those children must have standardized test scores high enough to be eligible for the entrance exam. They must pass the essay part of the test, but may have slightly lower scores on the multiple-choice section.

Seventh grade is the only year for which children are admitted.

Most students stay at Hunter through high school. A number leave in the 9th grade for Bronx Science or Stuyvesant, which some parents believe have science programs that are even more high-powered than Hunter's.

District 3

District 3, which encompasses the West Side between 122nd Street and 59th Street, includes elegant brownstones, doorman buildings on Central Park West, towering apartment blocks near Lincoln Center, faculty and student housing of Columbia University, as well as various public housing projects and (relatively) low-rent buildings.

For many years, the middle class shunned all but a tiny handful of District 3 middle schools, mostly sending their children out of district or to private schools. But activist parents in the late 1980s and 1990s pressured the district to offer more options than the chaotic and low-performing junior high schools and middle schools that had been the norm. By the end of the century, the district had shut down all zoned middle schools, replacing them with several dozen small schools organized around various themes. Some of these, needless to say, are better than others. But a district that once had almost no choices now has many. In fact, District 3 is one of the few in the city in which parents are *required* to choose a middle school. Priority is given to children living in the district, although there have been a limited number of spots for out of district children in recent years.

The new small programs or "option schools" are, for the most part, housed within gloomy old junior high school buildings. The programs are led by "directors," and generally occupy a floor or a wing in a building. Building principals are still in charge of administration. The amount of control the principals exert over each small program varies. Some programs operate autonomously. Others are nominally independent but in practice are merely corners of the old junior high schools that have been given new names. Some of the programs have a distinctive personality, with a clear mission, a sense of community, and a cohesive staff and student body. Others are struggling to gain their identity.

Most of the District 3 middle schools begin in the 6th grade. (The Center School starts in 5th grade.) Call the Office of School Choice at 212 678-2885 for a middle school directory, or write Lizabeth Sostre, the school choice coordinator, at the district office, 300 West 96th St., New York, N.Y., 10025.

The district holds middle school fairs in October, individual school tours take place in October and November. Tours fill up fast, so sign up early. Applications are due in December. Out-of-district children and those applying for 7th or 8th grades have until March. You must list your choices in order of preference. Several schools will consider your child's application only if listed as first choice. Most require an interview for admissions. Some require essays, and some accept children based on their scores on standardized tests. Acceptances are sent in May.

A school to watch: West Side Academy (MS 250), 735 West End Avenue, 10025, 212-856-6313, Jeanne Rotunda, director. Nestled on the top floor and attic of an elementary school, (PS 75), it has small classes, a dedicated staff, and a passionate director who's constantly fine-tuning teaching methods and curriculum. Arts are woven into the curriculum. Test scores are on the rise. The school has a special education inclusion program in which children with learning disabilities are included in regular classes, aided by a special ed teacher.

IS 243, Center School
270 West 70th Street
New York, N.Y. 10023

Elaine J. Schwartz, director
212-678-2791

Reading Scores: ★★★★★
Math Scores: ★★★★★
Eighth Grade Regents: yes
Grade Levels: 5–8
Admissions: Unzoned. By
interview and essay.
When to Apply: Weekly tours
October-November.
Class Size: 8–27
Free Lunch: 78%

Ethnicity: 42.7%W 25.1%B
26.3%H 5.8%A
Enrollment: 171
Capacity: 186
Suspensions: N/A
Incidents: N/A
High School Choices:
LaGuardia, Environmental
Studies, Stuyvesant

A tiny gem of a place, the Center School is one of the oldest and most popular alternative schools in the city. With very small classes and lots of attention for each child, the school combines a progressive attitude toward *how* children learn with a classical view of *what* they should learn.

Kids move around the classrooms and chat with one another as they work. Teachers and kids are informally dressed. Everyone—kids as well as grown-ups—is welcome to wander into the director's office.

The curriculum is traditional. Ancient Greek and Latin are mandatory. Everyone is expected to spell properly and to learn conventional geography and algebra. The subject matter is traditional.

The approach is extremely successful. The school has a very high rate of acceptance into selective high schools. More than 80 percent of graduates go either to the specialized high schools or to specialized programs known as educational option schools. Nearly one third of one recent graduating class went to LaGuardia and 17 percent went to Stuyvesant.

Director Elaine Schwartz founded the Center School in 1982 after coming to the conclusion that the traditional junior high school—with more than a thousand kids, forty minute classes, and lectures from textbooks—was simply the wrong way to teach young adolescents.

Children this age, she says, can't sit still and need to talk to their friends. They are beginning to move from concrete to abstract think-ing, but they can't absorb information solely from textbooks. They need materials they can see and touch. Schools that fail to recognize the realities of young adolescents' development, she says, won't be able to teach them. "If you accept the fact that they must socialize and they must make noise, you've won half the battle," says Ms. Schwartz. "Sitting still for hours and being quiet is not the way adults work, so why should children?"

The school allows ten minutes for class changes, not the three min-utes allocated at most schools. That gives children a longer break, so when their next class starts they're more ready to concentrate. Classes vary in length from forty minutes to two hours. The school goes from 5th to 8th grade, and children of different ages are assigned to classes together for most subjects. The mixing of ages provides a sense of family and belonging. But classes that are clearly sequential—math and Latin—are separated by age.

"Children this age are a mess of anxiety about everything," said teacher Judith Hartmann. "They are insecure emotionally, physically, every which way they can be. Most schools tend to make that even worse, exacerbating their insecurities." The ungraded classes, with children of different ages, she said, eases competition and allows chil-dren to relax about who they are. "What it teaches them is that not everyone is at the same place. They see 5th graders who know the answers and 8th graders who don't."

The staff has a mix of senior teachers, some of whom helped found the school, and young, new teachers. All the teachers I saw were extremely energetic and attentive to the children. They prided them-selves on their ability to teach different subjects. Gabrielle Castelnau, an English and social studies teacher, for example, gave a science unit on coral reefs, boning up on the subject herself over the summer. "We're expected to be flexible and to have enough intellectual curi-osity to delve into new subjects," said Ms. Castelnau. "We're not tied to one subject here." Interdisciplinary work comes naturally in a set-ting such as this. The unit on coral reefs, for example, included a lot of geography as well as science.

The teachers seem particularly well attuned to young adolescents and adapt their lessons to appeal to them. "They are really captivated by mayhem and disasters, so I did a science curriculum based on earthquakes, volcanoes and tidal waves," said Ms. Hartmann.

There isn't much fancy equipment. The small size means the school doesn't have labs. But teachers keep close tabs on each child. Each teacher acts as an adviser to eight to ten children, and meets with them as a group twice a week. "Their adviser knows every move they're making," said Indigo, the assistant to the director and who goes by one name only. One of the purposes of the advisory is to help develop study skills, particularly planning how to organize long assignments.

"The main purpose of the school is to make sure your child leaves us knowing how to learn," said Ms. Schwartz. "We never want to give so much homework that a student feels overloaded. Part of that feeling of 'too much' work comes from a student's lack of experience in planning. Our main job is to teach them to be responsible for themselves."

Instead of conventional report cards, children write their own evaluations in November. At the end of each trimester, teachers write long comments, and children add their own notes.

There are very few textbooks, except for math and Latin. Instead, teachers rely on works of literature and primary source materials such as diaries and historical documents. Trips to the New York Aquarium and the American Museum of Natural History are an important part of the coursework.

The Center School is on the top floor of a well-regarded and well-kept elementary school, PS 199. White wall tiles, white floors, and good lighting make the classrooms bright and appealing. Children's work covers the walls. There's a huge mural on brown paper tracing the history of life on Earth, from the simple one-celled animals through the age of the dinosaurs and up to the present. There are posters the kids made about the Russian Revolution, including portraits of the Czar and a timeline on the history of science.

The day I visited, a dozen prospective parents and pupils were also touring the school. We were ushered into a conference room, where Indigo, a gentle, welcoming teacher wearing a beard and overalls, introduced himself. He gave a general outline of the program and philosophy, and showed a videotape about the school. A girl who looked a little nervous held out her report card. "I don't need to look at that," Indigo said gently. "I love you without looking at those little marks." He made parents feel at ease, as well. "Please don't hesitate to call," he said as he rattled off the telephone number of the school. "It's never a bother."

The children sat in on classes for the morning, to give them an idea of whether they would like the school and to give teachers a feel for how the kids would do. Parents looked in on other classes.

In one 6th grade Latin class, children were using box cutters to build a Roman temple from cardboard. The lesson helped teach scale in making a model—a math skill—as well as teaching about Roman history and architecture. A couple of girls were chanting the Greek alphabet, apparently just for fun, while waiting for another class to begin. The Regents math class was the smallest I'd seen—just 11 pupils. Ms. Schwartz keeps classes small with careful scheduling. By restricting the administration, and by scheduling classes of 40 pupils for gym and swimming (children go across town to the sports complex at Asphalt Green) she can free up enough teachers to keep academic classes very small.

At the end of the morning visit, prospective students are asked to write the answer to a question such as "How did you feel when you came to the Center School?" The teachers then interview applicants, asking them questions about why they want to attend the Center School and what kind of books they like to read.

Parents are encouraged to call the school to arrange a tour and interview. Applications are due in December for in-district pupils, later for out of district.

The school has about 150 applicants for thirty-five spots in the 5th grade. A boy and a girl from each elementary school in the district are selected, and up to ten children from outside the district are accepted. The school generally has two or three spaces in the 6th grade, but never accepts children in the 7th grade. The entering class has a mix of children reading above grade level, at grade level, and below grade level. The school doesn't have separate special education classes, although it makes accommodations in regular classes for children with learning disabilities. The building is wheelchair accessible.

IS 245, The Computer Schools I and II
100 West 77th Street & 100 West 84th Street
New York, N.Y. 10024

Steven Siegelbaum, director
212-678-2785 & 678-2968

Reading Scores: ★★★★   **Free Lunch:** 56%
Math Scores: ★★★★   **Ethnicity:** 26.1%W 37.3%B
Eighth Grade Regents: yes   29.1%H 7.5%A
Grade Levels: 6–8   **Enrollment:** 268
Admissions: Unzoned. By   **Capacity:** N/A
   interview and essay.   **Suspensions:** N/A
When to Apply: Weekly tours   **Incidents:** N/A
   October-November.   **High School Choices:** Beacon,
Class Size: 23-30   LaGuardia, Vanguard

When the Computer School was founded in 1982, the idea of using computers in every classroom was considered offbeat, even weird. It has grown to serve 270 pupils on two sites, and has become one of the most popular and successful alternative schools in the city, with far more applicants than seats available. Nearly 80 percent of its graduates go to specialized high schools or to the alternative schools known as educational option schools, a figure four times the citywide average. The Computer School has an energetic and talented director, a cohesive staff, and a varied and imaginative student body. It also has very small classes: 23 to 28 students.

Students learn what's inside computers, how they work, and even how to fix them. "The philosophy of the Computer School is not to teach kids how to use a computer but to teach them how to *talk* to a computer," said PTA co-president Claudia Zangrillo. "Instead of giving games to the kids, you make your own games, which is very hard."

Computer School I is in the basement of IS 44 on West 77th Street, and Computer School II, on the third floor of PS 9 on West 84th Street. The director and founder, Steve Siegelbaum, runs back and forth between the two.

Both programs are tiny, with 180 children at I and 90 at CS II. Both have the relaxed atmosphere of a progressive school, combined with the intense individual attention available at a small school. The teachers are knowledgeable and concerned, constantly re-evaluating and adjusting their teaching techniques to accommodate different kinds of students. The staff seems to care as much about the low-achievers as the high-achievers, and struggles to make lessons interesting and exciting for all.

Siegelbaum (who sings and plays guitar in his spare time with the Walkabout Clearwater Chorus) has an open and relaxed demeanor that encourages kids to bring him their most intimate problems. But Siegelbaum is strict about certain things.

"I thought he was a hippie from the sixties, a great philosopher with curly hair and a beard," said Ms. Zangrillo. "But, academically and discipline-wise, he's very serious. Kids have to come to school on time. If you miss your homework, they send a letter home." She added that Siegelbaum took swift action when, for example, one child picked on another. He called the bully's parents and let the boy know his behavior was unacceptable and the bad behavior stopped.

"It's been a wonderful experience," added PTA co-president Mary Carson. "Siegelbaum's personality and vision are very important in what makes this school good. He seems to be able to find people who are very dedicated and very good to teach. The teachers genuinely like each other and communicate with each other."

The fact that teachers talk to one another means there is coordination between the disciplines. When one class studied evolution in science, for example, they read the story of the Scopes trial, *Inherit the Wind*, in social studies. Trips are a big part of the curriculum. Children attend rehearsals at Lincoln Center to learn about jazz and classical music. The integration of the curriculum, combined with the frequent trips, makes for what Ms. Carson called a "three-dimensional" education. CS is a member of the Coalition of Essential Schools.

The day I visited CS I, Siegelbaum invited me to look around on my own for as long as I wished. Throughout the school, kids were attentive, happy, and well-behaved. The classes are all along one hall, so it's impossible to get lost.

Eighth grade humanities teacher Ambar Panjabi was working to bring Shakespeare's *Julius Caesar* to life for his pupils. He played a dramatic reading of the script on the tape recorder, pausing to explain unfamiliar vocabulary, then asked the kids to take out their journals. "This is going to be fun," Panjabi said. "It's going to be a horror story." (Whoops from the kids.) "But it's connected to Julius Caesar." (Groans from the kids.) The teacher continued: "Imagine camping in the

Adirondacks or Montana and you're lost in the woods," he said, and told them to write a paragraph setting the mood. When the kids were done, he had them read Act I, scene 3, of the play and they noticed how Shakespeare used thunder and lightning to set an ominous mood just as some of them had used bad weather. "I'm trying to make Shakespeare accessible to kids and show them the kinds of decisions he makes as a writer are very similar to the decisions they make," Panjabi said.

Down the hall, fish tanks were bubbling and kids were looking through microscopes at samples of water and rocks they'd collected from Central Park. Earth Science teacher Henry Zymeck was discussing a class trip they had taken through the park to the Metropolitan Museum of Art.

In the park, he'd pointed out the effects of erosion and glaciers. In the museum, the kids had looked at different kinds of rocks and minerals in the Egyptian wing: granite sarcophagi and clay pottery and beads made of various minerals. "Rather than passing around a little piece of a rock in class, they can see what it's used for," Zymeck explained. "We ask, 'Where did these rocks come from? Where does clay come from?'" The trip piqued the kids' interest for a fifteen-minute video on "the rock cycle."

Zymeck was particularly proud of the way he'd managed to get a girl, who had been doing poorly in school, excited about Earth Science by assigning her to collect rock and water samples from the park. "You look for moments when you can take kids who are frustrated and build on their strengths," he said.

Teachers use a mixture of traditional and progressive techniques. I saw a math teacher offer by-the-book instruction on the Pythagorean theorem to the whole class, admonishing them to "keep your parentheses in the right place" and reminding them that "understanding and memorizing are two different things." And I saw a science teacher experiment with a lesson that melded social studies with the study of the human body, having kids research, for example, the effect of nineteenth-century coal mining on the respiratory systems of the miners.

Parents say the different techniques allow their children to move at their own pace and to explore their own interests while ensuring they get the basics. Ms. Carson, a teacher at nearby PS 87 said: "My daughter Maggie is getting plenty of skills and basics. She gets lots of grammar. She writes really good papers and they come back with red marks; fix this and fix that." As a result, Ms. Carson said, students are well-prepared for traditional high schools, but many also choose smaller, more progressive schools (such as the popular Beacon High School, an alternative West Side high school founded by former teachers at the Computer School).

Both Ms. Carson and Ms. Zandrillo praised the staff for helping kids choose good high schools.

Of the two, CS II in PS 9 is brighter and cheerier, and slightly better equipped, but the staff is first-rate at both buildings. Both have extremely good safety records with only a handful of suspensions reported each year. The relationship between CS I and the school it shares a building with, IS 44, could be better. The day I visited, IS 44 students passing through CS I on their way to lunch talked loudly, distracting students who were studying.

The Computer School has basic facilities. There is no instruction in musical instruments, and the art program is limited. Kids have to share microscopes. Parents say that's a shame, but high-quality staff counts more than than high-quality equipment. "They don't have the bells and whistles," said Ms. Carson. "I'd love to see a science room with the snazzy things. But it's the people who are the most important."

Children and parents are invited to tour the school in the fall. Teachers interview children in groups of eight to ten. There are typically three hundred applicants for ninety spots.

"We want to see if their learning style is amenable to what we do. If it's a kid who needs a lot of constant, direct supervision, he's not likely to do well here," Siegelbaum said. "What we look for is bright-eyed and cooperative kids. They don't have to be high achieving, but we like inquisitive kids."

IS 247, Dual Language Middle School
32 W. 92nd Street
New York, N.Y. 10025

Irma Marzan, director
212-678-2977

Reading Scores: ★★★
Math Scores: ★★★★
Eighth Grade Regents: yes
Grade Levels: 6–8
Admissions: Unzoned. By
  interview.
When to Apply: Weekly tours
  October-November.
Class Size: 13-25
Free Lunch: 87%

Ethnicity: 0.6%W 4.8%B
  94%H 0.6%A
Enrollment: 181
Capacity: 200
Suspensions: N/A
Incidents: N/A
High School Choices: Beacon,
  A. Philip Randolph, Art and
  Design

The Dual Language Middle School strives to teach children to speak and write fluently in both English and Spanish. Founded in 1990 by Irma Marzan and Ruthy Swinney (who is now at the Principals' Institute at Bank Street College), the school has a progressive curriculum in which Spanish and English alternate as the language of instruction. That means Spanish isn't isolated from the rest of children's studies and consigned to a forty minute period, as in most schools.

Located on the top floor of PS 84, a dual-language elementary school, the Dual Language Middle School attracts native speakers of both English and Spanish. The typical class size is extremely small, ranging from 13 for many literature classes, to 25 for most math and science classes. Parents comment that the school feels like a family. Students meet in a small group with an adviser once a week.

"The director, Irma Marzan, is a warm and loving person who brooks no nonsense," PEA's Judith Baum observed after a visit. "She expects hard work, good behavior, and high performance, and she gets them all."

More than half the 8th graders pass the demanding Regents exam in Spanish. That shows they've mastered the equivalent of *three years* of high school Spanish, completing their foreign language requirement before they even begin high school. More than half the 8th graders also pass the 9th grade math Regents, Sequential I.

Reading scores in English and math are above average, and the school has a good record of admissions to academic high schools. Roughly 10 percent of graduates pass the entrance exam for the specialized science high schools; roughly one-quarter attend the popular Beacon High School on the West Side.

Most of the staff of thirteen is bilingual in Spanish and English. The school has student teachers from Teachers College at Columbia University. About half the entering 6th grade class come from PS 84. The rest come mostly from other dual language programs in District 3 elementary schools. A handful come to the school with no knowledge of Spanish.

The vast majority of the pupils are of Hispanic origin, but about half speak English at home. English is the language of the playground. About half the kids are of Dominican origin. The rest have families that come from Central America, Mexico, South America, or Puerto Rico.

The school year is divided into trimesters. Math and science are taught in English. The other subjects—writer's workshop, social studies, and literature—are taught in English for two-thirds of the year, and Spanish for one-third the year. The curriculum is integrated, which means children studying, say, the history of immigration in social studies may read a novel about immigrant life in their literature class.

When possible, children read literature in its original language, not in translation. They read a variety of Latin American authors. In addition, children have a supplementary Spanish class twice a week in which they learn public speaking, theater arts, and grammar. The children read *La Noticias del Mundo*, a Spanish language daily published in New York, and many watch the news in Spanish at home.

"It was hard to find a good American history book in Spanish, but we found one," Ms. Marzan said. "We read stories written in Spanish about kids who have immigrated and are living here."

Ms. Marzan, a Puerto Rican who taught at PS 84 and who studied bilingual education at Bank Street College, founded the school as a way to continue the dual language programs that District 3 had established in several elementary schools. She found that students lost their fluency in Spanish if they didn't use the language continuously during the middle school years.

Test scores have steadily increased since the school opened. Most encouraging, the children's test scores rise the longer they stay at the school. Children typically gain more than 15 percentage points in both reading and math scores during their three years here, according to Ms. Marzan.

Part of the school's success comes from the passion that the staff has for teaching children this age. "I love middle school," Ms. Marzan says. "I love that you can talk to them about themselves, talk to them as adults, but they still have childlike qualities. They're so idealisitic. They're not jaded. They love to talk about right and wrong and fairness."

The school shares the library, gym, and lunchroom with PS 84. Kids can go out to lunch with parents' permission. Bathrooms are unlocked. Every Friday afternoon, there are "clubs." Children choose running, lacrosse, or photography. Ms. Baum called the fully equipped darkroom the school's "pride and joy."

Open from 7:30 a.m. to 5 p.m., there are after-school programs that include homework help, basketball, softball, dance, tai chi, chess, and crafts. There is an annual all-school trip—one year it was to Washington, D.C—and an annual camping trip to an environmental center.

Any interested pupil may apply. Parents are encouraged to call the school to arrange a tour. Children are interviewed and may be asked to submit a writing sample and a teacher recommendation.

IS 853, The Manhattan School for Children
234 West 109th Street/154 West 93rd Street
New York, N.Y. 10025

Susan Rappaport, principal
212-678-5856 & 212-222-1450

Reading Scores: ★★★
Math Scores: ★★★
Eighth Grade Regents: yes
Grade Levels: K–8
Admissions: Unzoned. By interview and teacher recommendation.
When to Apply: Weekly tours October-November.

Class Size: 29-30
Free Lunch: 30%
Ethnicity: 37.5%W 24.0%B 27.7%H 10.8%A
Enrollment: 395
Capacity: 520
Suspensions: N/A
Incidents: N/A
High School Choices: N/A

This progressive alternative school, founded in 1993 by a superactive, hyperinvolved group of parents, has become one of the most sought-after in Manhattan. Parents include an eclectic mix of West Side liberals, psychologists, journalists, Columbia University staffers, and mothers on public assistance who may not have much money or book learning themselves but who are willing to work hard for their children's education.

All are dedicated to a multiracial school in which children of various social classes and academic abilities work together and learn from one another. Parents are welcome, even encouraged, to hang out in their children's classrooms during the day. Children call teachers by their first names. Classrooms have rugs and sofas instead of desks and chairs, and mountains of children's literature rather than textbooks.

Classes for children in kindergarten through 4th grade are held on the top floor of PS 165 on 109th Street. The middle school, which will eventually serve grades 5 through 8, opened in the fall of 1998 on the third floor of the former Joan of Arc junior high school, a giant, eight-story Art Deco-style building on 93rd Street that's been turned over to various mini-schools and district offices.

The Joan of Arc building is dreary, half-empty because the junior high school it once housed was such a failure that parents did what they could to keep their kids out of it. But the parents of Manhattan School for Children have made the third floor an enormously cheery

115

place. Green-and-white checked cafe curtains deck the windows. Tall potted plants and purple sectional sofas line the corridor. Huge paintings by the children decorate the halls. Giant puppets in medieval dress, made by the kids for a project on the Middle Ages, occupy the display cases. Wooden benches, built by parents, provide seating in classrooms. Even the bathrooms are welcoming, decorated with waist-high potted plants. The sinks are skirted with green and white checked fabric to match the curtains. They are never locked, and they never have graffiti. Parents even provide toilet paper, towels, and soap—small necessities that are considered luxuries in most public schools.

Like the elementary grades, the middle school classes begin with a morning meeting with kids sitting on the rug or on benches in each room. Everyone then divides into small reading groups, seated around hexagonal tables in the hallways or in classrooms, discussing a book with a teacher. Every staff member, not just the classroom teachers, has a reading group and this brings the numbers down to fewer than ten in a group.

Teachers have volunteered to give up one of their two daily preparation periods, provided by their union contract, in exchange for much smaller class size than the maximum the contract allows. Teachers help out in one another's classes, parents volunteer, and student teachers get their training here, so it's not uncommon to see two or three grown-ups in each class.

"As children move into middle school, [too often] their interest drops, their academic achievement drops," said principal Susan Rappaport. Manhattan School for Children aims to keep children interested and engaged through these years by offering intense attention to individual kids and continuity.

The parents who founded Manhattan School for Children envisioned a K–8 school, perhaps even a K–12 school. Much as they rejected the idea of traditional elementary education, they also rejected the notion of sending kids to a large junior high school. Better, they said, to keep children with a small group of friends they had known since early childhood, in a building where they felt safe and where everyone knew them. The school, which began with only a kindergarten class, has been adding a grade each year and expects to graduate its first 8th grade class in 2002.

"It's a hard time of your life, and if you're with kids you've been with forever, it's a lot easier," said Judy Gilbert, a founding parent. "It's so small, every teacher knows every kid. You can call Susan (the principal) anytime; you can call her at home if you need her."

Struggles over space on 109th Street have kept Manhattan School for Children from expanding to include the upper grades, but parents and staff try to provide continuity for kids who are moving from the lower school to the upper school, sixteen blocks away. The principal shuttles back and forth between the two sites, exhausting for her but reassuring for the children. The art, music, and dance teachers teach classes at both buildings, and there is one PTA for the whole school. The school administration hopes eventually to unite the two halves under one roof.

The first year of the middle school was rocky. Many of the parents of the original 5th grade decided to send their children to well-established middle schools, rather than subject them to the uncertainties of being pioneers. Two 6th grade classes were hastily assembled in the summer of 1998, including some children who were reading on a 1st grade level, and two 5th grade classes were moved from the 109th Street building to the old junior high school.

The new quarters were in an appalling state of repair. Lockers were broken. There were two-foot holes in the walls, and windows were held together with tape. Paint was peeling. Desks were broken and bathrooms were covered with graffiti. Outraged parents set to work fixing the mess themselves, getting it shipshape by the time school opened in the fall.

"The birthing pains were quite intense, as they were for the elementary school," said Lucy Wicks, one of the founding parents. Putting the 5th graders, who had been in the school since kindergarten, together with the 6th graders—who were assigned to the school more or less at random—was a challenge. The solution: have all the kids and their parents spend a few days at a camp in upstate New York during the summer before school started. That, Ms. Rappaport said, helped build a sense of community so necessary for the functioning of a school.

However, their troubles continued. A teacher who disagreed with the school's philosophy was assigned to the school over the objections of the parents and the rest of the staff. After a long struggle, she eventually found a job elsewhere.

By spring 1999, the worst appeared to be over. The middle school had in place an expert staff, including several teachers from small progressive private schools such as City and Country and Trevor-Day. Only a handful of the 5th grade parents opted out of the 6th grade. The committee of parents and teachers working on curriculum expect that 8th graders will be prepared to take Regents-level exams in math and science. (Although the school is committed to having children of different abilities in the same classes, math classes in the upper grades are grouped by ability.)

Parents were impressed by the high quality of instruction and the imaginative projects the children were assigned. A 5th grade class, studying the Middle Ages, read the *Seven Voyages of Sinbad*. The children were then asked to write their own *Eighth Voyage*. Children studying *oblique* and *acute* angles in math were asked to find definitions for oblique and acute in the dictionary that had nothing to do with math, and write sentences that included these.

Most important, the chancellor granted the school independent status. Rather than being considered a mini-school-within-a-school, Manhattan School for Children was recognized as a full-fledged school, with Ms. Rappaport as principal. That gives the school considerable autonomy over budget and hiring, protecting it from random assignments of teachers.

Children who attend the elementary grades of Manhattan School for Children are automatically admitted to the middle school. Others may tour the school in the fall and complete an application. Entering 6th graders must apply by early December. Out-of-district 7th and 8th graders must apply by early March. Although the competition for entry into kindergarten is intense, the middle school had spaces in its first year of operation. The school accepts some pupils in special education, who are placed in regular classes and offered extra help when necesssary.

IS 246, Crossroads School
234 West 109th Street
New York, N.Y. 10025

Ann Wiener, director
212-678-5850

Reading Scores: ★★★
Math Scores: ★★★
Eighth Grade Regents: no
Grade Levels: 6–8
Admissions: Unzoned. By interview.
When to Apply: Weekly tours October-November.
Class Size: NA
Free Lunch: 62%

Ethnicity: 12.4%W 37.2%B 45.5%H 4.8%A
Enrollment: 145
Capacity: 145
Suspensions: N/A
Incidents: N/A
High School Choices: Coalition for Social Change, Environmental Studies, Landmark

The Crossroads School has a special talent for helping kids who are struggling, whether academically or socially, to find their strengths, gain self-confidence, and overcome any hurdles they've experienced in the past. It also challenges some bright kids who are bored or alienated in a traditional school. It attracts students from a wide range of income levels and racial and ethnic groups and prides itself on the fact that all kinds of kids learn to respect one another at Crossroads, to work together, and achieve academic success. The school is on the fifth floor of a building that also houses two elementary schools, PS 165 and Manhattan School for Children. Crossroads is open to kids of all abilities, from the most capable to those in special education.

On paper, its test scores are nothing spectacular. About half the kids are above the national average on standardized reading tests. What makes the school unusual is that it accepts children who've done poorly or only modestly well in elementary school and prepares them for very good high schools. Some go on to the specialized science schools, and of those who don't, nearly all go to the small alternative programs called educational option schools.

Crossroads, founded in 1990, was one of the first middle schools to offer "inclusion" classes for special education students. In these classes, children with learning disabilities (classified as MIS 1 in the bureaucratic jargon) are placed in classes with general education pupils. They receive extra help from a special ed teacher in the classroom with them. Several of these children have been "decertified"—determined to no longer need special services—and have gone on to regular high school classes, a rarity in the world of special education.

One father, Fernand Brunschwig, credits a "fabulous" special ed teacher, Lauren Katzman, with helping his son go from being a "tentative, uncertain, incompetent person" to one who excelled in most subjects. He said the teacher gets kids to be "conscious and articulate about their issues, not secretive," and made her son realize he had to do more work to get good results.

Another special ed child, who was dyslexic, flourished when he had a chance to study drama and was the lead in a class play. The fact that he struggled with reading didn't keep him from memorizing his lines or being the star of the show. Drama was just one way the boy was exposed to literature. He kept up with the rest of his class by using Books on Tape, which helped him to master the material the others were studying, despite his reading problems. General education kids in the class started using Books on Tape as well to reinforce their reading skills

Crossroads, a member of the Coalition of Essential Schools, was founded on the model of Central Park East Secondary School in East Harlem. It has a cohesive, idealistic, and committed staff that believes children must become political activists and advocates for their own education.

When the School Construction Authority halted a renovation project on the Crossroads School soon after it opened in 1990, students organized to protest. As director Ann Wiener tells the story, the scaffolding left standing by the SCA had become home to crack addicts. Students, armed only with rubber gloves they obtained from a nearby hospital, collected the empty crack vials. Then, students, parents, and members of community groups demanded a meeting with the SCA. After that dramatic appeal, the officials relented. Construction resumed and the crack addicts were ousted. Parents and community members have continued to pressure police to keep the area free of drug users, and the neighborhood is increasingly safe.

The century-old bulding is in good condition, but staircases are narrow and some rooms are quite small. The school safety officer is helpful and well-liked, and the building is very secure. Bathrooms are clean and unlocked. Students may go out for lunch or eat in the lunchroom shared with the other schools. Students who are late or

who violate school rules have lunchtime detention, known as PBL (peanut butter lunch).

School opens at 7:30 a.m, and there is an extended-day program. There are two advisories a week, where small groups of students meet with a teacher to discuss group concerns and personal issues. Students seem engaged and excited about their work.

Students have gym every day, including double periods twice a week. Swimming is offered at the pool at Riverbank State Park in Harlem. Many students take part in community service once a week, help out in the school library or office or at neighborhood daycare centers and elementary schools.

Ms. Wiener has high energy and a sense of mission that's contagious. "She's so clear about what she's doing. She's able to bring everyone on board, and they're so idealistic," Judy Baum said after a visit. "I think it's wonderful."

Crossroads requires prospective students to come to the school for an interview. Children are asked to provide a writing sample and a recommendation from their current teacher. Students may be asked to read aloud. In recent years, the school has had room for children from outside the district.

Delta Honors Program at Booker T. Washington Middle School, MS 54
103 West 107th Street
New York, N.Y. 10025

Frederick LaSenna, coordinator
212-678-5855

Reading Scores: ★★★★★
Math Scores: ★★★★★
Eighth Grade Regents: yes
Grade Levels: 6–8
Admissions: Selective. By exam
and interview.
When to Apply: Weekly tours
October-November.
Class Size: 29-30
Free Lunch: 40%

Ethnicity: 21.4%W 32.6%B
41%H 5%A
Enrollment: 512
Capacity: N/A
Suspensions: N/A
Incidents: N/A
High School Choices:
Stuyvesant, Bronx Science,
Brooklyn Tech

Don't be put off by the gloomy exterior of this school, a 50s-era brick-and-concrete building with a dark and foreboding entrance on a not terribly savory corner off Columbus Avenue. The Delta Honors Program, which includes about half of the approximately one thousand children in Booker T. Washington Middle School, is one of the most interesting, demanding, and successful in the city. The program has an extremely high acceptance rate at the city's most selective high schools, an able and energetic staff, and a student body that's hard-working, imaginative, and nice.

Founded with just fifty-four pupils in 1986 by director Frederick LaSenna and two other teachers, Delta Honors has grown to a three-year program with twenty teachers and more than five hundred students. Students are admitted based on the results of a competitive exam given in January, teacher recommendations, and an interview. Most successful candidates score in the 90th percentile or higher on standardized reading and math tests.

"Delta is the best program anyone can have their child in," said Millie Williams, a parent. "The teachers are all wonderful. You can come in the school anytime and sit in on your child's class. The teachers don't mind. The director, Fred LaSenna, is terrific. You can call him up anytime. You don't need an appointment."

"It has a very good spirit, a very lively atmosphere," said another mother, Miriam Jacob Stix. "The kids are animated and engaged." Her son, Benjamin, added: "I learned how to write amazingly well."

The entrance of the school, alas, has the feel of a minimum-security prison. Kids line up as a security guard checks their IDs. But get past the entrance and up a flight of stairs to the Delta Honors Program, and the atmosphere becomes cheerful and welcoming.

You might see a child standing on his head, eating a cracker, to demonstrate how the digestive system works, even upside down. You might hear a teacher chatting in Latin, not rattling off conjugations but actually speaking the language. You might hear a musician playing the fiddle and talking about the African roots of American music. You might see kids dressed up in the costumes of the ancient Greeks, putting on a mock trial of Clytemnestra from the play *Agamemnon* by Aeschylus. Or you might see children studying the principles of engineering by building model bridges from paper and cardboard as part of their math class.

It's common for schools to say their curriculm is interdisciplinary. At Delta Honors they really mean it. English, history, geography, art, and music appreciation are woven into a class called Humanities. Children studying the Age of Exploration read *Don Quixote*, both as a work of literature (learning, for example, the purpose of satire) and as a means to understand the mentality of the conquistadors and the events going on in Spain at the time of Columbus, such as the expulsion of the Jews. This requires teachers who are knowledgeable about a wide range of subjects, not just their specialities, and it makes for an exciting course of study.

The day I visited, a Symphony Space performer was singing "The Battle of New Orleans" for a 7th grade humanities class. The song recounts a battle at the very end of the War of 1812 after a truce had been signed but the soldiers didn't know it. The performer, Madeleine Loren, and classroom teacher Michelle Ajami explained that the seat of power was in New York City and that, before the invention of the telegraph, there was no quick way to get word to the soldiers that the war was over. The instructors went over the lyrics and expertly wove in tidbits of military history—how muskets, for example, had to be used at extremely close range. They went on to explain how songs, called broadsides, sung at taverns and carried from town to town, were used to transmit information in a time before television and radio. The result was a fascinating account, combining military and musical history.

Delta Honors has regular visitors from Symphony Space, professionals who help connect the music and dance of various periods in American history to the humanities curriculum.

Children learn how to research and interpret history, not just regurgitate dates and facts. Ms. Ajami wants children to move beyond "reports" based on information culled from textbooks, to analyze events in the past based on original documents, much as professional historians do. She takes them to the Mid-Manhattan branch of the New York Public Library after school to do research.

In another class I visited, children were watching a movie about the lost colony of Roanoke, one of the first European settlements in the New World. The mystery about what happened to the vanished colony has never been solved and therefore makes a useful theme for research papers. When there is no right "answer" to a question in history, children come up with their own theories.

"I try to choose a topic that you can impose your own interpretation on. That's what makes a research paper different from a report," says Ms. Ajami.

This emphasis on research and interpretation is carried out in other classes as well. I saw a math class where kids were working in groups to solve a problem about the most efficient route for a Zamboni to clear an ice rink. Twisting their rulers this way and that, and arguing over the best way to set out the problem, the kids were obviously having fun.

"In math, there is only one right answer, but there is always more than one way to get it," says teacher Carol Bleecker, who was one of the founders of the school. "This is the perfect activity for them because they never stop talking."

In one 6th grade science class, kids were working in groups mixing drops of iodine, water, and vinegar with salt, baking soda, and starch. As they mixed each substance, they had to determine whether a chemical change or a physical change had taken place. The kids seemed happy and engaged, shouting, "That's so cool!" or "Ooh, it turns purple," as teacher Timothy Ascolese walked from table to table, encouraging them and joking with them. "Table Two has created life!" he said. "What have the rest of you done?"

Foreign language classes attempt to blend language instruction with lessons about the history and culture of a country. In one French class, for example, a boy gave a report on Louis XIV that demonstrated his knowledge of political history, literature, and the scientific advances of the period in France.

Eight teachers at the school have attended summer school seminars under the direction of Lucy Calkins at Teachers College on how to teach writing. Children keep writers' notebooks, and go over one another's work. Ms. Michelle Sufrin reviews each child's work independently. When she notices that many of the kids are struggling with the same problem—the proper use of commas, for example—she'll give a group lesson based on that problem. Like the other humanities teachers, Ms. Sufrin blends history and literature, having children read novels that correspond to the period they're studying.

Unlike some schools-within-a-school, the Delta Honors Program has a good relationship with the other programs within Booker T. Washington. Parents and students I spoke to agreed the building is safe and, while there isn't a tremendous amount of mixing between children in the honors program and children in the rest of the building, there isn't friction, either.

The street outside the school has in the past been a site for drug dealing. Police have instituted a "safe corridor" between the school and subway and bus stops on Broadway, escorting children to and from school. Every parent I spoke to said the system seemed to work well.

Booker T. Washington is also home to a special education program, a bilingual program, and a general education program. The whole building shares facilities such as the computer lab, and children in the various programs study music and physical education together. The school has a building-wide P.T.A., and a building-wide "school-based planning team" of parents, teachers, and administrators.

"The program has a definite idea of who we are and what we're trying to do, but it's not isolated," says Delta director LaSenna. "We're very much a part of the fabric of this school."

Building principal Lawrence Lynch is a big fan of LaSenna and calls him a genius. "He takes on teachers who may be slightly burned out and gives them ways to renew themselves. Fred would be principal except he doesn't want to do the administrivia—dealing with the kids who act up, or the janitor."

Indeed, having an able administrator in the building allows LaSenna to concentrate on instruction and to help individual children with any problems they may have. The day I visited, he spent a lot of time chatting with a group of five girls who were troubled by plans for their class trip to Washington, D.C. The children were expected to bunk four to a hotel room, and the five friends didn't want to leave anyone out. LaSenna patiently discussed various ways they could work out their problem.

"Even though it's middle school, there's a lot of nurturing going on," La Senna explained to me. "There really aren't a bunch of rules here. It's really based on an idea of common respect." And, while children are expected to do well academically, learning to get along with one another is considered more important than scrambling to the top of the academic heap. "We really play down the competitive aspects," he said. "We want children to be stretching and doing the best they can, but not at the expense of other children."

The parents I spoke to were mostly enthusiastic about the school, although one father complained that there was too much homework and that some assignments seemed unfocused.

The school sends an unusually high proportion of its graduates to the selective high schools. More than 80 percent go to Stuyvesant, Bronx Science, Brooklyn Tech, or LaGuardia. Most children come from other District 3 schools, although there is occasionally room for students from outside the district. The admissions test, administered in January, consists of an essay and some math problems. LaSenna says he interviews every applicant and looks both for academic preparation and maturity. About 60 percent of those who apply are accepted.

PS 241, Family Academy
240 West 113th Street
New York, N.Y. 10026

David Liben, principal; Meredith Liben, middle school director
212-678-2941

Reading Scores: ★★★
Math Scores: ★★
Eighth Grade Regents: yes
Grade Levels: Pre-K–8
Admissions: Unzoned. By
 interview.
When to Apply: Weekly tours
 October-November.
Class Size: 30

Free Lunch: 75%
Ethnicity: 0.8%W 84.3%B
 11.1%H 3.8%A
Enrollment: 369
Capacity: 780
Suspensions: N/A
Incidents: N/A
High School Choices: N/A

Opened in 1991 as a year-round school with an extended day program, the Family Academy has developed a loyal following among parents who see it as a warm alternative to traditional schools in the neighborhood. A grade has been added each year, and there are plans to eventually include a high school. After years of temporary quarters, it finally got its own building in 1999, when the community school board voted to close a failing school, PS 113, and turn its classrooms over to the Family Academy.

Once serving mostly low-income families, it now attracts increasing numbers of middle-class families. The free lunch rate is about average for the city.

The Family Academy was founded by three idealistic and hard-working junior high school teachers who felt the normal 180-day school year just didn't give them enough time to teach city children what they needed to compete with more prosperous suburban kids.

The teachers were frustrated that kids arrived in middle school poorly prepared, and they were concerned about sending them off to an uncertain future in the city's high schools. They believed children needed more continuity between elementary school and middle school, and between middle school and high school, than is typically found in public schools.

So the teachers, David Liben, his wife Meredith Liben, and their friend and co-worker, Christina Giammalva, decided to create a school that would take children from the age of four and keep them through high school, a year-round school with classes until 5 p.m. four days a week and morning classes all of July.

The middle school boasts a traditional college-preparatory curriculum, with Latin for all pupils, Regents-level math, and Earth Science in the 8th grade. There are also four-day trips to other cities and an annual camping trip. The school has attracted enormous amounts of funding from private foundations and corporations, and is unusually well-equipped.

It has a special education class for children classified as MIS 1, or learning disabled. The building is wheelchair accessible.

Children who attend the elementary school are given priority for the middle school. In recent years, there have been a only a handful of seats in the 6th grade open for children from other District 3 schools. Selection is based on an interview and a writing sample. Priority is given to children who live within 10 blocks of the school.

District 4

District 4 in East Harlem, between 98th and 116 Street, Fifth Avenue and the East River, includes public housing blocks and run-down buildings as well as some posh Fifth Avenue apartments near Mt. Sinai Hospital. It also includes Spanish Harlem and a tiny Italian-American enclave.

An uncrowded district, it was one of the first in the country to allow parents to choose their child's public school. Two advocates of small alternative schools, Anthony J. Alvarado and Deborah Meier, were pioneers of the school choice movment here in the mid-1970s. Together they brought life and vigor to what had been a moribund district.

With Alvarado's encouragement as superintendent, Ms. Meier founded Central Park East Secondary School—still known as one of the most successful alternative schools in the country. The district boasts several of the city's most popular and high-achieving middle schools that attract children from as far away as Staten Island and the Bronx. Subway and bus connections to the neighborhood are good, so it's not difficult for students or staff to come from a distance. Each of the good schools has a distinctive personality, a level of enthusiasm, and sense of pride that's hard to match.

Unfortunately, the district's twenty-five-year history demonstrates that "choice" is not a cure-all for failing public schools. Many schools in the district still have very low levels of achievement. Strict admission requirements at some of the good schools have drained other schools of the best students, leaving them with pupils that many teachers have trouble reaching. School choice has not improved all schools, and may even have exacerbated the gaps between the best and the worst.

Some middle schools start in the 6th grade, others in the 7th grade. District 4 has no zoned middle schools. Rather, parents and children are expected to tour schools and to rank them in order of preference. The old junior high school buildings have been divided into small mini-schools, each with its own director. There are twenty programs to choose from. A directory is available from the district office at 319 East 117 Street, New York, N.Y., 10035, or by telephoning the director of options programs, at 212-828-3514.

A school fair is held in the fall. Parents then tour the schools. Children take admissions tests or fill out applications in January, and applications are due in March. Acceptance letters are sent in May.

For years, the schools accepted many children from outside the district. That changed somewhat in 1999 in response to local parents who complained that their children were shut out of the best schools. Now, District 4 children get priority, but there is still limited space for children from outside the district.

A school that's worth visiting.: The Academy of Environmental Science Secondary School, 410 E. 100 St., New York, N.Y., 10029, director Marty Schwartzfarb, telephone, 212-860-5979. This school, serving grades 7 through 12, has a dynamic principal, a rooftop garden where kids study science, and steadily increasing test scores. Both reading and math scores are above average.

IS 820, Manhattan East Center for Arts and Academics
410 East 100th Street
New York, N.Y. 10029

position vacant
212-860-6047

Reading Scores: ★★★★★
Math Scores: ★★★★★
Eighth Grade Regents: yes
Grade Levels: 6–8
Admissions: Selective. By interview and test.
When to Apply: Tour in fall.
Class Size: 30
Free Lunch: 38%

Ethnicity: 30.7%W 26.1%B 34.3%H 8.9%A
Enrollment: 280
Capacity: 280
Suspensions: N/A
Incidents: N/A
High School Choices: LaGuardia, Beacon, Manhattan Center

After you climb five flights of stairs, your heart still pounding, you're greeted by a sign that says: CONGRATULATIONS! YOU'VE MADE IT TO THE TOP!

Everyone at Manhattan East, a mini-school on the top floor of a junior high school built in 1923, is proud of the place and it shows. There's a joyful spirit that's shared by parents, teachers, and students. The building is immaculate, classrooms—all lined up along one corridor—are large and energized, and children's work is displayed everywhere.

Long one of the top-ranked middle schools in the city, Manhattan East attracts children from all over the borough as well as the Bronx, Queens, and Brooklyn. It's a traditional school, with desks in rows, teachers at the front, and a curriculum that concentrates on established books and methods, rather than innovation. What distinguishes the school is its tiny size, its homey atmosphere, and its extensive arts program.

"Even though we're traditional academically, there's a relaxed, nurturing, family environment," said former director Gail Kipper, who gave me my tour. "My vision of the school has been a family—a real sense of community."

There is an intimacy between students and staff that's unusual, even for alternative programs. Students and teachers eat lunch together.

131

The staff of fifteen teachers is small enough to fit around one table for their regular 7 a.m. staff meetings. And parents rave about the music, drama, and art teachers. Indeed, nearly one third of the Manhattan East graduating class goes on to LaGuardia High School, the city's premier school for music and art.

"We believe all kids can get into the arts, whether as a performer or as an audience," said Marsha Lipsitz, a former art teacher who helped found the school in 1981. "That was the idea behind the school." Children don't need to show a particular talent in the arts to be admitted and there is no audition to get in. But almost all children, Ms. Lipsitz said, learn to love the arts once they're enrolled. "A child will learn an instrument and get into the band, never having known he was good at music," she said. Some of the children are already professional performers: the lead for the Broadway play *The Lion King* was a Manhattan East student, as was at least one singer in the children's chorus at the Metropolitan Opera House.

"There is a wonderful drama teacher, Ann Ratray, who has had a great record of getting people into LaGuardia," said Mary Carroll, who transferred her daughter from a private school to Manhattan East and has found the education it offers comparable or better. "She manages to get a hundred or more kids up on stage once a year in a cohesive play where everyone gets to shine." The plays have had subjects ranging from the Underground Railroad to the Vietnam War.

The training in acting is all the more impressive, Ms. Carroll said, because "it isn't the 'Mother-Mother-pin-a-rose-on-me-TA DA!' obnoxious child actor that's she's creating," but a serious, thoughtful performance. Ms. Carroll had similarly high praise for the music and art teachers. The music teacher, Mike Rotello, is the leader of the citywide junior high school band.

Most important, Ms. Carroll said, is that the school has given her daughter a clear goal of becoming an actress and gaining admission to LaGuardia, at a time when many girls are obsessed with boys or clothes or anything but school. And the school has provided a peer group that supports her goal. "There are no peers telling her it's uncool to sit down and play jazz piano. It's okay to be a good actor. It's okay to play an instrument."

The school has a collaboration with Lincoln Center, and children regularly attend performances there.

The staff is quite senior, and all teachers have a high school license in their subject area—a rarity among middle schools.

The texts in the academic classes are old favorites such as *The Diary of Anne Frank, Animal Farm, Goodbye Mr. Chips, To Kill a Mockingbird, Kidnapped.* Some parents said the curriculum could use updating but agreed that all of the books on the reading list were good.

"The advantage of a traditional approach is that expectations are very clear, so the kids aren't all over the place," said Joyce Rittenberg, whose daughter attends. "They don't go with trends. They know what works." Ms. Rittenberg added: "One of the things that makes the school really special is that they really understand that sixth grade is a very difficult transition year for children." The school deals with this, she said, by emphasizing skills such as good study habits and how to take notes.

The kids I spoke to were happy and enthusiastic about the school, also a rarity among middle school students. "I never want to graduate, it's so warm and cozy," one girl said. "It's like a family and you can trust everyone," said another girl. "It's a community and we all work together." A third raved about her music teacher: "If you have a problem, he'll keep it in confidence. He's there for you. I used to be very shy and now I'm loud."

There is an unusual level of parent involvement. Between fifty and sixty parents usually show up for the monthy PA meetings, where speakers give parents tips on how to deal with adolescent issues such as peer pressure to have sex or use drugs. Ms. Kipper, who left in 1999, had an open door policy for parents and, indeed, with no secretary to protect her, anyone could walk into her office. Parents even have a say in how the budget is spent and what needs to be emphasized in the curriculum. If, for example, parents want more concentration on writing, the staff tries to oblige.

The building, the JHS 99 Educational Complex, is cheerful, well-kept, and safe, and there is none of the friction between Manhattan East kids and other programs in the building that sometimes exists in shared quarters. The building principal takes care of administrative problems and copes with tasks such as keeping the boilers running, which allowed Ms. Kipper the luxury of concentrating on curriculum and instruction. "I get into every class at least two times a day," she said.

The school has many student teachers, who offer individual attention to the children. There is no tracking and no honors classes, although some children take high school level Regents math and science in the 8th grade. More than 80 percent of graduates go to specialized high schools or to the alternative programs known as educational option schools.

Parents I spoke to agreed the school was extremely safe and had no concerns about their children taking public transportation to class each day. Some parents pay for private bus service as a matter of convenience. Parents were generally satisfied with the school. One mother, however, was disappointed that the school didn't offer an exam prep-course for the specialized science schools. "I'd like more support for children who don't want to do LaGuardia," the mother said.

The school has several special education classes for children identified as learning disabled and language delayed (MIS I and MIS III). The children are taught academic classes as a group, but integrated with other children for electives such as art. "They get a chance to interact with the mainstream kids and they aren't isolated," said Madeline Rubinow, a special education teacher.

The school offers weekly tours for prospective parents. Candidates must have reading and math scores at grade level or above. Children are given a writing test and a math test and are interviewed.

IS 816, Central Park East
Secondary School
1573 Madison Avenue
New York, N.Y. 10029

David Smith, principal
212-860-8935

Reading Scores: ★★
Math Scores: ★★
Eighth Grade Regents: no
Grade Levels: 7–12
Admissions: Unzoned. By
interview.
When to Apply: Tour in fall.
Class Size: 22
Free Lunch: 67%

Ethnicity: 3%W 50%B
46.5%H 0.5%A
Enrollment: 450
Capacity: 450
Suspensions: N/A
Incidents: N/A
High School Choices:
Manhattan Center, Central
Park East, Laguardia

Founded in 1985 by Deborah Meier, the extraordinary teacher who won a MacArthur Fellowship award for her work here, Central Park East Secondary School has become a national model of progressive education. *Time* magazine called it "one of the most celebrated alternative schools in the country." One of its directors, Paul Schwarz, went on to become an advisor to the Clinton administration in the U.S. Department of Education.

The genius of the teachers at Central Park East is their ability to prepare, for college, kids who would be forgotten or written-off elsewhere. It is a school that welcomes kids who don't fit the mold, who are bored or alienated by traditional programs, and who might drop out of school if Central Park East didn't exist.

There are high-achieving kids here, but there are also many who are struggling. One-third are classified as needing special education—either a MIS I class, for kids with learning disabilities, or resource room help for kids performing below grade level in reading or math.

Yet a remarkable 94 percent of graduates go on to college, and 87 percent get scholarships. The school has a dropout rate that's far, far below average—2.5 percent over a four-year period, compared to 15.9 percent for the city as a whole.

Daily attendance rates are well above average, and the school is unusually safe, with virtually no suspensions or incidents reported in the 7th and 8th grades and only a handful in the high school. Discipline is handled in-house. Children who misbehave are generally not sent home, but asked to leave their classrooms to work for a time in the school office.

Central Park East Secondary School, also called CPESS (pronounced "spess"), turns almost every feature of traditional education on its head. Children aren't grouped by ability. Even kids in special education are placed in classes with everyone else. Seventh and 8th graders are grouped together in what's called Division I; 9th and 10th graders are in Division II and 11th and 12th graders are in the Senior Institute.

Classes are small, some as small as 15, and may last two and a half hours. The school is founded on the belief that "less is more"—that it is more important to study a few disciplines in depth than to have a smattering of many subjects. There are very few electives. In 7th and 8th grades, children study humanities (history and English), math, science, and Spanish.

Children aren't expected to take Regents exams, the New York state-sponsored multiple-choice tests considered *de rigueur* for most college-bound high school students. Rather, to graduate, students are expected to show their mastery of various subject areas through "portfolio assessment," a combination of written essays, art, and oral presentations to the faculty on topics the students choose themselves. (The school has requested an exemption to new state requirements for Regents exams.)

While traditional schools expect children to master a body of knowledge—dates in history, quadratic equations, or the names of elements in the periodic table—CPESS expects students to develop what progressive educators call "habits of mind": the ability to examine evidence, to see the world from various points of view, to make connections between various disciplines, and to see patterns in history and the world at large. Children are asked to imagine alternatives. What if something else had happened? What is the significance of events? The idea is to foster lifelong learners.

Topics for portfolios vary. One student might show mastery of science by presenting a paper on "Theories of Ozone Layer Depletion," while another might choose "Waves and Hair Treatments." One might fulfill the history requirement by writing an oral history of women workers in World War II, another might study the black power movement. One might fufill a community service requirement by helping Planned Parenthood organize a march for abortion rights in Washington. Another might work as a sales assistant at a stock brokerage house.

Throughout, children are encouraged to look not for one right answer, but for an approach that will yield fruitful discussions, further questions, or more research.

David Smith, the director of the school and an unusually thoughtful, serious and well-read school leader, says the approach offers better preparation for the rigors of college life than the traditional education he received as a child, which he described as rote memorization of outdated facts. "I went to Bronx Science and my sister went to Stuyvesant [in the early 1970s]," Smith said. "I believe the education my students are getting is superior to our education." Smith said he spent a lot of time floundering in college because he didn't know what to make of all the information he'd accumulated, he wasn't used to thinking independently or doing his own research and, perhaps most important, he didn't know how to ask adults for help. At Central Park East, kids get plenty of attention from adults, lots of encouragement, and good career and college advice.

The building is nothing special. Inside the grim brick facade of the Jackie Robinson Educational Complex on the corner of 106th and Madison Avenue, CPESS occupies two floors. Its long corridors have ugly green walls, gray-and-black floor tiles, and flickering fluorescent lights that are just barely adequate. Kids mill around the halls in the standard uniform of urban youth: ski jackets, sweatshirts, jeans, and hats on backwards.

But stay a while and you'll see there's a sense of community and camaraderie that's palpable. Little kids from the elementary school in the building wave "hi" to the high school kids as they pass in the corridor. High school kids aren't afraid to ask grown-ups for help. Everyone knows everyone. Kids calls teachers by their first names.

Inside the classrooms, serious and talented teachers engage the kids in discussions that challenge both the brightest and the most troubled. History is presented not as a list of accomplishments of the rich and famous, but as the daily struggles of ordinary people. Rather than using textbooks, kids study history though biographies, historical fiction, or original sources such as newspaper accounts and slave narratives.

The day I visited, kids in a 7th and 8th grade humanities class were drawing "memorials" to the victims of slavery in the years before the Civil War. Made of construction paper, decorated with clay figures or crayon drawings, these memorials included handwritten quotes from famous abolitionists or contemporary accounts by the slaves themselves.

One girl wrote about a group of babies, left by the side of a field while their mothers worked, who drowned during a flash flood because the slave master wouldn't permit their mothers to retrieve them when the rain began.

The teacher, Richard Miller, wandered among the students, offering advice as they worked. One boy was about to draw a baseball bat to show a slave being beaten. Miller pointed out that "baseball wasn't invented until the 1870s" and suggested portraying a stick instead.

In a 7th and 8th grade science class across the hall, kids were studying "enzymes in action," looking for the answer to a question that has puzzled anyone who has read the back of a Jell-O box. Why can't you, as the box warns, put fresh pineapple in Jell-O? Kids made various hypotheses and tried putting fresh and canned pineapple in different cups with liquid gelatin. They discovered that the gelatin didn't jell in the cup with the fresh pineapple. They learned that fresh pineapple has live enzymes that break down the protein in the gelatin, while the process that is used to can pineapple kills the enzymes.

There's a certain amount of adolescent goofiness in the building. One kid threw a pencil at another in a math class the day I visited, and, although the teacher handled it promptly and professionally, instructional time for the other kids was lost. Another teacher acknowledged with a sigh that "classroom management is always a struggle."

But there is also a seriousness of purpose that permeates the school. The teachers are so well versed in their subject areas, so intensely concerned with the kids and with keeping them in school, that kids, who might otherwise give up, stay and graduate.

"My son always thought he couldn't go to college," said Sheila Lambright, the head of the PTA and one of my tour guides. "He's dyslexic and he always thought he was dumb. Now he knows what's wrong with him, and he sees he can go to college." Teachers helped him organize and focus on his work, she said, and his achievement improved.

Ms. Lambright says the school manages to challenge children who are high achievers as well. Her daughter, who was in "gifted and talented" classes in a public school on the West Side of Manhattan before coming to CPESS, found teachers who would give her extra assignments so she could work at her own pace.

In discussions of subjects that are by their nature ambiguous—the history of U.S. involvement in Vietnam, for example—the progressive approach takes in various points of view and is invaluable. The history of the Vietnam War is taught from the point of view of a Vietnamese peasant, or a U.S. soldier, not just from the point of view of the generals or the politicians or historians. Children read books such as *Born on the Fourth of July*, the travails of a American Vietnam War veteran, and *When Heaven and Earth Changed Places*, the autobiography of a Vietnamese girl who joined the Viet Cong, then changed sides. In analyzing broader themes—the origins of the war, the global perspective, the war in the context of the Cold War—children begin to draw conclusions about the nature of war, of nation-states, and of international relations.

I asked Smith about what I've always considered the central paradox of CPESS: How do children with low levels of skills—as measured by standardized tests—manage to do college-level work? About 35 percent of 6th through 8th graders score above the national average in reading; 48 percent score above the national average in math. None of the school's high school graduates receive a Regents diploma, yet nearly all go on to college. How do they do once they get there?

Smith gave me a report, written by the National Center for Restructuring Education, Schools and Teaching at Columbia University, that showed that CPESS graduates did well in writing, research, and "critical thinking" and less well in mathematics.

The students had trouble in classes that required memorization or multiple-choice exams, and were weak in lecture classes that required them to take notes, but they were successful in finding adults to give them help when they were floundering. In short, the graduates did well in the areas that CPESS emphasizes—writing and thinking—and less well in the areas it doesn't emphasize.

One of the most interesting findings: CPESS graduates were less likely to drop out of college than peers from similar socioeconomic backgrounds.

Central Park East Secondary School accepts children in 7th and 9th grades. It gives preference to children from District 4, but also attracts children from across the city. The admissions procedure is the same as for other District 4 schools. Parents should call the school to arrange a tour. Applications are due in March.

IS 838, Young Women's Leadership School
105 East 106th Street
New York, N.Y. 10029

Celenia Chevere, principal
212-289-7593

Reading Scores: ★★★★★   **Free Lunch:** 67%
Math Scores: ★★★★   **Ethnicity:** 8.8%W 39.8%B
Eighth Grade Regents: yes   46.9%H 4.4%A
Grade Levels: 7–12   **Enrollment:** 210
Admissions: Selective. By   **Capacity:** 400
  application and interview.   **Suspensions:** N/A
When to Apply: Tour in fall.   **Incidents:** N/A
Class Size: 9–25   **High School Choices:** N/A

Founded in 1996 as one of the few all-girls' public schools in the nation, Young Women's Leadership School has quickly gained a reputation as a serious, academically challenging college-preparatory school for girls who believe they can achieve more without the distraction and competition of sharing classes with boys.

Cheerful and well-equipped rooms, very small classes, attentive teachers, and a no-nonsense atmosphere combine to make this school a popular alternative to large neighborhood middle schools or high schools. The financial support of a private foundation, which helped start the school, and collaborations with institutions such as Smith College (which offers high school students summer school classes on its campus in Northhampton, Massachusetts,) provide unusual opportunities to the girls who attend Young Women's Leadership.

It has been adding a grade each year since it opened, with its first class graduating in 2001. The school is extremely small, with fewer than three hundred students, and girls get an unusual amount of individual attention from teachers. Occupying three floors in an office building at 106th Street between Lexington and Park Avenue, the school has pleasant quarters with commanding views of Central Park.

Uniforms are required—plaid skirts or navy-blue trousers with blue sweatshirts or blue blazers, emblazoned with a crest on the breast pocket. The director is a stickler for punctuality and good attendance, and homework is expected to be turned in regularly and on time. Good manners are emphasized. Class changes are nearly silent.

Yet there is a relaxed feel to the school. The walls are painted in soothing pastels of light pink and mauve, with navy-blue trim. Classrooms have framed art prints on the walls, cozy sofas, and tables instead of desks. Girls call their teachers by their first names (except for the Japanese teacher. That would run counter to Japanese culture, my student guide told me.) and think nothing of plunking themselves in a favorite teacher's office, without an appointment, to ask advice.

Instead of a noisy cafeteria, girls eat lunch in a place they call their "dining room," which has round tables suited for conversation, rather than the long, institutional tables typical of public school lunchrooms. Large windows let in the sun.

The instructional methods strike a balance between traditional and progressive. "I think there's a perception that progressive teaching is too loose and open, and traditional is too tight and closed," said Madelene Geswaldo, a 7th grade humanities teacher who came from PS 75 on the West Side of Manhattan and who trained at Bank Street College. Here, she said, "standards are high and clear" and traditional classroom instruction is enriched with frequent trips to museums such as the New York Historical Society and the Hall of Science in Queens, as well as various projects. For example, a dozen girls exhibited their photography and writing at El Museo del Barrio near the school.

In several classes I visited, teachers stood at the front of the room offering instruction to the entire class. They concentrated on eliciting facts from the kids: the accomplishments of Teddy Roosevelt, or the value of "x" in an algebraic equation. In other classes, there were lively discussions, ranging from the ways in which the Enlightenment changed European society to the character development in the play *A Raisin in the Sun*.

A chemistry class was run as a game of Jeopardy, with girls working in teams to answer questions about the Periodic Table, such as: "For which element would you expect the greatest jump between first ionization and second ionization?" No room for partial credit here. "There is only one right answer," the teacher admonished the girls. "If this were a Regents test, you would not be allowed more than one right answer."

In a biology class, girls conducted an experiment that demonstrated

Darwin's theory of adaptation. The girls had read about Darwin's finches, the birds he discovered on the Galapagos Islands. Each species had a beak with a slightly different shape, adapted to pick up different kinds of food. In the lab, the girls had paper plates with different kinds of candy—hard candy, lollipops, gum drops and candy corn—and different utensils: a spoon, a needle, forceps, an eye dropper and a pick. As they tried to pick up different kinds with different utensils, they learned how birds with differently shaped beaks adapted to different ecological niches.

The school was the brainchild of Ann Rubenstein Tisch, a journalist who believes that single sex education is an important way to counter what researchers see as a crisis of confidence that strikes young adolescent girls. "It seems to be where the unraveling begins, right out of elementary school," Ms. Tisch said. "Kids can go from being fairly stable, to getting into trouble socially and academically."

Carol Gilligan at Harvard University's School of Education, among others, has said that girls who are self-assured as pre-teens begin to change as they reach adolescence. Once fearless about raising their hands in class, the girls become shy and withdrawn. They begin to worry more about their looks and about pleasing boys than about academic achievement. Girls who are high-achievers in elementary school often begin to stumble in middle school, overtaken by boys whose confidence is increasing, the researchers say.

Ms. Tisch believes that single-sex education can overcome some of these problems. With the cooperation of District 4 and the Board of Education's high school division, she helped found the Young Women's Leadership School. A foundation she heads, The Young Women's Leadership Foundation, offers extra financial support.

The school isn't for everyone. A few girls have been asked to leave because they couldn't keep up with the academic pace, and a few have left voluntarily because they missed having boys in their classes. But most of the girls and parents I spoke to were enthusiastic. "She loves it," said Elena Feliciano, a mother who volunteers at the school.

Interested parents should call the school to arrange a tour in the fall. Girls must submit their elementary school records, a sample of their writing, and a recommendation from a teacher. Girls are screened for their academic achievement, but a willingness to work hard is just as important as grades. "We really push the girls," said the

school's director, Celenia Chevere. "If you have a problem with attendance and lateness, this is not the place for you."

Priority is given to students in District 4. Girls outside the district may be admitted as space permits to achieve racial and ethnic
balance.

IS 837, Talented and Gifted Institute for Young Scholars
240 East 109th Street
New York, N.Y. 10029

Sally Ann Perez, principal
212-860-6052

Reading Scores: ★★★★★
Math Scores: ★★★★★
Eighth Grade Regents: yes
Grade Levels: 6–8
How to Apply: Selective. By application and interview.
When to Apply: Tour in fall
Class Size: 28

Free Lunch: 52
Ethnicity: 1.5%W 63.7%B 33.3%H 1.5%A
Enrollment: 135
Capacity: N/A
Suspensions: N/A
Incidents: N/A
High School Choices: N/A

The continuation of a very popular and successful elementary school, the Talented and Gifted Institute for Young Scholars is an academically challenging program with a homey and gentle atmosphere. A lot of the children here are graduates of the Talented and Gifted (TAG) elementary school in the same building, but there are usually a few seats available in the upper grades for children coming to the school for the first time.

The TAG middle school program is one of several semi-autonomous schools in the IS 117 complex, a sleek, long, glass and brick structure built in 1957. The TAG program has classrooms on the first floor and in the basement of a building that's so clean the floors sparkle.

The day I visited, children ran up and hugged the head of the PTA, Reather Pinckney, who was chatting with kids in a corridor. A parent in a middle school is a rare sight. Hugs and kisses between grown-ups and kids are rarer still. "Because we're a small school, we have an open-door policy, not just for kids but for parents and teachers as well," said the director, Sally Ann Perez. Ms. Pinckney keeps an eye on kids in the park near the school where they eat their lunch and play. A member of the Chancellor's Parent Advisory Committee, she has also successfully lobbied in Albany for a parent "resource room" for District 4.

The TAG school sends many of its graduates to selective private high schools, including Catholic schools and New England boarding

145

schools. "A lot of them have their dreams come true," said Ms. Pinckney, whose own daughter was accepted at Cardinal Spellman High School.

The students are nearly all entirely black and Hispanic and came from as far away as the Bronx and Staten Island. The school is quiet and orderly, and children move smoothly from one activity to another. Almost all the kids in the elementary school wear uniforms: red plaid jumpers and white shirts for girls, gray trousers and red plaid neckties and vests for boys. But in the middle school there's more denim in evidence. Only a few big kids stick to the uniform.

The structure of the school is quite traditional. Textbooks are central to instruction, and many teachers offer lessons to the entire class, rather than encouraging kids to work in small groups. But teachers keep up-to-date with new teaching methods, such as the techniques for instruction in writing made popular by Lucy Calkins at Teachers College.

The level of children's writing I saw was quite high. Children's essays about their personal experiences—the death of a grandparent, their parents' divorce, the birth of a sibling—were moving. Ms. Perez said that sharing these experiences also helps build a sense of community in the school.

Some classes are interdisciplinary. History and English teachers co-ordinate their lessons, so that children studying World War II in history might have an English class in which they read an account of the experiences of Japanese-Americans in detention camps in the United States.

Most children take 9th grade Regents level math and Earth Science in the 8th grade.

The school is affiliated with the Center for Educational Innovation, a Manhattan school reform group.

Children who score above the 84th percentile in both reading and math are eligible for admission. Parents and children spend a morning at the school and fill out an application. Prospective parents may tour the school in the fall. In recent years, there were about 15 seats available in the 6th grade and a small handful in the 7th and 8th grades. The building is wheelchair accessible.

IS 826, Isaac Newton School for Science, Mathematics and Technology
East 116th Street & FDR Drive
New York, N.Y. 10029

Jeff Nelson, director
212-860-6006

Reading Scores: ★★★★
Math Scores: ★★★★★
Eighth Grade Regents: yes
Grade Levels: 7–8
Admissions: Selective. By exam.
When to Apply: Tour in fall.
Class Size: 30
Free Lunch: 82%

Ethnicity: 0.9%W 42.5%B 54.4%H 2.2%A
Enrollment: 226
Capacity: 240
Suspensions: N/A
Incidents: N/A
High School Choices: Manhattan Center, A. Philip Randolph, Vanguard

A small, traditional school with high-achieving kids and a stable, experienced staff, the Isaac Newton School combines old-fashioned ideas about how kids learn with an up-to-date science lab and new computers. Old wooden desks are in rows, some are even nailed to the floor, and teachers stand at the front of the room, writing on the blackboard. Kids are serious, attentive. "We're very traditional," said director Jeff Nelson. "The way we learned—sitting, taking notes—we think that's the best way."

No cooperative learning here. Textbooks are the main tools of instruction. Kids may do projects, such as building models of different kinds of Native American shelters, but the emphasis is on passing standardized tests.

"The teachers are just wonderful," said PTA president Jenneth Solomon. "They are there from seven in the morning to seven at night. The academic standards are very high. The teachers expect so much of the students and they get the best quality work from them." There seemed to be a nice rapport between the students and the staff. Children seemed respectful of the teachers, but also free to joke with them.

The school has received support from the Annenberg Foundation and the Center for Educational Innovation, a Manhattan school reform group. An Annenberg grant paid for a new science lab, where kids can do sophisticated chemistry experiments.

"They are doing things you wouldn't expect them to do until high school," said 7th grade science teacher Irwin Wein. "We don't just use salt and water. We use copper sulphate, copper nitrate, hydrochloric acid, sulfuric acid. They are making hydrogen with hydrochloric acid and a metal. It pops when it ignites. They jump out of their seats."

The chance to use a modern lab, Wein said, makes the kids serious about science. "If they are using burners, if they're using goggles, if they're using aprons, they feel like real scientists," he said. "I don't penalize them for wrong answers. I tell them, in a lab sometimes you don't get what you're supposed to get. I'm looking for them to explore logically and analyze their results. I want them to think."

Advanced 8th grade students may take Regents level (9th grade) math, called Sequential I, and Regents level Earth Science. A talented music and art teacher guides children in the elements of artistic composition and music projects on topics such as the history of jazz.

The school shares a large building with an elementary school, River East, and a high school, the Manhattan Center for Mathematics and Science. All the Isaac Newton classrooms are on one floor. Black tile floors, flickering fluorescent lights, buff colored wall tiles and terrible acoustics make for a physical plant that is adequate but not beautiful.

Both Nelson and Ms. Solomon acknowledged discipline is sometimes a problem. A number of children have been suspended for fighting; Nelson blamed it on the fact that children suspended for misbehavior in others schools are sometimes assigned to Isaac Newton against his wishes. Ms. Solomon said discipline might be improved with greater parent participation in the school and better communication between the staff and parents.

Until recently, the school accepted children from all over the city. New regulations give preference to District 4 residents, although there may be limited seats for children from outside the district. Teachers were concerned that the new policy would decrease the number of high-achieving kids accepted, because many of Issac Newton's best pupils have come from outside the district. In recent years, Isaac Newton has ranked among the top 15 percent of middle schools citywide.

Prospective parents are welcome to visit in the fall. Children seeking admission must take an admissions test. They are interviewed at the school, usually in January. "I don't look at standardized test scores. I look at them very little," said Nelson. "I look for kids who work very hard."

District 5

District 5 has long been one of the lowest-performing and most poorly managed districts in the city. Chancellor Rudy Crew dismissed the elected community school board in 1997 because of the district's low achievement and appointed Askia Davis as superintendent, along with a new board of trustees. Parents say Davis has made an effort to work with them, and the new administration is more open to their concerns. The rate of suspensions for the middle schools declined somewhat in the first years of his administration. However, the incident rate remained higher than the average for the city, attendance was poor, and reading scores were very low.

One notable exception to the poor performance in the district: The Frederick Douglass Academy, a school for high-achievers that consistently ranks at the very top of citywide lists.

For children with musical talent, the Harlem Choir Academy, a co-educational public school founded by Boys Choir of Harlem, is worth considering. The school, IS 469, at 2005 Madison Avenue, 10035, has 500 children in grades 4–12. It offers classes in the performing arts taught by professional musicians, dancers and actors, in addition to offering traditional academics.

The Boys Choir of Harlem was founded in 1968 by the Ephesus Seventh Day Adventist Church and has grown to include six different choirs, including two for girls. Children perform worldwide. Children may enter the school at the 4th and 7th grades. Auditions are held weekly. Call the principal, John Treadwell, at 212-289-6227 for details.

The district offers a "middle school fair" in February. Call the district office at 212-769-7500 for details.

IS 10, Frederick Douglass Academy
2581 Adam Clayton Powell, Jr. Boulevard
(149th Street)
New York, N.Y. 10039

Gregory Hodge, principal
212-491-4107

Reading Scores: ★★★★
Math Scores: ★★★★★
Eighth Grade Regents: yes
Grade Levels: 7–12
Admissions: Selective. By application.
When to Apply: Open house in February.
Class Size: 30-33
Free Lunch: 72%

Ethnicity: 1.3%W 83.8%B 13.8%H 1%A
Enrollment: 950
Capacity: 875
Suspensions: 6.1%
Incidents: 0.3%
High School Choices:
Frederick Douglass Academy, Brooklyn Tech, Martin Luther King, Jr

The Frederick Douglass Academy was founded in 1991 by an ambitious and charismatic educator, Dr. Lorraine Monroe, who sought to give the children of Harlem the rigorous preparation for college that's typical in a suburban high school but all too rare in low-income urban neighborhoods.

The school, which serves children in 7th through 12th grades, has succeeded admirably in its mission: It sent 92 percent of its first graduating class to college, including some to the Ivy League. The school's reading scores put it in the top 5 percent of middle schools in the city.

The school is a serious, traditional and highly structured place, where rules of behavior are carefully spelled out and infractions swiftly punished. Children are expected to complete two hours of homework a night and are sent to detention if they don't. A child arriving at school wearing boots, rather than the regulation black shoes (no sneakers allowed), is sent home.

Before enrolling a child, parents must sign a form agreeing to show up for parent-teacher conferences and to make sure homework gets done. The child must agree to abide by the written rules, called the "12 non-negotiables." Children who can't keep up with the heavy workload are asked to leave.

Crisp uniforms, with mandatory neckties for boys and skirts for girls (except in the winter months, when trousers are permitted), are a hallmark of Frederick Douglass. "We insist that everything they have on be either navy or white," Dorothy Haime, the assistant principal for the middle school, told me as she gave me my tour. "Uniforms are a big part of what we do."

Uniforms eliminate competition over clothes and therefore act as a great equalizer between poor and middle class children. Having children wear uniforms also allows the grown-ups to spot at a glance anybody who doesn't belong at the school—an important way to ensure security.

Dr. Monroe left Frederick Douglass in 1995 to become director of the School Leadership Academy at the Center for Educational Innovation, a school reform group formerly associated with the conservative think-tank called the Manhattan Institute. At the CEI, she teaches principals some of the techniques she developed in her years in the New York City public schools. Her successor, Gregory Hodge, declined to be interviewed for this book, although Ms. Haime arranged a long tour and several other assistant principals spoke to me at length.

I met many fine teachers and administrators. Two assistant principals, Ms. Haime and Howard Lew, are clearly committed to their students and impassioned about their work. But Dr. Monroe is a hard act to follow. Several students complained that the school no longer had the family-like feel it had when Dr. Monroe was principal, and that the new head was less involved in student life—unable, for example, to attend a student concert.

Still, the test scores remain extremely high. The course offerings are impressive, and the dedication of the staff is impressive. "Every teacher does something extra," Ms. Haime said. Everyone on the staff supervises at least one extra-curricular activity, such as coaching the soccer team or the debating team.

All children take high school level math and science in eighth grade. Japanese, Latin, music and dance are offered to all middle schoolers. Children study studio art as well as art appreciation. Two days a week, parents are invited to study how to use computers.

Students also take classes in what's called "whole life management," which, Ms. Haime said, helps ease the transition from elementary school by teaching study skills and other tips to get along in middle school. School trips include excursions to Paris, San Francisco, Israel, and South Africa.

The school has one special education class for children classified as MIS I. When I visited, the teaching and materials seemed favorably comparable to what was available in the rest of the school.

Students run the school store in collaboration with Gap, which supplies the school uniforms. Students learn business techniques by running the store, and one was flown to San Francisco to meet with Gap executives. In addition to school uniforms, the store sells notebooks and office supplies to students. Profits help pay fees for college applications.

The school has no playground and only a windswept cement patio as an entrance. Inside, some of the walls are standard issue: devoid of decoration and painted the drab gray and lime green tones so popular with the Board of Education painters. But there are also some cheerful yellow walls and some pleasant classrooms, well stocked with novels, biographies, and Aesop's fables, as well as standard textbooks.

The school seemed calm and orderly. Class changes were reasonable, and the building is not overcrowded. The high suspension rate seems to reflect the administration's hardline on discipline rather than a lack of control. Students I spoke to said the school is safe.

An extended-day program is available, and the building is open until 7 p.m. on weeknights.

Prospective students must fill out a two-page application and submit it along with their test scores and two handwritten recommendations from their teachers. Preference is given to students from District 5, but the school accepts 20-25 percent of its 7th grade class from outside the district. Several open houses are held in February.

District 6

District 6, which serves the upper Manhattan neighborhoods of northern Harlem, Washington Heights, and Inwood, is one of the most crowded in the city. School construction didn't keep pace with the waves of immigrants who moved to the area in the 1980s and 1990s, and hundreds of pupils are bused to less crowded schools downtown and in the Bronx. The southern boundary of the district is 135th Street, and the eastern boundary is St. Nicholas Avenue. (Curiously, Mott Hall, the district's crown jewel, is located in a leased building within the boundaries of District 5—although District 5 pupils are ineligible for admission.) The district office telephone is 212-795-4111.

Over the years, upper Manhattan has changed from being mostly Irish and Jewish to predominantly Dominican. Recently, Russian immigrants have moved to the area, along with artists and musicians escaping sky-high rents downtown. The most prosperous families live in large co-op apartments surrounded by formal gardens on Cabrini Boulevard and in Castle Hill Village overlooking the Hudson River. But most of the district consists of poor and working-class families living in rental apartment buildings, including some very run-down buildings in high crime areas.

The district, as a whole, is extremely traditional in its educaitonal philosophy. The long-time superintendent, Anthony Amato, who left the city to take a job in Hartford, Connecticut, in 1999, preferred tried-and-true teaching methods to experimentation. The district is home to one high-achieving K–8 neighborhood school and one program for gifted children in grades 4–8, both profiled here.

An interesting experiment, also profiled here, is the Community Service Academy, a progressive mini-school that does not group children by ability. It's part of the Children's Aid Society School at IS 218.

IS 223, Mott Hall School
Convent Avenue & 131st Street
New York, N.Y. 10027

Dr. Mirian Acosta-Sing, principal
212-927-9466

Reading Scores: ★★★★★
Math Scores: ★★★★★
Eighth Grade Regents: yes
Grade Levels: 4–8
How to Apply: Selective.
  By exam.
When to Apply: January
Class Size: 22
Free Lunch: 79%

Ethnicity: 1.8%W 8%B
  85.7%H 4.5%A
Enrollment: 445
Capacity: 359
Suspensions: 4.5%
Incidents: N/A
High School Choices: Brooklyn
  Tech, Manhattan Ctr., Bronx
  Science

The jewel of District 6 and consistently one of the very top-ranked middle schools in the city, Mott Hall chooses the best elementary school students in the district and pushes them to even greater heights. Founded in 1985 as a small, specialized program for gifted children, it is housed in a graceful brick building on the edge of the campus of the City College of New York.

Mott Hall has placed an extraordinary proportion of its children in specialized public high schools and in private schools, often on full scholarship. Students are admitted in 4th, 5th, 6th, and 7th grades based on their scores on standardized tests and on their teachers' recommendations. Admission is limited to children living in District 6.

The school is traditional in tone but many of the teachers use progressive methods. Teachers work in teams to offer children projects that integrate the disciplines of art, math, science, and literature.

Children may study Islamic art as a way of understanding geometry. They design, build, and launch their own model rockets as an introduction to Newton's Three Laws of Motion and the basics of trigonometry. One year, students researched the history of their school building, which was once a convent, and wrote and performed a cantata based on what they found.

"It's irresistible, because the people are very much committed to what they are doing," the Public Education Association's Judy Baum said after a visit. "The principal is constantly reaching out (to foundations and outside funders) and getting extra stuff for kids. She really sets the tone." A 1997 *New York Times* editorial extolled the teachers' "creativity and esprit de corps."

Everyone studies Spanish twice a week, and children learn a smattering of Japanese and Russian. Humanities is taught in two-hour blocks. Children participate in "literature circles," in which they discuss their reading with one another. But the major focus of the school is science and math. Children have a chance to work in labs at the City College Department of Engineering and Biomedicine, and the Columbia University School of Medicine. Students may communicate with scientists via e-mail, and a special program helps prepare kids for the Intel Science competition in high schools. Children have access to their own laptop computers, which they may take home. Video equipment is available for students to produce tapes of their projects.

After-school programs include dance classes sponsored by the National Dance Institute, acting classes sponsored by the Tisch School of the Arts at New York University, and chess. The school's team won the national chess championship twice in the 1990s. (Chess champion Gary Kasparov once made a surprise visit to the school and played chess with the students.) Mott Hall pupils teach chess to younger children at a nearby elementary school, PS 76. When teachers noticed that girls were dropping chess after the 6th grade, they invited the women's world chess champion to come and inspire them. The school also organized an all-girls' chess team.

In addition to regular academic courses, the school has a mentoring program that offers what the administration calls "positive adult role models" to every pupil. Volunteers from Morgan Stanley Dean Witter visit the school each week to teach basic concepts of business, finance, and economics. The volunteers help children open their own small businesses, including a keychain company and a T-shirt business.

The school understands that young adolescents need to connect classroom learning to experiences outside of school—and that one way to encourage children to act grown up is to give them grown-up responsibilities. Accordingly, 8th graders participate in a community service program, called Learning Service, for three hours a week. Children volunteer at a senior center, a library, a Head Start center, or in neighborhood elementary schools.

There is one special education class for learning-disabled children classified as MIS I. The school has plans to make the building wheelchair accessible. Special education children, who are screened for their academic abilities, are mainstreamed for some classes. Some are decertified—that is, determined to no longer need special services—when they go to high school. Mott Hall offers a bilingual enrichment program for Spanish-speaking children in the 4th and 5th grades.

The admissions process, which is daunting and complicated, begins in January. The school accepts about a hundred pupils from among 350 applicants each year. Children may be admitted in 4th, 5th, 6th or 7th grade.

Children entering the 4th grade must have reading and math scores in the 85th percentile or above. Entering 5th and 6th graders must score in the 80th percentile or higher in reading and math, and 7th graders must score in the 90th percentile or higher.

Students coming from private or parochial schools must have scores in the 80th percentile or above on a national standardized test such as the Stanford Achievement. Children applying for the bilingual enrichment program must score above the 80th percentile on the Spanish reading and math tests. Call the school or your child's elementary school guidance counselor for an application. Fill out the Parent Nomination Form and the Request for School Records and return it to your child's present school.

Children who pass the first round of admissions will be asked to take a written exam. Those who pass will then be interviewed, asked to present a writing sample, and evaluated on the basis of teacher recommendations. Each candidate receives a written score based on performance on each phase of the admissions process, and the highest ranking will be accepted. Children who are rejected one year may re-apply the next. There are no school tours.

PS 187, Hudson Cliffs
349 Cabrini Boulevard
New York, N.Y. 10040

Joan Harte, principal
212-927-8218

Reading Scores: ★★★★
Math Scores: ★★★★
Eighth Grade Regents: yes
Grade Levels: K–8
Admissions: Neighborhood school. Generally doesn't accept from outside zone.
When to Apply: Automatic registration by elementary school.
Class Size: 35

Free Lunch: 68%
Ethnicity: 14.9%W 4.6%B 77%H 3.6%A
Enrollment: 941
Capacity: 695
Suspensions: 0.6%
Incidents: N/A
High School Choices: Norman Thomas, Murrary Bergtraum, Environmental Studies

A highly structured, very traditional neighborhood school, PS 187 has long ranked among the top elementary and middle schools. The principal, Joan Harte, has poured her heart into the school for decades, and it shows. She's very involved in the daily life of the school, and even teaches an upper level math class herself.

Hudson Cliffs is run with military precision. Whistles and bells sound repeatedly during the day, signaling to children and teachers alike to fall silent and prepare for the next activity—to line up on the playground, to clean up the lunchroom after eating, or to listen to announcements over the loudspeaker. Little time is wasted moving between classes or getting children to settle down. A child who is momentarily distracted will be brought to task with a snap of the fingers.

Teachers say the discipline allows them to concentrate on teaching and not waste time getting children to pay attention. The results are impressive: The school is extremely safe and has a very high attendance rate. It has an excellent rate of admissions to specialized high schools and to other specialized programs known as known as educational options. Nearly two-thirds of 8th graders go on to those schools, triple the citywide average. The results are all the more impressive considering that the school accepts every child in the neighborhood, and that some of the very top pupils are lured away to the district's school for gifted children, Mott Hall.

"I personally believe kids do best when they know the expectations and the parameters," says the principal, who attended parochial school as a child not too far from PS 187. "There's nothing worse for a child than not knowing what's going to happen next."

Eighth graders may study Regents level math, taught by Ms. Harte herself, or read works by authors as varied as Rudyard Kipling, Edwin Way Teale, Alice Walker, and Russell Baker.

Like most of the programs in the district, PS 187 is badly overcrowded. Still, parents clamor to get a seat for their child. No variances are granted for children from outside the district. Legal variances for children from outside the immediate neighborhood zone but within the district are granted on a case-by-case basis. District officials acknowledge a certain number of parents falsify their addresses to get their children into the school.

The neighborhood is predominantly Dominican, with a large minority of Russian immigrants. Hudson Cliffs recently became eligible for federal money because of the large proportion of children whose families are poor.

Classes are heterogeneous through 3rd grade. After that, children are grouped by ability.

IS 218, The Salome Urena Middle Academy/ Children's Aid Society School
4600 Broadway
New York, N.Y. 10040

Luis Malave, principal
212-567-2322

Reading Scores: ★★
Math Scores: ★★
Eighth Grade Regents: no
Grade Levels: 5–8
Admissions: Neighborhood school. Generally doesn't accept from outside the zone.
When to Apply: Automatic registration by elementary school.
Class Size: 30

Free Lunch: 100%
Ethnicity: 1.2%W 4.3%B 93.9%H 0.6%A
Enrollment: 1476
Capacity: 1605
Suspensions: 8.3%
Incidents: 2.4%
High School Choices: John F. Kennedy, Norman Thomas, George Washington

IS 218 is a "community school" open from 7 a.m. to 10:30 p.m., six days a week. It is a collaboration between District 6 and the Children's Aid Society and offers medical, dental, and social services to everyone in the neighborhood. It also offers adult education classes, recreation programs, and after-school activities.

Just south of Dyckman Street, IS 218 is a jolly, spotless facility looking out on Fort Tryon Park. Opened in 1992, the four-story building is reminiscent of Art Deco design, with circular glass-brick lobbies on every floor. A garden in front has flowers and vegetables planted by the children. A cozy, well-equipped parents' room is just off the main entrance lobby, usually filled with parents who come to volunteer in the school or to take workshops for their own benefit.

The Public Education Association's Linda Pickett and Sheila Haber visited and observed a nutrition workshop, ESL-English as a Second Language, and GED (high school equivalency) classes for adults. An arts-and-crafts workshop was organized for parents together with their children. A cooking class taught parents the skills to make and sell cakes for weddings, birthdays, and holidays.

The school, named after a nineteenth-century advocate for educa- tion and women's rights in the Dominican Republic, is divided into four academies, each with its own personality. All the academies offer team-teaching, and there is a common prep time for teachers twice a week. That means teachers in different disciplines have a chance to talk to one another about children's progress. Small discussion groups, called advisories give children a chance to talk to teachers about any social or academic problems.

The strongest is the **Community Service Academy**. In this mini school, children work at a center for the elderly or tutor younger children in addition to their regular academic studies. In one unusual project, children teach police officers from the local precinct phrases in Spanish.

The director, Naomi Smith, is popular with students and particularly skilled with children who are struggling. "For much of the time we were with her, she had her arm around a forlorn-looking little fifth grader, who apparently needed a time-out from class," Ms. Haber said.

This academy has several inclusion classes for children in special education. Children with learning disabilities are placed together in a class with general education children, who are team-taught by a special education teacher and a general education teacher.

Seth Berry, who teaches science, social studies, and English, is in charge of the school garden. Some of the girls in his class were making muffins from pumpkins they had harvested themselves. Kids were working in small groups or alone, reading, inventing their own board games, or building vehicles with Lego blocks.

The other mini-schools in the building have some strong teachers as well. In the **Business Academy**, children manage their own school store. They make and sell silver jewelry and greeting cards, as well as standard school supplies. Children have mentors from the J.P. Morgan investment company and from several law firms. In one English class, the teacher was dressed as a witch, the better to pursue "grammar demons." Another class was working on "personal archaeologies," drawing conclusions about classmates from the contents of their pockets.

The school' s test scores in reading are below average, but math scores have been rising each year and are closing in on the national average. Attendance was higher than average for the district. Suspension and incident rates increased in the late 1990s, which teachers attributed to more diligent reporting and the hiring of additional school safety officers, rather than to any genuine increase in violence.

Parents were disappointed by the departure of Betty Rosa, the well-regarded principal of IS 218 who became superintendent of District 8 in the Bronx. Her replacement, Luis Malave. Nonetheless, IS 218 displays an impressive sense of community and camaraderie. "Everyone was working together, parents, teachers, students," said Ms. Pickett. "It was very, very obvious."

The school is open to children who live within its zone, and generally doesn't have room for others.

Reading Scores

Math Scores

Eighth Grade Regents

Grade Levels

Admissions

When to Apply

Class Size

Free Lunch

Ethnicity

Enrollment

Capacity

Suspensions

Incidents

High School Choices

BRONX

THE BRONX

From the mansions of Riverdale to the tenements of the South Bronx, from the high-rise apartments of Co-op City to the seaside bungalows of City Island, the Bronx encompasses rich and poor, urban and suburban, new immigrants and longtime New Yorkers.

Many of its public schools have suffered in past years from poor leadership, political infighting, and even outright corruption of local school boards. Several boards were mired in various scandals in the late 1980s and early 1990s involving ballot stuffing, patronage, kickbacks from vendors, and payments solicited from job applicants.

New state legislation, that stripped the local school boards of their power to hire and gave more authority to the city's schools chancellor, was intended to cut down on local corruption, so some of the most obvious abuses of power seem to have been curbed. Improving student achievement is another story, however. The schools vary tremendously in quality, and only a few offer a first-class education. Most districts discourage school choice because of severe overcrowding.

The best-educated and most prosperous parents tend to send their children to Riverdale's private schools or to bus them to alternative public schools in Manhattan. Even parents of very modest means sometimes send their children to parochial schools, particularly once they reach middle school.

However, in a borough where most middle schools had nowhere to go but up, there have been some encouraging signs in recent years. District 10, a huge district that runs from Riverdale to the central Bronx, has opened some promising alternative programs. The zoned middle school for Riverdale, despite recent turmoil, still sends many students to the super-selective Bronx High School of Science. District 11, in the northeast corner of the borough, and District 12, in the central Bronx, have embraced the Middle School Initiative and have begun to reorganize their large junior high schools into small minischools. District 8, which runs from Throgs Neck to Hunts Point, has a new, well-regarded superintendent who promises to bring some life to the schools. Even District 7 in the South Bronx has some new alternative schools that are flourishing with the help of private foundations.

District 7

District 7 in the south Bronx has long been one of the worst school districts in the city, scoring low in student performance and high in ugly school board politics. The district has been the subject of numerous probes by the Board of Education's special investigator. The chancellor suspended the superintendent and several board members for financial irregularities in 1996. The district is in the poorest congressional district in the country. Despite the obstacles, a few schools have flourished.

JHS 149, at 360 E. 145 Street, Bronx, 10454, houses the district's "special progress," or gifted program. The school has very low rates of suspensions and incidents (less than 1 percent for each). JHS 149, which has 687 children in grades 6 through 9, offers a continuation of PS 31's gifted and talented program. The school has a family room, which is open each day for parents to discuss school and family issues, and offers monthly parenting workshops. Test scores for children outside the SP class are disappointing. The principal is John Piazza. The telephone is 718-292-2211.

The Academy of Future Technologies, IS 162, 600 St. Ann's Avenue, Bronx, 10455, also has a gifted program and a low rate of suspensions and incidents. Its test scores, while still below average, have risen dramatically in recent years. Call Clara Katz, director of recruitment, at 718-292-0880.

Susan Winston, the school choice coordinator for the district, can be reached at 718-292-0481, ext. 209

District 8

District 8 is a racially divided district in the southeast corner of the Bronx. The western edge of the district includes some of the poorest neighborhoods in the city, such as Hunts Point, while the eastern and northern edge includes more suburban settings, such as Throgs Neck, which has a mix of modest single-family houses, low-income projects and expensive beachfront condominiums.

For many years, the district had an administration that was unresponsive to parents and fearful of anything new. The middle schools have long had low reading scores and high rates of violence. The statistics for suspensions and incidents for the district were more than double the citywide average in 1997. When the longtime superintendent, Max Messer, retired in 1997, many parents yearned for new ideas that might turn the middle schools around.

They got their wish: the new superintendent, Dr. Betty Rosa, appointed in 1998, is attentive to parents, knowledgeable about adolescent development, and serious about reorganizing the schools to make them safe and welcoming. She was the founding principal of IS 218, a successful alternative school in District 6 in upper Manhattan (see page 160) that is divided into four semiautonomous academies. Dr. Rosa brought two of the well-regarded directors from IS 218, Lydia Bassett and Freda Carter, to be her deputies in District 8. At Dr. Rosa's urging, District 8 applied to and was accepted in 1999 into the Middle School Initiative—the Board of Education's program to reorganize large, anonymous, dangerous schools into small, intimate minischools where every teacher knows the name of every child and no one gets lost. One of the new administration's first experiments is a maritime academy, in collaboration with the State University of New York, on the waterfront under the Throgs Neck Bridge. This academy is a magnet school, open to children across the district. Call the district at 718-842-2224 for details.

Bringing life and vigor to the district is a Herculean task. But at least there is now hope for change. One parent said of Dr. Rosa, "She recognizes talent when she sees it." Another said: "She's got some good ideas to jump start a district that's been lagging."

District 9

District 9 in the south-central Bronx has mostly low-performing middle schools with poor attendance rates and high rates of suspensions and incidents.

Worth watching: The Health Opportunities Middle School, IS 327, 350 Gerard Avenue, 10451. A new, small school serving grades 7 through 12, Health Opportunities has the highest reading scores in the district, with 55 percent of children reading above the national average in 1999. Principal Donald Sexton may be reached at 718-401-1826.

The district telephone is 718-681-6160.

District 10

One of the city's most overcrowded is District 10, stretching from the hilly, leafy reaches of Riverdale—with its huge houses and fine apartment buildings overlooking the Hudson River—to the bombed-out neighborhoods of the central Bronx. With forty-three thousand pupils in grades K through 8, the district is by far the largest in the city. The huge size makes it an administrative nightmare. Endless political battles on the school board and friction between those seen as the "haves" of Riverdale and the "have-nots" from "down the hill" have demoralized parents and teachers alike.

The district superintendent, Irma Zardoya, is an energetic and passionate defender of small alternative schools and schools of choice, and a few new small schools have opened under her leadership. But the sheer numbers of kids to be placed has thwarted her efforts at school improvement, and many of the schools in the district are low-performing.

A new school of choice that's open to all in the district: The Bronx Dance Academy, at 286 E. 204 Street. The director is Lisa Paolo and the telephone is 718-405-0580. Opened in 1995, the Dance Academy sent ten of its first twenty-seven graduates to LaGuardia High School.

Also included in this chapter is a 6 through 12 school that's part of the alternative high school division, University Heights Secondary School.

The District 10 office number is 718-329-8000.

at IS 151, KIPP Academy of PS 156
250 East 156th Street, Room 418
Bronx, N.Y. 10451

David Levin, principal
718-665-3555

Reading Scores: N/A   **Free Lunch:** 97%
Math Scores: N/A   **Ethnicity:** 0%W 49%B 51%H
Eighth Grade Regents: yes   0%A
Grade Levels: 5–8   **Enrollment:** 223
Admissions: Unzoned. First   **Capacity:** N/A
   come, first served.   **Suspensions:** N/A
When to Apply: January   **Incidents:** N/A
Class Size: 30   **High School Choices:** N/A

KIPP Academy is for children who are willing to get up early, to work late every day, to come in on Saturday, and to attend summer school. Classes start at 7:25 a.m. and last until at least 5 p.m. every weekday. Classes are also held for four hours each Saturday, and fulltime all during July.

The hard work pays off. The strategy has been very effective with kids who are reading below grade level and in boosting their skills to prepare them for demanding high schools. Test scores have risen dramatically since the school opened in 1995: 78 percent of 7th graders, who had been in the school three years, scored above the national average on a recent citywide reading test.

KIPP Academy is the brainchild of David Levin, an energetic, self-confident History of Education major at Yale Unversity who joined Teach for America, a program designed to attract Ivy League graduates to teaching. He became smitten with teaching at his first assignment in a Houston elementary school, and he and a friend started a school there called KIPP (the initials stand for Knowledge is Power Program). Levin won a grant from the Annenberg Foundation to replicate it in New York.

Levin believes the average child is often neglected by an educational system that offers special classes for the gifted and for children with learning disabilities. "We believe there are really not that many places for the middle 80 percent," Levin said. "What we've shown is that they can outperform the 'gifted and talented' kids."

The secret to success? Quality teaching, support from parents and the school administration, and an increase in what educators call "time on task" or, as Levin puts it: "The more you work, the better you do." KIPP kids spend 67 percent more time in class than average American student, Levin said.

The school is affiliated with the Center for Educational Innovation, a reform group formerly associated with the Manhattan Institute. It has attracted considerable support from corporations and foundations to pay for its extended day and summer school programs, as well as special activities such as a nine-day student camping trip to Zion National Park in Utah.

The academy is on the fourth floor of IS 151, an immaculate building. (For complicated administrative reasons, the Board of Education considers KIPP part of the elementary school around the corner, PS 156, rather than part of the school with which it shares a building.)

KIPP Academy is traditional both in tone and in teaching methods. Male teachers wear suits and ties; female teachers, suits with skirts and stockings. Children wear uniforms: blue-and-white Gap-style clothes. In a nod to modernity, girls are permitted to wear pants.

Teachers mostly stand at the front of the room and offer lessons to the entire class. "There is plenty of exhortation to do it the right way, to pay attention to form and to protocol, to do homework, and to be on time," said Judy Baum of Public Education Association, who visited. "The level of work is high. Kids do algebra in the seventh grade, for example, and everything is done by the book."

She said the teachers were entertaining and held the children's attention. A nice touch: Class periods are marked by jingling bells instead of an intrusive siren. After 3:15, children have physical education, orchestra, reading groups, and study hall. On Saturdays, there are classes in art, dance, music, karate, touch football, and chess.

The extended year allows children to take long out-of-town trips without jeopardizing their classroom studies: a six-day trip to Washington, a five-day ski trip. They have attended Broadway productions such as *Cats, Beauty and the Beast*, and *The Diary of Anne Frank*, and regularly visit New York museums.

Board of Education data on test scores isn't available for KIPP Academy, because its students are included in the data for the elementary school around the corner, PS 156. But Levin says test scores have steadily risen since the school opened in 1995-96. Fewer than one quarter of the kids in the first 5th grade class were reading on grade level when they entered KIPP. By the time they were in 7th grade, 78 percent were at grade level, Levin said. In math, 82 percent of 7th graders scored at or above the national average. Fewer than one-third were scoring at grade level in math when they entered.

The administration says its success comes not only from the quality of instruction and the extended day, but also from the school's emphasis on developing character, a sense of community, and ties between school and home. Teachers visit students at home throughout the year and give their own phone numbers to students who might need homework help at night. Staff development is also emphasized. Teachers are expected to seek out more experienced staffers and to share ideas on new and effective methods.

In the fifth grade, KIPP Academy accepts any child who agrees to work hard and who has a family willing to help with homework and to make sure the child gets to school on time. In the upper grades, applicants are screened for achievement. Applications are available in January, and children and parents are invited to visit the school. Children are admitted on a first-come, first-served basis.

MS 118, William Niles School
577 East 179th Street
Bronx, N.Y. 10457

Robert Schreier, principal
718-584-2330

Reading Scores: ★★★
Math Scores: ★★★
Eighth Grade Regents: yes
Grade Levels: 6–8
Admissions: Neighborhood
   school. By application for
   gifted program.
When to Apply: Contact school.
Class Size: 32

Free Lunch: 90%
Ethnicity: 1.1%W 33%B
   61.9%H 4%A
Enrollment: 1235
Capacity: 1245
Suspensions: 2.8%
Incidents: 0.6%
High School Choices: N/A

Willam Niles is a find. I visited MS 118 to see the "gifted and talented" program, called the Pace Academy, but I came away impressed by the entire place. Teachers here manage to make every child feel important, from the high achievers who win scholarships to private high schools, to the emotionally troubled children in special education who go out to breakfast once a week with a favorite teacher.

Lots of school administrators talk about breaking up big, anonymous buildings into warm and intimate mini-schools, but here they've really done it. Each small program of 100 to 300 children has its own personality and flavor, its own identity, its own sense of pride, and that gives kids a feeling of belonging. Each school has its own leader: either a director, or a teacher who acts as a team-leader. Each leader has an unusual degree of autonomy, even controlling budgets for each mini-school. Teamwork isn't just a slogan here. Teachers really plan their lessons together and shape each program according to what the kids need.

The feeling of community translates into very low rates of student suspensions and incidents. Kids talk freely to adults when they have problems, and are under the watchful eye of grown-ups who feel responsible for them.

Tucked in the southernmost corner of the district in East Tremont, MS 118 is in a neighborhood that's undergone the devastation and renewal that marks the history of the Bronx over the last 30 years.

Once an Irish, Italian, and Jewish neighborhood, it became predominantly black and Puerto Rican as whites moved to the suburbs. Abandonment by landlords and arson followed, and some teachers remember blocks around the school being burned by arsonists during the 1970s.

More recently, new immigrants have moved to the neighborhood from the Dominican Republic, West Africa, Bangladesh, southeast Asia, the Caribbean, India, and Latin America. Garbage-strewn vacant lots and boarded-up ruins are being replaced with trim brick townhouses and new apartment buildings. Greengrocers and clothing stores along the main commercial streets are bustling.

Through the changes, teachers say, the school has remained strong, held together by stable, effective leadership and a corps of teachers who came in the 1960s and 1970s and never left. Robert Schreier, now the principal, started teaching here in 1969, attracted to the profession because it offered a deferral from the draft during the Vietnam War.

"We're all draft dodgers," he said with an ironic smile. "But we dodged the draft for children, and we're still fighting for them." Indeed, the school has an unusual number of middle-aged male teachers with long hair, jeans, or an odd earring or two. Joined by younger teachers, both men and women, the faculty has an esprit that is palpable and a commitment to teach whoever comes to them, whatever demographic changes may transpire.

At first glance, the school's test scores are nothing special. Kids' reading scores are just a hair above the national average, and math scores, while a bit higher, aren't spectacular. What the test scores don't show, however, is the tremendous progress that children make while they are here, and the good high schools they attend when they leave.

Kids, who come in to MS 118 reading very, very poorly, are almost at grade level when they leave, while kids who come in at the very top find enough challenges to keep them there. The school's reading scores have been the highest in the district in recent years, edging out IS 141 in Riverdale, a much more prosperous neighborhood. The Board of Education ranked MS 118 "well above average" when compared to schools with similar demographics.

The school administration makes it a point of pride not to send a single graduate to a general program in the zoned neighborhood high school. Instead, guidance counselors work to place children in smaller, specialized public high schools or private or parochial schools with scholarships.

I started my tour on the top floor, where the three hundred kids in the **Pace Academy** study with sixteen teachers, under the direction of director Joe Landes.

Fluorescent lights have replaced the chandeliers that Landes remembers when he first arrived in the late 1960s, and lots of computers have been installed, but otherwise the building looks much as it must have when it opened in 1938. The corridors have black linoleum floors and buff-colored wall tiles. Classrooms have lime green walls, old wooden coat closets, and large casement windows that let in lots of light. Paint is worn away, leaving bare spots on the walls, but the classrooms are otherwise well-equipped. There's a nice library and an adequate gym, and student work is displayed on bulletin boards in the halls.

Kids are quiet, eager, and well-behaved. The teaching methods and curriculum are, for the most part, traditional. Latin is taught "as it has been in Catholic schools since time immemorial" Landes said, although there is a chance to study Roman culture as well as declensions. I saw a geography lesson in which the teacher was asking kids for facts about cities in Canada, and a geometry class in which kids were bisecting angles in their workbooks. Kids discuss novels with one another in groups called "literature circles." Top 8th graders take 9th grade math, called Sequential I and 9th grade Earth Science (although the school has no labs and teachers must improvise).

Computers are used throughout. I saw two computer labs in which kids were hooked up to the Internet, and new computers for classrooms were being delivered. The school has a full-time band instructor, and kids from the Pace Academy make up the lion's share of the musicians.

The program's teachers are organized in teams for the 6th, 7th, and 8th grades. Each team meets formally each week, and informally each day, to plan lessons and discuss individual kids' progress. There is a sense of camaraderie among the teachers. "These programs don't work unless the teachers feel dedicated to the team," said Landes.

Parents praise the staff's tireless efforts at getting kids into good high schools and the accessibility of the director. "He answers his own phone," said Lois Harr, whose daughter attended and is now at the High School for Environmental Studies in Manhattan. The program's promotional leaflet boasts that Pace graduates have gone on to universities such as Colgate, Cornell, Fordham, even Yale.

Children from throughout the district are eligible for the Pace Academy. Half the seats are allocated to children whose test scores are above the 70th percentile; the other half are allocated according to a lottery. Children with test scores above the 80th percentile are automatically admitted; those with lower scores may gain admittance by teacher's recommendation.

Downstairs, the building principal, Schreier, proudly showed me the rooms that most principals hide—special education classes, and classes for chronic truants whose reading scores he said were in "the single digits" in terms of percentiles. A MIS II class for emotionally disturbed children was beautifully equipped, with tanks of fish and large iguanas that the kids cared for. But the kids were out at a diner having breakfast with their teacher. A MIS III class for children with speech and language delays had the same cheerful aspect as regular classes: walls were decorated with Caribbean papier mache masks and brown paper Egyptian mummies made by the kids.

Schreier is a proponent of "inclusion" for kids in special education. Children with learning disabilities classifed as MIS I are integrated into classes with general education pupils. These classes have two teachers—a regular teacher, and one who specializes in special education. Both the general education and bilingual classes were pleasant; students and teachers seemed conscientious and serious.

In the schoolyard are eight new prefabricated classrooms—modern, brightly lit rooms with sparkling white walls. The rooms are connected by a corridor that has a royal-blue tile floor decorated with a yellow stripe. This mini-school has its own cafeteria.

"I put the neediest kids in the most luxurious space," Schreier said as he showed off **Camelot**, the program for kids with the most problems, both academic and social. Why the name Camelot? "An ideal place where dreams come true and visions are realized," replied Schreier.

Rather than a dumping ground, this program feels like an extra-special place. It has teachers who have asked to work with the most troubled kids and with one another, and who are proud of the progress the kids make. No watered-down curriculum here: Kids were watching a film production of *Hamlet* in one class, and reading and discussing intelligently a novel, *Fast Sam, Cool Clyde and Stuff* in another.

"I have more requests from teachers to go to Camelot than to Pace," Schreier said. Smaller class-size makes a difference, as does the autonomy provided by having control over the mini-school's budget. Teachers decide as a group whether they need books, supplies, or new furniture in any given year.

Children living in the zone for MS 118 are automatically admitted;

others outside the zone but inside the district may apply for a variance to attend. A lottery for admissions is held in March. Children applying to the Pace Academy gifted program are admitted according to their scores on standardized tests.

Parents are encouraged to visit the school on tours organized by elementary school PTAs. Until 1999, MS 118 accepted children from outside the district, and, because it is closer geographically to District 9 and District 12 than to the northern reaches of District 10, it attracted many children from the south central Bronx. Overcrowding forced the school to limit admission to children living within the district.

X495, University Heights High School
University Avenue & West 181st Street
Bronx, N.Y. 10456

Deborah Harris, principal
718-289-5300

Reading Scores: ★★
Math Scores: ★★
Eighth Grade Regents: no
Grade Levels: 6–12
Admissions: Unzoned. Parents and children visit school for one full day.
When to Apply: February
Class Size: 20
Free Lunch: 75%

Ethnicity: N/A W 40%B 60%H N/A A
Enrollment: 450
Capacity: 450
Suspensions: N/A
Incidents: N/A
High School Choices: University Heights, Art and Design

Even as you walk into this tiny alternative school, you have the feeling you're arriving at a place where learning is valued and students are respected. Climb the hill from the subway, past a guardhouse and the well-kept buildings of Bronx Community College, and you come to Nichols Hall at the heart of the campus. Walk inside the ornate gothic revival building and you'll find University Heights High School, which, despite its name, serves children in grades 6 through 12.

Just walking to school each day, as they pass college students clutching their books, University Heights students can see, quite concretely, where their studies might lead them. The most advanced high school students can even choose to take college-level courses.

University Heights was founded in 1986 as a "transfer alternative" or "second chance" high school for students who were floundering, who couldn't cope with the anonymity of big schools. It has become so successful that it now attracts students who are doing well elsewhere, but who prefer the intimacy and personal attention a small school provides.

University Heights opened a middle school in 1994 with just sixty-five children in grades 6, 7, and 8. It has grown to eighty pupils. It has sincere, well trained teachers who love teaching this age group. At first, the middle school attracted brothers and sisters of students at the

179

high school; as word of mouth about the school spread; others from around the Bronx came as well.

The middle school is organized into four "family groups" of twenty students who meet each day for one hour to discuss everything from health and friendships to current events and conflict resolution among students. The teacher may pose a philosophical question to be discussed, such as, "Is life choice or chance?"

"You hope to be able to pass the tests, but we also hope it's more than that," said Ruth Smith, who is team leader, the teacher who acts as head of the middle school. "We want them to become more responsible, conscious citizens."

University Heights is a member of the Coalition of Essential Schools, the national network of small progressive schools based on the principles of Brown University's Theodore Sizer. The atmosphere is very informal, with teachers in jeans and kids calling grown-ups by their first names. Children are expected to conduct portfolio assessments of their work, and the staff places much more emphasis on these written and oral reports than on the results of the standardized tests required by the Board of Education.

There are no bells. Middle school children stay with one teacher for several hours, rather than switch classes every forty-three minutes. The teachers decide among themselves how to divide the schoolday and the subject matter to be taught. One teacher might give lessons in both history and English, another in science and math. "We're generalists," Ms. Smith said. "But we've decided to teach to our strengths."

The teachers are keen to present material in ways that are interesting to young adolescents, but they also work to make sure all acquire the basic skills.

The day I visited, kids in a science class were sitting in groups of four, playing a board game designed to teach basic facts about chemistry. As the players rolled the dice, they moved pieces across boards with the periodic table printed on them. They drew cards that said, *Go to the next halogen* or *Move ahead to the next element that is a gas at room temperature.* Their teacher moved around the room, helping as needed.

Across the hall, the children were discussing trench warfare in World War I, based on their reading of *All Quiet on the Western Front.* Later a teacher read aloud from a picture book about four British boys who lied about their age to join the army and were sent to the trenches.

In an English class, children were working on conventional

grammar execises, learning the difference between *to* and *too* and between *they're* and *their* and composing three paragraphs with an introduction, a body, and conclusion.

It sometimes took the children a few minutes to settle down at the beginning of class. One or two fidgeted with rubber bands or stared off into space, but most seemed intent on their lessons. The school is safe, with a suspension rate of 2.2 percent, far below the citywide average.

The students I spoke to loved University Heights. "The teachers help the kids a lot," one girl said, "and we can go out at lunch." "They stay after school to help you," a boy said, "I was bored at my old school. This is more challenging."

Interested parents are encouraged to call in February for an application. Children must score in the 28th percentile or above on standardized reading tests and must have a recommendation from a teacher and one other adult. Children are asked to write a short essay about themselves. Parents and potential students are welcome to visit. "Parents come in anytime and they stay as long as they like," said Ms. Smith.

The school accommodates a handful of special education pupils classified as MIS I (learning disabled) and MIS II (emotionally troubled). They are integrated into the regular classrooms, and two assistant teachers are assigned to help the classroom teachers.

MS 45, Thomas C. Giordano School
2502 Lorrilard Place
Bronx, N.Y. 10458

Joseph Solanto, principal
718-584-1660

Reading Scores: ★★
Math Scores: ★★★
Eighth Grade Regents: no
Grade Levels: 6–8
Admissions: Neighborhood
   school. Rarely accepts from
   outside zone.
When to Apply: Automatic
   registration by elementary
   school.
Class Size: N/A

Free Lunch: 94.4%
Ethnicity: 7.7%W 16.1%B
   70%H 6.1%A
Enrollment: 1562
Capacity: 1192
Suspensions: 3.1%
Incidents: 0.5%
High School Choices:
   Theodore Roosevelt, Evander
   Childs, Herbert H. Lehman

Just south of Fordham Road near the Bronx Botanical Gardens in the Belmont section, IS 45 was one of the first in the city to adopt the Middle School Initiative. This large former elementary school is divided into thirteen mini-schools, each with its own personality and vision.

Giordano is unusually safe, with rates of suspensions and incidents well below average. The organization of the school into mini-schools means each child stays with a group of teachers on one wing or one floor for all three years. Children and teachers get to know one another well, congestion in the halls during class changes is reduced, and the friction that's typical in large, overcrowded schools is lessened.

"The approach seems to breed high morale on the part of teachers and allows for some strong academics," said PEA's Judy Baum. "There's a tremendous spirit and concern and caring for the kids. The school has a great atmosphere and great potential."

The day Ms. Baum visited, the school band was off to the Metropolitan Opera to watch a rehearsal. Boys and girls were learning how to sew in a home economics class. Kid were reading *The Jungle Book* by Rudyard Kipling in an English class. A cooking club was preparing for their tour of Le Cirque, where they would dine! The chess club was practicing during lunch.

The mini-schools vary in size and quality. **Aurora,** an accelerated program for children who are bilingual in Spanish, and **Giordano Prep**, also an accelerated or gifted and talented program, are the strongest academically. The Aurora program has a functioning weather station on the roof of the school.

The school has below average test scores overall, possibly because it has an unusual number of new immigrants and children with limited proficiency in English. (Recent immigrants include children from Vietnam and Cambodia). But Board of Education statistics place the school above average when compared to others with similar demographics.

Designated as a Beacon School, the building is open to the community for various activities from early in the morning to late in the evening. For instance, parents meet with a nurse practioner and a doctor who have a clinic on the premises. During our visit, parents were also discussing special education with a school board member, Diana Pelaez Tabacco, herself an IS 45 alumna.

The school is extremely overcrowded and rarely accepts children from outside its zone.

MS 141, Riverdale/David Stein School
660 West 237th Street
Bronx, N.Y. 10463

Michael Taub, principal
718-796-8516

Reading Scores: ★★★
Math Scores: ★★★
Eighth Grade Regents: yes
Grade Levels: 6–8
Admissions: Neighborhood
school.
When to Apply: Automatic
registration by elementary
school.
Class Size: N/A

Free Lunch: 66%
Ethnicity: 17.9%W 18.3%B
54.9%H 8.9%A
Enrollment: 1419
Capacity: 1200
Suspensions: 8.7%
Incidents: 2.9%
High School Choices: 57%
JFK; 7% Bronx Science

Located in the heart of Riverdale, MS 141 has experienced an upheaval in the past decade. Zoning changes in 1992 brought poor and working class black and Hispanic children from overcrowded schools in Marble Hill into what had been a whiter and more middle class neighborhood school. Subsequent racial friction has alienated parents of all ethnic groups. This is a place where everyone, it seems, feels like a member of a beleaguered minority.

The school has had four principals in fifteen years, and staff turnover has been high. Many senior teachers left in the early 1990s, prompted by the Board of Education's budget-cutting offers of early retirement and, some parents claim, by fear of the changing demographics. Some Riverdale parents withdrew their children, sending them to private schools, or to public schools in Manhattan. An increase in the population of Orthodox Jews, who send their children to religious schools, has further contributed to the decline in the number of neighborhood parents who choose MS 141.

A proposal by parents to reorganize the school into a "Kingsbridge-Riverdale Academy," that would serve children in grade 6 through 12 and, in essence, reestablish the pre-1992 zoning lines, inflamed passions and polarized the previous local school board. A new board was elected in 1999, and seven of the nine members were from Riverdale and supported the new Academy. However, it wasn't clear when the

184

district might find the space to house Marble Hill children, now zoned for MS 141, to make space for a high school for children from Riverdale and Kingsbridge.

As it stands, MS 141 has some enduring strengths: a cadre of good teachers who will stay on regardless of what the school board decides, an involved parent body, solid honors classes for high-achieving students, and excellent programs in art, music and sports. Riverdale itself has become racially integrated, and white and black parents I spoke to were happy to live in such a community.

"By and large, it's an extremely dedicated staff who really take an interest in the children," said Diana Pelaez Tabacco, a school board member who sent her six children to MS 141. "Parents really take an active role."

"I've seen it go down, but it's bouncing back," said another parent, Michael DeCasseres. "You're getting a lot of young teachers who care. There's so much money for computers. There's dance. There's a band essemble. Whatever your kid is interested in, it's there."

A large, T-shaped building constructed in 1958, the school has long corridors with buff-colored wall tiles, red linoleum floors, and shaky fluorescent lights. The standard junior high school gloom is alleviated by colorful wall murals of jungle animals painted by the kids. The day I visited, thirty bulletin boards were being delivered to better display children's work.

Several of the rooms have million-dollar views of the Hudson River and the Palisades. There is a cheery, sunny, and well-equipped library and an impressive ceramics lab complete with two kilns and three pottery wheels. Class changes are crowded, but the atmosphere is orderly and I didn't see kids milling around in the halls. Bathrooms are locked; children must ask permission to use them.

The style of teaching is mostly traditional. Both parents and staff prefer tried-and-true methods to what they derided as "fuzzy wuzzy" innovations. But it's not all desks-in-rows and lectures. One social studies teacher, for example, gave a spirited reading of Patrick Henry's speech "Give me liberty . . ." and the class responded: "Or give me death," before launching into a lively discussion of the Continental Congress.

The teachers have a number of interdisciplinary projects. Children studying ancient civilizations in social studies, for example, might paint in the style of the ancient Egyptians in art class.

In a Regents Earth Science class, kids were working in groups, making time lines of the history of the earth on long strips of paper.

The project combined scientific concepts of geological events with mathematical problems in ratios and proportions. They translated dates such as the age of the earth (4.5×10^9 years), into centimeters on their strips of paper.

Children had writing assignments in every class I visited, even physical education. In science, they might write a report on the circulatory system; in math, an explanation of a mathematical problem; in art, they might write an autobiography to go with a self-portrait. In physical education, they were required to write a two-page report on their favorite basketball player or on the history of basketball.

Parents said the honors track was adequate and even good. Some complained that, outside of the honors, the academic programs' classes were weak. One father said some teachers of the students in the low tracks have low expectations for their kids. Even in the honors track, one mother complained that her daughter got lost in the huge size of the school and that administrators didn't know her name.

Parents and children agreed that there are too many squabbles, rude comments, pushing in overcrowded hallways, or minor spats on the playground. Quarrels often divide along racial lines. "Nobody gets along," one black girl commented.

"Kids have an attitude at this age. That's part of their development," said Ms. Tabacco, who is white. "My daughter walked in with an attitude problem. She had a confrontation with another student, and she's learned to be more tolerant."

Research has shown that small schools, where everyone knows everyone, are safer than large, anonymous schools. Administrators are working to make the numbers more manageable.

Although it had been divided into three "academies," or three mini-schools, the structure never really worked. Officials say it might be better to have teachers volunteer to work in teams or in a particular mini-school, as they did at MS 118, than to be arbitrarily assigned to one. "Everybody has to have a stake in what's going on," former principal Ira Gurkin said. "People have felt disenfranchised, because they weren't consulted. You have to allow teachers to be masters of their own destiny." MS 141, despite the recent turmoil, is worth investigating.

Jonas Bronck Academy
4525 Manhattan College Parkway
Bronx, N.Y.

Mercedes Boothe, principal
718-884-6673

Reading Scores: N/A
Math Scores: N/A
Eighth Grade Regents: no
Grade Levels: 6–8
Admissions: Unzoned. By lottery.
When to Apply: Spring
Class Size: 27

Free Lunch: N/A
Ethnicity: N/A
Enrollment: 130
Capacity: 160
Suspensions: N/A
Incidents: N/A
High School Choices: N/A

Jonas Bronck Academy, which opened in 1997 with a grant from the educational reform group called New Visions for Public Schools, has just two classes in each grade. With seven teachers and 130 pupils, everyone knows everyone, no one gets lost. This tiny, jolly middle school on the campus of Manhattan College is the continuation of the Bronx New School, a progressive elementary school founded by District 10 parents on the model of Central Park East in East Harlem. Director Mercedes Boothe, and several of the teachers came from MS 141, the large middle school in Riverdale. For the staff, the contrast is enormous. "There I taught a hundred and fifty kids a day. Here I teach fifty-five," said the humanities teacher, Andrew Halpern. When the school has grown to its full enrollment it will have 160 kids.

Like its fellow members of the Coalition of Essential Schools, Jonas Bronk is based on the principle that less is more, teaching a few subjects well, rather than offering a potpourri of every imaginable elective. Kids here study humanities (which combines history and English), math, science, art, and Spanish—and not much else. They go by bus to the gym at Lehman College for physical education. Classes may last as long as two and a half hours.

The school leases space in a pretty brick building, with white trimmed-casement windows. Surrounded by large shade trees, it is on the community college campus. As you enter, the first thing you see is a sofa in the hall, which the kids call their "sick bay," a place to rest and recharge when the trials of the day stress them out. The day I visited, a teacher draped an arm around a tearful girl, comforting her in hushed tones.

There are no desks, just tables and chairs. Kids call teachers by their first names. There is no tracking. Children of different abilities work together in "cooperative learning" groups. Every class has a student teacher, and some have two.

Some parents swear by the cooperative learning methods. One mother said the small group gave her shy daughter the confidence she needed to speak in class. Another said she's sure her child would have dropped out of school were it not for the educational approach of Jonas Bronck. One mother, however, complained that the cooperative learning cheated the high-achievers, who acted as peer-tutors to the group and weren't able to move ahead at their own pace.

Acknowledging this dilemma, teachers have taken steps to make sure the strongest students are challenged. In math, where the divisions between strong and weak pupils seem the hardest to breach, children are sometimes grouped by ability. The school offers test preparation classes for children who want to take the entrance exam for Bronx High School of Science and the other specialized science high schools. For children who are struggling and need extra help, small "resource room" classes are offered after school.

The science program was not fully developed when I visited, but the school has been working on a promising collaboration with Manhattan College. Jonas Bronck students have biology labs on the campus of the college, assisted by undergraduates majoring in biology and engineering.

"Besides cutting up the crawfish, they would say, 'What is it like to go to college? Is it a lot of work?' " said Lois Harr, one of the parents who helped found Jonas Bronck. "They have a sense that college is a good place to go." The collaboration with Manhattan College also offers Jonas Bronck teachers a chance to take continuing education courses and gives education majors a place to do student teaching. In addition, a staff developer from Manhattan College works with Jonas Bronck teachers on fine-tuning curriculum and teaching methods.

The school hopes to expand to include grades 6 through 12. However, like every other school in District 10, space is at a premium and it's uncertain when, if ever, the expansion might occur.

Graduates of the Bronx New School are automatically admitted to

Jonas Bronck. Others are admitted by a lottery conducted by the district office in May. Only District 10 residents may apply. There are generally ten seats available in the 6th grade. The school is wheelchair accessible. It doesn't have special education classes, although a few of the pupils might have been classified as special education students if they attended a traditional school.

District 11

District 11, which encompasses the northeast corner of the Bronx, includes the leafy neighborhoods of Pelham Park, Eastchester, and Woodlawn; the high-rise towers of Co-op City; the tiny seaside community of City Island; and the low-rise apartment buildings around Albert Einstein Hospital. This racially mixed district has a combination of expensive and moderately priced single-family homes as well as co-ops and rentals. The district is overcrowded, but not as seriously as the adjoining District 10.

The middle schools, as a whole, have below average scores and above average suspension rates. District 11 has embraced the Middle School Initiative, which aims to make schools safer and more intimate by breaking up large institutions into mini-schools in which teachers work in teams and know every child. As this initiative has taken hold, attendance rates have increased and suspension rates have decreased, although student performance is still disappointing.

The district has retained a number of K though 8th grade schools, which many parents prefer to the large middle schools. Children tend to go to their neighborhood schools. The district doesn't offer parents a choice among middle schools, with two exceptions: The gifted program at MS 181 and the arts program at MS 180, both in Co-op City. Both accept children from around the district. Barbara A. Neuner, the district's coordiantor for admissions to those programs, can be reached at 718-904-5563. The district office is 718-519-2672.

Pablo Casals School, IS 181, at 800 Baychester Avenue, 10475, is the site of the district's gifted program. The school has the highest middle school test scores in the Bronx, with 57 percent of children reading at or above the national average. It sends an unusaually high proportion of its graduates to the Bronx High School of Science. It is a traditional school with a very low rate of suspensions and incidents. It has 837 children in grades 5 through 8. Principal Stephen Bennett can be reached at 718-904-5600.

District 12

A low-performing district in the south central Bronx, District 12 has myriad problems. The schools chancellor repeatedly removed the school board in the early 1990s for various misdeeds. A well-regarded former principal, Mary Rivera, was installed as superintendent in 1996, and then removed by the chancellor three years later.

The district joined the Middle School Initiative in 1997, and, with the help of Fordham Univeristy, began reorganizing. Teachers and administrators were invited to visit model institutions such as MS 45 in Belmont. Fordham offered "coaches"—retired middle school principals—to give administrators day-to-day advice. Teachers were invited to take graduate courses at Fordham on topics such as interdisciplinary learning. High turnover among teachers and administrators has made it particularly difficult for the district to make progress, but at least there are a few signs of hope.

PS 61 is a safe and promising school with 659 children in prekindergarten through 8th grade at 1550 Crotona Parkway, 10460. Test scores rose from 28.8 percent reading at grade level in 1995 to 39 percent in 1999. Math scores rose from 33.5 percent to 47 percent at grade level in the same period. The school telephone is 718-542-7230.

Juan Fonseca, a special consultant to the superintendent, is knowledgeable about middle schools in the district. He can be reached at 718-328-2318, ext. 627.

MS 180, Daniel Hale Williams Middle School for the Arts
700 Baychester Avenue
Bronx, N.Y. 10475

James Duffy, principal
718-904-5650

Reading Scores: ★★★
Math Scores: ★★★★
Eighth Grade Regents: yes
Grade Levels: 5–8
Admissions: Neighborhood school. By audition for talent program.
When to Apply: May
Class Size: 30

Free Lunch: 67%
Ethnicity: 4.4%W 62.6%B 31.1%H 1.9%A
Enrollment: 1113
Capacity: 1130
Suspensions: 8.0%
Incidents: 2.2%
High School Choices: Truman, Dewitt Clinton

MS 180, called the Middle School for the Arts, draws children from across the district to its magnet program in art, dance, drama, vocal, music, and instrumental music. The school has been reorganizing into small teams of teachers who plan lessons together and who get to know a small group of students well, thereby reducing the sense of alienation common in old-fashioned junior highs.

Built in 1972, the concrete, nearly windowless building in Co-op City has all the charm of a bunker. But colorful murals decorate the walls inside. Girls in black leotards and blue jeans dance to African rhythms on a polished dance floor surrounded by floor-to-ceiling mirrors. A teacher leads the school orchestra, with the help of an assistant teacher who once played bass with Lionel Hampton and Stevie Wonder. Fifth graders have a cozy "enrichment center" with a sofa and rug, a teddy bear, a chess set, a Scrabble game and a microscope. They go as a treat between classes.

The school's test scores are only fair, with reading scores just above the national average. But the principal, James Duffy, has a human touch with kids and with his staff, an openness to parents, and the energy to help the staff adapt to new teaching methods. He spends most of his day in the halls and in classrooms, not locked away in his office, and he seems to know every child by name.

The school has a large special education program, including children classified as MIS I and MIS II (learning disabled,) MIS III (speech and language delayed) and MIS V (mentally retarded.) The school is wheelchair accessible. I was impressed by the way in which special education teachers marked children's progress.

In a class for the mentally retarded, children learned basic skills for independent living such as how to peel vegetables, how to make beds, and how to dust furniture in a classroom furnished like an apartment. They also learned social skills. As their final exams, they helped cook a Thanksgiving feast for the whole school and they attended the school prom with general education kids. Both events were the source of enormous pride.

The school accepts between 90 and 115 children from outside the zone for the arts magnet program, based on the results of auditions given in May. The school has no regular tours, but interested parents may arrange a visit by calling the school.

PS 175, City Island School
200 City Island Avenue
Bronx, N.Y. 10464

Ena P. Ellwanger, principal
718-885-1093

Reading Scores: ★★★★
Math Scores: ★★★★
Eighth Grade Regents: yes
Grade Levels: K–8
Admissions: Neighborhood
school. Rarely accepts from
outside its zone.
When to Apply: Automatic
registration by elementary
school.

Class Size: 33
Free Lunch: 32%
Ethnicity: 69.9%W 6.9%B
18.2%H 5%A
Enrollment: 505
Capacity: 337
Suspensions: 1.8%
Incidents: N/A
High School Choices: Lehman,
Truman, School of the Future

City Island looks more like a New England fishing village than most
people's idea of the Bronx. Surrounded by Long Island Sound and
connected to the mainland by a bridge, it has inlets, sailboats, Victorian houses with big porches, summer beach bungalows that have
been converted for year-round use, and one commercial main street
with seafood restaurants, sailmakers, and antique shops. It's the kind
of place where lots of mothers stay at home with their kids, where parents keep an eye on one another's children, and where kids can walk or
ride their bikes to school.

The cheerful, well-kept PS 175, with more than five hundred children in grades K through 8, features many reminders of the seaside
community it serves: giant windows overlooking the sound, a large
papier-mâché dolphin in the cafeteria, and huge saltwater fish tanks
filled with flora and fauna from the ocean. The school has received a
grant from the Annenberg Foundation to build a center to be used by
children from all over the city for the study of the marine environment. Work began in 1998 to reconstruct rotting bulkheads above the
salt marshes and to build the center on the adjacent shore.

In many respects, PS 175 is very traditional. There are lots of desks
in rows and teachers at the front giving lessons to the entire class.
Spelling, grammar, algebra, and history are taught the old-fashioned

way. But the architecture is modern, even bizarre. The program in marine studies lends a progressive feel, and the tiny size of the school means teachers naturally talk to one another and coordinate their lessons. A new program that mixes special education with general education children, shows the administration is open to innovation.

First the architecture: Built in 1975, the school was an apparent attempt to turn the educational philosophy of the "open classroom" into an architectural style. Rather than classrooms with walls, the second floor of the building is one large, open space, divided only by brick pillars holding up the roof.

What the architect had in mind in terms of teaching is unclear. However, the school administration has set up movable blackboards and bookshelves to divide the space into teaching areas, and teachers have set up desks in their designated spaces. The school is extremely overcrowded, and several classes are held in the cafeteria. Children seem to be able to concentrate despite this, and the school is an orderly, generally quiet place.

There are constant reminders of water. The playground, with climbing structures made to look like boats, overlooks the real docks. In a science project, 4th graders seeded oysters and learned how oysters are a natural filter for water. Seventh graders stocked the giant fish tanks in the open area on the first floor that serves as an auditorium and cafeteria. They put on hip-high wading boots and set up a bucket brigade to bring water from salt marshes at nearby Orchard Beach. Another watery (and memorable) lesson: a 7th grade science teacher plunged his head into a tank of water to teach kids how to measure the volume of an irregular object (his head) through displacement.

In a new district-wide special education program, learning disabled children classified as MIS I and their teacher work together with general ed kids and their teacher. The general ed teacher gives lessons to the entire group for part of the day. Then they break into two smaller groups. The special ed teacher works with any kids who are struggling on a particular lesson (special ed or general ed), and the general ed teacher works with the rest.

The advantage of the system is that special ed kids who are strong in one subject can move ahead while still getting extra help in their areas of weakness. General ed kids who need help on one lesson, but not another, can also get it. And special education becomes a flexible grouping, rather than the lifetime sentence it is at many schools.

The school also has self-contained or segregated special education classes for children who can't cope in larger classes. But these, too, have the gentle, welcoming feel of the school as a whole.

City Island has high test scores, with 72 percent of children reading at or above the national average and 76 percent at or above the national average in math. (Because it is a K–8 school, its test scores are ranked among elementary, not middle schools.)

Alas, it is extremely overcrowded. It has no room for children from outside the zone (the zone is the entire island) except for special education pupils, who are assigned by the district office and bused to the school.

Reading Scores   Free Lunch

Math Scores   Ethnicity

Eighth Grade Regents   Enrollment

Grade Levels   Capacity

Admissions   Suspensions

When to Apply   Incidents

Class Size   High School Choices

BROOKLYN

BROOKLYN

From the elegant nineteenth-century brownstones of Brooklyn Heights to the dilapidated public housing towers of Coney Island, the city's most populous borough has an extraordinary variety of people, places—and schools. Brooklyn has some of the best schools in the city—and some of the worst. Half a dozen selective schools for the "gifted and talented" draw children from across the borough. Unfortunately, the establishment of these schools has also drained some of the energy and life from the zoned neighborhood middle schools, many of which remain dull and listless places. As a whole, the neighborhood middle schools are too big, too crowded, and too run-down. Many parents expend considerable energy trying to find a way to keep their children out of what one father—recalling William Blake—called the "dark Satanic mills" of Brooklyn's middle schools.

Although school choice is the official policy of the Board of Education (which means you can theoretically apply to any school in the city) each of the twleve districts in Brooklyn operates as its own fiefdom. Each tries to lure the best students from other districts, while making it next to impossible for its own children to find out anything about schools outisde its borders.

Basic information, such as test scores and safety records, is hard to come by. Tours for parents are perfunctory or nonexistent in most middle schools. Each district—and sometimes each school—has its own admissions criteria. One Brooklyn mother had her daughter sit for five different entrance exams on five different Saturdays.

Thankfully, there have been some improvements in the past decade. District 15, which runs from Cobble Hill to Sunset Park, decided to close all but two of its middle schools and start from scratch. In an ambitious—some say overly so—move, the district reorganized its giant buildings. In 1998, it opened ten mini-schools, each with its own new director and staff. Some are quite promising. These mini-schools eschew the notion of special classes for the gifted. They do not group children by ability and strive to give all kids a first-rate education.

District 22, which runs from Ditmas Park to Bergen Beach in southern Brooklyn, has developed some excellent special education programs as well as a "second chance" program for kids on the verge of dropping out. District 21, which runs from Bensonhurst to

Sheepshead Bay, has expanded its gifted and talented programs, opening up possibilites for more out-of-district pupils. District 20, which includes Bay Ridge and Dyker Heights, has several new, small schools. So look around. New programs are opening all the time.

District 13

District 13 has mostly African-American neighborhoods, including the ninetheenth-century brownstones of Bedford-Stuyvesant and the gentrifying areas of Fort Greene, as well as run-down housing projects. Brooklyn Heights residents, who are mostly white, generally send their children out of district or to private schools. One middle school in the district stands out: the Ronald Edmonds Learning Center. The district telephone: 718-636-3220.

District 14

Recent Polish immigrants, artists and bohemians priced out of Manhattan, ultra-Orthodox Jews, and Hispanic families inhabit the neighborhoods of Williamsburg and Greenpoint, the area of Brooklyn just over the Williamsburg Bridge from Manhattan. District 14 middle schools have low levels of achievement and high rates of suspensions and incidents. IS 318, at 101 Walton Street, 11206, telephone 718-782-0589, has average test scores, above-average attendance rates, and a suspension rate of 6.8 percent. (That's about average for the city, but half the district's rate.) The incident rate is well below average: 0.8 percent. The school's gifted program offers children Regents-level courses in the 8th grade. The district office: 718-963-4800.

A public school that's located within the geographical boundaries of the district, but which reports directly to the chancellor, is Beginning with Children school, a small K–8 school supported by a foundation of the same name. The school, at 11 Bartlett Street, 11206, has both general education and special education children. The school has a long waiting list and generally doesn't accept new pupils in the upper grades. Telephone: 718-388-8847

District 15

From the desolate housing projects of Red Hook to the glorious brownstones facing Prospect Park, from Sunset Park's new immigrant communities to the longtime Italian-American neighborhood of Carroll Gardens, District 15 includes families from a wide range of income levels, political persuasions, sexual orientations, races, religions, and ethnic groups.

Relations on the local school board are sometimes fractious. Poor and working class black and Hispanic parents have complained that schools in their neighborhoods were shortchanged. Upper middle class whites say that while the schools of Red Hook may be dismal, the schools in their neighborhoods are nothing to write home about, either. The one point that everyone agreed on was this: The district's middle schools were in terrible shape. Francis J. DeStefano, the well-regarded principal of a Greenwich Village school, was appointed superintendent in the summer of 1997 with a four-word mandate from parents: Fix the middle schools.

DeStefano has gone about his work with energy and vision. A disciple of former District 2 superintendent Anthony J. Alvarado, DeStefano understands that a strong, effective principal and good staff development are the key to school improvement. He was instrumental in attracting good people as directors of his new mini-schools and in encouraging teachers to hone their skills with summer school courses and special programs. A master fundraiser, DeStefano won a giant federal magnet grant to give principals the money they need to set up new programs. DeStefano is also a magician when it comes to manipulating the school system's construction and maintenance bureaucracy. Under his leadership, floors of buildings that had been vacant or in serious disrepair for years got new paint jobs, new wiring, repaired roofs, and adequate plumbing.

DeStefano decided to keep open two middle schools and a secondary (6th though 12th grade) school that were functioning adequately: MS 51, MS 88 and the Brooklyn School for Global Studies. Everything else was shut down and reopened under new management. Several small middle schools were opened on vacant floors in elementary school buildings. Others were set up in the old junior high school buildings. In all, eight new schools were opened in 1998, and two more opened in 1999.

The sweeping changes have made DeStefano some enemies. Some parents complain that he dictates minutiae—such as how desks should be aligned. But District 15 schools, which had been losing students to other districts for years, have begun to win them back. In 1999, five hundred parents from outside the district applied for their children to be placed in one of the newly organized schools.

The changes, of course, have left parents dizzy. How do you judge a new school? The quality of the teaching is probably more important than the level of kids' achievement. A school with good teachers will attract bright kids as word gets out.

District 15 is one of the few in the city that has a rational and tolerable—if time consuming—admissions process. Kids get a catalogue of middle school options in the fall. The district holds several middle school-choice fairs in the fall and winter, and parents are encouraged to visit individual schools in January and February. Applications are due in February. Notifications of acceptance are sent in April. Preference is given to children living in District 15, but some programs have room for children from outside the district. The district office can be reached at 718-330-9252 or 718-330-9386.

Three fledging programs that are worth a visit: The Manuel de Dios Uname Journalism School at MS 142, 610 Henry Street, Alison Sheehan, director, 718-330-9106. It became an "inclusion" program in its first year, with special education pupils working alongside general ed pupils. Kids have professional journalists as mentors.

The Math Academy at MS 293, 284 Baltic Street, Rosemary Stuart, director, 718-330-9390. Parents describe the director as a "genius" and say the school attracts a "terrific caliber of student."

The School for Leadership in the Environment at PS 27, 27 Huntington Street, Pat Poole, director, 718-330-1832. An Expeditionary Learning–Outward Bound School, built on the same model as IS 30 in Bay Ridge (see page 231), this Red Hook middle school has close ties to community-based organizations such as Good Shepherd Services.

IS 113, Ronald Edmonds Learning Center
300 Adelphi Street
Brooklyn, N.Y. 11205

Katherine Corbett, principal; Kalek Kirkland, gifted coordinator
718-834-6735

Reading Scores: ★★★
Math Scores: ★★★★
Eighth Grade Regents: yes
Grade Levels: 7–8
Admissions: Unzoned. By exam
 for gifted program, audition
 for talent program.
When to Apply: February
Class Size: 22-25
Free Lunch: 81%

Ethnicity: 0.8%W 87.7%B
 9.8%H 1.7%A
Enrollment: 859
Capacity: 1223
Suspensions: 3.3%
Incidents: 1.7%
High School Choices: Boys &
 Girls, A. Philip Randolph,
 Brooklyn Tech

IS 113 is clean and safe, with a strong gifted program. It was one of the first in the city to establish small, semiautonomous programs within a large building as a way of controlling the chaos and violence that plague so many junior high schools. As the programs took hold in the early 1980s, the anonymity typical of a large school disappeared, enrollment increased, and the school's safety record improved. Test scores rose from a low of 27.1 percent of children reading at or above the national average in 1980, to 61 percent. The Board of Education said IS 113's test scores were far above those of other schools with similar demographics.

Children feel a loyalty to their school-within-a-school. Teachers know each child, and every child knows every other child. That feeling of belonging means kids are more likely to talk through their problems with adults or other kids rather than resort to violence. IS 113's rates of suspensions and incidents are far below average. In 1998, the U.S. Department of Education named it a Title I Distinguished School because of its record of achievement in a high-poverty area.

The school has four programs, each occupying a different floor or wing of the building. They include **Summit**, for children who pass a written entrance exam; the **Academy of Performing Arts** and the **School of Fine Arts and Design**, for children with demonstrated artistic, musical, or theatrical ability; and the subschool of **Environmental Studies and Technology**, for children interested in using neighboring Fort Greene Park as a laboratory.

PEA's Judith Baum and Jessica Wolff visited. Kids were singing gospel tunes in a large music room, there was a band rehearsal in the basement, and children in T-shirts and tights—a surprising number of the boys—incorporated traditional African steps in a modern dance number they performed in the auditorium.

"The kids looked really happy—engaged in the material and engaged with one another—in the dance classes, the music classes and the art classes," Ms. Wolff said. "The school is extremely clean. I have never seen an old school so polished up."

Academic classes were mostly traditional, with desks in rows and teachers at the front giving instruction to the entire class. The staff, which is almost entirely African-American, had a "sense of purpose, an air of professionalism, and a sense of community," said Ms. Wolff. The district gives its own tests every two months to mark children's progress.

"Katherine Corbett runs a tight ship," said a mother, Theresa Daughtry, whose daughter was in the Summit program for gifted children. "I found all the teachers to be well educated and good. They have an open-door policy. Parents can always go in and see what's going on." Ms. Daughtry said the school provided her daughter excellent preparation for the rigors of high school. "Sometimes I thought she was overwhelmed with work but the teachers seemed to know what they were doing. Now I see the children weren't overwhelmed, they were challenged."

Children in the Summit program may take Regents-level, 9th grade math and science in the 8th grade.

Parents may attend an open house at the school in February. Children applying to the Summit program should take an exam offered by the district office. Children applying to the arts programs should contact the school to arrange an audition.

IS 429, The Brooklyn School For Global Studies
284 Baltic Street
Brooklyn, N.Y. 11201

Lawrence Abrams, principal
718-694-9741

Reading Scores: ★★★
Math Scores: ★★★
Eighth Grade Regents: yes
Grade Levels: 6–12
Admissions: Unzoned. By lottery.
When to Apply: Tours in January, February
Class Size: 5–25

Free Lunch: 58%
Ethnicity: 19.7%W 36.8%B 35%H 8.5%A
Enrollment: 525
Capacity: N/A
Suspensions: N/A
Incidents: N/A
High School Choices: Global Studies, John Jay, Murrow

A collaboration between District 15 and the high school division, The Brooklyn School for Global Studies opened in 1995 with the support of New Visions for Public Schools, a Manhattan-based reform group.

Global Studies has won a following among parents, who say their children get an unusual degree of attention from their teachers.

"If you want your child to use up-to-date technology, if you want your child to use the Internet as a research tool, if you want you child to learn to work in groups, this is the place for you," said Mykele Westervelt, a Park Slope mother. Her son, whom she described as mildly dyslexic, flourished at Global Studies. "This year he was in the ninety-ninth percentile in reading. He's been in the ninetieth percentile ever since he went to Global. For me, it worked."

PTA president Lisa Espinoza, whose two sons travel from Canarsie to the school each day, said the staff expects hard work and good behavior. The kids comply. They sign a contract agreeing to the school's rules. "They learn there are consequences for their actions," Ms. Espinoza said. "If you're late, you get detention. If you don't do your homework, you get detention."

She said her older son was only an average pupil in elementary school. Teachers pushed him to work hard at Global Studies, and by the end of 8th grade he was a top student, preparing to take Regents-level exams in math and science. Small classes and a curriculum that allows kids to visit museums or to work on projects outdoors, measuring shadows in math or digging soil for experiment in science, make a difference.

"You can hide in a class of thirty-eight," Ms. Espinoza said. "You can't hide in a class of twenty-five. You're under a microscope. They won't let them get away with anything. And when you touch something with your hands, as opposed to reading it in a textbook, you're always going to remember it."

The school is based on the less-is-more model of Central Park East Secondary School, where children are expected to master a few key subjects well rather than skim many disciplines. Class sizes are very small and often run for two hours. A few have five children or even fewer, all working closely with a teacher when they need extra help. The kids seemed serious. "If you're looking for a fashion show, or if you're just interested in boys, this is not the place for you," one girl said. "This is a place to study."

The building is grim—the standard ugly junior high school architecture of the mid 1960s—but the classrooms are bright and cheerful, with nice class libraries, kids' work on the walls, and colorful mobiles hanging from the ceilings.

Global Studies has an effective and popular Spanish teacher, Luz Delgado. Her class was one of the few foreign language classes I have seen in which the kids were actually speaking the language they were studying.

Parents may visit the school in January and February. Admission is by lottery.

MS 828, New Horizons School at PS 32
317 Hoyt Street
Brooklyn, N.Y. 11231

Mary Lou Aranyos, director
718-330-9228

Reading Scores: ★★★
Math Scores: ★★★
Eighth Grade Regents: N/A
Grade Levels: 6–8
Admissions: Unzoned. By
lottery.
When to Apply: Tours in
January-February.

Class Size: 28
Free Lunch: N/A
Ethnicity: N/A
Enrollment: 60
Capacity: 180
Suspensions: N/A
Incidents: N/A
High School Choices: N/A

The New Horizons School is an extension of the Children's School, the city's most radical experiment in integrating severely handicapped children with children in general education, side by side, in the same classes, all day, every day.

While the Children's School offers classes for children in kindergarten through 5th grade, New Horizons, which opened in 1998, has 6th through 8th grades. Each class has 28 children—8 in special education and 20 in general education—and three grown-ups, a special education teacher, a regular classroom teacher, and an assistant teacher. Each of the assistant teachers had training at the Children's School.

The team-teaching approach allows kids to get much more attention than they would in a traditional class, teachers say, allowing both disabled children and those who are high-achievers to work at their own pace.

"When you're alone, you're so busy helping the kids who need help, you never get to the kid who can go further," said Rose Ann Gonzalez, a math teacher. "We have a lot of very bright kids. Here, they have someone to take them beyond where I could if I were alone."

I visited the school a few months after it opened, when it had only three classes. I was impressed by the quality of teaching and by the dedication, experience, and competence of the staff.

The day I visited, an autistic girl, whose native language was

Chinese, spoke in class for the first time. She read a journal entry about the police in her neighborhood, and I was moved by the way in which both teachers and classmates encouraged her. In a lively history class, kids discussed questions such as "What's the point of studying history?" and "Who cares what happened long ago?" and "How is the author drawing us into this book?"

One mother said the teachers adapt the curriculum to serve the various abilities of the kids. Her son, who has severe learning disabilities and who reads at a 1st grade level, studied ancient Greece along with the rest of his class. Together with a classmate, he made a model of a Greek temple from cardboard paper towel tubes and Styrofoam, and learned how the Greeks raised pieces of the columns with winches and pulleys. "The school doesn't treat him as a kid who can't learn," the mother said.

Students read books that are appropriate for their age, while her son works on easy-to-read books such as *Frog and Toad*. But when he makes classroom presentations, "the kids high-five him and cheer him on," the mother said.

The school is on the top floor of an elementary school, PS 32. The rooms are cheerful and well equipped. Irritating buildingwide announcements over the loudspeaker interrupt the tranquillity of the top floor from time to time, but the physical plant is more than adequate. The building is not wheelchair accessible, a pity for a program that has so many children with special needs.

Inclusion programs—classses which combine special ed and general ed kids—are rare and mostly untested in middle schools. Even among the successful inclusion programs in the city's middle schools, few, if any, have as great a range of abilities as is found in New Horizons. Whether the school will attract high-achieving kids as it grows— as the Children's School has done successfully—remains an open question. But the staff clearly knows what it is doing, and New Horizons is off to a fine start. It's worth a visit by any parent looking for a small, intimate school where children get lots of attention from grownups and learn to be tolerant of differences.

Admission is by lottery. Parents may tour the school in January and February.

MS 51, William Alexander School
350 Fifth Avenue
Brooklyn, N.Y. 11215

Michael Schlar, principal
718-330-9315

Reading Scores: ★★★★
Math Scores: ★★★★
Eighth Grade Regents: yes
Grade Levels: 6–8
Admissions: Selective.
Applicants with scores above
85th percentile in reading, for
gifted program. By interview
and audition for talent
program.
When to Apply: Tours in
January-February.

Class Size: 29-33
Free Lunch: 45%
Ethnicity: 25.1%W 19.7%B
45.7%H 9.5%A
Enrollment: 1173
Capacity: 1042
Suspensions: 2%
Incidents: N/A
High School Choices: John Jay,
Murrow, Midwood

William Alexander School has been a top-ranking school in the district for many years. MS 51 has a long history of preparing its best students for the specialized high schools. It has an excellent choir, a popular photography program, and classes in computer graphics that attract all children, from the highest achieving in the gifted program to those in special education.

It is divided into two magnet programs, the **Rainbow Academy for the Intellectually Gifted**, for children who score high on standardized tests, and the **Academy for Arts and Creative Education**, or AACE program, for children who show a talent in writing, fine arts, photography, and music. The school also has special education classes for children with learning disabilities (MIS I) and emotional problems (MIS II).

In many respects, MS 51 is a traditional school. Its long corridors with fluorescent lights, crowded class changes, and gloomy 1950s architecture, are reminiscent of junior high schools of a generation ago. Black tile floors, gray wall tiles, lime green walls, and beat-up desks add little to the ambiance. Teachers tend to work the old-fashioned way—at the blackboard at the front of the class. But there are signs of life and change throughout the building. The school's staff

211

developer attended a course at Columbia University's Teachers College on the Writing Process, and has trained all the English teachers in this new method of teaching writing. A staff developer from Teachers College visits MS 51 weekly and works with faculty on how best to help children learn to write well. Kids learn to edit one another's work, revising it many times before presenting it for "publication" to the rest of the class. The method allows teachers to work individually with pupils, without being swamped by dozens of papers, and allows children to improve their work even without the teacher's help. The results are impressive. Eighth graders, for example, produced high-quality essays on their personal experiences: an eye operation, a father's accident, a trip to Yemen, and a child's first haircut.

The day I visited, principal Michael Schlar had just returned from a conference at the University of Pittsburgh on ways to raise school standards. He was bubbling with new ideas on how to motivate what he called "reluctant readers." The conference, he said, taught him to be a "teacher-researcher . . . I have to know *why* a kid isn't learning."

Schlar, who has spent his entire thirty-year career in the building, said his philosophy has evolved in his many years as principal. "Fifteen years ago, I considered myself a benevolent despot. But when we started the gifted program, we got parents who were more involved, who were more inquisitive." That is, parents who didn't accept the principal's word for everything just because he was principal. Accordingly he adopted a more collaborative approach.

At the same time, he was influenced by the philosophy of the Middle School Initiative—that children in early adolescence need close contact with nurturing adults, not just instruction in subject matter. He began to hire teachers who he saw as warm and comforting, not merely those who had a command of their disciplines.

Parents describe the staff as dedicated. One teacher sacrifices her lunch hour to play basketball with the kids. Another helps edit the school newspaper.

"The teachers genuinely like the kids," said one mother, whose daughter chose MS 51 over the super-selective Mark Twain school in Coney Island. "Although it's a traditional school, my daughter felt it was freer, and that she would have a more cordial relationship with her teachers than she anticipated at Mark Twain."

Although the quality of teaching is not uniformly stellar, parents said the assistant principals are masters at developing faculty talent and renewing the enthusiasm of burned-out or mediocre teachers. "Some of the teachers have been terrible, but the school has been very good about encouraging them to improve," one mother said. "They recognize when the teachers are poor."

Of the two programs in the building, Rainbow has livelier classes and more attentive pupils. I saw a number of heads on desks in the AACE program. In the Rainbow program, an energetic male teacher with a ponytail helped his 7th grade science pupils figure the area and volume of their classroom with yardsticks. A brisk and competent math teacher drilled 8th graders in Regents-level (9th grade) class called Sequential I. A history teacher held an interesting discussion of the concept of "total war" in the Civil War, and kids wrote their own newspaper called *The Abolitionist Times.*

Children in AACE, in Rainbow, and in special education are all entitled to take part in the school choir, which has performed on Broadway, for the mayor, and even for the president. One mother called choral director Alan Zwirn a genius for his ability to bring out talent in every child.

A photography class, in which kids travel around Brooklyn and take black and white photos of landmarks such as Coney Island, and the computer graphics classes are open to kids from all of the programs.

The school's bathrooms are unlocked. Students are allowed to leave the school at lunchtime, and many go out to enjoy a nearby park.

Parents are invited to tour the school in January and February. Children are eligible for admission to the Rainbow program if they have test scores above the 85th percentile in reading and the 71st percentile in math. Children must have an audition for entry to the AACE program.

MS 827, New Voices School of Academic and Creative Excellence at PS 146
330 18th Street
Brooklyn, N.Y. 11215

Erika Gundersen, director
718-330-2232

Reading Scores: ★★★
Math Scores: ★★★★
Eighth Grade Regents: N/A
Grade Levels: 6–8
Admissions: Unzoned. By lottery.
When to Apply: Tours in
   January-February
Class Size: 18-28

Free Lunch: N/A
Ethnicity: N/A
Enrollment: 180
Capacity: 300
Suspensions: N/A
Incidents: N/A
High School Choices: N/A

This sweet middle school has strong programs in dance and the arts, a cohesive and collegial staff, and a capable and conscientious director who has a good understanding of children this age. New Voices opened in the fall of 1998 but it doesn't have the raw, unfinished feel typical of new schools, possibly because many of its students and staff came from the same elementary school, PS 172, in Sunset Park.

On the border between Sunset Park and Park Slope, New Voices occupies the top floor of a sunny, turn-of the-century building with high ceilings, big windows, shiny hardwood floors, and freshly painted white walls. There are no desks, only hexagonal tables and chairs. A room with a sofa is set aside as a student lounge where pupils who complete their homework on time and maintain good attendance records can relax or listen to the radio during free periods.

Originally built as a high school, the building, PS 146, also houses two small alternative elementary schools, Brooklyn New School and PS 295. The arrangement allows New Voices to share art and dance teachers with other programs in the school, giving children a chance to study a range of subjects unusual in a school so small.

The dance teacher, Candace Tovar, is popular not only with girls, but with boys too. Ms. Tovar once taught ballet to the football players of the Houston Oilers.

The art teacher uses projects to reinforce what the kids are studying in other subjects. Those studying China in social studies, for example, might look at how Chinese porcelain is made and discuss the different dynasties as seen through the history of art, then build a colorful 3-D paper dragon to hang in the hall. She combines lessons in art and science in a unit on anatomy. Children measure their faces and discover, for example, that their noses are not in the center of their faces, but in the lower third.

The school uses textbooks for math and science, but history and English are taught entirely from novels, biographies, and various reference books found in the classroom. Each room has bins of books with novels by Beverly Cleary and Roald Dahl and other authors favored among kids this age.

One humanities class discussed *The Lion, the Witch, and the Wardrobe* by C. S. Lewis, analyzing the motivations of characters, using the chapter headings to predict what might happen next. Writing assignments included exercises using "descriptive" or "figurative" language. Humanities classes, which combine English and history, last from an hour and a half to just over two hours.

In another room, a teacher was reading aloud from a book called *Homesick: My Own Story*, an autobiographical novel by Jean Fritz, the child of a missionary living in China in the 1920s. "They're not too old to be read to," the director, Erika Gundersen, said. "Everybody loves to be exposed to beautiful language."

The children then read by themselves, each choosing a different book: books about Arthur, or the Teenage Mutant Ninja Turtles, or children' classics by Tommie de Paola or C.S. Lewis, or adult classics such as Jack London's *Call of the Wild*.

In math, kids were studying arithmetic and pre-algebra problems that seemed standard and appropriate for their age. Students were a bit fidgety in science class, and I got the impression the school's science program wasn't yet fully developed.

Students were attentive and serious, class changes were reasonable, and the school felt extremely safe. Parents credit Ms. Gundersen for creating an atmosphere where standards of behavior are high. "My daughter says she's very strict, but as a parent I love that she is the way she is," said Annette Hendrickson, the PTA president. "At regular junior high schools, at three o'clock, you're on your own and anything can happen. But Erika is out there making sure they get home safely. She's on top of every problem."

My impression is that the quality of teaching is superior at New Voices. But, because many of the children have modest skills levels, I wondered whether very bright kids would be challenged here.

Ms. Hendrickson, whose own children are high achievers, said the school offers so much individual attention that everyone may work at his or her own level.

"Once my son had an easy book, and Erika, who'd had my son as a fourth grade teacher at PS 172, said, 'Jason, you read that in fourth grade!' She pushes him to read harder books." She said her son and daughter, both in the school, had regular homework, even over school vacations. One project included watching three hours of cartoons, counting the incidents of violence in each one, and then writing a paper on the effect of violence in children's programs. She said her children kept regular "writers' journals" to comment on the books they read.

The first year the school opened, it attracted mostly children from PS 172 and from nearby blocks in Sunset Park. It had a free lunch rate of more than 90 percent, and nearly 80 percent of the pupils were Hispanic.

Parents may tour the school in the fall and winter. Children are admitted by lottery.

MS 825, The New School for Research in the Natural and Social Sciences at PS 230
1 Albermarle Road
Brooklyn, N.Y. 11218

Dr. Anthony Galitsis, Christine Mineo, co-directors
718-834-9645

Reading Scores: ★★★
Math Scores: ★★★★
Eighth Grade Regents: N/A
Grade Levels: 6–8
Admissions: Unzoned. By lottery.
When to Apply: Tours in January-February.

Class Size: 22-31
Free Lunch: N/A
Ethnicity: N/A
Enrollment: 194
Capacity: 400
Suspensions: N/A
Incidents: N/A
High School Choices: N/A

The director of this new middle school, Tony Galitsis, is a member of a rare breed. A Ph.D. in physical chemistry, he has an extensive knowledge of the subject areas his pupils need to learn. But he also has a good feel for young adolescents and what they need socially and academically. It's like finding a surgeon with a good bedside manner. He is competent as well as comforting.

The school, which opened in the fall of 1998 on the top floor of a well-regarded elementary school, PS 230, is off to a fine start. Earnest, sweet, attentive teachers, an active PTA, and a pleasant building combine to make the New School for Research in the Natural and Social Sciences a promising place for kids. (The only trouble I was able to spot on my visit is the unwieldy name.)

This is a science school without labs. Galitsis, formerly head of science curriculum for the central Board of Education, says kids can learn all the science they need in middle school without expensive equipment. All they require, he says, are simple kitchen supplies for basic chemistry; things like roller skates, stopwatches, and toy sailboats to understand the principles of physics; and trips to the park to learn about biology.

"I don't want labs," said Galitsis. "That kind of stuff belongs in college. We're dealing with little kids. You need running water? Get it from a faucet! No bunsen burners? Use a hotplate. Take them to Prospect Park. Let them look at the things that are living in the water."

Rather than dissecting a frog in class, kids go to the Brooklyn Center for the Urban Environment in Prospect Park to study invertebrate zoology, better known to the kids as "bugs and worms." The school has microscopes, but Galitsis says they're "strictly for PR"—to impress the parents touring the building. He prefers to have kids do experiments with their hands, such as testing the acidity of vinegar, milk, juice and sugar.

Similarly, he thinks kids are generally better off without textbooks. Although the school does have some textbooks for math and science, teachers don't use them extensively. Rather, kids work on big projects that integrate math and science, such as a project analyzing the design and construction of their school building.

"How many facts do you know? I'm not into that," Galitsis said. "We're interested in having the student do investigations, and, through research, they understand what a scientist does for a living."

Built in 1930, PS 230 is a large building in a fairly good state of repair. The school became extremely overcrowded in the early 1990s, as new immigrants moved to this neighborhood south of Prospect Park. A new annex for the early elementary grades opened in 1996, easing overcrowding in the main building and making room for a new middle school. About one-third of the first class at the New School for Research came from PS 230.

Galitsis hired a group of teachers who seem to love their work, including several recent graduates of The New School for Social Research in Manhattan. In a humanities class, an earnest young man was helping kids plot military strategy in an imaginary country in 1500 b.c. Kids thought up ways they might storm a fortress using only pieces of wood, ropes, swords, shields, and axes. The exercise was an introduction to the Trojan War and military history of ancient Greece. The kids, working in groups, were excited to shout out different ideas of how they could deceive the enemy.

"Even the students who aren't motivated under normal circumstances become very animated, and that's encouraging," said the teacher, George Perros, who is a Ph.D. candidate in political science at The New School. "Education can be a very noisy affair."

Kids in a 6th grade class that combines math and science were studying "super even numbers," learning about the power of 2. The kids also summarized newspaper articles on scientific topics, such as the findings of the *Pathfinder* probe to Mars, or new research into osteoporosis. One child wrote a research paper on the history of the subway.

In a writing class, four student "experts" were editing the work of pupils. Kids were working on the fourth draft of their essays on personal experiences such as "The first time I joined a basketball team" and "My first day in the United States."

Classes last up to two hours and twenty minutes. English and history are taught together in humanities. Similarly, math and science are taught by one teacher. Even art class offers interdisciplinary lessons: the art teacher took kids to a cemetery to do gravestone rubbings and combined their project with a lesson in American history.

I visited the school only a few months after it opened, but it didn't feel brand new. Perhaps that's because many of the children came from the elementary school downstairs. About 65 percent of the first year's pupils qualified for free hot lunch, which means the parents' income levels is about the same as that at the elementary school.

Parents say the staff is responsive and that it is easy to meet with teachers or the director whenever problems arise. Parents are encouraged to tour the school in January and February. Admission is by lottery.

District 16

One of the lowest performing districts in the city, District 16 in Bedford-Stuyvesant has suffered from ugly school board politics and a rapid turnover of superintendents. The chancellor has suspended the local board for poor performance on various occasions. The district office telephone number is 718-919-4112.

District 17

District 17 in Brooklyn encompasses East Flatbush and Crown Heights, home of the annual Caribbean Day parade on Labor Day, when one million people revel in North America's verison of Carnival. It also includes snippets of gentrifying neighborhoods near Prospect Park, including Prospect Heights and Park Slope. The district has a mix of large Victorian houses on tree-lined streets and more modest apartment buildings.

Much of the neighborhood is divided between blacks and Hasidic Jews, who generally send their children to private yeshivas. As a result, the public schools are almost entirely black.

The district has a solid base of middle- and working-class parents. The high free lunch rate reflects the fact that many parents work at low-wage jobs, not that they are unemployed or on public assistance.

For years, the district suffered from poor leadership but Dr. Evelyn Castro, the well-regarded former prinicpal of the superselective Hunter Elementary School, was named superintendent in 1996. Since then, there have been signs of improvment, paticularly at the elementary school level.

Among middle schools, two high-performing programs are profiled here. Two others worth watching are: The Mary McLeod Bethune Academy at MS 394, at 188 Rochester Avenue, 718-756-3164, director Linda Barnette, a selective school for children who score above the 50th percentile on standardized reading tests and who pass an exam administered by the district office in March. For chidren in special education, look at the inclusion program at MS 2, 655 Parkside Avenue, 718-462-8202, principal Joan King. MS 2 also has a gifted program, called the Apex Academy.

The district office telephone number is 718-826-7800.

IS 308, Clara Cardwell
616 Quincy Street
Brooklyn, N.Y. 11221

Dr. Gail Bell-Baptiste, principal
718-574-2372

Reading Scores: ★★★★
Math Scores: ★★★★★
Eighth Grade Regents: yes
Grade Levels: K–8
Admissions: Selective. By exam in February.
When to Apply: Contact school.
Class Size: 25-28
Free Lunch: 87%

Ethnicity: 0%W 94.7%B 3.4%H 1.9%A
Enrollment: 1016
Capacity: N/A
Suspensions: 2.2%
Incidents: 0.2%
High School Choices: Boys and Girls, Brooklyn Technical, Philippa Schuyler

This K–8 school for the gifted in the heart of Bedford-Stuyvesant has long been the crown jewel of a low-performing district. It offers high school math classes to children as early as the 7th grade, and accelerated courses in science and English. Children can study African dancing and drumming, chorus, and various forms of studio art.

The tone is traditional. Children wear uniforms—yellow or white shirts and navy blue trousers or skirts. "Everybody is friendly and all the kids are respectful," one mother said.

Children who are zoned for the school are automatically admitted. Others may take an entrance exam offered by the district office in February. Scores in the 80th percentile or above in reading and math are required for admission. Children are admitted at various ages, including 6th and 7th grades.

It is by far the highest performing school in the district and one of the highest performing in Brooklyn. Top graduates attend Stuyvesant, Brooklyn Tech, and private schools.

Clara Cardwell has embraced the Middle School Initiative, which stresses team teaching and interdisciplinary instruction. Teachers stay after school to plan lessons together, and guidance counselors have a chance to meet with children individually and in small groups to talk about whatever problems they may have.

The school has abandoned its previous policy of requiring students who are zoned for the school to take a test to continue after 2nd grade. Under current policy, zoned children may stay in the school through 8th grade without taking the entrance exam. However, the principal stresses that the school hasn't lowered its expectations: "We say, 'If you want to stay with us, you have to work, because we're not dropping the standards for some kids,' " said Dr. Gail Bell-Baptiste, "For some, it's too much pressure and they drop out," to transfer to less demanding programs.

Clara Cardwell operates on the so-called Renzulli model, a teaching method based on the work of the University of Connecticut researcher Joseph Renzulli, and the model of Bloom's taxonomy, which suggests that children must go beyond rote learning to gain real understanding of a subject. "Teaching should not just be memorizing," Dr. Bell-Baptiste said. "Instruction should give the opportunity to evaluate what you've learned, to do something with it."

Say the kids are studying jazz: The way Dr. Bell-Baptiste describes it, children must first be introduced to a new concept. So they listen to a piece of music. Then they must research it by reading biographies of musicians or studying music theory. Finally they learn to write their own music. These steps are followed whatever the subject area.

Although these methods were originated as ways to help gifted children, Dr. Bell-Baptiste believes they are applicable for all children. "I really believe that gifted education is what all education should be about. The only difference in a gifted school is that expectations are higher," she said.

Dr. Bell-Baptiste said teachers combine lessons, geared toward competence on standardized tests, with projects that are engaging. For example, a social studies teacher encourages kids to write their own newspapers set during the Civil War.

Teachers voted to make Clara Cardwell a "school-based-option" school. That means staff is chosen by a committee of parents, administrators, and staff, rather than assigned by the district office, as was the case previously.

The administration has had repeated squabbles with the district office. The principal was removed in 1997 after being accused of "fiscal irregularities," including giving free school lunches to parents; she was restored to her post after the chancellor intervened. The squabbles seem likely to continue. Dr. Bell-Baptiste is defiant about the school lunch issue—an apparent violation of Board of Education regulations that got her in hot water: "When food is left over, I let the grandparents eat it rather than throw it away. So sue me," she said. But she is confident that with the support of her teachers, parents, and students ("My babies," as she calls them) Clara Cardwell will remain strong.

The school has a parents' room. Tours are provided in the spring for prospective students who have passed the admissions exam.

IS 340, North Star Academy
277 Sterling Place
Brooklyn, N.Y. 11238

Gloria J. Dupree, principal
718-857-5516

Reading Scores: ★★★★   **Free Lunch:** 100%
Math Scores: ★★★★   **Ethnicity:** 0.7%W 90.9%B
Eighth Grade Regents: yes   6.7%H 1.7%A
Grade Levels: 6–8   **Enrollment:** 297
Admissions: Selective. By exam.   **Capacity:** 400
When to Apply: Apply in   **Suspensions:** 7.4%
    December, exam in February   **Incidents:** 1.3%
Class Size: 28   **High School Choices:** N/A

North Star Academy, a new, selective middle school in a hundred-year-old building, graduated its first 8th grade class in 1998 and has quickly become a favorite among people in the know in District 17. "Most of the staff in the district office sends their kids there," said one mother. "It's the best kept secret in Brooklyn."

Kids don't change classes here. Teachers do. That's because the halls in the old building are so narrow that having students change classes could result in chaos. But the policy has the effect of giving kids a sense of belonging to their classroom as well as to their school.

Teachers plan their lessons together, so kids might read an historical novel in their English class that takes place in the period they're studying in social studies. Arts projects are integrated into social studies as well: a class builds models of Roman cities with cardboard and gravel.

"Our expectations are very high," said former principal Gloria Dupree. "We have an interdisciplinary approach, with a lot of hands-on projects, a lot of research. We're far from traditional."

Sixth graders have their major academic subjects with one classroom teacher. In 7th and 8th grades they have different teachers for different subjects. Parents say teachers typically are at school until 5 p.m., preparing for the next day.

There is a student-run bookstore, which parents say gives students a sense of pride.

The application deadline is December, and an entrance exam takes place in February. Children whose combined reading and math scores are 110 or above are eligible.

The majority of children come from District 17, although there are limited spots for children from outside the district. Parents are welcome to tour.

Crown School for Law & Journalism, at PS 161
330 Crown Street
Brooklyn, N.Y. 11225

Principal (position vacant)
718-756-3100

Reading Scores: ★★★★★   **Ethnicity:** 0.4%W 90.9%B
Math Scores: ★★★★★   7.6%H 1%A
Eighth Grade Regents: yes   **Enrollment:** 180
Grade Levels: 6–8   **Capacity:** 180
Admissions: Selective. By exam. **Suspensions:** 0.2%
When to Apply: January exam   **Incidents:** N/A
Class Size: 25-30   **High School Choices:** N/A
Free Lunch: 96.6%

The Crown School for Law and Journalism is a tiny, highly selective middle school on the top floor of a gigantic elementary school. Children wear navy blue and gray uniforms. Students have internships with judges, lawyers, and journalists who are part of the curriculum, and pupils can study science with professors at nearby Medgar Evers College.

"It's traditional, but not oppressive," said PTA president Gloria Arthur. "It's a small setting, and the children get individualized attention. They get to know one another. There's a lot of class discussion, and children have the opportunity to give their opinions." Many teachers have creative ideas for projects, she said, such as the Spanish teacher who had kids write their own comic books in Spanish.

The mini-school was founded in 1995 by three PS 161 teachers who, as parents, found that many children were lost in large, anonymous junior highs. With the backing of their principal, they set up their own program for 6th, 7th, and 8th grades in PS 161.

The teachers believed it was important for students to have more contact with teachers than is typical in junior high school. Instead of changing classes for every subject, students might have math and science with one teacher, and English and history with another. Teachers spend time with children outside regular school hours, as well. A music teacher, for example, takes children to the opera.

Writing is emphasized. Children are expected to write multiple drafts of their papers, correcting and improving them each time. An English class I visited combined the rigor of sentence diagramming and drills on subject-verb agreement with a subtle discussion of the use of irony in a book about the introduction of Western customs to an Indian village in the Pacific Northwest. The children were serious and attentive, and the classes were very orderly.

A school newspaper is part of the journalism program. In the law classes, pupils study the Bill of Rights and the Constitution, visit courts, and put on mock trials. One teacher said kids are so wrapped up in the study of the Constitution that when they bump one another in the hall they say, "Hey! You're violating my Fourth Amendment rights!"

Ms. Arthur said the admissions process is competitive, but once children are enrolled they help one another in class and the competition isn't cutthroat. She said two to four hours of homework a night is typical. In addition to academics, there are arts and crafts after school and a step dancing team. The chorus sings classical music such as Handel's *Messiah* and *Jesu, Joy of Man's Desiring* in four-part harmony. Eighth graders may take Regents-level (9th grade) math and science.

About one-third of the students come from PS 161, the elementary school in the same building. The rest come from other schools in the district. Children must score above the 75th percentile in both reading and math, and must be recommended by their elementary school teachers. Children take an entrance exam in January and are interviewed at the school. More than four hundred children are tested in a typical year, and only sixty are admitted. The average score for children admitted in recent years was the 93rd percentile in reading and the 94th percentile in math.

A large number of graduates go to Stuyvesant or to other selective high schools. Some are part of Prep for Prep, an organization that helps kids prepare for admissions to selective private day and boarding schools.

Tours are offered to prospective students who pass the admissions test.

District 18

District 18 includes the neighborhoods of East Flatbush, which has seen immigration from the Caribbean in recent years, and Carnarsie, which used to be mostly white but is now ethnically mixed. Although the district has several fine elementary schools that attract children from across the borough, until recently it lost its best students to middle schools in other districts.

Change is being wrought by strong leadership at a few middle schools, combined with a reorganization of some old buildings into smaller mini-schools according to the principles of the Middle School Inititative, making them safer, more attractive places. "I think all five schools in the district are really moving forward," said Kenneth E. Jewell, director of the Center for School Restructuring at Bank Street College in Manhattan, who has assisted in the reorganization.

IS 285, at 5909 Beverly Road, 11203, telephone 718-451-2200, in East Flatbush, is worth a visit. Principal Stephen Hinds runs a magnet school for the performing arts that also has a gifted program called Astral. Test scores have been steadily increasing in recent years. A colleague calls Hinds an "extraordinary principal who really feels the pulse of the community." With 1,388 pupils, IS 285 is well over its capacity of 1,159. Teachers say that's a sign that parents clamor to get their children in, despite overcrowding.

The Lenox Academy is a small new middle school program housed in a successful elementary school, PS 235, at 525 Lenox Road, 11203, telephone 718-773-4869. Inaugurated in 1998, the program is projected to have 270 children in grades 6 through 8. The school offers advanced instruction in math and science. Teachers meet weekly to plan lessons together and discuss each child's progress.

The district has a number of magnet programs to encourage racial integration and several gifted programs not listed here. Children applying for the gifted programs are tested in December or January. Those who qualify are invited to open houses. Call Joel Rubenfeld at the district office at 718-927-5125 for more information.

District 19

District 19, which includes Starrett City and Cypress Hills, has long had low-performing schools. An energetic superintendent, Robert

Riccobono, linked up his principals with mentors in Manhattan's successful, high-performing District 2. His principals "shadowed" their mentors for three weeks, picking up ideas on running a good school. Riccobono was credited with ridding the district of some ineffective principals, and he cooperated with a community group, East Brooklyn Congregations, that's organizing parents to work for school reform. However, test scores failed to improve quickly, and he was removed by the chancellor in 1999. Call the district office at 718-257-6900 for information, or call EBC at 718-498-4095.

District 20

District 20 includes the pleasant residential neighborhoods near the Verrazano Narrows Bridge: Bensonhurst, Bay Ridge, Borough Park, and parts of Sunset Park, many of which have a small-town feel. Kids still go trick-or-treating door to door on Halloween. With a mixture of single-family houses and small apartment buildings, the area has long had large Italian and Norwegian populations and is now home to immigrants from the former Soviet Union, China, and Central America. Borough Park is predominantly inhabited by Orthodox Jews, most of whom send their children to private yeshivas.

Children are assigned to neighborhood schools according to their addresses. However, many parents shop around and send their offspring outside their immediate zone. In addition, some pupils from outside the district seek admission to its middle schools.

Those who score above the 90th percentile in reading and math on standardized tests may take an exam in January to qualify for the "superintendent's" or high honors program offered at many schools.

In addition, children of all achievement levels may apply to magnet programs outside their neighborhood school. Originally established with federal funds, magnet programs were designed to encourage racial integration by luring children outside of their immediate neighborhood to schools organized around a theme, such as the study of law. Federal funding for the program has expired, but District 20 has continued what one district official calls the "magnet concept" on a limited basis. That means the district attempts to maintain a balance of different races and ethnic groups at each school, but doesn't keep precisely to the formulas required in programs supported by federal funds. Children are admitted by a lottery that takes race and ethnicity into account. As a rule of thumb, schools that are more than 50 percent white favor nonwhites, schools that are less than 50 percent white favor white admission.

Most of the schools have an open house for parents in the fall. The district also has an "informational" meeting for parents in December. For more information, call Jack J. Gursky, coordinator of gifted programs, at 718-692-5241 or Barry R. Feldman, magnet coordinator, at 718-692-5201.

The general number for the district office is 718-692-5200.

IS 30
415 Ovington Avenue
Brooklyn, N.Y. 11209

Linda Viggiano, principal
718-491-5684

Reading Scores: ★★★★
Math Scores: ★★★★
Eighth Grade Regents: N/A
Grade Levels: 6–8
Admissions: Neighborhood school. Doesn't accept from outside zone.
When to Apply: Automatic registration by elementary school.

Class Size: 30-33
Free Lunch: 52%
Ethnicity: 62.6%W 0.8%B 19.8%H 16.8%A
Enrollment: 131
Capacity: 400
Suspensions: 6.1%
Incidents: 0.8%
High School Choices: N/A

IS 30 is one of the most interesting experiments in public education in Brooklyn. Children start the year by climbing the Alpine Tower in Gateway National Recreation Area, they camp in lean-tos in Jacob Riis Park, interview retired neighbors to write an oral history of Bay Ridge, and study the history of mathematics in ancient Egypt and Babylon. These varied activities are intended to build self-confidence and a sense of community, to strengthen character as well as academic skills. The school attempts to engage children who might be bored in a traditional setting and to challenge everyone, not just those at the top of the academic ladder.

Opened in 1997, IS 30 is one of fifty-three Expeditionary Learning Centers in the nation. (There are several others in New York City, including the School of the Physical City in Manhattan and the Active Learning Prep School in Queens). It is part of a progressive network of schools committed to the belief that learning is best fostered in small groups in which a caring adult looks after the progress of each child.

"We provide students with seemingly impossible challenges and the tools they need to meet them," said Laura Flaxman, New York coordinator for the Expeditionary Learning schools. To climb the Alpine Tower, for example, children and teachers belay each other with ropes up the three sixty-foot telephone poles that make up the base. This

231

activity builds trust among children and adults and helps create what Flaxman calls a "positive peer group" for children at an age when peers are all important and bad influences abound. This may sound like a year-round Boy Scout camp, but the expeditions are only the beginning. Serious academics go on in the classroom. The subject matter is related to children's interests outside school and to the frequent trips the kids take.

IS 30 has leased space in a building that once housed a Lutheran day school and which still has private apartments. The place is bright and pleasant, with white tiled walls, good lighting, and sun-filled windows. The entrance resembled the lobby of a posh apartment house, with a rug on the floor, a poster of scenes of Rome on one wall and a vase of flowers on a small table. On the day I visited, the building was spotless. Even the bathrooms—pink for girls, blue for boys—sparkled.

There were no desks in rows; kids aren't expected to sit still and listen to a teacher for long periods of time. "The nice thing we have is the freedom to move around," said Principal Linda Viggiano. "I don't believe in chalk-and-talk."

In the art studio, students were putting finishing touches on oil portraits of people they had met at the local senior center, part of an extensive oral history project. The children had interviewed retired people about what their neighborhood was like fifty years ago and compiled their findings for an exhibit at the Bay Ridge Historical Society.

In the next room, art and computer teacher Katherine Tsamasiros was helping kids put together an "Egyptian myth" home page incorporating pictures, music, text, and graphics on their computers. Tsamasiros, who has a doctorate in education from Teachers College, explained that the English and social studies teachers had collaborated on a unit on Egypt in which children learned, among other things, that the Cinderella story had its origins as an Egyptian myth.

Computers are also used to help children with weak writing skills. One child was asked to create a computer program that would teach kindergarteners how to count from one to ten. The exercise encouraged the child to figure out "how to communicate what they have to say to another person," Dr. Tsamasiros said.

Down the hall, math teacher Felloy Galanis was preparing her next class. Her room was decorated with colorful polyhedrons made from origami paper and posters describing the lives of great mathematicians. Ms. Galanis favors math problems with real-life applications. Kids clip the ads for apartment rentals in the *Daily News* to figure problems such as "If you want to rent an apartment in Bay Ridge, how much money do you need to make?" They calculate water quality with samples drawn from below the Carnarsie Pier. They figure the number of square feet needed for a community garden, and calculate the height of trees on excursions to the Brooklyn Botanical Gardens.

"I just do what excites me, and I figure it will excite them," says Ms. Galanis. She has a particular passion for the history of math, and kids in her class learn various idiosyncratic facts: The ancient Babylonians had a number system based on 60, which is why we have 360 degrees in a circle. One large unit the Aztecs had was the number of cocoa beans that fit in a sack. Egyptians used the lotus flower as a symbol for 1,000. Einstein wore no socks. Each of her students must write a biography of a famous mathematician on their birthdays. Topics include the feud Newton and Leibniz had over who really invented calculus.

The school doesn't have an organized sports program or an outdoor playground. In place of gym, children play volleyball with a beach ball in a large classroom. There is a small recreation room in the basement where children can play Ping-Pong or bumper pool.

The school doesn't have a high honors superintendent's program or a magnet grant. It does have a "special placement" class, with 33 students per class. Regular classes have fewer than 30 children; English as a Second Language classes have 16. The school is open to children who live within the zone; there is no provision for variances for children outside the zone.

IS 259, William McKinley
7301 Fort Hamilton Parkway
Brooklyn, N.Y. 11228

Iris Baum, principal
718-833-1000

Reading Scores: ★★★
Math Scores: ★★★★
Eighth Grade Regents: yes
Grade Levels: 6–8
Admissions: Neighborhood
school. Test for gifted
program, lottery for magnet
program. January test for
superintendent's program.
November open house.
When to Apply: November

Class Size: 33
Free Lunch: 63%
Ethnicity: 48.7%W 4.4%B
23.9%H 22.9%A
Enrollment: 1266
Capacity: 1036
Suspensions: 7.7%
Incidents: 0.9%
High School Choices:
Franklin D. Roosevelt, Fort
Hamilton, Brooklyn Tech

One of the first things Principal Iris Baum did when she took over
William McKinley Intermediate School in 1997 was to persuade the
custodians to take the plastic covers off the fluorescent lights and wash
off years of grime. After a fresh coat of white paint (replacing dark
blue and yellow walls) the dingy halls looked like new. Built in 1938,
the building is pretty and has large windows, hardwood floors, and
charming dark-stained wooden coat closets.

Although it attracts children from outside the zone and the district,
McKinley has the ambiance of a neighborhood school. Recently hon-
ored were three generations—a grandmother, mother and child—for
perfect attendance at the school. Many teachers live in the neighborhood, and half a dozen have chosen McKinley for their own children.
Its eighty-five-piece band offers entertainment to the community with
outdoor concerts in McKinley Park.

The neighborhood, once mostly Irish and Italian, now has large
numbers of new immigrants. Bilingual classes are offered in Arabic,
Chinese, Russian, and Spanish. About 20 percent of the school is
Muslim.

"It's a socially and economically integrated school," said UFT repre-
sentative Jim Kenna, who has taught there for more than thirty years.

"We never had a single dominant ethnic group. That makes it an egalitarian and tolerant school. We have a staff that's been here a long time. An enormous percentage of the faculty lives in the neighborhood."

The day I visited, the honors debating team was preparing arguments on the question "Is adopting English as the official language consistent with American values?" The room was cluttered with dismantled computers the teacher repairs in his spare time. Discussion was lively, and the children were attentive and polite.

An English class discussed whether a character in *To Kill a Mockingbird* fell on his knife or was stabbed. In one science class, children copied facts about sea salt from the blackboard. In social studies, a teacher read aloud from a textbook, then asked students to consider why railroad workers in the early twentieth century might be resentful toward immigrants.

Teaching methods are, for the most part, very traditional. The reading lists include such classics as *Julius Caesar*, *Oliver Twist*, and *Of Mice and Men*. Advanced students may take two years of high school math, Sequential I and Sequential II, in the 7th and 8th grades.

The school has one high honors class, called the superintendent's program, and three honors classes in each grade. The most successful students go to Fort Hamilton High School, Brooklyn Tech, and Stuyvesant.

"It's a warm, friendly, cozy, cuddly place," said one mother. "The teachers are willing to be open and caring about the kids." The teachers are comfortable balancing discipline with fun, and many take part in events such as a teacher-student basketball game that allows them to mix informally with the children.

Overcrowding has been a persistent problem. The school has no homeroom period or lockers, which means children must carry their heavy books around with them each day and take them home each night.

The opening of two new schools in the district has eased the overcrowding somewhat, and Ms. Baum says she hopes to reduce the school's enrollment to about a thousand, the number the building was originally built to hold. The suspension rate has declined as the school has become less crowded.

There are two ways to get into McKinley from outside the zone (besides the inventive use of addresses—always a popular method).

One is the magnet program. Schools do not consider test scores when admitting children under the magnet program.

The other is the superintendent's program, for honors students. Fifth graders take a test in January and are also required to complete a writing sample. The school holds an open house for prospective parents before Thanksgiving.

IS 201, Dyker Heights Intermediate School
8010 12th Avenue
Brooklyn, N.Y. 11228

Madeleine Brennan, principal
718-833-9363

Reading Scores: ★★★★
Math Scores: ★★★★
Eighth Grade Regents: yes
Grade Levels: 6–8
Admissions: November open house. Neighborhood school. By test for gifted program, lottery for magnet program. January test for superintendent's program.
When to Apply: November

Class Size: 30-33
Free Lunch: 55%
Ethnicity: 50%W 8.8%B 18%H 23.2%A
Enrollment: 1240
Capacity: 1350
Suspensions: 7.3%
Incidents: 1.5%
High School Choices: New Utrecht, Fort Hamilton, Brooklyn Tech

The Italian-American community of Dyker Heights is widely known for the elaborate Christmas tree lights and decorations on its large, single-family houses—a fantastic display of toy soldiers and Santa's elves that draws visitors from across the city during the month of December.

The community's middle school, IS 201, is less flamboyant, but it, too, draws from outside the neighborhood. Children who are not zoned for the school may apply either to the superintendent's program for gifted children or to a magnet program in law.

Madeleine Brennan, who has been principal of the school since 1963, says she's is "traditional in attitudes toward discipline, honoring the flag, character development, and good citizenship" but also open to creative teaching ideas. In the law program, children have a chance to put on mock trials; they may also run their own small businesses, setting up a sweet shop to sell candy in the school, for example. Children in the superintendent's program build architectural models according to methods developed by the late Mario Salvadori, an engineeer and educator who believed children could learn everything from mathematics to social studies through the study of architecture.

Built in 1924, IS 201 has a stable, experienced staff. Its rate of suspensions and incidents are about average for the city.

School spirit is built with a student-teacher volleyball game and a parent-teacher softball game. The school has a large special education program for children with learning disabilities classified as MIS I.

Reading and math scores above the 90th percentile are required to apply to the superintendent's program, as is a test given by the district office, usually in early January.

Any child may apply to the magnet program. Deadlines vary, but they are usually in February. Children are admitted according to a lottery that is designed to ensure ethnic balance.

IS 187, Christa McAuliffe School
1171 65th Street
Brooklyn, N.Y. 11219

John Q. Adams, principal
718-236-3394

Reading Scores: ★★★★
Math Scores: ★★★★
Eighth Grade Regents: no
Grade Levels: 6–8
Admissions: November open house. Neighborhood school. Test for gifted program, lottery for magnet program. January test for superintendent's program.

When to Apply: November
Class Size: 30-33
Free Lunch: 77%
Ethnicity: 42.9%W 3.7%B 21.6%H 31.8%A
Enrollment: 1127
Capacity: 852
Suspensions: 2.5%
Incidents: 0.9%
High School Choices: N/A

"Small is better" is the mantra at Christa McAuliffe School, founded in 1994 and based on the premise that the huge, old-fashioned junior high school, simply doesn't work anymore, if it ever did.

Christa McAuliffe is made up of three mini-schools, each with about 350 children, its own pesonality, and its own director (called "a teacher-facilitator" in the current jargon). Each mini-school or academy has its own floor. Students stay on the same floor for all their academic classes.

The building was constructed in the 1920s as an elementary school, and it has the homey feel of a school for little kids rather than the factory-like feel of so many junior high schools. There are lots of floor-to-ceiling murals in the corridors and colorful bulletin boards covered with the children's work. The school is overcrowded and the halls are jammed during class changes. But kids are serious and attentive and also seem to be having fun.

Children with a wide range of abilities and family backgrounds are well served. There is a special education class for developmentally delayed children who run their own cafe in the school, bilingual classes in Spanish and Chinese, honors classes called Special Placement Enrichment, and a high honors class called the superintendent's program. A few children who have been transferred out of other schools for misbehavior have flourished here. Teachers say the small setting and individual attention seems to make them calm down.

"If you want children to respond to you, you have to respond to them," says principal John Q. Adams. "You have to give them activities—things to do they enjoy." When children help paint a mural, or take part in an all-school production of *Grease*, or go to Washington for a three-day class trip, they become protective of their school. That feeling of belonging fosters discipline and safety better than bullhorns and security guards. The school's suspension rate is half the citywide average; the rate of incidents is one-third the citywide averarge.

On the first floor is the **Academy for Scientific Research**. This mini-school has the most experienced teachers and the most traditional approach to learning. Parents said it is also the most demanding. The classrooms are mostly organized with desks in rows and teachers at the front.

There's nothing fancy here. There are no regular science labs, and the teachers carry their materials around on rolling carts. But the pleasant atmosphere seems to make up for the lack of elaborate equipment.

The day I visited, a science teacher was burning various compounds with a propane torch, teaching kids to identify the component elements. "Look at that flame!" one kid shouted gleefully. "It's like the sun!" The teacher, Avrum Leaf, then crumbled the powdery remains of the compound in his fingers. "It's not hot," he said. "That's something we'll work on later. But it's a powder. There has been a chemical reaction." Students were excited to learn that steel wool is heavier after it burns because iron combines with oxygen to form a compound. When the kids burned paper, they found it weighed less and had to come up with a hypotheses to explain why. The kids' hands flashed as they offered their explanations.

Many junior high schools mark their success in science by how many high school Regents exams the children can pass before they get to high school. Here, the approach is different. Rather than racing through a textbook so children can a pass a standardized exam in the spring, teachers concentrate on exploring a few topics in depth.

On the first floor is a coffee shop run by special education children who are classified as MIS V, or developmentally disabled. The children prepare lunch for staffers and any school visitors who want to eat. They learn arithmetic by making change, learn reading and writing by making signs. The children are paid a dollar a week and open their own bank accounts.

On the second floor is the **Academy for Global Communication**, led by teacher-facilitator Frank Sollazzo. The teaching style here is middle of the road—neither strictly traditional nor very progressive. "We don't like to go for the fads," says Sollazzo. "We want good, solid instruction." The halls are lined with colorful bulletin boards covered with children's work. The classrooms have more maps and globes than you might see in other programs, and computers are an integral part of instruction. Kids learn geography on the Internet and correspond with foreign penpals via e-mail.

The theme of the 6th grade is "Who are we?" Children study their own cultural roots and look for common values among different ethnic groups. "We're using that diversity to say people are more the same than they are different," says Sollazzo.

Seventh graders study "Peace through the Rule of Law," and examine civil and criminal law. They go on trips to courts and prisons and conduct mock trials in a "courtroom" set up in the school. Eighth graders study "World Peace through Understanding." They visit the United Nations, and spend three days in Washington. Sollazzo organized an exchange program with middle school students in Italy. Eleven children from Christa McAuliffe flew to Fabriano, Italy, and fifteen children from Fabriano stayed with families in Bensonhurst.

The school's classes in English as a Second Language and bilingual classes in Spanish and Chinese are part of the Academy for Global Communication. In bilingual classes, children study in both English and their native language, reading novels in Chinese, for example, but also boning up on English vocabulary as they practice how to multiply fractions or record their observations of zebrafish and iguanas in large glass cases. The school also has instruction in English as a second language for children from Poland, Russia, and the Ukraine, among other countries.

On the third floor is the **Academy for Arts and Humanities**, which has the most progressive approach to teaching of the three mini-schools. Teacher-facilitator Albert Catasus has a beard and wore a black turtleneck and jeans the day I visited. His favorite word is "cool" and he's as likely to be found sitting on a child's desk and chatting with kids as he is in his office, where he's posted a sign with a twist on a quote from Dante's Inferno: "Abandon all despair ye who enter here."

The walls of the corridor are covered with giant murals painted by the kids on subjects related to their studies: Street scenes from Verona, to tie in with their reading of *Romeo and Juliet*; a painting of rural China, to go along with *The Good Earth*; ancient Athens and Egypt, to go along with the study of ancient civilizations.

Teachers integrate different subjects in the curriculum, assigning works of literature such as *Tom Sawyer* or *Old Yeller* in history class. Children draw on both art and science for an "invention convention" when they construct Rube Goldberg-style gadgets. One child built an automatic spaghetti twirler by connecting a fork to a handheld fan.

Social studies projects, too, combine art with history and writing. A student wrote a fifteen-page paper and constructed an elaborate poster about the Cherokees' Trail of Tears, when Indians were evicted from the South and forced into exile. Teachers may use paintings as a primary source for information about an historic period. Sixth graders may study Latin, learning roots that are useful in their English writing.

Catasus believes in a collaborative approach with his staff; "I sit with the teachers and say, 'What do you want to do this year?' " And he's not afraid to get down on the floor and paint with the kids. "A little chaos is good once in a while," he says.

The staff of Christa McAuliffe has voted to retain homerooms, which give children a base to begin their day. The school receives grants from the Annenberg Foundation and is a member of the Center for Educational Innovation, formerly part of the Manhattan Institute, a conservative think tank.

One area of weakness: the writing program. One parent complained that children didn't have enough writing assignments. The principal said he planned to concentrate staff development on ways to improve the teaching of writing.

Each of the academies has some children in the superintendent's program, the districtwide high honors track. The principal said the school is also concentrating on ways to make the superintendent's program as challenging as possible.

The school has more requests for variances than it can accommodate.

Parents agreed that their children were well adjusted socially.

"I love it," said PTA President Margaret Philipps. "It's like a second home for the kids." Christa McAuliffe is also home to the district's **Saturday Academy**, a special program in American History led by teachers from around the city. Some three hundred kids come each week just for the love of learning. No tests are given, and there's no formal academic credit. One teacher brought an elaborate model railroad and spoke about the role of trains in history. Children might have a mock trial, or debate ideas that shaped the nation, such as: "Do you think we have the right to overthrow the government if it doesn't meet our needs?" Children from across the district are eligible to attend.

The Christa McAuliffe School is open to all children who live in the zone. Children outside the zone may be admitted under the superintendent's program or under the provisions of a magnet grant intended to maintain racial integration. Because the school is less than 50 percent white, preference is generally given to whites applying under the magnet program. Preference is also given to siblings of children already enrolled. About twenty-five to thirty children are admitted from outside the zone each year.

There is an open house in November. Children applying for the superintendent's program take an exam in January.

District 21

District 21 encompasses a stretch of southern Brooklyn from Bensonhurst and Midwood to Coney Island and Sheepshead Bay. Bensonhurst, once largely Italian-American, now has a sizable Asian population. Midwood is increasingly an Orthodox Jewish community. Coney Island is largely African-American. Sheepshead Bay has many new immigrant communities, particularly families from Russia.

A long sandy beach, the New York Aquarium, a boardwalk stretching for several miles from Coney Island to Brighton Beach and, of course, the amusement park at Coney Island make these Brooklyn neighborhoods a popular tourist destination.

The district is unusual in that it has retained many of its K–8 schools—so many pupils don't need to choose a middle school at all, but many simply continue at their elementary school.

The district has established six gifted-and-talented programs that attract children from across the borough and even from Queens. The best known of these is the Mark Twain School for the Gifted and Talented, but others are gaining in popularity. Be sure to call the district office for an updated brochure. Some of the newest programs opened too recently to be included here.

The district has a program to integrate special education and general education children in "inclusion" classes at the Brooklyn Studio School in Bensonhurst. It also has a promising transfer alternative program for children who have been removed from other schools for misbehavior. This program, called Project Adapt, is in a school that's otherwise reserved for gifted children, the Bay Academy in Sheepshead Bay.

The admissions process for the gifted-and-talented programs isn't a lot of fun, but it's pretty clear-cut. Parents of 5th graders may receive an application and brochure about the programs by calling the district at 718-714-2500 or Mark Twain at 718-266-0814. Each of the six schools with a gifted-and-talented program has an open house in November or December. Application deadlines are in December.

Children applying to gifted and talented programs must be tested in two areas of "talent"—such as science, music, art, drama—in January. Not all schools have the same talent areas, so read the brochures carefully. Out-of-district pupils may apply to any of the gifted-and-talented programs. Local children may apply to Mark Twain and to their neighborhood school.

Anita Malta, executive assistant to the superintendent, is knowledgeable about middle school programs and admissions procedures for the district. She can be reached at 718-714-2500.

IS 280, Brooklyn Studio Secondary School
8310 21st Avenue
Brooklyn, N.Y. 11214

Harold Epstein, principal
718-266-5032

Reading Scores: ★★★
Math Scores: ★★★★
Eighth Grade Regents: yes
Grade Levels: 6–12
Admissions: Neighborhood school. Accepts from outside zone.
When to Apply: Tours: call anytime. Application deadline: March.

Class Size: 16-33
Free Lunch: 81%
Ethnicity: 58.5%W 14.5%B 12%H 15%A
Enrollment: 200
Capacity: N/A
Suspensions: 7.5%
Incidents: 5%
High School Choices: N/A

Brooklyn Studio Secondary School opened in 1994 as an "inclusion" school, meaning that some children in special education get the extra help they need in general education classes, without being segregated. Brooklyn Studio offers general education, relatively small classes, a principal who knows students by name, and the intimacy of a neighborhood school.

Studio shares a building with an elementary school, PS 128. Students may attend school in the same building from kindergarten through 12th grade, just by moving from one wing to another—a plus for parents who are nervous about sending their children to large junior highs far from home.

Principal Harold Epstein, the former supervisor for speech services for the district, says having special ed kids mix with general ed kids is good for everyone. An inclusion class may have twenty-five general ed children, three children who are classified as learning disabled—and two teachers or a teacher and an assistant. The special ed kids tend to perform better when they're with kids who are higher achievers, and the general ed children get more attention than they otherwise would.

"We don't believe in isolation," Epstein said. "We believe in providing support in the classroom." Even children who are classified as emotionally disturbed may benefit from an inclusion class, he insists.

To persuade me, Epstein showed me a 7th grade English class where the children, who obviously loved their teacher, were discussing a novel called *The Outsiders*, about a fourteen-year-old orphan and gang member. He challenged me to pick out the emotionally disturbed child and the learning disabled child in the class. I could not.

"When you put twelve emotionally disturbed kids together in class, what they learn is how to be emotionally disturbed," Epstein said. "Kids who had antisocial tendencies in other schools fit in here."

Inclusion is not the answer for all special ed children, of course. The school also has "self-contained" or separate classes for children with speech and language delays, for learning disabled children, and for the emotionally disturbed children who can't cope in regular classrooms.

Sometimes kids in the inclusion class need extra help outside of the regular classroom. For example, learning disabled pupils might be assigned to a regular biology class, and then have special sessions where a teacher explains the science vocabulary they might not understand.

The teaching at the Brooklyn Studio School is, for the most part, traditional, with desks in rows and lots of blackboard-aided lecturing. The day I visited, there were some lively teachers who engaged the kids, and some who were not-so-lively and whose students looked bored.

The building, while light and cheery, needed work. Blasts of cold air came through antique windows in some rooms, while other spaces were overheated. New television equipment, valued at one million dollars, hadn't been unpacked because the wiring couldn't support it. The school, originally built in 1900, was being renovated during my visit, and the principal told me he expected the problems to be solved shortly.

PTA president Theresa Hernandez says the pluses of the school far outweigh the minuses. The small size means everyone knows everyone else. Nobody gets away with cutting class. If your child is absent for two days, the office calls home. Ms. Hernandez is thrilled to have her children right around the corner from where they live and not far away at a large junior high.

Her son, who needed extra help in reading, was happy to have a resource room teacher come into his regular class. In his previous school, he had been taken out for resource room and missed regular class time.

For her daughter, attending a school with grades 6 through 12 allowed her to keep contact with a beloved middle school math teacher when she moved on to high school. "Her math teacher said, 'If you ever have a problem, you know where I am. My door is open.' " Ms. Hernandez said. "It's like a family. All the teachers work together."

Although the school doesn't have a large sports program, it has a pleasant mirrored dance studio and a very popular dance teacher. Ms. Hernandez was working to organize a swim team at a nearby pool.

Test scores put the school in the top 20 percent of middle schools city wide. (Special ed children are exempt from the test.) Advanced students may take high school math (Sequential I) in the 8th grade.

The school has a higher than average suspension rate and a higher than average incident rate. Ms. Hernandez says the school is generally safe, but acknowledges there are occasional fights. "I'm not going to say everything is peaches and cream," she said. "You can't have everyone get along 24-7. But I've yet to see any major catastrophes." After a disturbance in the lunchroom, the administration decided to have the children in the self-contained class for the emotionally disturbed eat lunch in their rooms.

Children who attended PS 128 are automatically admitted to the Brooklyn Studio School. Others are admitted as space permits. The principal welcomes visits by parents. Children from outside the immediate zone for the school must submit an application for admission in March.

IS 228, David A. Boody School
228 Avenue S
Brooklyn, N.Y. 11223

Ralph DiBugnara/Marion Lish, magnet coordinator
718-375-7635

Reading Scores: ★★★★
Math Scores: ★★★★
Eighth Grade Regents: yes
Grade Levels: 6–8
Admissions: November open house. Neighborhood school. By exam and audition for talent program.
When to Apply: December application deadline; test in January.

Class Size: 30
Free Lunch: 66%
Ethnicity: 51.8%W 19.6%B 12.1%H 16.5%A
Enrollment: 1300
Capacity: 1457
Suspensions: 9.1%
Incidents: 0.8%
High School Choices: Abraham Lincoln, John Dewey, Lafayette

The halls of David A. Boody are lined with painted murals and dotted with papier-mâché creations, constructed by the children. A large papier-mâché tree climbs one wall, and painted stars twinkle through the branches. There's a huge Caribbean mask in bold colors on another wall, as well as a space ship. Hanging from the ceiling is a big papier-mâché leg and foot in a red high-heeled shoe.

The botany lab has the feel of a lush tropical rain forest. Flowering bromeliads, ferns, garden vegetables, and cactus fill the classroom so completely I was reminded of the scene in the children's book *Where the Wild Things Are* in which a boy's room is transformed by magic into a jungle.

The building is one of the oldest junior high schools in the city, built in 1929. It has pleasant big windows and high ceilings, although there's a bit of peeling plaster and some of the rooms could use a paint job. Some of the desks and chairs are pretty beaten up.

"It's a comfortable, warm place." said one mother, "The new principal is open to new ideas, very open to parents."

PTA co-president Enrica Fontana says the school has a relaxed atmosphere, and there is a good rapport between teachers and children. "Academics are important, but the kids are not pushed to the point of stress," Ms. Fontana said. "They try to look at the whole child, the social and emotional side as well. Kids talk about their teachers as if they were favorite uncles."

The day I visited, I saw some excellent teachers and, alas, a few who seemed rather dull.

One science teacher had children collect live turtles, bullfrogs, and other wildlife in Jamaica Bay, and brought them back to the classroom where they lived in a "pond" made from a tub. They looked at algae in the water under a microscope.

Combining the study of art with mythology, children were making giant dragons from papier-mâché, a quilt with scenes from Greek myths, and a huge unicorn.

A math teacher, Joyce Sigona, showed kids the connections between math and art, bringing both subjects to life. Children studied symmetry in nature and the patterns in Islamic art. They made kites shaped like polyhedra and studied transformational geometry by constructing shapes from origami paper. They study statistics using basketball scores and topology using Mobius strips.

"It adds a spark to the room when they see, 'Hey! I couldn't have done that if I didn't know angles," Ms. Sigona said. "I ask, 'Why does a kite fly if it's symmetrical, and why doesn't it fly if it's not symmetrical?' " Ms. Sigona said the kids are amazed by her math tricks. "I say: 'Pick a number and do this and do that and I bet I can guess the number," she said. "They say: 'She's a magician.' I have fun. If I have fun, the kids do too."

I saw a cozy special education class, for children classified as MIS I, or learning disabled, with a rattan sofa and chairs and teddy bears.

I saw teachers and children chatting informally between classes. "You see, there are always children hanging out with teachers," said Marion Lish, the assistant principal who led my tour.

Like Mark Twain and Bay Academy, applicants take "talent" tests to be admitted to Boody's "magnet" program from outside the neighborhood. Unlike Twain and Bay, Boody is also a neighborhood school. Children who live within the school zone are automatically admitted.

"Talents" include: art, athletics, band, creative writing, dance, drama, keyboards, mathematics/computer, vocal music and science.

The science talent classes are among the most appealing in the school. The 6th graders have an environmental science lab with doves, rabbits, gerbils, snakes, lots of fish and even a tarantula. Seventh graders study botany, including genetics, for the first half of the year and herpetology—amphibians and reptiles—the second half a year. The herpetology lab has live geckos, snakes, lizards and turtles. Seventh graders study marine biology at the New York City aquarium, and astronomy.

Unfortunately, children who are not in science talent are not allowed to use these facilities. "The other kids just get textbooks, and some of the textbooks are the pits," said one mother. She described her son's Regents science teacher as one whose teaching style was to have "his back to the kids, writing on the board and if you didn't get it—too bad."

The school is tracked: children are grouped by ability.

Parents agree the school is safe, and they praised the principal, Ralph DiBugnara, for dealing promptly with potential problems. For example, when a parent called to say she had heard a group of girls had threatened another group of children, DiBugnara called the local precinct to have a police officer on hand when school let out that day and he called individual parents of children who were believed to be involved, and spoke to the girls themselves warning them of consequences. He alerted the teachers who routinely monitor school dismissal to be extra observant. Everyone left safely that day.

Parents I spoke to called DiBugnara, who was appointed in 1998, a warm and nurturing man who, as the father of teen-age children himself, had a particular affinity for and understanding of children of middle school age.

IS 239, Mark Twain Intermediate School for the Gifted and Talented
2401 Neptune Avenue
Brooklyn, N.Y. 11224

Gary Goldstein, principal
718-266-0814

Reading Scores: ★★★★★
Math Scores: ★★★★★
Eighth Grade Regents: yes
Grade Levels: 6–8
Admissions: Selective. By tests or audition. November open house.
When to Apply: December application deadline; January test.
Class Size: 35

Free Lunch: 29%
Ethnicity: 58.8%W 9.9%B 7.7%H 23.6%A
Enrollment: 1202
Capacity: 1244
Suspensions: 2.5%
Incidents: 1.3%
High School Choices:
Stuyvesant, Brooklyn Technical, Midwood, Murrow

A beautifully-equipped, first-rate school in a desolate corner of Brooklyn, Mark Twain Intermediate School for the Gifted and Talented is one of the highest-ranking and most sought after schools in the city. A magnet school, created as part of a court-ordered desegregation plan in the 1970s, it attracts children from all over Brooklyn and even parts of Queens, despite its grim setting amid vacant lots and dirty marshes on a nearly abandoned spit of land west of Coney Island.

With three or four applicants for every spot, the administration can afford to be picky. Don't expect kid glove treatment when your child applies. If the people you talk to act as if they can live without you and your child—well, they probably can. But if your child should make it through the daunting, peculiar, and even arbitrary admissions process, chances are it'll be worth it.

The parents I talked to agreed Mark Twain provides a firm foundation for the most rigorous high schools. The school typically sends 16 to 18 percent of its graduates to Stuyvesant, 10 percent to Brooklyn Tech, 15 percent to Midwood, and 15 percent to Murrow—an unusually high rate of acceptance to selective high schools.

Mark Twain is predominantly white (and increasingly Asian), in an area of Brooklyn that's mostly black and Hispanic. Some black parents have complained that the admissions test effectively excludes most of the children, who go to low-performing elementary schools nearby. The administration has taken some steps to increase black enrollment, but progess has been slow.

The building is one of the oldest junior high schools in the city, built in 1936 and is still heated by a coal-burning furnace. Recently renovated, the school is spotless and light, with two giant, sunny gymnasiums, a pleasant library filled with plants, colorful murals and papier-mâché figures made by the kids. The classrooms are big and bright, with wood floors, wood coat closets and cabinets, and large windows.

The school seems to offer something for students of every conceivable academic bent or artistic talent. It has a drama department that puts on plays and musicals worthy of Broadway. It has a sports department with elaborate gymnastics equipment and tournament-level tennis competitions. It has an extensive music department with an impressive orchestra and full band, and a vocal department in which children learn both sight-reading and music theory.

Mark Twain has three math labs where kids study 3-D geometry on computers; science labs where kids may study microbiology and organic chemistry for three years; a television studio and darkroom equipped with free cameras for kids to study photography, a mirrored dance studio, an art studio, woodworking lab, sewing room—a staggering array of special programs.

"What really puts our school on the map is the talent program," says Principal Gary Goldstein. Children are admitted either on the basis of their overall academic achievement, or on the basis of a demonstrated "talent" in one of ten areas: art, athletics, creative writing, dance, drama, instrumental music, media, science, or vocal music.

Each child takes a test or audition in two "talent" areas. Once enrolled, a child is assigned to one talent, which becomes a sort of super-major for his or her three years at Mark Twain. In addition to regular coursework, children take six extra periods a week in their talent area. That means, for example, if your specialty is science, you'll take five periods a week of science with your regular classmates, plus another six periods of science with your talent class.

The parents I spoke to were uniformly enthusiastic about the talent classes. "Extraordinary!" "Extra-extraordinary!" "Incredible!" "First rate!" "Best vocal instructor I've ever seen," and "She loved it!" were typical comments.

One mother said her son was able to complete a full high school science curriculum before he graduated from 8th grade. Another said her daughter was thrilled to study solid geometry on the computer, and to learn how to build complex geometric solids from construction paper.

The drama teacher, Michael Polenski, is particularly well-loved. The day I visited, kids were practicing a play called *Frankenstein Slept Here* in the school auditorium. "Murder! Monsters! Mayhem!" Polenski shouted and the kids screamed "Help! Help!" They were practicing falling, knocked over by invisible monsters. "More noise, Anthony!" Polenski shouted. "Roll over, Anthony!" And Anthony happily complied.

In the dance studio, children were practicing a number from *Cats*, combining steps from ballet and jazz dance. In the art studio, children were making high-quality papier-mâché masks and inventive caricatures of their teachers for the school yearbook.

The teachers, for the most part, are old-fashioned, or as Goldstein puts it, "Traditional, but nobody falls asleep." Most are experienced, relaxed, and happy to be teaching. In the regular classes, outside the talent areas, I saw some teachers who invigorated class discussions with interesting questions and projects, and others who were a bit dull.

One social studies teacher, for example, led a lively discussion of the civil rights movement, based on a segment of the PBS documentary *Eyes on the Prize*. As the children talked about the battle for school desegregation in Boston, the teacher expertly wove in discussion of the history of their own school, which was established as a magnet school in 1975 after the NAACP sued the Board of Education, claiming the school was illegally segregated. The kids—alert, attentive and well-behaved—clearly enjoyed learning how the civil rights movement had repercussions in their own lives.

Another social studies teacher helped children understand the American Revolution by reminding them that many of the soldiers were teenagers not much older than they are now. The children watched a movie version of *April Morning*, the story of a young boy in the Battle of Lexington and Concord, and then discussed the origins of the Revolution. "Is there no Tory here? No one who will defend the British?" the teacher said, encouraging children to see history as a debate, not a list of dates and facts.

I also saw some teachers going over practice tests ad nauseum. Some parents complain of teachers who rely on boring textbooks, rather than giving children experiments to do in science, or works of literature to read in English.

"In every subject, there are great teachers and not-so-great teachers," said Iris Gersten, whose daughter attends the school. "One teacher, I called seven times and she didn't return my call. Another teacher calls home every time there's a little problem, or even with good news."

The school is extremely safe, orderly and disciplined. "We've had maybe half a dozen incidents in the past twenty years," said Goldstein, who began teaching at the school in 1965 and has been principal since 1988. Children lock their coats in wooden coat closets in their homerooms. Bathrooms are unlocked, and children may use them when they please.

Members of the staff wait outside in the morning and afternoon to make sure kids come and go without incident. Since the school is far from the nearest subway stop and few children live within walking distrance, nearly everyone comes by bus—free yellow buses for kids within the district, private buses paid for individually by parents for those living outside of it.

The fact that children are bused means there is "zero after-school life," one mother said. Children leave the school promptly and have no time for informal socializing or after-school programs.

The school has no bells. Class changes are boisterous but not unpleasant. "We're not fussy about decorum, about talking in the halls," said Goldstein as he gave me a tour. "We think it's a good outlet."

The only teacher I heard yelling was the one assigned to lunchroom duty who barked directions on clean-up over an annoying loud speaker. One mother complained to me later about "rigid" rules in the lunchroom, where children are required to line up in a certain way and eat with a set group of children. But she acknowledged that the school's record of safety was linked to the fact that there are clear, consistently enforced rules.

There is no tracking for most subjects, although some children are assigned to honors classes in math and science. Students are assigned to a "cluster" of five teachers, who have a common preparation period and who are supposed to coordinate their lessons. Some parents say the coordination is imperfect, and that, for example, several teachers may give an exam on the same day.

There are 400 children in each grade, and an assistant principal is assigned to stay with them through their three years at the school. That means the assistant principal will know the children well and it breaks down the anonymity of an otherwise large middle school. Class size ranges from 15 for minor subjects, such as photography, to 37 for general academic classes.

A few parents complain that certain activities are limited to children with a particular "talent." If you're in the science talent, for example, you can't work on the student newspaper; if you're in the creative writing "talent," you can't take tennis.

Chris Armao, PTA co-chair, said scheduling makes it impossible for children to study everything. "Where in the course of a day can you possibly fit it in?" she asked.

The workload is heavy. "Depending on what 'talent' you were in and what teacher you had, you could have reasonable amounts of work or oppressive amounts of work," said one mother, Karen Greenberg.

"It's an excellent education, but it has to be right for your child," said another mother. "My daughter was happy, but she did complain about not having a social life. She would be up to 10, 11 o'clock at night studying. Sometimes, it would go over to the weekend and you'd have to cancel plans so she could work."

But, overall, parents are positive about their children's experiences.

"I put my kids on the bus and they can't wait to get to school every day," said Ms. Armao, who lives in Howard Beach, Queens. "The teachers really know the children and care about them. If you walk through the building you see a lot of chatty, happy kids. When you have a happy environment, kids thrive."

The legacy of the court decision integrating the school is an extremely complex admissions formula. Children are admitted based on a combination of factors, including their race, their test scores, and the results of their "talent" test.

Under the terms of the court order, the racial balance must be within five percentage points of the racial makeup of the district, which is 50 percent white and 50 percent non-white. Blacks, Hispanics and Asians are grouped together and compete against one another for spots; whites compete against other whites for spots.

About 60 percent of the pupils are admitted on the basis of their standardized test scores in fourth grade, which make them eligible for special placement (SP). They must also take two "talent" tests or auditions. The other 40 percent are admitted on the basis of their "talent," which includes anything from athletic ability to proficiency in science.

"You have to tell your child, 'You're probably not going to get accepted,' and tell them it's not their fault," Goldstein said. "Blame it on me. Blame it on the testing procedure. Blame it on the judge. Ethnicity is a factor. Where you live is a factor. SP or non-SP is a factor."

African-American parents have complained that their children face enormous hurdles gaining admission to Mark Twain. Ronald Stewart, the only black member of the community school board for District 21, a Mark Twain alumnus and the father of three alumni, said that the quality of the neighborhood schools has been poor, so children are badly prepared either to be admitted on the basis of their overall academic achievement or to pass the academic "talent" exams in science, math or creative writing.

Goldstein says the school has taken steps to increase black enrollment. One promising program brings children from neighborhood elementary schools to Mark Twain to study science on a regular basis, making use of the middle school's sophisticated lab equipment and preparing neighborhood children for the demanding exam.

Anita Malta, an official in the district office, said more than 120 children from neighborhood schools were accepted in 1999—a number far higher than previous years—because of improvements in those schools.

Both white and black parents told me the admissions process can be unpleasant. If you live in District 21, it's fairly straightforward and your elementary school will guide you through. If you live out of district, chances are your home district will make it difficult for you to collect the necessary paperwork. Districts are loath to lose their best students and don't make it easy for a child to leave.

All applicants must have good records of attendance and behavior. Children applying for SP must have standardized test scores in the 83rd percentile for reading and the 75th percentile for math. All children must score at least in the 40th percentile in reading. (Exceptions are made for children in two special education classes, MIS I and MIS II, and children with limited proficiency in English. Special education students are assigned by the district office.)

Out-of-district children should call the district office or the school in the fall to request an application. Parents may also attend an open house in November to get general information about the school. Parents describe the open house as a mob scene of more than 800, in which overwhelmed staffers can't possibly answer all questions.

Because of the number of applicants, parents aren't permitted to tour the school.

Children are assigned a date in January for their talent tests and auditions at the school. Each child must take two. Parents are herded into the auditorium to watch a slide show about the school while the children sweat out the tests. Some parents told me the tests were no big deal, no worse than ordinary standardized test. But one mother recounted how a teacher giggled at a child who did poorly in the audition for drama.

Your chances of getting in are somewhat dependent on the "talent" you choose. Some "talent" programs have many, many more applicants than others. About 900 children a year take the math test, for example, but only 125 audition for the band.

If your child is admitted, he or she must accept immediately or face losing the spot. Try not to let the process get to you. If your child gets in, it's a nice place to go. If not, there are other fine schools he or she might like just as well.

IS 98, Bay Academy For Arts & Sciences
1401 Emmons Avenue
Brooklyn, N.Y 11235

Marian Nagler, principal
718-891-9005

Reading Scores: ★★★★★
Math Scores: ★★★★★
Eighth Grade Regents: yes
Grade Levels: 6–8
Admissions: Selective. By test or audition. November open house.
When to Apply: December application deadline; January test.

Class Size: 30
Free Lunch: 34%
Ethnicity: 67.4%W 15.9%B 7.5%H 9.2%A
Enrollment: 861
Capacity: N/A
Suspensions: 2.9%
Incidents: 0.7%
High School Choices: N/A

The Bay Academy for Arts and Sciences was founded in 1995-96 to enable the district to build on the enormous success of Mark Twain's gifted and talented program and to provide an appealing alternative for children who might not be admitted to Twain. Some parents now choose Bay Academy over Mark Twain. It's a smaller, more relaxed school, and the atmosphere is a bit less competitive. Class sizes are manageable, and the school isn't overcrowded. It is extremely safe. Bay Academy has managed in just a few years to attract high-achieving children from all over Brooklyn.

Principal Marian Nagler is a serious, hard-working traditionalist described by parents as both "a tough cookie" and a "very sweet lady." Parents say she is accessible and that the traditional approach she favors is good preparation for high school.

"At this age, children need to know their limits, they need the structure," says Judi Aronson, the principal of PS 261 in Boerum Hill, whose son attends the Bay Academy. "The school is very strict, and my son knows what's expected. The principal runs a very tight ship."

The building faces Sheepshead Bay, a narrow inlet crisscrossed by bridges. A tiny park nearby has a memorial to the Russian Jews who died in World War II, a touchpoint for the Jewish community of Manhattan Beach across the bay.

Built in the 1960s, the school has a prisonlike exterior of gray concrete. But it has a cheerful, brightly lit entry hall, and the classrooms are sunny and attractive, with plain white plaster walls and lots of children's work displayed. There is an interior courtyard filled with plants, and many classrooms display plants as well.

Much of the teaching is by the book, with an emphasis on textbooks and worksheets to prepare children for standardized tests. But the staff also makes use of the school's location by the sea, and teachers often take their classes to the beach to study ecology and to the aquarium in Coney Island to study marine biology.

Sixth graders have four workshops a year that take them behind the scenes at the aquarium. Seventh graders take a morning sea cruise to study oceanography on a boat owned by Kingsborough Community College. Children also attend classes at the Poconos Environment Education Center.

The teachers I spoke to were happy to be there, and praised Mrs. Nagler for giving them the leeway to teach as they saw fit. "She believes as long as the students are learning, it's up to the teacher to determine the method," one teacher said. However, another complained that the school didn't schedule time for teachers to plan lessons together.

Students praise the small size: "I had the chance to meet every single kid in the school over the course of three years," said Zachary Adlouni, a recent graduate. "If you needed help, the teachers would give you extra attention." His mother, Laurel Adlouni, said she liked the fact that the children were pushed to excel without fostering unpleasant competition. "You have to try hard, but the kids are nice to each other," she said.

The school stresses social development as well as academic achievement, offering, for example, five or six dances a year. Mrs. Nagler believes academics shouldn't crowd out all other aspects of a child's life. "Let children be children," said Mrs. Nagler, herself the mother of seven children, all grown.

Tiny problems are dealt with in a mock law court, where students reprimand each other for infractions such as cuttting class or chewing gum. The principal ensures the teachers follow all the rules, as well. The day I visited, she reprimanded one staff member for going out the "in" door in a stairwell, and admonished another teacher, whose children were talking to one another as they worked on class projects, to have the pupils work more quietly.

There are several special education programs, including classes for autistic children, the emotionally disturbed, and the hearing impaired (taught in American Sign Language), and an innovative and successful class called **Project ADAPT**, a transfer alternative program for children who have been suspended from other schools for misbehavior.

Mrs. Nagler clearly feels she is principal for all the children in the school—not just the "gifted"—and she is just as proud of the children in special education. "The whole school is Bay Academy," she says. Her formula for success is the same for all children: "A lot of love, a lot of special attention."

The teachers I saw in the class for autistic children were loving and attentive. They guided children in reading books such as *Charlotte's Web* and *Island of the Blue Dolphins*. They also helped those with severely impaired motor abilities to master basic living skills such as how to chew and swallow without spitting and how to walk in a straight line in the corridor without flailing their limbs.

Most of the special education children are separated from the rest of the school, but I saw hearing impaired children integrated into regular art classes. Hearing children may learn from the deaf, as well. American Sign Language is one of the languages offered at the Bay Academy, along with Spanish and Italian.

Project ADAPT is a promising "second-chance" program for children who have been thrown out of other schools for serious infractions such as assaulting a teacher or carrying a weapon. They spend a year in the program with ten kids and two teachers, where they get extraordinary attention from the staff. The day I visited, kids were having a birthday party for a classmate who'd been a habitual truant. The fact that he attended school regularly was something to celebrate. "In the beginning of the year, we'd go to his house at seven in the morning to get him out of bed," said teacher Mark Goldberg. After the party, a girl gave a touching and dramatic reading of the Langston Hughes poem "Mother to Son" with the line: "Life for me ain't been no crystal stair." When she finished, a teacher, moved almost to tears, gave her a kiss.

The program uses positive incentives, rather than punishments, to motivate children. For example, kids earn "money"—school-printed scrip—for arriving at class on time. The scrip can be redeemed for pizza on an outing with the teachers. Although the program's fifty children have classes on their own, the director, Joel Chapnik, says they benefit from being in an orderly school with high-achieving kids. "We put them where the youngsters could see learning going on," Chapnik said.

Chapnik also credits the program with dramatically improving safety in other middle schools in the district. Rather than transferring kids from one large middle school to another when they are suspended as many districts do, the most serious behavior problems come to Project ADAPT. "We've cut the number of suspensions by 90 percent by removing these kids from the neighborhood schools," said Chapnik.

Parents interested in Project ADAPT may call Barry Fein 718-714-2547 in the district office.

Admissions to the gifted-and-talented classes at the Bay Academy is the same as for Mark Twain. Parents attend an open house and fill out an application in November. Exams and auditions are held at Mark Twain in January. Children must take tests for two "talents."

District 22

District 22, which stretches from Ditmas Park in central Brooklyn to Marine Park on Jamaica Bay, is one of the few in the city in which most parents have confidence in their neighborhood middle schools. Achievement levels are fairly high, the schools tend to be safe and orderly, and parents say their children are prepared for the rigors of high school.

The schools are organized as traditional junior high schools, with 1,200 or more, long, crowded corridors, bells and class changes every forty-three minutes. But there are innovations in the curriculum and teaching methods that make the schools more interesting than your standard-issue junior high.

The district has adopted an imaginative approach to teaching mathematics, pioneered at Johns Hopkins University in Baltimore. Instead of having the teacher stand at the front and lecture to the entire class, each child works at his or her own pace. When a student needs help, he or she may go to the teacher for individual instruction.

The district is known for its attention to children in special education, who are integrated into general education classes more often than is typical in New York City. The district also has had success with many children on the brink of failing or dropping out entirely. In the district's "second-chance scholars program," selected children who are on the verge of flunking 7th grade are given a chance to complete 7th and 8th grades in one intensive year. The small class size—15—and the extra attention seem to pay off. Principals say the vast majority of kids in the "second-chance scholars" program go on successfully to high school.

Parents are encouraged to shop around for a middle school. Children from outside the district are eligible for admission, either by applying for the gifted program, called The Center for Intellectually Gifted (CIG), or through the magnet programs at each school. Each school has an open house for parents in the fall.

Those scoring above the 90th percentile in reading and math are eligible to take the CIG exam, called the "gifted intermediate admissions exam," in 5th grade. Those who pass are offered a seat either in the CIG program at Hudde Intermediate School in Midwood or at Shellbank Intermediate School in the southern end of the district. (The same exam is used to determine eligibility for gifted programs at two neighborhood schools, Marine Park and Cunningham.) The test is generally offered in December at the district's elementary schools or at a place determined by the district office. Call the CIG office for details: 718-368-8035.

There is no district-wide exam for the magnet programs. Each school sets its own admissions criteria. Hudde's math and science magnet program requires an exam offered at Hudde in December or January. (This exam is different from the one for the gifted programs.) Other schools rely on interviews, teacher recommendations, or other evaluations. Call the individual school for details.

A school that's not administered by the district—but that is situated within its boundaries—is the Brooklyn College Academy, a secondary school serving four hundred kids in grades 7 through 12. This is a "second chance" or "transfer alternative" school administered by the division of alternative high schools program for children who have floundered in traditional schools.

An annex, serving kids in grades 7 through 10, is called Bridges to Brooklyn. It's at 350 Coney Island Avenue. The 11th and 12th grades are housed on the Brooklyn College Campus. The school, founded with a grant from New Visions for Public Schools school reform group, uses the borough of Brooklyn as a huge research site. Children may visit the Brooklyn Museum to study paintings or walk across the Brooklyn Bridge to learn about architectural design. For information, call principal Madeline Lumachi at 718-951-5941 or assistant principal Rosemary Maher at 718-853-6184.

IS 240, Andries Hudde School
2500 Nostrand Avenue
Brooklyn, N.Y. 11210

Julia Bove, principal; Susan Forster, magnet coordinator
718-253-3700

Reading Scores: ★★★★
Math Scores: ★★★★
Eighth Grade Regents: yes
Grade Levels: 6–8
Admissions: Neighborhood school. Tests for gifted programs in December-January. Fall open house.
When to Apply: N/A
Class Size: 28-32

Free Lunch: 48%
Ethnicity: 23.1%W 62.7%B 7.2%H 7%A
Enrollment: 2123
Capacity: 1946
Suspensions: 3.9%
Incidents: 1.2%
High School Choices: Edward R. Murrow, South Shore, Midwood

Andries Hudde Intermediate School is a gigantic neighborhood school with two programs for high-achieving kids that attract applicants from all over Brooklyn. It's an old-fashioned school in terms of organization, and has some of the flaws common to big junior high schools. Kids complain of irritating announcements over the public address system and "halls sweeps" meant to punish kids who are in the corridors when they are supposed to be in class. Bathrooms are often locked, and kids need permission to use them.

But if you can get past the overwhelming size and sometimes rigid structure of the place and look inside the classrooms, you'll see that there's a lot of first-rate teaching by a staff that keeps up to date with the latest methods. Here you'll find traditional structure but progressive pedagogy.

The school is home to a new way of teaching kids math pioneered by researchers at Johns Hopkins University in Baltimore. Rather than having the teacher stand at the front of the classroom and write exercises on the blackboard, kids work individually, at their own pace, and the teacher helps each one as needed. The program has allowed strong students in math to move far ahead of their grade level, and has given those who are struggling the individual attention they need.

Many of the teachers have adopted projects that engage kids on their own level and encourage them to work in groups or on their own. There's very little lecturing and teachers don't rely heavily on textbooks.

Kids studying ancient Egypt made their own mummies—from supermarket chickens. They learned how corpses were prepared for burial and reproduced the process, carefully wrapping the chickens in long strips of cloth and allowing them to dry, decorating the "tombs" (cardboard boxes) with ancient designs and filling them with precious objects such as pretend jewelry. Kids studying the Age of Exploration made maps of the world. Then they purchased packets of spices and attached them to the maps to show where each came from in the Far East and where they were used in Europe.

The school has unusually good art and music programs. The most advanced students can study high school biology in 7th grade. Not every teacher is a star. One father complained that his daughter's Spanish instructor showed movies endlessly in class and never showed up for parent-teacher conferences. The day I visited, however, I saw a nice rapport between the students and their teachers, between the the principal and the kids, and between the principal and the staff.

The new head, Julia Bove, is a rarity among principals: She is both a strong educational leader and an able administrator. Parents give her high marks for her enormous energy, and talent. "The kids love her. Respect is like her middle name. She respects the kids and she expects them to respect her," said Anne Mackinnon, a school board member and parent. "She is very serious and has very high expectations. She works like a dog, and she doesn't accept anything less from anyone else."

"Ms. Bove is willing to try almost anything new in terms of teaching methods, but never forgets that what students learn is more important than the method by which they learn it," Ms. Mackinnon said. "It's content, content, content," Ms. Mackinnon continues. "They stuff them full of knowledge. Ms. Bove says to the teachers, 'Okay, you love the kids. What have you taught them today?' " Teachers are expected to pay attention to children's social and emotional development, but never at the expense of academic achievement.

In the past, some parents have complained that Hudde was a school of the haves and the have-nots, with the children in the two gifted programs getting the most energetic teachers and the best equipment and supplies. The divisions have sometimes taken on racial overtones. The children who are zoned for the school are mostly black, while those who come in through the district-wide gifted program are more likely to be white or Asian. Children in the school's annex have felt particularly isolated.

Ms. Bove has taken steps to alleviate the worst of the inequities. She has insisted that teachers divide their time between general ed pupils and the high-achieving kids so everyone gets a chance at having the best teachers. And the district office is working to improve conditions for children assigned to the annex, which in the fall of 1999 was to become its own school, with its own administration. That move should reduce the Hudde population to a more manageable size, and eliminate the orphanlike status attached to being schooled in an annex.

Hudde has a rate of suspensions and incidents that's below average for the city. When incidents do occur, Ms. Bove is credited with taking swift action, and kids say they feel the administration takes their concerns seriously. When children were having trouble with high school students pestering them after school, Ms. Bove set up an extended-day program that allowed her students to stay until 4 p.m., long after the troublesome high schoolers had left the area.

An open house is held in early December. Children who are zoned for the school are automatically admitted. (The surrounding neighborhood is increasingly made up of Orthodox Jews, who generally send their children to private religious schools. Most of the children who are zoned for the school are African-Americans from the northern part of the district.)

Children who want to be admitted from outside the zone, or who want to attend the accelerated programs for high-achieving students, must take an exam to be admitted. The highest track in the school is the Center for the Intellectually Gifted or CIG program (pronounced sig as in the first syllable of cigarette.) The second-highest track at the school is the magnet program. Both are accelerated for high achieving pupils. The CIG exam is offfered by the district office; the magnet exam is offered by the school itself. See page 263 for details.

IS 234, W. Arthur
Cunningham School
1875 East 17th Street
Brooklyn, N.Y. 11229

Jeffrey Latto, principal
718-645-1334

Reading Scores: ★★★★
Math Scores: ★★★★★
Eighth Grade Regents: yes
Grade Levels: 6–8
Admissions: Neighborhood
school. By January exam for
gifted program, lottery for
magnet program. Fall open
house.
When to Apply: N/A
Class Size: 33

Free Lunch: 53%
Ethnicity: 55.9%W 19.6%B
8.4%H 16.1%A
Enrollment: 1598
Capacity: 1233
Suspensions: 4.7%
Incidents: 0.3%
High School Choices:
Edward R. Murrow, James
Madison, Midwood

A traditional school in an old-fashioned building—there are still some wooden desks (with inkwells) nailed to the floor—Cunningham has a reputation as a safe school that delivers above-average test scores despite enormous overcrowding. It's the school of choice for recent immigrants from Russia, one mother said, adding, "There's a huge amount of lying about addresses to get in."

The school ranks in the top 20 percent of citywide reading scores. It has a math program developed at Johns Hopkins University that allows each child to move at his or her own pace. Some kids complete three years of high school math before they graduate from 8th grade.

Tucked in the neighborhood between Midwood and Sheepshead Bay, IS 234 has a stable staff and a principal who grew up in the community. "I'm a graduate of this school," said the principal, Jeffrey Latto. "We have a lot of teachers who graduated from here, and a lot of my teachers have their own kids come here."

The school has a mix of new immigrants from China, South America, the Middle East, and India, as well as students from the Italian-American, Irish-American, African-American, and Jewish families who have lived in the neighborhood for a long time. Cunningham has retained the vocational training that many other junior high schools have eliminated as passé. There is a functioning woodworking shop, a ceramics studio with a kiln, a darkroom, a print shop, and classes in cooking and sewing.

"I'm a big proponent of school-to-work programs," Latto said. "For some of the kids who really don't shine academically, it gives them a chance to build up their self-esteem." Some students run their own small businesses, selling holiday greeting cards or T-shirts imprinted with school designs or special messages.

There is a "second-chance scholars program" for children on the verge of failing 7th grade. Extra-small classes allow kids to fill in the material they missed in 7th grade while completing 8th grade requirements—all in one year.

Special education classes are offered for children diagnosed as learning disabled (MIS I) or emotionally troubled (MIS II). An inclusion class puts special education children together with general education children and two teachers. Children who need extra help in reading come in early, rather than being pulled out of their regular classes.

The school has an active School Leadership Team. Members of the team—parents, teachers, and the principal—make many crucial decisions together. For example, when teachers felt it was important for some struggling kids to work in a smaller classes, the team agreed, even if it meant extra-large classes for children in the higher tracks. The fact that parents and teachers agreed in advance to the large classes for high-achieving students meant there would be little resentment when the change was instituted. Class size ranges from 15 to 37.

There is an orientation for incoming 6th graders in June, when parents and students come to the school in the evening and sit in on mini-lessons offered by the staff. It helps the kids prepare for the rigors of middle school, Latto said, adding that for some kids who are not ready to change rooms for every subject, the school offers classes in which most subjects are taught by a classroom teacher, just like in elementary school. Class size for those kids is limited to 25.

Children who live in the zone for the school are automatically admitted. Others may apply to a computer "magnet" program, or to the Vanguard Academy, a program for high-achieving kids. Children are accepted in the magnet program according to a lottery and are admitted to the Vanguard Academy based on an entrance exam given at Hudde, another middle school in the district. The higher rents and real estate values in the zone are indicative of IS 234's desirability. Prospective parents may visit the school during an open house in December.

IS 278, Marine Park School
1925 Stuart Street
Brooklyn, N.Y. 11229

Mary Barton, principal
718-375-3523

Reading Scores: ★★★
Math Scores: ★★★
Eighth Grade Regents: yes
Grade Levels: 6–8
Admissions: Neighborhood school. By January exam for gifted program, application for magnet program. Fall open house.
When to Apply: N/A

Class Size: 30
Free Lunch: 51.2%
Ethnicity: 46.2%W 39.8%B 10.1%H 3.9%A
Enrollment: 1372
Capacity: 1528
Suspensions: 4.2%
Incidents: 1.2%
High School Choices: N/A

This not-terribly-overcrowded school, in a sleepy corner of Brooklyn, boasts an unusual level of community involvement. There's a senior citizens' center attached to the school, and several dozen retired people volunteer on a regular basis to give kids individual help in their studies.

The School Leadership Team—the committee of parents and staff that makes many key decisions—is particularly active, which gives parents a chance to make their opinions known on a wide range of school issues, such as the budget. For example, the committee decided it was more important for the school to have more guidance counselors, even if it meant having fewer "paraprofessionals" or assistant teachers. One result is that there are more adults kids can turn to if they are having trouble in school or at home.

Principal Mary Barton, the former assistant principal for magnet programs at Hudde Intermediate School, brings enthusiasm and energy to her job. Many of the teachers are traditional in approach, but some have instituted interdisciplinary cooperation. An English class historical novel is about the period they're studying in social studies. Ms. Barton said she hopes to incorporate some progressive teaching techniques.

There is a magnet program, called the Olympic Academy, that offers extra classes in physical education along with regular academic studies. Children might study the history of sports or take backstage tours of Madison Square Garden. Physical education classes five days a week in the school gym and in Marine Park next to the school. Children from inside and outside the district are eligible for the program. Admission is based on an application that includes a teacher's recommendation.

The school's Park Prep Academy is for high-achieving children. Admission is based on the entrance exam for gifted programs given by the district office.

There are several inclusion classes for special education children classified as learning disabled (MIS I). Children in special education take classes with general education students, and two teachers team teach. The special ed and general ed teachers meet once a day to plan lessons and discuss children's progress.

Marine Park, like the other schools in the district, has a "second chance scholars program" for kids who are held back in 7th grade. They are placed in a class of 15 and given intensive instruction which allows them to complete 7th and 8th grades in one year, so they can start high school with children their own age, rather than losing a year.

Tours are available by appointment, and there is an open house for parents in the late fall or early winter. "Parents are welcome to come anytime," Ms. Barton said.

Children zoned for the school are automatically admitted. Others may apply to the magnet program or to the gifted program. Call the school for details.

District 23

For years, this has been a bleak district with low-performing schools, in the neighborhoods of Ocean Hill and Brownsville. However, the district has a well-respected new superintendent, Dr. Kathleen Cashin, and there is a glimmer of hope for the future. The district office telephone is 718-270-8600. A community group, East Brooklyn Congregations, is working with the cooperation of the superintendent to organize parents for school reform. EBC's Sister Kathy Maire at 718-498-4095 is a helpful, independent source of information about schools in the district.

District 32

Another bleak district with low-performing schools, District 32 in Bushwick, at least has one first-rate school for the gifted: Philippa Schuyler. However, children attending District 32 middle schools generally have reading scores that are too low to gain admission to Schuyler, which draws kids from across the city. The district office is 718-574-1125.

IS 383, Philippa Schuyler School
for the Gifted and Talented
1300 Greene Avenue
Brooklyn, N.Y. 11237

Mildred Boyce, principal
718-574-0390

Reading Scores: ★★★★★
Math Scores: ★★★★★
Eighth Grade Regents: yes
Grade Levels: 5–8
Admissions: Selective. By exam.
When to Apply: Applications available in October; admissions test available on 4 Saturdays between December and March.
Class Size: 25-36

Free Lunch: 57%
Ethnicity: 00.9%W 74.5%B 22.2%H 2.4%A
Enrollment: 1335
Capacity: 1667
Suspensions: 1.2%
Incidents: N/A
High School Choices: Brooklyn Technical, Edward R. Murrow, Clara Barton

Philippa Schuyler School for the Gifted and Talented is one of the highest-performing schools in the city, with an excellent record for getting children into some of the best high schools, public and private, in the country. It draws from a wide spectrum of social classes: from families on public assistance to the children of doctors and lawyers. Children come from as far as Staten Island and the Bronx to the school next to the rumbling Elevated tracks in the Bushwick section of Brooklyn.

The PTA handbook for parents describes Philippa Schuyler as "an oasis in the desert, a true oasis and not a mirage." Indeed, this is a school that lives up to advance billing, a serious, no-nonsense kind of place, with lots of homework. Plaid uniforms set the tone. Safe and orderly, class changes are smooth. Teachers are strict without being dictatorial. The staff believes in keeping order by engaging children in interesting work, not barking at them through bullhorns. "If you have good teaching, you don't have a problem with discipline," said assistant principal Tina Reina.

A good mix of classical and progressive teaching techniques is evident. Teachers drill children in the basic skills of grammar and insist they use proper diction. All children are expected to write research papers and essays frequently. Classics such as George Orwell's *Animal Farm* are required reading. Kids dissect frogs in biology, as they have for generations.

The teachers also expose their children to many experiences outside the traditional curriculum. In social studies, kids might write a journal of an imaginary trip by traders across Africa in the Middle Ages. In science, they walk across the George Washington Bridge to study first hand the rock formations of the Palisades in New Jersey. They calculate the circumference of the Earth by comparing the length of shadows cast by pins in a globe and the shadows cast by sticks on the playground, reproducing the calculations of the Ancient Greek mathematician Archimedes.

Unusually attractive science labs are located in a sunny, modern area the size of several ordinary classrooms. Children compare the growth rates of kidney beans and radishes in the school greenhouse, or chart the behavior of gerbils, lizards, and frogs who live in big glass tanks. An aquarium has zebrafish that lay transparent eggs. Children can use a microscope to see the embryos develop inside the eggs.

The science teachers share materials and ideas, as well as the large science area that's only partly broken up by room dividers. "The science department is the best because we feed off each other," says Steve Appelman, its head. "Whatever the kids need, we have, because we have people fighting for us," he said, nodding toward Principal Mildred Boyce, a formidable fund-raiser. An active alumni association and the PTA have raised enough money to make IS 383 better equipped than most public schools.

Lessons in ballet, jazz, and modern dance are part of a program that's as serious and rigorous as the academic courses. "Lift the passe higher! Pack up the inner thigh muscle!" I heard a teacher exhort the students in black leotards, short skirts and pink tights as they practiced their jumps.

Even home economics is taught with a serious purpose. Children not only learn table manners and how to cook, but also tour the Culinary Institute to learn about possible career applications of their lessons.

Philippa Schuyler is the brainchild of Ms. Boyce, who transformed it from a dumping ground for low-performing kids to one of the best schools in the city. Bushwick had suffered a decline in the 1970s, as waves of arson and abandonment decimated the neighborhood. "When they had riots in the 1970s, what wasn't burned or bombed was just left in disrepair," says Ms. Boyce.

When IS 383 was built in 1977, the neighborhood was depressed and the school had the lowest performing kids in the district, she said. Ms. Boyce, who was an English teacher at the school, got the idea of setting up a "gifted and talented" program to attract children from outside the immediate neighborhood. Her idea worked.

The neighborhood itself is making a comeback and, while there are still some boarded-up buildings nearby, there is new housing construction, a new police station, and busy commercial streets that have made the surrounding blocks more inviting.

Parents are enthusiastic. They appreciate the challenging curriculum and the frequent contacts with teachers. They enjoy the fact that PTA meetings are held on Saturday mornings—a more convenient time than weeknights—and that parents are made to feel welcome.

The one criticism I heard is that teachers sometimes forget how young the children are and give lessons more appropriate for high schoolers than middle schoolers. Even if they are academically capable, they need to have assignments spelled out more precisely, one mother said.

The provision in the teachers' contract that eliminates homeroom and teacher supervision of the lunchroom has been a problem, parents say. Although the school is very safe, bathrooms are locked and children must all have their midday meal together in a very crowded lunchroom because there aren't enough aides to supervise numerous lunch periods. Children are not allowed to play in the playground afterward because there are no teachers to supervise them.

Homework is heavy. Every subject has homework every night and children generally need to study two, three, sometimes four hours a night. Parents are expected to help children with their homework and to help them organize their assignments, buying, for example, poster board and foam balls for science projects.

"I wouldn't say it's competitive, but everyone is expected to do their best," said PTA president JoAnn Robinson. "It's not just the child doing the work. You as a parent have to be on top of it as well. If a parent is not willing to be involved, there are going to be problems."

Children who do not perform satisfactory work are put on probation. If they fail persistently, they are asked to leave. Boys, particularly, seem to have trouble keeping up. The school accepts equal numbers of boys and girls. By graduation, the class is about 60 percent female.

A large proportion, perhaps one-third of the class, goes to Brooklyn Technical High School. Others win scholarships to independent day schools such as Dalton and boarding schools such as Phillips Andover Academy in Andover, Mass.

Any child who lives in the city may apply for admission. Children are required to take an entrance exam, offered four or five times from December to March. Parents watch a video about the school while their children take the Saturday morning test. There are no organized tours for prospective parents, although there is an open house for parents whose children have been offered admission.

The entrance exam consists of 100 multiple choice questions, similar to the standardized citywide reading test, plus a writing sample. Any child who answers half the questions correctly will be offered a spot. "I will not refuse a child who passes the test and who wants to come," says Ms. Boyce. Chlldren who fail the test in the 4th grade may take it again in 5th grade.

The school has come under attack from neighborhood parents because only a few children from District 32 elementary schools pass the admissions test. Until recently there were no provisions for Spanish-speaking children or for children in special education.

Under pressure from the district office, the school set up a special education program as well as a bilingual program. Children with language delays are admitted to the special education program under criteria set by the district office. Children are admitted to the bilingual program according to their scores on a Spanish version of the entrance exam. I visited both bilingual and special ed classrooms and found the quality of teaching and the materials to be comparable to the rest of the school.

Reading Scores

Math Scores

Eighth Grade Regents

Grade Levels

Admissions

When to Apply

Class Size

Free Lunch

Ethnicity

Enrollment

Capacity

Suspensions

Incidents

High School Choices

QUEENS

QUEENS

Queens was once a place of scattered villages set amidst farmland. Today the farmland is gone, but the identity of the old villages remains. Ask people where they live, and they're likely to say Richmond Hill or Woodside or Douglaston—rather than Queens.

Some neighborhoods have a distinctive ethnic atmosphere. You're just as likely to hear Greek as English spoken on the busy streets on Astoria, where the music from bouzoukis fills the air late at night. In Little India in Jackson Heights, there are more women dressed in saris than in blue jeans, and the perfume of curry spices wafts through the streets. Other neighborhoods are polyglot, where you'll see newsstands selling papers with a dozen different languages. More than one hundred languages are spoken in the borough today.

Much of Queens was rural until World War II, and there are still many suburban neighborhoods with single-family homes and large lawns. Junior high schools came relatively late. Borough children went to small neighborhood K–8 schools until the 1950s, when the population finally was large enough to justify the construction of the large junior high schools still in use today

The population boomed again in the 1980s and 1990s with newcomers from all over the world, particularly Asia. Single-family homes were divided into many small apartments, often in violation of zoning regulations. School construction didn't keep pace with immigration, and many of the schools are badly overcrowded.

Traditional for the most part, the schools reflect the values of the communities they serve. Quality varies. Several schools in Little Neck and Bayside rank at the very top, and one in the Rockaway peninsula ranks near the bottom of the Board of Education's annual ratings.

School choice in Queens is very limited, because of the overcrowding, because the bureaucracy discourages it, and because it's inconvenient to get from one school to another. The borough is large—almost as large in area as Manhattan, the Bronx and Brooklyn combined—and many neighborhoods are not particularly well served by public transportation.

Still, if you're unsatisfied with your neighborhood school, there are options. Several of the districts allow parents to choose a school within their district—even though they refuse admission to children who live outside their boundaries. Several schools in District 30, which includes the neighborhoods closest to Manhattan, accept children from outside the district. Some parents pay for private buses to transport their children to good public schools in Brooklyn, and some parents commute with their children to Manhattan.

Don't overlook mini-schools or programs within your neighborhood middle school. There are a few excellent small programs within otherwise undistinguished large schools.

District 24

This district, which includes Elmhurst, Middle Village, Corona, and Glendale, has long been one of the most overcrowded in the city. School construction fell short of what was needed to accommodate the immigration of the 1980s and 1990s, and school choice is next to impossible because of overcrowding. Variances—special permission to attend a school other than a child's zoned school—are granted only occasionally, usually for reasons of health and safety. Try Linda Ciborowski at the district office 718-417-2600 to make your case.

The middle schools are, overall, fairly safe and competently run. Test scores are mostly average. The number of children suspended for misbehavior is about average for the city, but the number of incidents—cases involving school safety officers—is well below average. The schools are, for the most part, traditional. The highest test scores for the district are at IS 119 at 78th Avenue and 74th Street in Glendale, 11385, telephone 718-326-8261. A colleague describes IS 119 as "very traditional," serving a community whose unofficial motto might be "The way it is, is the way it was."

Parents looking for a more innovative approach might consider IS 125, at 46-02 47th Avenue in Woodside, 11377, 718-937-0320, IS 93 at 66-56 Forest Avenue in Ridgewood, 11385, 718-821-4882, and IS 5, at 50-40 Jacobus Street, Elmhurst, 11373 718-205-6788. All three are large schools with average test scores that have adopted the principles of the Middle School Initiative, in which children are grouped in teams or houses to break down the anonymity of a big institution.

The schools do not offer regular tours, but you might consider attending a PTA meeting, or visiting schools during the evening when parent-teacher conferences are held. The principal of IS 5, Steve Katz, welcomes visits by parents.

The best-established and most sought-after alternative for children living in District 24 is the Louis Armstrong Middle School in East Elmhurst, which draws children from throughout the borough. The vagaries of a federal court decision on desegregation put Louis Armstrong into a district of its own, District 33, which is also called the Chancellor's District. (See pages 330, 341.)

District 25

From Flushing's bustling Chinatown to Whitestone's quiet residential streets, District 25 includes varied neighborhoods in north-central Queens. Many newcomers from Korea, India, and China have moved here recently. The southern part of the district feels very much a part of the city, with busy commercial streets and apartment buildings and a fast connection to Manhattan via the number 7 train. The northern part is more suburban, with big trees and single-family houses and stops on the Long Island Railroad. Schools tend to be smaller and less crowded in the northern end of the district.

The middle schools are mostly traditional, with above average reading scores. The district takes a hard line on disciplinary infractions, and has a higher than average rate of suspension of children for misbehavior. However, the incident rate—the number of problems reported to school safety officers—is less than half the citywide average. The district takes a particularly tough line on suspensions, and my impression from visiting the schools and talking to parents is that the high suspension rate reflects the district's hard line, rather than unsafe conditions.

The district encourages parents to visit schools, and children may apply to a school outside their immediate zone, space permitting. Children living outside the district may not apply, but those living within the district are free to shop around. The district publishes a brochure outlining the options under the magnet program, which allows kids to transfer from one school to another. Call the district at 718-281-7600 for information.

JHS 194, William H. Carr School
154–60 17th Avenue
Whitestone, N.Y. 11357

Anita Sobol, principal
718-746-0818

Reading Scores: ★★★★
Math Scores: ★★★★
Eighth Grade Regents: yes
Grade Levels: 7–9
Admissions: Neighborhood school. By application for magnet program. January open house.
When to Apply: N/A
Class Size: 33

Free Lunch: 23%
Ethnicity: 49%W 3.6%B 18.4%H 28.9%A
Enrollment: 906
Capacity: 1310
Suspensions: 11.5%
Incidents: 1.4%
High School Choices: Robert F. Kennedy, Cardoza, Bayside

The heart of JHS 194 is its architecture and engineering studio, where children can design anything from a portable homeless shelter to their own dream house. Kids may build a tiny Indian village or Colonial American settlement from cardboard, integrating their history lessons with a study of measurements and design.

The studio is based on the principles of the late Mario Salvadori, a Columbia University professor who believed the basics of engineering and architecture could be taught to young children. It allows children to use their academic work in various subjects to solve real-life problems. "This is the place where they begin to apply all the things they are learning in the other classrooms," says former principal Michelle Fratti, who studied with Salvadori. Ms. Fratti, who gave me my tour, was subsequently named District 25 superintendent.

Sometimes the children come up with a creative answer to a social problem, such as the portable homeless shelter. Sometimes they consider land-use decisions, such the best place to build a village. Sometimes they walk around their locale and analyze what makes a neighborhood work.

JHS 194 is a clean, happy school, with a well-equipped library and pleasant classrooms. It's not overcrowded, and class size, while not ideal, isn't as large as some schools.

Although the suspension rate is above average for the city, the incident rate is well below. That means a fairly large number of kids are suspended for misbehavior, but there are few incidents of violence. PTA president Irene Kouba said, "The high suspension rate reflects the fact that the administration follows district policy by the letter. Rather than covering up or ignoring problems, school officials deal with them promptly," Ms. Kouba said. Other parents and students I spoke to agreed, saying the school is "definitely safe."

"If you go up the down staircase, you get reprimanded," Ms. Kouba said. "The cafeteria is run like an army camp, but you know, the kids don't mind it. They appreciate it."

Said a parent, "They'll be outside the building at two thirty every afternoon, making sure there are no kids smoking on school property, making sure there are no fights. If a kid is smoking, they'll take the cigarettes and call the parents."

Seventh graders are divided into three teams, each taught by a group of teachers. That means kids don't go all over the building for their classes, and teachers get a chance to meet with one another to talk about kids' progress. The day I visited, I saw students and teachers talking informally to one another in small groups and in the halls between classes.

"In most ways we're very traditional," said Ms. Fratti. "For the most part, you still have teachers in the front of the room. What is not traditional is people really talk to each other."

Ms. Kouba agrees. "The teachers meet constantly," she said, "If one teacher is giving a test on a Tuesday, the other will give a test on a Wednesday so the kids are not overwhelmed."

Ms. Kouba was particularly impressed by the way in which teachers and guidance counselors helped her son after his father died. "They rallied round my kid more than I could help him, because I was wallowing in my grief. Every single one came to the wake." The teachers were sympathetic, but "never let him off the hook" in his studies and, as a result, the boy stayed on the honor roll throughout his ordeal. "Nothing but wonderful," she said. "It's really an exceptional school."

The staff has voted to retain homeroom, and a teacher supervises the cafeteria.

Children are not grouped by ability, except for 8th and 9th grade Regents classes.

Nearly half of the 8th grade class takes Regents level (9th grade) classes in Earth Science, Sequential I math, English acceleration, and

Spanish proficiency. In 9th grade, every student takes either Sequential I or II math, and half take the Biology Regents, usually given in 10th grade.

Children from outside the zone (but inside the district) are eligible for admission. Ms. Fratti says the district office chooses about thirty-five such children each year from some two hundred applicants.

JHS 185, Edward Bleeker School
147–26 25th Drive
Flushing, N.Y. 11354

Barbara Rubin, principal
718-445-3232

Reading Scores: ★★★★
Math Scores: ★★★★
Eighth Grade Regents: yes
Grade Levels: 7–9
Admissions: Neighborhood school. Doesn't accept from outside its zone.
When to Apply: Automatic registration by elementary school.

Class Size: 30
Free Lunch: 40%
Ethnicity: 33.7%W 9%B 30%H 27.3%A
Enrollment: 918
Capacity: 1162
Suspensions: 6%
Incidents: 1.5%
High School Choices: Robert F. Kennedy, Flushing, Bayside

A traditional junior high school with reading scores that put it in the top 15 percent of schools in the city, JHS 185 offers high school math to selected 7th graders. That means some children complete Regents exams for both 9th and 10th grade math before they leave 8th grade.

Its desks are in rows and teachers are at the front of the class. Textbooks are central to instruction. Discipline is strict. A traditional school with a traditional curriculum.

The school has a large bilingual program for Spanish-speaking children, and a sizable special education program. Test scores of the bilingual and special ed children, who together make up nearly one-third of population, are not included in calculating the overall test scores.

The school is the only one in the district that doesn't have a magnet program. Only children who are zoned for the school may attend. There is no provision for "school choice."

JHS 189, Daniel Carter Beard School
144–80 Barclay Avenue
Flushing, N.Y. 11355

Emily Tom, principal
718-359-6676

Reading Scores: ★★★
Math Scores: ★★★★
Eighth Grade Regents: yes
Grade Levels: 7–9
Admissions: Neighborhood
school. By application for
magnet program. January open
house.
When to Apply: N/A
Class Size: N/A

Free Lunch: 60%
Ethnicity: 9.6%W 9.3%B
30%H 51.1%A
Enrollment: 1224
Capacity: 1266
Suspensions: 11.6%
Incidents: 0.5%
High School Choices: Francis
Lewis, Flushing, Bayside

JHS 189 has a magnet grant to offer international studies and is part of the Urban Systemic Initiative, which trains teachers and kids in the latest hands-on technologies used in science and math.

The theme of international studies is carried out in the multicultural library and media center, and is integrated into regular classes in history and geography. Children operate their own weather station, work on the New York History Fair, and participate in the *Where in the World is Carmen San Diego* television show.

Ranked in the top 25 percent of middle schools in the city in terms of reading scores, JHS 189 was rated above average by the Board of Education when compared to schools with similar demographics and non-English speakers.

The principal didn't respond to my request to visit. There is limited room for children from outside the immediate zone. Prospective parents may attend an open house in January or February.

JHS 25, Adrien Block School
34–65 192nd Street
Flushing, N.Y. 11358

Dorita Gibson, principal
718-961-3480

Reading Scores: ★★★★
Math Scores: ★★★★
Eighth Grade Regents: yes
Grade Levels: 7–9
Admissions: Neighborhood
school. By application for
magnet program. January open
house.
When to Apply: N/A
Class Size: 30-33

Free Lunch: 22%
Ethnicity: 41.3%W 4.1%B
19.3%H 35.4%A
Enrollment: 1209
Capacity: 1555
Suspensions: 11.1%
Incidents: 1.2%
High School Choices: Cardozo,
Francis Lewis, Bayside

Principal Dorita Gibson describes the Adrien Block School as a "very traditional school" with "very traditional parents." It's a clean, brightly lit place, with orderly—if crowded—class changes and a principal who's confident enough about safety to leave the boys' and girls' bathrooms unlocked at all times.

There are students from sixty nations, including Korea, China, Russia, Lithuania, Greece, India, Bangladesh, Colombia, Ecuador, the Domincan Republic, and Vietnam. Ms. Gibson describes the parents as "upwardly mobile" and committed to getting their children into good high schools and good colleges. "They like to see homework. They like to see high test scores," said Ms. Gibson. She welcomes visits by prospective parents.

In each grade, the school has one class of 30 very high-achieving children in the "Intellectually Gifted Class" or IGC. Children who score in the 90th percentile or above are eligible. Each grade also has five "Special Placement" or SP classes for children in the 80th percentile or above, and five general classes.

Teachers are grouped in teams in the 7th grade, with classes of children of different abilities in each team or house. That means children get the same teachers and the same curriculum whatever track they are on. After the first marking period, children may move in or out of the honors classes, depending on their grades, while keeping the same teachers.

PTA co-president Angela Bartolini said the teachers get to know the children better with the house system. Teachers also coordinate their lessons. For example, one class read *To Kill a Mockingbird* in English class and studied the U.S. legal system in social studies at the same time.

The school has a bilingual program for Korean-speaking children, who study English and Social Studies in English with an English-speaker. But while English-speaking kids are studying Spanish and math, the Korean-speakers are pulled out for special classes in math and science taught in Korean. That way they have a great deal of exposure to English each day, but they don't fall far behind in math and science while they are learning English.

The staff is senior, and their methods of teaching are the most tried and true. Teachers are strict. I heard at least one shouting at students who were talking out of turn; desks are mostly in rows; and textbooks are central to instruction.

I saw kids copy vocabulary words in Spanish from the blackboard, underline subjects and verbs in English, and listen to a teacher read aloud from a geography textbook about changes in farming in the nineteenth century.

The school is working to implement the "new standards" curriculum, which includes more emphasis on writing poetry, essays, and short stories (rather than short paragraphs) and on reading complete works of literature (rather than excerpts from anthologies or textbooks.) Qualified 8th graders may take Regents level (9th grade) math. The math classes I visited were both lively and serious, as children wrestled with questions of probabilty with a deck of cards.

There is a nice ceramics lab, a full orchestra and band, and a dance studio.

The school has a higher-than-average suspension rate but a lower-than-average rate of incidents. Parents and students say part of the reason for the high suspension rate is the school's policy of suspending children caught fighting outside the school, not just inside the building. That makes for a higher rate on paper, but increases children's feeling of security because they know bad behavior will be punished, whether on campus or off. The parents I spoke to were confident of their children's safety.

One student complained of the strictness of the discipline—how an assistant principal barred him from attending the school prom because he was late, how one teacher sent him to the dean's office for talking in class, and another refused him permission to go to the bathroom.

Ms. Gibson makes no apologies for running a tight ship. "You can't educate without discipline," she said. "I do suspend children. In my school, you can be a wimp. I suspend for fights, and I suspend both children who are involved."

Prospective parents may visit during an open house in January or February.

JHS 237, Rachel L. Carson School
46–21 Colden Street
Flushing, N.Y. 11355

Joseph Cantara, principal
718-353-6464

Reading Scores: ★★★
Math Scores: ★★★★
Eighth Grade Regents: yes
Grade Levels: 7–9
Admissions: Neighborhood
school. By application for
magnet program. January open
house.
When to Apply: N/A
Class Size: 33

Free Lunch: 62%
Ethnicity: 13.5%W 16.4%B
20.8%H 49.2%A
Enrollment: 1329
Capacity: 1562
Suspensions: 7.4%
Incidents: 1%
High School Choices: Francis
Lewis, John Bowne, Bayside

Principal Joseph Cantara describes himself as a "junior high school principal with an elementary school philosophy." Since he took over the leadership of JHS 237 in 1995, he's worked at transforming the school into an innovative place where kids and grown-ups can take risks, and where standardized tests are not the only measure of success. He strives to supply some of the warmth and intimacy of an elementary school by dividing up the large building into "houses" in which teachers work cooperatively and have time to plan their lessons together.

The school was built in 1973, at a time when the notion of "houses" was already coming into vogue. Accordingly, the building has classrooms clustered together, with short hallways separating each cluster from the main corridors. It's clean, if not spotless, with decent lighting, and halls tiled a rich green.

"I believe in creating a place where children are excited and where teachers can try new things," Cantara said. "We're here to help kids think and to solve problems. We're not teaching to the test." Even so, the school has respectable test scores. It ranks in the top 20 percent of middle schools citywide. The Board of Education rated it "far above average," compared to schools with similar demographics. The incident and suspension rates are well below average.

When Cantara became principal, only those children who scored above average on standardized reading tests were permitted to take part in the chorus, band, art programs, or gymnastics. He opened those classes to all, believing that success in nonacademic courses can lead to success in academics. "Without the arts, we wouldn't have anything to read or write about," he said.

There is an "artists in residence" program, as well as classes in drama and dance. Cantara also encourages class trips to see dramatic performances. The whole 9th grade went to see the movie *Amistad*, as well as stage productions of *Evita* and *Romeo and Juliet*.

"School should be a happy, fun place. Schools are not just the academics," Cantara said. "We also have to concentrate on social and emotional aspects" of children's lives. One way to do that is exemplified by the "service learning" program, in which children volunteer in hospitals, libraries, and animal shelters.

In the classes I visited, the textbooks were a bit worn but the discussions were lively. Kids were excited, raising their hands, throwing out a lot of ideas as their teachers drew them out. Most of the classes had desks in rows, and the methods of instruction were generally traditional.

JHS 237 is in a blue-collar neighborhood where most families rent apartments rather than own homes. Some forty languages are spoken by the children. The latest wave of immigration is changing the school. Once, Cantara said, the new arrivals came from well-off and well-educated Chinese and Korean families, now they tend to include children from working-class families with weaker academic preparation.

Cantara believes the new approach to teaching, in line with the Middle School Initiative, is more appropriate for children who have not received a first-rate elementary education.

The challenge for Cantara is to persuade teachers, many of whom are very senior, to buy into his way of doing things. He lost one early battle: When the UFT contract relieved teachers of the responsiblity of supervising homerooms, halls, bathrooms, and the cafeteria, Cantara wasn't able to persuade them to continue on a voluntary basis. As a result, a parent leader told me, the unsupervised bathrooms on two floors had to be locked, and kids had nowhere secure to put their coats. (Coats had been put in the homerooms, with teachers on hand most of the time to make sure they were safe.) A few children's coats were stolen. Some kids started cutting class, in part because they had their coats with them and it was therefore easier to leave the school grounds.

Cantara hopes to persuade the teachers to reinstate homerooms; in the meantime, the kids have standard lockers, which seems to have solved the immediate problem of theft. And many parents and teachers are enthusiastic about his leadership. "He's very innovative," one parent leader said. "He's young at heart and that's good for the kids." Another parent, Loretta Girard, was even more enthusiastic, "He's wonderful," she said of Cantara. "I love the teachers. I love the school. I love the neighborhood."

"He's very flexible at the administrative level," said social studies teacher Steve Stroh. "It really feels like a team effort."

The school has space for a handful of children from outside its zone.

IS 250, Robert Francis Kennedy Community MS/HS
75–40 Parsons Boulevard
Flushing, N.Y. 11366

Marc P. Rosenberg, principal
718-591-3015

Reading Scores: ★★★★
Math Scores: ★★★★
Eighth Grade Regents: no
Grade Levels: 5–8
Admissions: Unzoned. By teacher recommendation and lottery. January open house.
When to Apply: N/A
Class Size: 20
Free Lunch: 22%

Ethnicity: 58.4%W 9.9%B 18%H 13.7%A
Enrollment: 161
Capacity: N/A
Suspensions: N/A
Incidents: N/A
High School Choices: Robert F. Kennedy, LaGuardia, Bayside

Robert Francis Kennedy Community Middle School was founded in 1992 as a place for underachievers of average intelligence to get a boost in a very small school with extra-small classes and especially attentive teachers. It quickly became one of the most popular schools in Queens. Parents now clamor to prove their offspring are—well— underachievers of average intelligence, so they can get in.

Principal Marc Rosenberg says the school is good for those who might get chewed up in a traditional junior high school. With only 20 kids in a class and 160 in the middle school, everyone knows everyone. The sister high school in the same building has 350 kids. That makes a nice transition for children, who may stay in the building from 5th grade all the way through 12th grade.

"Kids who might be stigmatized as nerds are accepted here. We're all a little bit different," said Rosenberg. "We've also had one or two merry-go-round kids"—students thrown out of other schools for bad behavior. What's interesting is that the troublemakers seem to settle down once they get to RFK. The school has a very low incident rate, and the suspension rate is a shade lower than average.

Rosenberg credits the intensive attention kids get, not only to their academic performance, but also to any problems they may be having at home. Safety for children leaving school is made easier by staggered dismissal times: RFK dismisses at 2:20; the high school dismisses at 2:05; and Parsons Junior High School, just down the street, dismisses at 2:40.

The school isn't limited to struggling students. It also attracts high-achieving and well-behaved children who simply don't like the anonymity and scariness of the big junior high schools. They are children who do quite well, but not as well as their teachers feel they could be doing.

"My son does well academically, but he was incredibly shy," said PTA president Debbie Fine. "He would just look down when someone called on him. Here, the teachers have the time and the experience to draw the children out."

Parents are called promptly if a child doesn't show up for school. When one student was disruptive in class, his teachers called his mother and, as a group, met with her for an hour and a half. She talked about her divorce, her child's psychological problems, the medication he'd been taking. "She realized we're not just calling to complain—that this was a genuine problem," said Rosenberg.

"Some of our more difficult kids have become the stars here," Ms. Fine added. "Put in the postion of older brother or sister [in a class with mixed ages] they come through with flying colors."

Ms. Fine believes the mixed ages, and having 5th grades in the same school as 12th grades, is part of the reason for the school's success. "We segregate kids in school, but we don't segregate them at home. At home, we expect a kindergartner to get along with a high schooler."

There are no bells, and the class changes are pleasant and uncrowded. Bathrooms are unlocked and children are allowed to use them when they please. The school has just thirteen teachers, which means the whole staff can fit around a table and talk.

Built in 1972 as a Jewish day school, the building is spotless, well-lit, and cheerful. The walls are white tiled, and cinderblocks painted yellow. There's a large gym, a nice computer lab, and a pretty art room. Space is extremely tight. A second gym has been clumsily converted into classroom space, with three or sometimes even four teachers sharing the same large area. The day I visited, the kids were surprisingly attentive, serious and quiet given the difficult physical conditions. The administration planned to install room dividers.

English and social studies are integrated. In one class, children studying Colonial American history read *The Witch of Blackbird Pond*, a novel set in 1687 about an orphaned teenager from Barbados who lives in Connecticut with an aunt. The child is accused of witchcraft and put on trial. After reading the book, the children had a mock trial.

In one math class, students were working on problems individually and in small groups, as the teacher went around the room helping each individual. In a science class, children were converting fathoms to meters and back. A social studies teacher was going over multiple choice questions in a textbook. In a Spanish class, an animated teacher was regaling everyone with his imaginary ailments: *"Tengo dolor de cabeza!"* he said, patting his head. *"Tengo dolor de estomago!"* he said, patting his belly.

"I don't think we're reinventing education," Rosenberg says. "We have a small size, and kids don't get lost. It's traditional, with some nice pieces to it." One of the "nice pieces" is the community service all children perform one morning a week for two hours. One child did volunteer work with an occupational therapist. Another worked with autistic children.

"I'm delighted we have RFK," said Ronnie Schraud, who sent two daughters to the school, one who needed extra help in reading and one who was a high achiever. "It's been the most delightful school of my life."

Although the school admits mostly kids who score average or low-average on standardized tests, it brings them along so well that the overall scores are well above average for the city. The Board of Education ranked RFK in the top 20 percent of middle schools citywide. Most of the students stay on for high school.

Children are eligible for admission if their "academic performance is not consistent with their ability and if they have been recommended for the program by adminstrators, teachers, and staff," according to a brochure. "An initial selection will be made by the Middle School staff. A final selection may be made by interview and random selection from the pool of eligible youngsters."

According to district policy, the school should have the same ethnic makeup as the district. It is disproportionately white, school officials said, because the children who apply are mostly white. There are between 200 and 250 applicants for 40 places. Anyone in the district may apply.

JHS 168, Parsons School
158–40 76th Road
Flushing, N.Y. 11366

David Mitchell, principal
718-591-9000

Reading Scores: ★★★
Math Scores: ★★★
Eighth Grade Regents: yes
Grade Levels: 7–9
Admissions: Neighborhood school. By application for magnet program. January open house.
When to Apply: N/A
Class Size: 33

Free Lunch: 49%
Ethnicity: 31.7%W 22.2%B 21.6%H 24.5%A
Enrollment: 833
Capacity: 848
Suspensions: 15%
Incidents: 1.9%
High School Choices: Robert F. Kennedy Community HS, Francis Lewis, Bayside

Parsons School has a first-rate music and dance program, a creative and energetic principal, some serious students and a cadre of excellent, dedicated teachers. The honors program, called Special Placement Enrichment, is particularly strong.

The day I visited, kids in an 8th grade honors social studies class were making their own videos about topics such as the organization of unions and the women's suffrage movement before World War I. Some 7th grade science students were using yeast to blow up a balloon. Other 7th graders were writing and illustrating their own children's books. An 8th grade English class was having a lively discussion about the author Richard Wright, and thinking about why a black American might prefer to live in Paris.

The rooms were well equipped and cheerful, with colorful bulletin boards and rich class libraries filled with novels, dictionaries, and useful reference books on grammar and style. One English teacher takes classes to the theater in Manhattan. Students have community service projects in nursing homes, at police stations, and working with handicapped children.

Regents level classes are offered in Earth Science and Sequential I math. "At other schools, only the hand-picked, select few can take the Regents exam," says Principal David Mitchell. "Here, anyone who wants to can sign up."

The school has created an extensive performing arts program made possible by a magnet grant. Students attend dance workshops in the school and visit City Center to see performances by the Martha Graham and Twyla Tharp companies and others. A drama specialist teaches improvisation and pantomine; helps children write and direct their own plays, movies and videos; and takes children to see live theater productions. The music department has both instrumental and vocal programs and children are exposed to classical, pop, jazz, electronic, and modern musical forms.

The principal impressed me as a soft-spoken, sweet man who clearly loves his job, his kids, and his staff. The class changes I saw were orderly, the school isn't overwhelmingly big, and the place felt safe.

Mitchell said the high school's suspension rate reflects its careful adherence to district policy on discipline and its policy of reporting every problem. "We're stricter, and we don't let kids get away with anything," he said. Kids told me they felt safe, and that incidents included such things as fistfights and thefts of jackets—unpleasant, but, as one girl said, "not weapons, or anything like that." Mitchell is exploring alternatives to suspension that will keep kids in school, while still holding them accountable for bad behavior. For example, kids who misbehave may be required to stay after school to help school custodians with various errands.

The impression I got from my visit, and from interviews with parents, is that the school has its share of goofy, immature kids, but that kids who are serious can get a good education from its many imaginative teachers and rich programs in the arts.

Prospective parents may attend an open house in January.

District 26

District 26 in northeast Queens, which includes the prosperous communities of Bayside, Little Neck, and Douglaston, has the highest test scores in the city. Every single school in the district consistently scores well above the national average on standardized reading tests. Parents buy houses in this district just because of the schools.

The district has a suburban feel, with single-family houses, large yards and big shade trees, particularly in the neighborhoods that border on Long Island Sound. But, unlike Nassau County, just over the city line, this section of Queens hasn't totally succumbed to car culture and shopping malls. The old villages retain their pre-automobile charm, and it's possible to buy a quart of milk without first climbing into a car. Many families own only one car and the adults commute to Manhattan via the Long Island Railroad. New immigrants from Korea, China, and Japan have moved into the district in recent years.

Children are assigned to neighborhood schools according to their address. Parents are welcome to visit schools during open houses held in the winter, and there is some room for movement within the district. Children may apply to a school outside their zone, space permitting. There is occasionally room for students from outside the district. Unfortunately, there are usually three to four times as many out-of-district applicants as seats. Call Joan Gewurz at the district office, 718-631-6900 for information about variances—special permission to attend a school outside your zone.

JHS 216, George Ryan School
64–20 175th Street
Fresh Meadows, N.Y. 11365

Janice Imundi, principal
718-358-2005

Reading Scores: ★★★★
Math Scores: ★★★★★
Eighth Grade Regents: yes
Grade Levels: 6–9
Admissions: Neighborhood
    school. By application and
    lottery from outside zone.
    January open house.
When to Apply: N/A
Class Size: 30

Free Lunch: 27%
Ethnicity: 23.2%W 19.1%B
    15.7%H 42.1%A
Enrollment: 1160
Capacity: 1121
Suspensions: 9.6%
Incidents: 2.1%
High School Choices: Francis
    Lewis, Benjamin Cardozo,
    Jamaica

George Ryan Junior High School ranks in the top 10 percent of middle schools citywide. Its test scores are well above average, and a large proportion of students master high school math and science while still in 8th grade. Nearly 20 percent of its graduates go to the prestigious Benjamin Cardozo High School in Bayside, and another 20 percent go to the specialized high schools or to the specialized programs called educational option schools.

In any other district, Ryan would be the crown jewel. But in District 26, parents have treated the school like a poor relation. Its gloomy physical plant—yellow walls, gray tiles and not-quite-adequate lighting—and high rates of suspensions and incidents have contributed to Ryan's less than stellar reputation. The proportion of children suspended for misbehavior, while about average for the city, is double the district-wide average.

On the other hand, the school has some energetic and talented teachers, and the program in English as a second language is inspiring. Children in ESL gain proficiency in English at twice the rate of the city schools as a whole.

Ryan offers a refuge for some children from low-performing schools in adjoining districts. The school is not terribly overcrowded, and generally has room for a dozen children from outside its immediate zone.

I visited the school before the new principal, Janice Imundi, took the reins. She planned to divide the school into three "academies"—a move which, if properly done, may improve discipline considerably. In other schools that have successfully adopted the principles of the Middle School Initiative, behavior problems decrease because grown-ups can keep track of kids better and children feel they belong to a small school where everyone knows everyone.

One of the proposed mini-schools—an Academy of Medical Sciences—sounds particularly interesting. The plan called for professors from Queens College medical school to offer classes at Ryan.

The school has an open house for prospective parents in January.

MS 158, Marie Curie School
46–35 Oceania Street
Bayside, N.Y. 11361

Anita Gomez-Palacio, principal
718-423-8100

Reading Scores: ★★★★
Math Scores: ★★★★★
Eighth Grade Regents: yes
Grade Levels: 6–9
Admissions: Neighborhood
school. By application and
lottery, from outside zone.
January open house.
When to Apply: N/A
Class Size: 32-38

Free Lunch: 27%
Ethnicity: 33.9%W 12.8%B
11.9%H 41.4%A
Enrollment: 1179
Capacity: 1282
Suspensions: 3.1%
Incidents: 0.4%
High School Choices:
Benjamin Cardozo, Francis
Lewis, Bayside

If you ignore the size of the kids and the sophisticated level of their work, you might think you were in an elementary school when you first walk into Marie Curie Middle School. Colorful bulletin boards cover the walls. Mobiles made by the kids and construction paper projects hang by clothespins on strings from the ceiling.

Bins of fun-to-read books, ranging from biographies of sports figures to teen romances, and manipulatives (specially-designed plastic blocks used to teach math) fill the classrooms.

In some classes, desks are pushed together in groups and kids are working together quietly on projects. Classes don't change every forty-three minutes. Instead, children may stay in a class for several hours, studying history and English with one teacher.

Marie Curie was one of the first schools in the city to switch from being a junior high school to a middle school. Now, with a decade's experience adopting the principles of the Middle School Initiative, the administration and staff are comfortable with the new ways of organizing the day and the new ways of introducing material.

Principal Anita Gomez-Palacio, who has led the school since 1995, says the new methods are more appropriate for young adolescents than were traditional junior high schools with desks in rigid arrangements and teachers lecturing from textbooks.

"Adolescents love to talk," Ms. Gomez-Palacio says. "Adolescents love to intereact. Adolescents love to show off. We try to have children work together on projects" to channel that energy productively.

Junior high schools, she says, are "content-oriented." That is, children are expected to master a body of knowledge on which they are tested at the end of the year. Middle schools, on the other hand, are "child-oriented." That is, teachers try to adopt their methods to accommodate each child's different way of learning. For example, children are allowed to select books that interest them or to write on topics of their own choosing, rather than reading from textbooks. "You've got to teach them the content no matter what," said Ms. Gomez-Palacio. "But the question is, how do children learn? Not all children learn the same way."

The school still has many of the trappings of a traditional junior high school. The halls are extremely crowded during class changes, and the principal patrols with a walkie-talkie to keep in touch with the distant office. There are still many teachers who feel most comfortable with aligned desks and formal lessons, particularly in math and science, and particularly in the 8th and 9th grades. Some parents complain that giant class size mean kids don't get individual attention. On my tour, I saw some ancient lab tables and some bored kids.

But the administration makes attempts to give children a sense of belonging, to break through the anonymity common to junior high schools. Once a week, pupils meet with a teacher and nine other children for an "advisory" to talk about any problems they may be having in school or out. "This is the way we try to see children bond with one adult in the school," Ms. Gomez-Palacio said.

The children are organized into teams of four or five classes. Each team shares the same teachers, and the teachers meet regularly to discuss their lessons, to plan trips and interdisciplinary projects, and to talk about their students. Parents are welcome to attend the team meetings.

"I like what they do for the individual child," said Kathy Nadime, a parent who gave me my tour of the school. "It's not as if the child is just passing through. The teachers know the child, his strengths and weak points."

The building is well kept and properly lit and, although it was built in the charm-free architectural style of the 1950s, it doesn't have the prisonlike atmosphere of so many junior high schools.

Staff morale has improved since Ms. Gomez-Palacio became principal, offering stability after a few years of rapid turnover in leadership. The rate of suspensions, once above average for the district, has dropped dramatically. The staff has voted to keep homeroom and teachers volunteer to supervise the cafeteria, eliminating a possible source of disorder.

In the 6th grade, children study reading, writing, and history with one core teacher, and change classes for other subjects. The "core" teachers integrate English and social studies, so that students might read an historical novel set in the Middle Ages, about a boy who becomes a knight in England and saves his father from the Scots.

In the upper grades, children have different teachers for each subject, but many projects involve several disciplines. In a 7th grade math class, children wrote papers on the discoveries of famous mathematicians and in science they wrote about the lives of scientists such as Thomas Edison and Louis Pasteur. One 8th grade history teacher brought her subject matter alive with the kind of gritty details that young adolescents love. The kids were assigned to write and illustrate a report about a social problem that existed at the end of the nineteenth century, and the Progressive Era laws that were passed to alleviate it. They wrote about child labor, poor housing, and sanitation. The teacher gently drew them out as they discussed their reports.

"If you wanted to go to the bathroom, you had to go outside to an outhouse in the middle of Manhattan," she said. "There were no washing machines, no garbage collection. Imagine the smell in the middle of summer. The heat is beaming down on you and you have garbage in the street." Textbooks were supplemented with contemporary accounts by Jacob Riis and Upton Sinclair, as well as videotapes on the history of settlement houses.

Staff development is an important part of Marie Curie. The day I visited, English teachers met with a teacher-trainer from Teachers College to learn the Writing Process, the new technique for teaching writing. Children share their drafts with each other, and offer suggestions for changes. In this way, they learn to write for an audience, rather than just the teacher. The topics come from the children themselves. A child who is interested in sports may write a biography of a sports figure. One who is interested in fiction may invent his own stories.

The school has a "gifted magnet program," for children who graduated from the gifted class of PS 31, a nearby elementary school. The "gifted" children scored in the 97th percentile or above in their elementary school. The rest of the 6th grade mixes children of different abilities.

In 7th grade, children are placed in "Special Progress Enrichment"

(SPE) or a general academic track, based on their achievement in 6th grade. Most SPE students score in the 80th percentile or above.

Some children, particularly those in the "gifted magnet program," leave the school after 6th grade for Hunter High School in Manhattan. That opens up a few spots—sometimes as many as twelve—in the 7th grade gifted magnet program.

In addition, the school has room for a dozen or so children from outside the immediate zone in its regular and SPE classes. Under the terms of the federal magnet grant to encourage racial integration, preference is given to white children living in District 26.

The school has an extensive after-school program, as well as some Saturday and summer classes.

Prospective parents may attend an open house in January.

MS 67, Louis Pasteur
51–60 Marathon Parkway
Little Neck, N.Y. 11362

Mae Fong, principal
718-423-8138

Reading Scores: ★★★★★
Math Scores: ★★★★★
Eighth Grade Regents: yes
Grade Levels: 6–9
Admissions: Neighborhood school. Generally doesn't accept from outside zone. January open house.
When to Apply: N/A
Class Size: 27-34

Free Lunch: 13%
Ethnicity: 43.4%W 10.5%B 8.9%H 37.2%A
Enrollment: 1189
Capacity: 1357
Suspensions: 2.2%
Incidents: 0.2%
High School Choices:
Benjamin Cardozo, Bronx Science, Stuyvesant

Louis Pasteur seems to have it all: A lush country-club campus complete with tennis courts and softball fields. Science labs, a full band and orchestra, and a well-equipped library. Hard-working, serious, high-achieving kids. An involved parent body, a dynamic principal, and teachers who love their assignments so much, they feel as if they've died and gone to heaven. "The number one school in the number one district," principal Mae Fong says simply. It's easy to see why people buy houses in Little Neck just to send their kids to MS 67, and on to one of the best neighborhood high schools in the city, Benjamin Cardozo.

For those who want to send their kids to specialized high schools, MS 67 paves the way: More than one-third of the 8th graders are offered spots either at the selective science schools—Bronx Science, Stuyvesant and Brooklyn Tech—or the selective school for humanities, Townsend Harris in Queens.

The school has a suburban feel. It's spotless and shiny, with cheerful yellow wall tiles and wide corridors. It's an orderly place. Rules of conduct are clearly outlined in a student handbook given to all entering students. Class changes are smooth and quiet, and children settle down quickly to study at the beginning of lessons. Discipline is strict, which parents appreciate even if some of the kids may chafe a bit.

Consistent rules—such as no hats or coats in school—help keep the school safe.

"The deans stand at the door and say: 'Coat! Take it off!' " says Carol Wilk, a parent. "They may be abrasive but it works. I see their strictness as a godsend." In many respects, Louis Pasteur is a traditional junior high school. Class changes are marked by bells. Children are tracked by ability, with the gifted classes reserved for the top 2 to 3 percent of the students (who move up as a class from the district's elementary school gifted program at nearby PS 221), "special progress" for those in the top 20 percent; regular academic for average students; special education for those with special needs. It's a big school and, unlike most of the the rest of middle schools in the city, it has retained its 9th grade.

Teachers emphasize the basic skills of grammar and spelling, and much time is spent on test preparation. Many classes have desks in rows, and textbooks are central to instruction. The staff is very senior, and many keep to time-tested teaching methods. But the administration also keeps abreast of the times. Teachers are encouraged to go back to school for training, and new teaching methods are introduced when they seem appropriate.

Several teachers have adopted the University of Chicago Math Project, which shows students that there's more than one way to solve a problem. A 6th grade teacher, for example, might help students find three ways to compare fractions: changing them to decimals, making them into fractions with the same denominator, or multiplying the denominators by the opposite numerators.

Three 6th grade teachers have studied the Writing Process with Lucy Calkins at Teachers' College. They encourage students to keep their own journals, which the teachers don't grade. The hope is that allowing children some leeway to write from the heart, without fear of being graded, enourages them to stretch their writing.

The school has adopted many of the principles of the Middle School Initiative. Instead of changing classes every period, 6th graders have three periods of English and social studies in one room with the same teacher. Math and science are taught by specialists.

"They have one teacher who knows them particularly well," says Assistant Principal Kenneth Morris. "And that teacher has sixty students instead of 120 or more."

In seventh grade, the school is organized into "houses" or "minischools" of four classes each. Math, science, English and social studies teachers work as a team, and children stay in their house for most subjects. The teachers have time set aside during the day to plan lessons together.

Even though the new teachers' contract relieves teachers of homeroom and cafeteria duty, Pasteur teachers have voted to retain homerooms, and one teacher patrols the lunchroom. Teachers are also on the sidewalks before and after school to make sure kids come and go safely.

"Mae Fong is an excellent educator and a good administrator," says Dalia Blanco, whose two sons attended the school. "This lady goes in at six or seven in the morning and doesn't leave until late in the afternoon. She's very reachable and very approachable. It's a very strict school, and it's really a place kids go to learn and not to fool around."

The school concentrates on academics more than on children's social and emotional development. Parents I spoke to say the atmosphere is competitive but that the children seem to handle the competition well.

"It's a traditional community with very high expectations," said Ms. Fong. "We fit into the cultural values of our community." Parents say the various ethnic groups, including Chinese, Korean, Jewish, and Iranian, get along well.

Ms. Fong, who started her career teaching chemistry at Stuyvesant High School, is admired for her loyalty to her teachers. Once, a minicontroversy erupted in a local newspaper after a teacher, as part of a project on the legal system, took children to a criminal court where they heard some sexually explicit testimony in a rape trial. Some community members complained that the teacher had acted inappropriately, but Ms. Fong defended her. "She has some backbone," said one father. "She stuck by her teachers."

Ms. Blanco admires the changes Ms. Fong instituted after she became principal in 1991. Although the school always had good test scores, it was poorly equipped and maintained, and had developed a reputation for stale teaching and a disorderly atmosphere. "The roof was leaky. The fence was broken and stayed broken for years," Ms. Blanco said. "She got new furniture, new desks, and fixed the tiles."

Ms. Fong opened the music and art rooms that had been closed, encouraged the staff to receive training in new teaching methods, and brought the school up to date in computer technology. There is now an extensive music program, with a chorus in each grade, the orchestra, and band, a jazz band and a pep squad.

Law is one of the themes of the school. Children study the U.S. legal system and the Constitution, visit the state supreme court in

Queens, and apply what they learn to organizing their own system of justice within the school. In a peer mediation program, for example, children act as "prosecutors" and "defenders" in resolving disputes among pupils. Children wrote their own Bill of Rights for the school, outlining what they said was their right to be treated fairly regardless of race or academic achievement.

Children who live in the school zone, which includes Little Neck and Douglaston, are automatically admitted, as are those in the gifted program at PS 221. No children from outside the district are admitted (except those already attending District 26 schools). A few children from outside the immediate zone (but within the district) are admitted by a lottery organized by the district office.

There are no organized tours, but prospective parents are enouraged to contact the guidance counselor to arrange a visit. The school has an open house in January.

MS 172, Irwin Altman School
81–14 257 Street
Floral Park, N.Y. 11004

Dr. Barry Friedman, principal
718-831-4000

Reading Scores: ★★★★
Math Scores: ★★★★★
Eighth Grade Regents: yes
Grade Levels: 6–9
Admissions: Neighborhood school. By application and lottery from outside zone. January open house.
When to Apply: N/A
Class Size: 27-37

Free Lunch: 19%
Ethnicity: 36.1%W 14.5%B 14.3%H 35.2%A
Enrollment: 1237
Capacity: 1369
Suspensions: 4.5%
Incidents: 0.2%
High School Choices: Martin Van Buren, Cardozo, Bayside

Walk into MS 172, and you might see the principal chatting with students in the hall, or a teacher with his arm draped around a child's shoulder. You'll see classrooms with plants, fish tanks, rabbits and gerbils; a video studio decorated with movie posters; and an art studio where kids are splattering paint in the style of Jackson Pollock.

Floral Park is a sleepy, residential community with big trees and modest single-family homes. Once made up primarily of families of Irish and Italian descent, it now has a large number of recent immigrants from India and Pakistan.

MS 172's building is a drab, standard-issue junior high built in the 1950s, with gray tiles, green walls, and just adequate lighting. But somehow, despite the gloomy surroundings, the school manages to be a cheerful place. Parents credit the leadership of Barry Friedman, who became principal in 1997. "I think Barry has brought a lot of sunshine in," says Dave Chowdhury, whose two children attended the school. "He's involved. He loves his job. He interacts with the children." "He's a genuine, caring person," says PTA co-chair Elaine Davidow. "He's out in the hallways, he's outside after school, he's not in his office behind a computer. Students talk to him and he loves it."

Teachers, too, are willing to talk to pupils after class, and eager to learn about new teaching techniques. "There's a warmth between the staff and the children that you don't find in other schools," says assistant principal Helaine Kobrin. "The teachers are very eager to buy into staff development. They don't ask, 'What am I going to get paid for it.' They ask, 'What am I going to learn?' "

Friedman is a traditionalist when it comes to discipline. The school's suspension rate went up when he took over, parents say, because he cracked down on violations of the discipline code that had been ignored in the past. When a girl wore a too-short skirt to school one day, the school called the girl's mother and asked her to bring in more appropriate clothing. Parents say they appreciate the security that strict discipline offers. "I think the most important aspect is the tone of the school—a sense of safety, discipline and order," says Ms. Davidow.

The academic program is traditional as well. Teachers concentrate on study skills and preparation for tests. Many rely on textbooks as the major source of reading material. Class changes are noisy and crowded, as children shift from one subject to another in the large building.

The academic program is evolving, however, as the school adopts the Middle School Initiative. MS 172 is experimenting with team-teaching and block-programming, which will allow children to study a subject—say, a combined class in English and history—for a whole morning, rather than a forty-minute period. The block scheduling will also cut down on the human traffic jams in the halls during class changes.

Already, some teachers have integrated English and history so that children studying ancient civilizations might read a mystery story set in ancient Egypt. Children studying the American Revolution might read an historical novel about a young man who joined the Minute-men although his father was loyal to England.

In science, many teachers supplement textbooks with hands-on learning. One teacher encourages children to care for animals in the classroom. Another teaches about vacuums by lighting a candle inside an overturned beaker placed in a dish of water. When the oxygen is gone, the candle goes out, and the water rises in the beaker.

Friedman, who has a Ph.D. in educational research from Hofstra and who teaches at Adelphi, is familar with the latest teaching methods but is not a sucker for fads. Parents say he has a good handle on which teachers are performing well, and which ones need help.

The principal says he is dedicated to offering wide opportunities to all children, from those in the advanced "special progress" class to those in special education.

"Special education is very integrated," Friedman says. "Every one of my children is mainstreamed"—integrated with other classes for nonacademic subjects. He also hopes to arrange schedules so children who are not in "special progress" classes will be allowed to take Regents exams.

The school has room for a handful of children from outside the district, admitted under the provisions of a federal magnet grant to achieve racial integration.

Prospective parents may visit during an open house in January.

MS 74, Nathaniel Hawthorne School
61–15 Oceania Street
Bayside, N.Y. 11364

Michael Mazun, principal
718-631-6800

Reading Scores: ★★★★★
Math Scores: ★★★★★
Eighth Grade Regents: yes
Grade Levels: 6–8
Admissions: Neighborhood
school. By application and
lottery from outside zone.
January open house.
When to Apply: N/A
Class Size: 31–38

Free Lunch: 21%
Ethnicity: 34.7%W 19.7%B
8.7%H 37%A
Enrollment: 1104
Capacity: 940
Suspensions: 3.4%
Incidents: 0.5%
High School Choices:
Benjamin Cardozo, Bronx
Science, Stuyvesant

The kids were on the floor with a glue gun, putting together corrugated cardboard walls for their model of the Lower East Side at the
turn of the last century. You could see a tiny scale model of the
Eldridge Street Synagogue, the Grand Theater, and the Kletzer
Brotherly Aid Association, each with careful renderings of every architectural detail. The project was part of an elaborate study that incorporated history, math, writing and art—typical of the interdisciplinary
work that makes Nathaniel Hawthorne School such an interesting and
appealing place. This study began with a trip to the Tenement
Museum on the Lower East Side of Manhattan, to study the history of
the neighborhood. They students used math to make the scale models,
kept journals about their work, and put the whole thing together in
the art room. "They learn that everything has a connection, and that
everything has a purpose somewhere else," said art teacher Mary
Belfi.

Michael Shyman, who retired as principal in 1999, built his school
on the belief that there should be more to school than racing through
the curriculum to pass a test at the end of the year. "We used to teach
kids a lot of stuff—facts, concepts. But teaching kids to think was not
really a considered thing," he told me on my tour. At Nathaniel
Hawthorne, children are challenged to come up with their own solu-

tions to problems. Teachers work in teams, go in and out of one another's classrooms, or chat informally in common rooms adjacent to their classes.

When you walk around the school, you can't always figure out what subject the kids are studying, and that's part of the charm of the place. Those kids on the floor of the corridor, putting, together a cardboard Sphinx and pyramid—is that a geography project or an art project? And that puppet show about the charge of the Redcoats, is that drama or history? What about the skit on how industrialization in the nineteenth century changed the roles of women and family life? Those kids with the video camera in the hallway, what are they up to? What's going on in the former woodworking shop, where kids are growing plants in gravel and water?

Trips are an important starting point for many lessons. Kids might take a trip to Great Adventure theme park, then build a cardboard scale model of an amusement park with rides that actually work, and study the principles of acceleration in the process.

To study the development of industry and commerce in the nineteenth century, kids might go to Mystic Seaport in Connecticut and return to build a scale model of a nineteenth century fishing village from (you guessed it) corrugated cardboard. "The biggest sin in this building is throwing away a piece of cardboard," Shyman said.

The kids seem to be having a good time, but the school isn't just fun and games. You see traditional classrooms, as well, with desks in ranks and teachers lecturing at the front. "We do have chalk-and-talk. It's necessary," said Shyman. Throughout, kids seem cheerful and attentive. In one math class, kids cooed, "Oh, cool," as the teacher explained a formula on the board. A weekly class is about how to take notes, how to study efficiently, and the basics of how to look things up in the library.

The proportion of students taking and passing accelerated courses in math and science is comparable to other high-ranking District 26 schools: 14 percent took the 9th grade Sequential I math exam and 20 percent took the 9th grade science exam in the 8th grade.

The school has a federal magnet grant to maintain racial integration, and with the grant goes the unwieldly name of Magnet School of Global Communication and Information Studies. The school is well equipped, with computers and video equipment. It has a high-speed Internet connection. New digital cameras are used to photograph children's artwork and store it on computer disks.

The day I visited, kids were using a CD-ROM encyclopedia to look up primary source material on slavery in the American South, including an invoice for a slave purchase and fliers for a slave auction. Other children were working on various mini-documentaries for their video teachers on topics such as drug abuse by parents, giving kids tips on where to go for help.

Video teacher Harvey Kay said making videos strengthens children's academic skills as they write scripts and time segments to the fraction of a second. They also learn less tangible skills such as patience, self-control, and seeing a project through to its conclusion, he said. The work draws in children who might otherwise lose interest in school. "You can always capture the honor roll kids, but most schools tend to roll over the kids who are not ready," Kay said. "This helps engage that youngster who normally doesn't feel wonderful about himself."

In a woodworking lab that's been converted to a technology lab, teacher Eric Steinberg echoed that sentiment. "It's not the end product—the candy dish or the end table," he says. "It's learning how to do it that counts. It doesn't have to be something the parent puts on the coffee table. Let the kids run with it. If they make a mistake, it's not the end of the world."

The school, alas, has many of the problems common to New York City schools. Classes are large. Half have more than 33 pupils, and some reach 38. Class changes are horrible, and the halls are so crowded that a certain amount of jostling is inevitable. Students acting as "hall guards" try to direct traffic.

As in most other city schools, homerooms have been eliminated, although there is a brief "attendance period." Teachers no longer do cafeteria duty. Bathrooms are occasionally scarred with grafitti. Some desks are so old they could be museum pieces—if only they were museum quality.

The principal, like his colleagues, must accept teacher transfers to his school based on seniority and isn't allowed to hire his own staff. But Shyman, like his most clever colleagues, used what he calls "magic and lying" to get his preferred candidates. A favorite trick: He advertised openings in licenses that nobody has, such as home economics. When no one applied, he hired whomever he pleased and assigned the new teacher to do whatever was needed.

There is room for sixty to eighty kids from outside the zone each year. Shyman said children are accepted more or less at random, but adds, "I'm not going to bring a child in who has caused havoc."

Children in special education are mainstreamed for nonacademic subjects.

The school has an early morning gifted and talented program, and extended after-school programs, as well as optional Saturday and summer classes.

District 27

District 27, which includes Howard Beach, Ozone Park, Richmond Hill, and the Rockaway peninsula, is an overcrowded district whose test scores range from average to abysmal. The district has long suffered a brain drain of its best middle school students to schools in Brooklyn and other parts of Queens.

That may change in the coming years. The district has adopted the Middle School Initiative, which attempts to break big, factorylike junior high schools into smaller and more manageable "houses" in which teachers work in teams and children stay together with their classmates as they change classes for different subjects.

In a traditional junior high school, a child might have English on the first floor, math on the third floor, and science on the second floor. Class changes can be chaotic, and teachers never get a chance to talk to one another. On the other hand, in a house system, where teachers are organized in teams, five teachers are clustered together along a corridor. Children stay within their "house" for all classes. Teachers have common preparation periods, so they have a chance to meet regularly to discuss children's work.

When it works, the result is higher attendance rates, decreased rates of suspension, and incidents and improved staff morale. Reading scores in the district are still disappointing—the three mainland middle schools have reading scores that are merely average, and the three on the Rockaway peninsula range from average to bleak. And there's still lots of room for improvement in the safety department. But the district seems to be moving in the right direction.

For high-achieving students, the benefit of District 27 is class size. The "gifted" programs have far smaller classes than is typical in middle schools—22 or 24 kids.

The district welcomes school visits, and encourages parents to shop around for the best program for their child. It publishes a brochure on middle school choice. Call the Middle School coordinator Joel Rosenweig at 718-642-5819. The district and the schools have open houses for prospective parents in the fall.

JHS 226 at 121-10 Rockaway Boulevard, South Ozone Park, 11440, has steadily rising tests scores and a good safety record under the strong leadership of Principal Rhia Warren. The school has pupils from sixty-five countries and the city's only bilingual class in Punjabi. The building is gigantic—more than 1900 kids jammed into a school designed for 1683—but the architectural design is conducive to team-teaching. Each group of four classrooms is clustered on a mini-wing, separated by a wall from the rest of the building. Ms. Warren, whose office is filled with stuffed animals and pots of flowers, has a warmth and dedication that seems to spread through the building. Parents help as volunteers. The school's telephone is 718-843-2260.

The Advanced Learning Institute housed in IS 53 at 1045 Nameoke Street, Far Rockaway, 11691, is a first-rate gifted program inside an otherwise low-performing and chaotic middle school on the Rockaway peninsula. About half the students in the gifted programs are recent immigrants from Afghanistan, Korea, Jamaica, Barbados and other countries. The program successfully prepares kids for the city's most selective high schools, including Brooklyn Tech and Townsend Harris, and some children win scholarships to private boarding schools. Particularly impressive was a math teacher, John Johnson, who spends his lunch period teaching kids advanced topics such as Euclidian geometry and quadratic equations. Principal Charlotte Powell can be reached at 718-471-6900.

An experimental program worth watching is the Capt. Michael Healy Maritime Academy, housed in JHS 198, 365 Beach 56th St., Arverne, 11692. In this program, housed in another low-performing school on the Rockaway peninsula, regular classroom instruction is combined with frequent field trips to coast guard stations. On one trip, children visited the "vessel traffic service" on Staten Island and learned how the coast guard guides boats through New York Harbor much as an air traffic controller clears airplanes for takeoff and landing. Principal Beth Longo can be reached at 718-945-3300.

The Active Learning Prep School (ALPS), at JHS 180, 320 Beach 104th Street, 11694, is the brainchild of program director Patricia Tubridy. This small program, with 150 students, has an intimate atmosphere. One classroom has a rocking chair and overstuffed armchairs. Classes are small and include children of all abilities. Parents must sign a contract promising to attend teacher conferences and to participate in various activities, such as a family astronomy night at a local restaurant, when teachers, parents, and children gaze at Saturn through telescopes.

Children explore their own beach community on frequent class trips. A research boat from City University of New York took the youngsters across Jamaica Bay. The children studied the history of the bay and learned how to read maritime maps and how to test the water for cleanliness.

Teachers use trips to introduce textbook material. The day I visited, 6th graders had just returned from a visit to the Native American Museum in Manhattan. They compared how Spanish explorers were portrayed in their textbooks with how they were portrayed in the museum. The program was founded with support from New Visions for Public Schools, the Manhattan-based reform organization. ALPS is an Expeditionary Learning Center, part of a network of alternative schools. Contact JHS 180 Principal Robert Spata at 718-634-1555 for details.

District 28

District 28, which includes the mansions of Forest Hills and the modest bungalows of Jamaica, is a district divided by race and class. There are, unfortunately, frequent quarrels between school board members representing the northern, richer, and whiter end of the district and those representing the southern, poorer and blacker end. Huge numbers of immigrants from Asia and the former Soviet Union have moved to the district in recent years, particularly to Rego Park, a pleasant middle-class neighborhood where large apartment buildings are shaded by trees and shrubs.

The district is badly overcrowded, and parents are strongly encouraged to send their children to their neighborhood school. Some folks lie about their address to get their child into a better school—but it's risky. One mother told me a school actually sent a truant officer to her home to see if she lived there. The official, called an attendance teacher, demanded to look in the closets to see if there were enough clothes and toys to demonstrate that she was in permanent residence, not merely visiting.

The district gives out a handful of variances for children to attend school outside their zone, but be prepared to have a good reason for the transfer. Variances are generally given only if a child's health and safety is endangered at his neighborhood school. Forget about getting your child in from out of district.

There is one unzoned school open to everyone in the district, the Gateway to Health Services Secondary School.

The district office telephone number is 718-830-8800.

JHS 157, Stephen Halsey School
64th Avenue and 102nd Street
Rego Park, N.Y. 11374

Martin Mayerson, principal
718-830-4910

Reading Scores: ★★★★
Math Scores: ★★★★
Eighth Grade Regents: yes
Grade Levels: 6–9
Admissions: Neighborhood school. Doesn't accept from outside zone.
When to Apply: Automatic registration by elementary school.
Class Size: 30-33

Free Lunch: 48%
Ethnicity: 48.9%W 14%B 15.4%H 21.8%A
Enrollment: 1806
Capacity: 1534
Suspensions: 6.6%
Incidents: 0.3%
High School Choices: Forest Hills, Stuyvesant, Bowne

More than one hundred tiny flags of the United Nations decorate the walls of the entry hall at JHS 157, representing of the countries of origin of the pupils at this pleasant but extremely overcrowded school. "It's why everyone gets along so well," said Assistant Principal Richard Dodici as he swept his arm in an arc past the flags. "Everybody here is from somewhere else." About one in six children at JHS 157 has arrived in the United States in the past three years; about one-fifth have limited proficiency in English.

The children come from Korea, India, Pakistan, Bangladesh, Russia and Georgia, among many other countries, and speak 43 different languages. Teachers carry a list of dozens of religious holidays so when a child misses school, the staff can tell whether the excuse of a religious holiday was real or made up.

The school is traditional in many respects. Children are tracked by ability. Bells mark the end of classes, and children must move from one end of the huge building to the other side to change classes.

Principal Martin Mayerson said he experimented with the idea of houses. It worked well in the 6th grade, he said, but he abandoned the house system in the upper grades because it didn't give the flexibility necessary to group children by ability. "We have kids who are just off the boat, and we have kids who are four or five years above grade level," Mayerson said. "How can you put them in the same class and do justice to them?" A new immigrant with limited knowledge of English might be assigned to a slow class for language arts and social studies but to an advanced class for math where language skills are not as important.

The halls of the school are about as appealing as a poorly lit factory, but the classrooms are cheerful and bright. The atmosphere is relaxed, and class discussions are more common than straight lectures. The 6th grade is in a new wing. It feels more like an elementary school than a typical junior high school, with colorful bulletin boards and projects made out of cardboard decorating the classrooms. The library is cheerful, if a bit run down, and decorated with kids' Rube Goldberg machines made out of papier-mâché.

"A lot of times, the more noise you hear, the more things are going on," Dodici said. "This is not a convent school. The kids should be buzzing. There should be interaction in the classroom. Kids, when they walk around, should be talking."

Most children walk to school, which gives the place a feeling of community. Children feel loyalty to JHS 157 even after they graduate. The day I visited, a boy who had graduated returned to tell the principal he'd been accepted to college. Dodici describes the parents as "very concerned, very active and very involved."

Whatever the staff is doing, it seems to be working: The school has a better than average record of teaching English to new arrivals. Reading scores put it in the top 20 percent of middle schools citywide. About two-thirds of the school's graduates go to the highly regarded neighborhood high school, Forest Hills, and a dozen or so go to Stuyvesant. The suspension rate is high, but the rate of incidents is low.

Dodici says the school's biggest problem is overcrowding. "For a while we had students without chairs. Kids were sitting on tables, on window ledges." When I visited, all the children had desks, but the school is nevertheless very, very big and crowded.

Admission is generally limited to children living in the school zone, although it's no secret that parents lie about their addresses to get

their children in. There's an open house for parents in May, but Mayerson said he welcomes visits anytime. "Come and see the school the
way it is," he said. "Come in without an appointment. I try not to put
on a show."

JHS 190, Russell Sage
68–17 Austin Street
Forest Hills, N.Y. 11375

Stuart Mulnick, principal
718-830-4970

Reading Scores: ★★★★
Math Scores: ★★★★
Eighth Grade Regents: yes
Grade Levels: 7–9
Admissions: Neighborhood
school. Doesn't accept from
outside zone.
When to Apply: Automatic
registration by elementary
school.

Class Size: 33
Free Lunch: 33%
Ethnicity: 42.1%W 7.6%B
19.3%H 31%A
Enrollment: 1410
Capacity: 1263
Suspensions: 4.6%
Incidents: 0.6%
High School Choices: Forest
Hills, Hillcrest, Brooklyn Tech

Stuart Mulnick is an old-fashioned junior high school principal and proud of it. His school, Russell Sage Junior High School, hasn't changed its teaching methods or style of discipline much since it was first opened in the 1950s.

It's a clean and brightly lit building. You'll see desks in rows and teachers reading aloud from textbooks, quizzing kids on geography facts and dates in history, administering fill-in-the-blank quizzes on parts of the respiratory system. There's a nice feeling of camaraderie among the faculty, and a rapport between teachers and kids.

"Our school works wonderfully," says Mulnick "Why change it?" One way the school has changed: Immigration has brought children from dozens of countries around the globe, particularly from China, India, Russia, and Bangladesh. Mulnick says the children and parents are highly motivated. "The kids are like sponges. The parents say in broken English, 'How do I get my child into Stuyvesant?' "

Children are tracked according to their ability. In the highest track, called "enrichment" or E track, children stay together for all their classes. In other tracks—A, B, and C—children may be assigned a high class for one subject and a low class for another. Bells mark class changes. Mulnick keeps order with periodic "sweeps."

"If I feel the building is a little rowdy," Mulnick says, "I'll get on the PA and announce: 'This is a sweep. All children must be in their rooms in thirty seconds,' The doors will be locked and anyone caught in the halls will be brought to the dean's office." The "sweeps" usually catch about ten children. The dean either scolds them in his office or calls their homes. The school's incident rate is well below average.

Parents and children I talked to said the school was safe and highly structured, that children knew what was expected of them and that assignments were clear.

"I had a prejudice against Russell Sage," said one mother who attended the school herself as a child. "I felt it was too rigid and uncreative. But it's a really good program for my son." She said there is a "wonderful band," and a Latin teacher who brings the language alive. She finds the structured approach to writing works well. "You have to write a certain paragraph a certain way," she said. "They are very specific about what they want. For a lot of kids, it makes things easier."

Admission is mostly limited to children who live in the school zone. Each year the district office grants six or seven variances, or special permission to attend the school from out of the zone. Variances are granted only if a child's health or safety is threatened in another school. There are no scheduled tours, but there is an open house one evening in May for new parents.

JHS 680, Gateway to Health Services Scondary School
150–91 87th Road
Jamaica, N.Y. 11432

Joan Pinard, principal
718-739-8080

Reading Scores: ★★★★★
Math Scores: ★★★★★
Eighth Grade Regents: no
Grade Levels: 7–12
Admissions: Unzoned. By application and essay.
When to Apply: March
Class Size: N/A
Free Lunch: 23%

Ethnicity: 1.8%W 80.1%B 6.4%H 11.7%A
Enrollment: 171
Capacity: 220
Suspensions: 5.3%
Incidents: 2.3%
High School Choices: most continue at Gateway

A small alternative school in southeast Queens, Gateway to Health Services was set up as a collaboration with Queens Hospital Center and Mount Sinai School of Medicine to encourage children to consider hospital careers. Children have six-week internships at Queens Hospital and "shadow" professionals at Mt. Sinai.

The day I visited, I saw some very bright and attentive kids discussing questions such as "Why do you think the Crusades were called a successful failure?" and "How did the role of women change during the American Revolution?" Kids were dissecting grasshoppers in the biology lab. In an English class they were reading a poem about America written by an immigrant, and considering how the poem might be different if it had been writltten by someone of another ethnic group.

"I love this school," said Mark Spina, a math teacher. "I feel like I've hit the the lottery. If you have an idea and you are willing to put the time and energy behind it, the administration will back you."

Founded in 1995, Gateway has encountered the struggles common to many new schools. It has suffered from a high staff turnover. The day I visited, I saw a few kids with their eyes closed and their heads on their desks. One or two teachers had to shout to get their classes to settle down. But the school is a promising experiment and definitely worth watching.

There is no test for admission. Children are asked to write an essay about why they want to attend Gateway, and the school reviews a child's school records, including reading scores, math scores, and attendance. Children in special education are admitted on a case-by-case basis. The school has hearing and speech-impaired students.

District 29

District 29 includes the middle-class, mostly African-American neighborhoods of St. Albans, Hollis, and Springfield Gardens and the ethnically mixed neighborhoods of Holliswood and Queens Village. The schools have average to below-average test scores. Each school has a "gifted" program. Children go to their zoned schools, and there is no provision for school choice.

The highest performing school in the district is IS 59, at 132-55 Ridgedale Street, Springfield Gardens, 11413, principal Antonio J. K'Tori, telephone 718-527-3501. The school ranks in the top third of middle schools citywide. It has a high attendance rate and low rates of suspensions and incidents. It offers a continuation of the gifted track for children from PS 176, a well-regarded elementary school. Classical music is piped into the halls for a soothing effect. Children have a chance to study genetics with professional scientists at the DNA Learning Center at Cold Spring Harbor Laboratory on Long Island.

A school to watch is IS 109 at 213-10 92nd Ave., Queens Village, 11428, telephone 718-465-0651. Principal Caryn Frange is a dynamic and popular leader who was credited with transforming a district elementary school, PS 15. She is working to reorganize IS 109 according to the principles of the Middle School Initiative, using successful Queens schools such as Louis Armstrong Middle School (see page 330, 341) as a model. IS 109 has a strong music program that includes a jazz band, a string ensemble, and an orchestra. Like the students at IS 109 pupils may study genetics at the DNA Learning Center at Cold Spring Harbor.

There are no scheduled tours, but the district's middle school liaison, Diane Ehrlich, said, "Any parent really just has to make a phone call" to visit a school. Call her at 718-978-5900.

District 30

The Queens neighborhoods closest to Manhattan—Long Island City, Astoria, Sunnyside, and Jackson Heights—make up District 30. Although the district as a whole is overcrowded, some of the schools in Long Island City are below capacity and accept children from outside the district. The district's middle schools have average test scores, but the Board of Education's "similar schools report" ranks them well above average when compared to schools with similar rates of poverty and children with limited proficiency in English.

Parents are encouraged to visit schools. They may transfer their child from the neighborhood school to another in the district, space permitting. The district offers a brochure listing the options. Call the district office at 718-777-4600 for information.

The district has one middle school program for very high achievers, called The Academy Program at PS 122. Call the district coordinator for gifted programs, Stephanie Thier, at 718-777-4600, ext. 641, for details.

Another noteworthy school is IS 145 at 33-84 80th Street in Jackson Heights, 11372, 718-457-1242. The school is gigantic—with an enrollment of 2140—and many find its size overwhelming. But others swear by its vast array of special programs. Kids visit places as varied as Japan, the Caribbean, and France in a student exchange program. They also host students visiting from around the world.

IS 145 features an unusual emphasis on foreign language instruction. Children may study Russian, Japanese, Mandarin, Cantonese, French, Spanish, and German.

A popular alternative for District 30 parents is The Louis Armstrong Middle School in East Elmhurst. The school gives preference to children from District 30, even though it is not part of the district.

District 33

District 33 is a unique district with only one school—The Louis Armstrong Middle School. The district was established in 1979 as a result of a federal court order on desegregation, and reports directly to the schools chancellor. When Louis Armstrong was being built, there were quarrels over whether it would be part of District 30 (the most crowded district at the time) or District 24 (which had several very overcrowded schools that were mostly non-white).

As a compromise, a federal judge set up a new district just for the school and established a complicated admissions formula intended to relieve overcrowding and achieve racial integration.

JHS 204, Oliver Wendell Holmes Middle School
36–41 28th Street
Long Island City, N.Y. 11106

Philip A. Composto, principal
718-937-1463

Reading Scores: ★★★
Math Scores: ★★★
Eighth Grade Regents: yes
Grade Levels: 6–8
Admissions: Neighborhood school. By application from outside zone. March open house.
When to Apply: N/A
Class Size: 30

Free Lunch: 89%
Ethnicity: 10.5%W 28.7%B 42.6%H 18.1%A
Enrollment: 1176
Capacity: 1448
Suspensions: 2.5%
Incidents: 1.1%
High School Choices: Long Island City, William C. Bryant, Queens Vocational

When Phil Composto took over as principal of IS 204 in 1991, one of the first things he did was ask the children how they felt about their school. The kids told him they hated the fact that bathrooms were locked and that they could only use them while accompanied by an adult. The kids complained they were cooped up inside all day, and not allowed to play in the playground. And they wanted to have some fun, maybe hold a school dance.

Composto opened up the bathrooms, let the kids play in the playground after lunch, and helped organize school social activities such as dances. He found that those simple measures increased school spirit and helped pave the way for improved student achievement.

"Our philosophy is this: If kids enjoy coming to school, they are going to perform better and act out less," Composto says. "The children have developed a sense that they belong here. We ask them: 'What do you need to be a better student?' "

PTA president Janice McCollin says the school has changed "almost one hundred percent" under Composto's leadership. Before he became principal, she said, children used to fight in the halls; many teachers were alienated or even hostile to the children; and parents were asked to come to the school only if their child was having problems.

Composto restored order, helped motivate the staff, and welcomed parents into the school, she said. "He's really encouraging to the kids," McCollin said. "He's from the neighborhood himself, and he has his own children in the public schools." Now, parents and teachers work together on various projects, such as organizing an international potluck supper at the school once a year. Parents are invited to play volleyball with their children in the evening, with day care provided for younger siblings.

Teachers say they appreciate the way Composto listens to their ideas and lets them start new programs. For example, a gym teacher suggested that kids use a paved area across the street from the school as a roller-skating rink. The principal endorsed the idea, and the school now has roller hockey as a regular part of the physical education program.

The school's test scores are far above average when compared to schools with a similar poverty rate and proportion of non-English speaking children. The teaching methods and curriculum are fairly traditional, but the school is organized in a way that reduces the anonymity of a typical large junior high.

Sixth graders have two main subject teachers: one for math and science, and one for reading and social studies. Children aren't overwhelmed by changing classes for each subject in their first year.

By 7th grade, they are are more able to cope with having five teachers, one for each subject. Teachers are organized in teams and have common preparation periods, so they have a chance to talk to one another about an individual child's progress.

All children study piano in the 7th grade. Children shoot and edit their own dramatic films in the school's video production studio. A computerized CD-ROM database research library was paid for with a magnet grant. Designated as a Beacon School, IS 204 has after-school programs and community activities until 10 p.m.

Children from all over the district are eligible to attend; children from outside the district may be admittted with the superintendent's approval. Some parents have organized private bus service to transport children to the school who live outside the neigbhorhood. There is an open house in March, and prospective parents are welcome anytime.

Q560, Robert Wagner Institute for Arts and Sciences
47–07 30th Place
Long Island City, N.Y. 11101

Terry Born, Juliana Rogers, co-directors
718-472-5671

Reading Scores: ★★★★★
Math Scores: ★★★★
Eighth Grade Regents: yes
Grade Levels: 7–12
Admissions: Unzoned. By application, and interview in April.
When to Apply: N/A
Class Size: 22

Free Lunch: 39.7%
Ethnicity: 20.6%W 24.2%B 46.0%H 9.3%A
Enrollment: 400
Capacity: 500
Suspensions: 5.1 (HS)
Incidents: 2.7 (HS)
High School Choices: N/A

Here's a find: a small, experimental school with strong programs in art and technology, hidden away in a converted Macy's warehouse in an industrial neighborhood in Long Island City. Robert Wagner Institute for Arts and Technology has a fine staff, a beautiful new building, small classes and an unusual and innovative approach to education.

Founded as a high school in 1993 with grants from New Visions for Public Education and the Annenberg Foundation, the Institute for Arts and Sciences added its middle school in 1996. It offers an intimate, familylike atmosphere, with only sixty kids in the 7th and 8th grades.

The school provides a smooth transition from the 7th and 8th grades to high school, located in the same building. And the institute has a collaboration with LaGuardia Community College a few blocks away. High school students may take certain college classes for free and may use the college library and other facilities such as the swimming pool.

The school has a high-tech, gleaming white design, with wide halls and carpeted areas where kids can relax. Most of the rooms don't have windows, but they're brightly lit and connected to one another with glass brick walls that combine a sense of light with privacy. (Teachers complained the ventilation was poor, giving them headaches.)

Long Island City—the Queens neighborhood closest to Manhattan—has become an artists' community in the past fifteen years. Painters and sculptors, pushed out of Manhattan by high rents, have carved lofts out of vacant industrial buildings. PS 1, a century-old public school abandoned in the early 1980s, has been converted to a large exhibition space.

The Institute for Arts and Technology draws on this community, inviting twenty artists to the school each week to work with kids. The school has a theater, a dance studio, an exhibition hall, a beautiful library, and a video studio. Children study topics such as comedy improvisation, photography, street theater, video production, life drawing, and instrumental music.

The day I visited, the art gallery had a photo exhibit on the history of the civil rights movement, put together by students from a sister school in Manhattan, the Urban Academy. Called "Doors to Freedom," the exhibit had a "white entrance" and a "colored entrance," giving viewers a vivid reference to the era of segregation.

Students claim the school has a strong sense of community: "We know all the teachers," 8th grader Janet Nunez told me, as she and two friends chatted between classes.

"We call them by first name," 8th grader Larry Alvarado added. Kids said they even go over to teachers' houses for dinner.

"In my old school, I'd be too shy to ask anything," 8th grader Legren Ball said. "Here, the teacher puts me next to a smart person in the class to help me or helps me herself."

"She's also teaching us to teach each other," Janet added.

"If kids see a paper on the floor here, they're not obligated to pick it up, but they do because they feel it's their house," Larry said.

The middle school is adminstratively part of the alternative high school division. One sign of its academic success is its rate of admission to the specialized high schools. In 1999, two 8th graders won spots at Bronx High School of Science and one was admitted to Brooklyn Tech—an impressive number given that the school had only nineteen 8th graders to begin with.

Regents-level (9th grade) Earth Science is offered in the 8th grade.

Children from District 30 and District 24 are given preference for admission to the middle school, but anyone in the city may apply. As an educational option or "ed-op" school, the institute attempts to maintain a balance of children of different abilities: 16 percent have above average reading scores, 16 percent have below, and the rest have average scores.

Terry Born, one of the school's founders and codirectors, says the school has good luck with children who have had trouble elsewhere. There is no test for admission. Staffers interview children and parents. The school is looking for children with an interest in art and technology who are mature enough to attend a school with high schoolers in the same building. The school also wants assurance that parents will attend parent-teacher conferences.

Parents should call the school in April to arrange a visit.

The Academy, at PS 122
21–21 Ditmars Boulevard
Long Island City, N.Y. 11105

Mary Kojes , principal
718-721-6410

Reading Scores: ★★★★★
Math Scores: ★★★★
Eighth Grade Regents: yes
Grade Levels: 6–8
Admissions: Selective. By exam
When to Apply: Spring
Class Size: 25-30
Free Lunch: 64%

Ethnicity: 37.7%W 9.9%B
31.5%H 20.9%A
Enrollment: 195
Capacity: N/A
Suspensions: 1.1%
Incidents: 0.2%
High School Choices: N/A

Housed in graceful old elementary school PS 122, the Academy is a tiny middle school program for high-achieving kids. It offers a close-knit and attentive staff, some interesting projects and so much homework that one graduate said the work at the Bronx High School of Science was a breeze by comparison.

Children from the district's two elementary schools "gifted and talented" programs at PS 150 in Sunnyside and PS 122 are admitted automatically. Others must score above the 90th percentile on standardized reading and math tests and must take an entrance exam given by the district office in the spring. There are three 6th grade classes. Many of the children leave the Academy for Hunter High School in Manhattan in 7th grade, and there are just two 7th and 8th grade classes.

The curriculum is based on the work of Joseph Renzulli, a University of Connecticut professor whose approach to education for the gifted encourages children to work independently. Instead of listening exclusively to lectures by a teacher, children work on interdisciplinary projects on a wide range of subjects.

In one class, for example, children studied the history of various aspects of rock bands. One child wrote about the history of the electric guitar. The project required research skills, the ability to write, an understanding of music, history, and even a bit of science as the pupil investigated the materials used to make guitars and the way sounds are made.

In an English class, children made their own crossword puzzles with clues based on the works of a particular author. One girl chose Dr. Seuss, and the clues in her puzzle involved the titles of well-known children's books. In a project combining math and architecture, children make scale models of structures ranging from bridges to the pyramids using Popsicle sticks.

"The academics are excellent," PTA president Michele Basco said. "The teachers really listen. The children build a close relationship with the staff, and they really grow, emotionally and socially."

Ms. Basco said there are pluses and minuses to a school as small as the Academy. When everyone knows everyone, no one gets lost. The bonds between the students and teachers are strong, particularly since children often have the same teachers for 7th and 8th grades. But the school doesn't offer the frequent dances, social activities, sports programs and other extra curricular events possible at a large school. And it's sometimes hard to make friends when you have only sixty kids in a grade to choose among.

The PS 122 building, completed in 1924, is clean and orderly, with large windows and an ample playground.

The school was ranked the highest in the state in 1999, based on reading scores of the Academy's 6th graders, 100 percent of whom scored at the highest level on the state reading exam. The state test measured whether children could read material similar in difficulty to the *New York Times* or *Moby Dick*. Principal Mary Kojes said she was particularly proud of the school's achievement because many of the children are immigrants who speak English as a second language. In addition to native born African-Americans, Greek-Americans and Italian-Americans, the school has new immigrants from Mexico, Pakistan, Bangladesh, China, Korea, Greece and India.

The Academy is open to all children in the district. Call Stephanie Thier, the district's gifted program coordinator, at 718-777-4600 for details.

IS 675, Renaissance School
35–55 81st Street
Jackson Heights, N.Y. 11372

Monte Joffee, principal
718-803-0060

Reading Scores: ★★★★
Math Scores: ★★★★
Eighth Grade Regents: yes
Grade Levels: K–12
Admissions: Unzoned. By lottery.
When to Apply: Call in
  December for tour dates;
  application deadline in
  February.
Class Size: 25-30

Free Lunch: 52%
Ethnicity: 36.8%W 24.2%B
  25.8%H 13.2%A
Enrollment: 302
Capacity: N/A
Suspensions: 10.3%
Incidents: 3.3%
High School Choices:
  Renaissance, John Bowne,
  Environmental Studies

The Renaissance School was founded in 1993 by a group of teachers with a grand vision: to build a progressive and democratically run school that would spark a revival of the city itself. It quickly became one of the most sought after in the district, with hundreds of applicants for twenty-five seats in the kindergarten class and a long waiting list.

This school, K to 12, has one class per grade in kindergarten through 5th grade. In 6th grade, it expands to include two classes per grade, so parents who are interested in having their child transfer to Renaissance might consider it for the middle school years.

Children concentrate their studies on the history, people, and culture of New York, with traditional disciplines of math and English woven into this theme. They may spend months designing and constructing a scale model of an ideal city, and then use what they've learned to think of ways to improve the real place they live in.

The school is committed to teaching children of all races and income levels, and each class mixes kids who are high-achieving with those who are struggling, including some in special education. Teachers manage to accommodate a wide range of abilities by allowing children to work independently.

The day I visited, 8th graders were building bridges out of tooth-picks and 3-by-5 index cards. Some were quite basic; others extremely sophisticated. Teacher Richard Doherty introduced the lesson in "static force" by arm wrestling with the kids. "That's zero force—nothing is moving," he said. "Ideally, when you cross a bridge, you want nothing to move." Then he held up an index card and showed how easily it bends. Children experimented with ways to make it stronger by, for example, folding up edges of the card. With a box of toothpicks and a bottle of glue, they set to work making their own suspension bridges. Doherty tested each bridge for strength, piling it with pebbles until it broke.

The school has an unusual approach to studying foreign language which, parents say, is very successful. On another visit, PEA's Sheila Haber saw an 8th grade class designed to teach English-speaking kids Spanish and Spanish-speaking kids English. The teacher and students alternated the use of each language in class in conversation, and then the teacher gave an explanation of the verb "to be" in both languages as kids conjugated the verb. At the end of the lesson, she invited anyone who had questions to call her at home, surely a sign of dedication.

In a 7th grade social studies class, children were writing 350-500 word essays comparing London and New York, using the Internet and reference books in their class for research. Ms. Haber said the quality of writing was good. Children were expected to write three drafts before handing in a completed essay. Ms. Haber was also impressed with the quality of instruction in math, which is influenced by the work of the late Mario Salvadori, an engineer who pioneered techniques of teaching principles of architecture to young children.

Housed in a converted department store, the Renaissance School has an unusual floorplan. It has no hallways. Instead, central common rooms open onto classrooms. The result is a homey environment; there are spots where children can gather to chat with friends and display their projects, as well as more formal classrooms. The cafeteria has round tables, rather than the long institutional ones common at most schools, and teachers eat with the kids. The noise level is low enough that people can actually carry on a conversation.

Like all new schools, Renaissance has had its share of ups and downs. In the first few years of operation, it moved to three different locations. Some parents, who decided they wanted a more traditional education, transferred their children out. But the school now boasts a solid, enthusiastic group of parents who volunteer tons of time to make sure it works. The staff is energetic and passionate about their work, and teachers appreciate the notion that decisions are made jointly, not dictated by the principal.

"This is such a gold mine because there is nothing like it in all of Queens," said PTA co-chair Barbara Lombardo Reynolds. "The middle school has really come into its own this year."

The school has a complicated admissions procedure. Half the seats are allocated by lottery. Half are chosen by a committee set up to ensure a racial and ethnic balance, as well as a mix of children of different abilities. Preference is given to siblings, and 90 percent of the seats in grades K through 8 are reserved for children living in District 30. The school has frequent tours for prospective parents.

IS 227, Louis Armstrong Middle School
32–02 Junction Boulevard
East Elmhurst, N.Y. 11369

Elizabeth Ophals, principal;
Richard Siegal, admissions director
718-335-7500

Reading Scores: ★★★★
Math Scores: ★★★★
Eighth Grade Regents: yes
Grade Levels: 5–8
Admissions: Unzoned. By
lottery. January open house.
When to Apply: December.
Class Size: 32-34
Free Lunch: 44%

Ethnicity: 40.8%W 17.8%B
27.7%H 13.7%A
Enrollment: 1540
Capacity: 1653
Suspensions: 3.4%
Incidents: 1.8%
High School Choices: John
Bowne, Newton, Townsend
Harris

The Louis Armstrong Middle School, founded in 1979 as a court ordered experiment in racial integration, embodies the philosophy that children learn best when they have classmates of varying academic ability, from different ethnic groups and neighborhoods. The administration prides itself on giving all children the chance to try all subjects. At IS 227 you don't need to audition to play in the band.

The school is a laboratory for new teaching techniques. Teachers work in teams and decide among themselves which methods work best for their students. An experienced, enthusiastic staff, a well-equipped building, and a long-term collaboration with Queens College have made IS 227 one of the most sought after schools in Queens.

The school is open to all children in the borough, from the most disabled in special education, to high-achievers who can do high school work while still in middle school. There are far more applicants than spots: four for every seat in special education, five for every seat in 5th grade, and seven or eight for every seat in 6th grade.

Classes, for the most part, mix children of different abilities. Teachers try to draw on children's interests, and it's not a super-competitive school. "We don't push kids," says principal Elizabeth Ophals. "We invite invite them, we motivate them. It's academically rigorous. But I think learning is noisy and messy. There's nothing I hate more than desks in rows."

Professors of education from Queens College help develop the curriculum, student teachers work in the classrooms, and IS 227 teachers are expected to keep up to date on new methods. About 40 percent of the teachers were trained at Queens College, and many student taught at IS 227.

"After thirty years, I'm still excited about teaching," said Arthur Shield, a 7th grade social studies teacher. "This is the way a school should be run—not just for children, but for the teachers as well."

The day I visited, Shield and a few other teachers were having lunch together in a classroom, chatting informally about how best to help a bright girl who was goofing off in class. In another classroom, I saw a math teacher give a special ed teacher tips on how to use computers, also during their lunch breaks. This kind of informal meeting is common. Teachers routinely talk to one another about what they're teaching and exchange tips about how to handle a difficult student. IS 227 is unusual in that most teachers have their own offices, a sign, teachers say, that they are considered professionals.

The atmosphere is cheerful and orderly. Children I spoke to said race relations are good. The school is safe. Bathrooms are unlocked, and children are allowed to use them when they please. The number of children suspended for misbehavior is far lower than for the typical junior high school.

Teaching techniques are a mixture of traditional and progressive. The lower grades look more like an elementary school than a traditional junior high school. Desks are in groups. There are lots of colorful bulletin boards. Teachers help children with individual projects. By 8th grade, the school seems more like a traditional high school, with desks in rows and teachers standing at the front lecturing.

There are strong programs in art, music, and dance and some parents say the electives are the school's most attractive feature. Some children take art as many as nine periods a week.

Large schools have gone out of fashion in recent years, but visit IS 227 and you'll see why large schools were built in the first place. The school has equipment and labs that would be too expensive for a small school to provide: a woodworking shop, a plastic and metal shop, and a print shop. Three full-time music teachers offer classes in music appreciation as well as band, orchestra and chorus. The school has a large auditorium, a dance studio and a licensed dance teacher. (Swimming is offered at two pools in the neighborhood.)

The school librarian boasts that the IS 227 library is "hands down, the best middle school library in New York City." Two full-time librarians, a library aide, high-speed Internet connections, and access to the Queens public library database enable children to do sophisticated research projects. If a book is not available in the school library, it's easy to find a branch of the public library near a child's home that has it. Children can even dial into the school library and the Queens public libraries from their homes, if they have their own computer and modem.

The school was one of the first in the city to recognize that children in early adolescence often need more individual attention than a traditional junior high school provides. Accordingly, IS 227 is divided into three "houses" of about five hundred pupils, each with its own assistant principal. Children spend three years in a house and get to know the assistant principal and the guidance counselor.

Each house is divided into "clusters" of four to six classes. Teachers in each cluster work as a team, plan lessons together, and talk about each child's progress. Each cluster of classrooms is connected by a common hall. When classes change, kids mostly stay within their cluster: the changes don't feel like rush hour.

Each team of teachers decides how best to organize its classes. In the 5th grade, for example, children study all their academic subjects (except science) with their classroom teacher. In the 6th grade, some teams have decided that each teacher will specialize in different subjects, while others continue to teach all subjects. By 8th grade, each subject is taught by a different teacher, although children stay within their cluster of five classrooms for most of the day.

Some of the teachers give up their school vacations to take students on trips. One year a group went to New Orleans to study the roots of jazz. And five teachers once combined forces to organize a trip to France for fifty youngsters. A favorite science teacher takes thirty or forty kids to the Epcot Center in Florida and to a space camp organized by NASA in Huntsville, Alabama.

The building is wheelchair accessible. Children with disabilities are integrated into regular classes whenever possible, sometimes with full-time aides helping them. The day I visited, a boy with cerebral palsy was seated in his wheelchair in a regular English class, listening intently while an aide took notes for him. The aide told me the boy learned best by listening and had a phenomenal memory, but he had trouble writing. With her help, he was able to keep up with a regular class.

Special education children are assigned to "clusters" with three or four regular classes and one special education class. That means children in special education have the same teachers as other children. If a child needs special education for one subject, say reading, but can cope in a regular class for other subjects, the cluster can accommodate him.

The school has classes in English as a second language for new immigrants, but doesn't have bilingual classes.

The school has no "special progress" track with accelerated courses for advanced students. It has only two classes each for Regents math and biology, high-school-level courses offered to unusually competent 8th graders.

"We believe all youngsters are qualified to take all courses," says Jay Stonehill, a school adminstrator who gave me my tour. "We try to offer everything to everyone."

The school strictly limits the number of children taking Regents-level classes to sixty in math and sixty in biology. Only those who score in the very top of their grade are allowed to register for Regents courses. This is frustrating to children who just miss the cutoff, who in another school might be able to take Regents classes. But Stonehilll says that keeping strong students in regular classes lifts the level of those classes. "We don't want to isolate the remaining youngsters," he said. As a compromise, some children who miss the cutoff are allowed to take a special Regents class after school.

Not every teacher is a star. One mother complained that teachers allowed her daughter to get-by doing the bare minimum of work. She called the Regents math class "a disaster" the year her daughter took it.

But the good teachers are extraordinary. A parent described how a shy, quiet boy blossomed and grew self confident when exposed to a challenging art curriculum. Another said her daughter consistently had teachers who were "challenging, creative, interesting, and hard-working." The mother, Lori Lustig, said, "What I liked best was not the meat and potatoes but the extras—the dance, the plays, the band. The school has an unusually high proportion of teachers' children."

Test scores are well above average in reading and math—a remarkable achievement considering the school goes out of its way to admit a student body that's average in every way. It has a high percentage of admissions to the specialized science high schools and sends more children to the selective Townsend Harris High School than does any other middle school in Queens.

Louis Armstrong has a complicated admissions process, the result of the stormy history that preceded its opening in 1979. Officials in two adjoining districts—30 and 24—each claimed they needed the new school the most. District 30, which includes Astoria and Long Island City in western Queens, was the most overcrowded, and was mostly white at the time; District 24, which includes Corona, Elmhurst and Middle Village, had several overcrowded schools that were mostly nonwhite.

The NAACP filed suit saying the new building should be part of District 24 and should be racially integrated. A court decided that the school should attempt to both relieve overcrowding and achieve racial integration, and that it shouldn't be part of either district but should report directly to the schools chancellor.

The admissions formula is a result of that court order. A certain number of seats are reserved for children from District 30 and District 24, but children from all over Queens may apply. Bus transportation is provided for children from outside the neighborhood.

Children are admitted according to an extremely complex lottery designed to maintain the school's racial balance without upsetting the racial balance in neighboring schools. The lottery also ensures that the school has a mix of children of different abilities: 25 percent of the seats are reserved for children who score below average on standardized tests; 50 percent are for children with average scores; and 25 percent are for children with above average scores.

The racial quotas were determined by the 1980 census for the borough of Queens. (Queens today is much less white than it was then, so the quotas give whites an advantage in admissions.)

According to the formula, the school is supposed to maintain a racial balance of 45 percent white and 55 percent nonwhite. It is also supposed to give preference to children who would otherwise attend schools where most children are of their own race, rather than children whose presence in their neighborhood school serves what the bureaucrats call an "integrative function."

In plain English, Stonehill says, that means: "If you are white, and you live in, or your zoned junior high school is in, a nonwhite area, your chances of getting in are slim. If you are a minority, and you live in a mostly white area, your chances of getting in are slim."

More nonwhites than whites apply, and that generally gives whites an edge in admissions. "The federal requirement for integration is to retain whites," Stonehill says.

Interested parents should attend an open house at the school in

December or January. Usually one open house is on a Saturday morning and one is on a weekday evening, and some eight hundred parents attend. In mid-January, parents can pick up an application from their child's elementary school.

The first round of acceptances goes out in April, to children living in the immediate neighborhood. The second round goes out in May. Stonehill advises parents who have their heart set on Louis Armstrong to send a letter explaining why they believe the school would be the best for their child. If their child is placed on a waiting list, there's still a possibility he or she will be admitted over the summer. For those willing to wait, some children are even accepted in September.

Reading Scores

Math Scores

Eighth Grade Regents

Grade Levels

Admissions

When to Apply

Class Size

Free Lunch

Ethnicity

Enrollment

Capacity

Suspensions

Incidents

High School Choices

STATEN ISLAND

STATEN ISLAND

District 31

The magnolias are in bloom, and you drive by houses with swing sets and above-ground pools in the backyards, patio furniture on the decks, and mini-vans in the driveways. Can this really be New York City?

Well, yes and no. New York City police patrol the streets and your Metrocard works on the buses here, but Staten Island is culturally and psychologically a world apart. Sleepy, suburban, even rural in part, Staten Island attracts people who are looking for quiet neighborhoods and reasonably priced housing. Many people both live and work on Staten Island, and refer to their infrequent jaunts to Manhattan as an excursion to "the city." They refer to people who live elsewhere as "off-islanders."

Politically conservative, Staten Island has long been a Republican stronghold in a predominately Democratic city. For many years, the borough was mostly white, attracting blue-collar, Italian-American and Irish-American families with stay-at-home moms, and dads who worked in construction, or who were firefighters or police officers. Those families still make up a large part of the population, but they have been joined in recent years by African-Americans and immigrants from the Caribbean, Central America, India, Korea, and other Asian countries.

The population grew quite dramatically after the construction of the Verrazano Narrows Bridge in 1964, which connected the island to Brooklyn for the first time. Junior high schools were built to accommodate the increase in school-age kids. Most of those buildings are still used as middle schools. They are generally bright, cheerful, well equipped, and well maintained. Staten Island is one area of the city where parents are generally satisfied with their neighborhood middle schools.

Children usually go to their zoned schools, and the district discourages shopping around. Two exceptions: The Michael Petrides School, at 715 Ocean Terrace, Building B, 10301, is a K–12 school open to all children in the district by lottery. Principal Michael Davino can be reached at 718-815-0186. The Petrides School generally has vacancies for only a few children in middle school.

IS 61 in Brighton Heights has a federal magnet grant to maintain racial intergration and accepts children from outside its immediate zone.

Occasionally the district office grants variances or special permission to children wishing to attend a school outside their zone. Call the district office at 718-390-1608 for information.

IS 61, William Morris School
445 Castleton Avenue
Staten Island, N.Y. 10301

Richard Gallo, principal
718-727-8481

Reading Scores: ★★★
Math Scores: ★★★
Eighth Grade Regents: yes
Grade Levels: 6–8
Admissions: Neighborhood
school. By test or audition for
magnet program. January open
house.
When to Apply: N/A
Class Size: 25-36

Free Lunch: 71%
Ethnicity: 30.4%W 41.1%B
24.6%H 4%A
Enrollment: 1212
Capacity: 1467
Suspensions: 10.1%
Incidents: 0.4%
High School Choices: Curtis,
Ralph McKee, Tottenville

In a city that's often divided by race and class, IS 61 stands out as a school where children of all colors and family backgrounds seem to get along. In the lunchroom, you'll see students of different races sitting at the same tables and chatting—an all-too rare occurrence in many city schools.

IS 61 has a well-clipped lawn, shaded by pink-flowering trees. There's a park in back. It looks more like a suburban school than what you'd expect in an urban neighborhood like Brighton Heights. On one side there are large Victorian and Tudor houses with mature shade trees. On the other, public housing projects and a homeless shelter. The school draws from the professional families on one side as well as the working poor and the unemployed on the other.

"We're all one great big happy family," one student said. "We're like brothers and sisters," said another.

The school has a federal magnet grant intended to maintain its racial balance. The special programs in music and journalism that the extra money provides have attracted children from outside the neighborhood. A drama class puts on elaborate plays. Journalism students write their own literary magazine, put on their own television show, and publish the yearbook. Children may study violin or flute or clarinet. There's a jazz band, a regular band, and an orchestra. There is also an extensive visual arts program in sculpture and drawing.

"The white students are from families who are receptive to being in a mixed school, so it really works," said Marge Hack, an education reporter for the *Staten Island Advance* and an IS 61 parent. "It has kids who are very affluent and kids who are dirt poor."

The school adopted the Middle School Initiative in the late 1980s. Each child is assigned to a "team" of five classes within a "division" made up of three teams. Each team is named after a professional football, basketball, or baseball team, and children make their own felt banner, which they keep through their three years at the school. "If you ask kids their homeroom, they'll give you the name of the team, rather than the room number," Principal Richard Gallo told me as he gave me a tour.

The architecture of the school, built in 1972, lends itself to the system of teams. Rather than the long corridors typical of junior high schools, IS 61 has small wings, divided by walls. Each wing has five classrooms and a few smaller offices where teachers can meet to plan lessons or discuss. Children change classes within the wing so halls aren't as congested as they are at a typical large junior high school.

"The teachers buy into it. They feel it's their area, their kids, their team," Gallo said. Each team competes for prizes such as pizzas given to the group that accumulates the most "points" for good behavior. According to Gallo, "Everyone has a reason to cooperate and do well."

One teacher, Brian Sharkey, said one of the reasons kids get along is that they know each other from elementary school. In many city neighborhoods, the elementary schools are largely segregated and kids get to know children of other races only when they reach the turbulent adolescent years. But the elementary schools that feed into IS 61 are integrated, Sharkey said.

Children living within the zone are automatically admitted. Those outside the zone must take a test or be auditioned for the "talent" or magnet programs. Children who are zoned for the school may also audition for the magnet program. Parents may visit during Open School Week in November, on a "magnet night" in January, or during a dramatic performance in March.

IS 24, Myra S. Barnes School
225 Cleveland Avenue
Staten Island, N.Y. 10308

Richard Spisto, principal
718-356-4200

Reading Scores: ★★★★
Math Scores: ★★★★
Eighth Grade Regents: yes
Grade Levels: 6–8
Admissions: Neighborhood school.
When to Apply: Automatic registration by elementary school.

Class Size: 33
Free Lunch: 24%
Ethnicity: 89.2%W 2%B 5.4%H 3.4%A
Enrollment: 1176
Capacity: 1558
Suspensions: 6%
Incidents: 2.6%
High School Choices: N/A

This neighborhood school ranks in the top 20 percent of middle schools citywide. Richard Spisto, who was named principal in 1998, hopes to bring a warmth and cheerfulness to a school that has long had high test scores, but which one mother said was once run "like a military school."

"I'm very people oriented," Spisto said. "I want to make sure the children and the staff are happy coming into the school building. We want a pleasant environment where everyone works as a team."

The school has had a suspension rate that's higher than average for the district, and Spisto hopes to bring that down. He said he's trying to spend more time in the halls and classrooms talking to kids and teachers, and less time in the office on administrative tasks. He said the suspension rate was down 70 percent in his first year.

IS 24 has adopted the Middle School Initiative and has been divided into eight "teams" of five classes each. Each team of 175 kids is identified by a banner of its own design.

Each team of teachers meets once a week to plan lessons together, allowing them to organize interdisciplinary projects. For one project, children studied the Industrial Revolution in social studies, did research on famous inventors in science, and read a biography of Thomas Edison.

A popular nonacademic course is stagecraft. Children design and build sets and props for elaborate school plays.

IS 24 is a major feeder school to a selective high school, Staten Island Technical School. Of the high school's entering class of 165, one-quarter typically come from IS 24, Spisto said.

IS 24 has a special education class for nonaggressive, emotionally troubled children classified as MIS II, children who are anxious, depressed, or withdrawn. A social worker said the class is valuable because "these kids would have been eaten up in other MIS II classes," which often have a concentration of aggressive children.

Five or ten children a year at IS 24 receive variances—special permission to attend a school outside their zone. Contact the district office for details.

IS 7, Elias Berstein School
1270 Huguenot Avenue
Staten Island, N.Y. 10312

Nancy Lisiewski, principal
718-356-2314

Reading Scores: ★★★★
Math Scores: ★★★★
Eighth Grade Regents: yes
Grade Levels: 6–8
Admissions: Neighborhood school.
When to Apply: Automatic registration by elementary school.
Class Size: 33

Free Lunch: 12%
Ethnicity: 88.4%W 2%B 3.9%H 5.7%A
Enrollment: 900
Capacity: 1441
Suspensions: 5.1%
Incidents: 2.3%
High School Choices: most go to Tottenville, 5% to SI Tech 1% to LaGuardia

IS 7 ranks in the top 15 percent of middle schools. It was one of the first on Staten Island to adopt the Middle School Initiative, where teachers and kids are divided into teams with names such as "Voyagers" or "Pathfinders" as a way of making a large school more intimate.

"There's little glitz or glamour here," Principal Nancy Lisiewski said. "It's pretty much three Rs. This school is run collaboratively and teachers help formulate policy."

The day PEA's Jessica Wolff visited, kids in a 6th grade social studies class were talking about Plato and Socrates. "What's a three-year-old's favorite word?" the teacher asked. After some prodding, the kids answered "Why." The teacher then began to ask, "Why?" every time the kids answered a question, as a way of getting them to understand what philosophy is all about.

"What were the philosophers looking for?" she asked.

"They were trying to understand the world they lived in," one child answered

"Why?" asked the teacher.

"Because they were curious," a child replied.

"Why were they curious?" the teacher asked, and so on.

In a math class, kids clustered around the teacher—some on the floor, some in chairs, some sitting on desks—as she read an amusing book with questions and answers about shapes: What is the shape of the place where our government plans military strategy? (Pentagon) What shape stops traffic? (A hexagon.)

In a Regents-level (9th grade) Earth Science class, 8th graders were using a laser disc program on a computer to learn about different strata of soil. They also passed around a clear beaker filled with dirt to see the different layers. Ms. Wolff described the teacher as dynamic, funny, and confident.

The school's most popular nonacademic class is one in which children take care of animals in cages and tanks in a classroom: guinea pigs, gerbils, a lizard, snakes, doves, an iguana, rabbits, mice, turtles, and a parrot.

A local bank has sponsored a computer program that simulates the situation that employees might face working in a bank. Children start out as "tellers" and work their way up as they solve various problems.

The school also offers classes in cooking.

Trips are a big part of the curriculum, and children have a chance to visit the Liberty Science Center in New Jersey, as well as various museums in Manhattan.

The teachers have volunteered to keep homerooms, even though their new contract excuses them from such administrative tasks. "This age group needs a home and the structure of a homeroom to organize themselves," Ms. Lisiewski said

IS 7 graduates go on to twenty or more different high schools, in Manhattan and Brooklyn as well as on Staten Island. Guidance counselor Stanley Siesel said he wants parents to be aware of all available options, rather than automatically sending kids off to their neighborhood high school.

IS 75, Frank D. Paulo School
455 Huguenot Avenue
Staten Island, N.Y. 10312

Julie El Saieh-Wolfe, principal
718-356-0130

Reading Scores: ★★★★
Math Scores: ★★★★
Eighth Grade Regents: yes
Grade Levels: 6–8
Admissions: Neighborhood
school.
When to Apply: Automatic
registration by elementary
school.
Class Size: 32

Free Lunch: 13%
Ethnicity: 90%W 0.8%B 4.4%H
4.8%A
Enrollment: 1429
Capacity: 1640
Suspensions: 1.6%
Incidents: 0.6%
High School Choices:
Tottenville; Susan Wagner;
SI Tech

IS 75 is a traditional school in a large, modern building on a street lined with flowering white pears. The facility, opened in 1985, has spotless, wide corridors and big display cases with trophies and shelves showing off children's ceramics. Large pastel drawings made by students decorate the walls. The band was practicing the theme song from the Disney movie *Aladdin* when PEA's Jessica Wolff arrived for her tour.

Even the lunchroom is bright and cheery, with tile mosaics on one wall. It was quiet during Ms. Wolff's visit. Kids were reading to themselves in what's called "sustained silent reading." The quiet time after lunch gives kids a chance to calm down before they go back to class, administrators said.

The school has test scores that put it in the top 20 percent of middle schools citywide. It's safe and orderly, with a very low suspension rate and almost no reported incidents. The kids are well-behaved and attentive.

Principal Julie El Saieh-Wolfe calls herself a "meat and potatoes administrator" who prefers perennial methods of instruction. IS 75 does not have teams or houses, but is organized as a traditional junior high school. Ms. El Saieh-Wolfe said that allows for individualized programming. For example, a child may be assigned to an advanced class for math, a regular class for science, and a remedial class for

English. Desks are mostly in rows, and teachers mostly give instruction to the entire class, rather than having them work individually or in small groups.

The principal is particularly proud of the school's nonacademic programs, which include classes in television production, a band, a chorus, and an award-winning debate team. The school has partnerships with the Staten Island Symphony, the Staten Island Children's Museum, Young Audiences, and the Metropolitan Opera in Manhattan. One staffer teaches kids to write their own operas.

The school has a well-equipped library, a large metal shop, a ceramics studio, a graphics design studio, and a woodworking shop.

One mother described the principal as "very bubbly, very up" and said parents are "incredibly supportive" of the adminstration. Ms. Wolff called her "an enthusiastic cheerleader for her teachers."

IS 34, Tottenville Intermediate School
528 Academy Avenue
Staten Island, N.Y. 10307

Jeff Preston, principal
718-984-0772

Reading Scores: ★★★★
Math Scores: ★★★★
Eighth Grade Regents: yes
Grade Levels: 6–8
Admissions: Neighborhood school.
When to Apply: Automatic registration by elementary school.
Class Size: 30-33

Free Lunch: 16%
Ethnicity: 89.3%W 0.8%B 5.2%H 4.7%A
Enrollment: 1239
Capacity: 1162
Suspensions: 2.3%
Incidents: 0.4%
High School Choices: Tottenville, SI Tech, Stuyvesant

An old, well-kept building on the very southern tip on Staten Island, IS 34 is the southern most school in the state of New York. It ranks in the top 15 percent of middle schools citywide.

Before the advent of railroads, the village of Tottenville was a major stagecoach stop on the route from Manhattan to Philadelphia. Travelers would alternate between ferries and stagecoaches. The village still has an old-time feel to it, with many buildings dating to the early nineteenth century. The surrounding area is one of the fastest growing in Staten Island, and many new houses are under construction.

IS 34 is an integral part of the community. Students are involved in projects such as planting trees and giving a band concert on the town green. Built in 1936, the school has a bell choir, a jazz band, and an orchestra. The bell choir, in particular, helps children, who've had little exposure to music, read musical notation quickly and efficiently, principal Jeff Preston said. There is also a ceramics studio, a stained-glass studio, a woodworking shop, and classes in calligraphy.

The school is adopting the Middle School Initiative, with five teachers in different subject areas working in a team and planning lessons together. In one class combining English and art, children made their own pop up books.

The school has an inclusion class for children in special education

361

classified as emotionally disturbed, or SIE 7. Special education and general education children are in the same class, with two teachers.

Occasionally children attend the school from outside the immediate neighborhood. Contact the district office for details.

Index